SENTENCED TO TROLL 4

S.L. ROWLAND

AETHERVALE PUBLISHING

ALSO BY S.L. ROWLAND

Tales of Aedrea

Cursed Cocktails

Sword & Thistle

The Halfling's Harvest

There Be Dragons Here

Pangea Online

Pangea Online: Death and Axes

Pangea Online 2: Magic and Mayhem

Pangea Online 3: Vials and Tribulations

Sentenced to Troll 1-6

Path to Villainy: An NPC Kobold's Tale

Collected Editions

Pangea Online: The Complete Trilogy

Sentenced to Troll Compendium: Books 1-3

Sentenced to Troll Compendium 2: Books 4-6

ISBN 978-1-964567-08-2 *(Paperback)*

ISBN 978-1-964567-09-9 *(Hardback)*

Published by Aethervale Publishing

Sign up for S.L. Rowland's Newsletter

For signed copies and advanced chapters visit Patreon at patreon.com/slrowland

 Formatted with Vellum

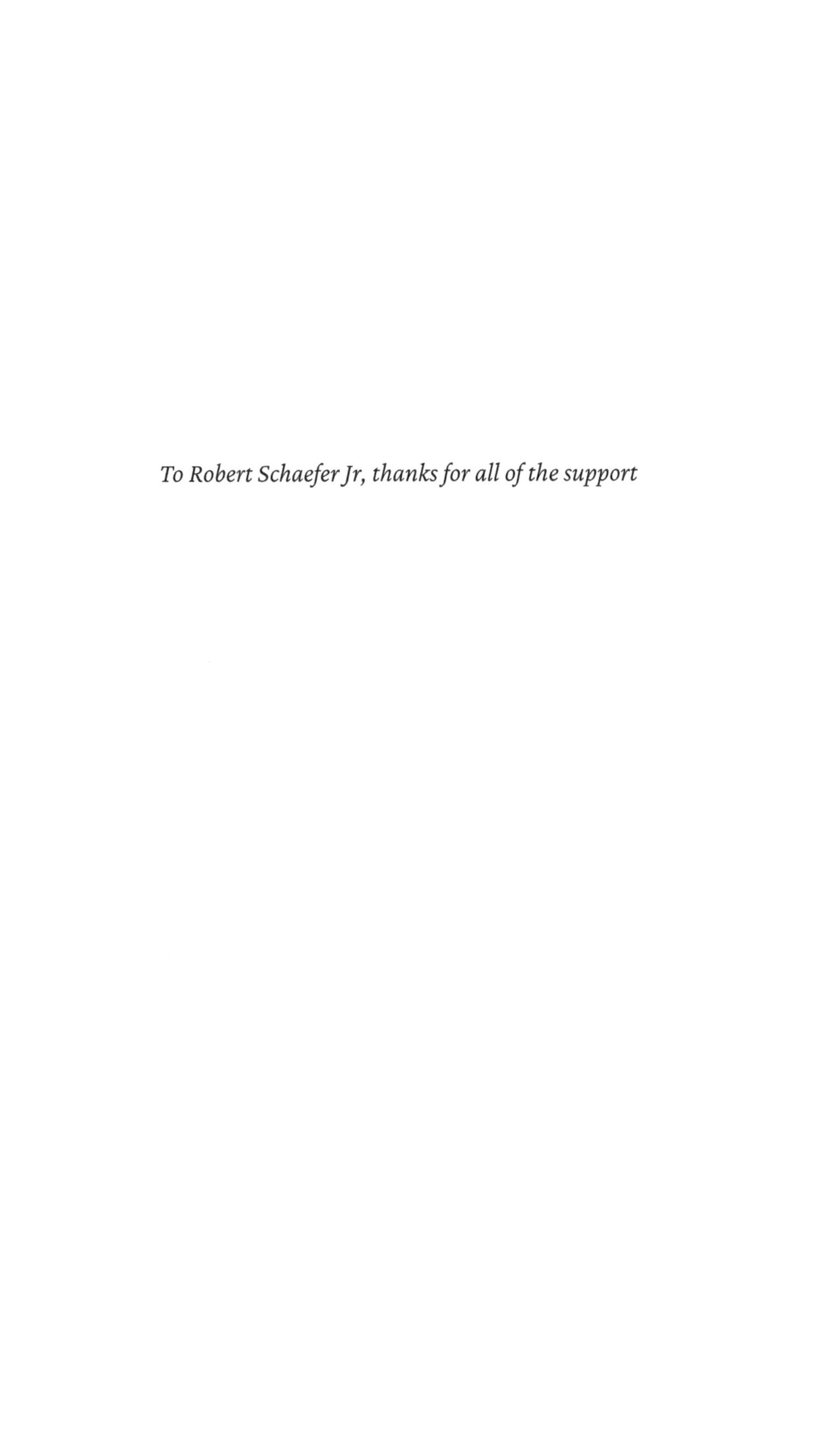

To Robert Schaefer Jr, thanks for all of the support

CURRENT STATS

Chod, Level 24 Barbarian/Summoner Forest Troll
HP: 5880/5880
Mana: 5000/5000
Rage: 0/100
XP: 603,208/665,000

Strength: 41
Dexterity: 24
Constitution: 42
Intelligence: 10
Wisdom: 15
Charisma: 6

+1 Strength and Constitution racial bonus per level.

+1 Ability point per odd level.

5 stat points available.

1 ability point available.

Abilities:

Bite. *Using your massive tusks and powerful jaw, you take a bite out of an opponent, dealing immense damage. Cost: 10 rage Level 2.*

Claw. *You attack with sharp claws, swiping at an opponent and dealing extra damage. Cost: 5 rage. Level 2.*

Intimidation. *You stare down your opponent, confusing them so that they are unable to attack for two seconds. Cost: 10 rage.*

Berserker Rage. *(Ultimate) Attacks and physical damage build your rage meter. 5 rage per attack. Rage meter deteriorates over time when out of combat at a rate of 5 rage per second. Activating Berserker Rage fills rage meter. For 30 seconds, rage meter does not decrease, deal increased damage, health regenerates at 5x the normal rate, cannot be stunned, slowed or otherwise affected. Cooldown: 10 minutes.*

I'm Always Angry *(Passive. Available at level 10). Once rage meter is at 50%, it will not deteriorate below 50% when out of combat.*

Increased Regeneration. *(Passive) Regenerate health at a faster rate. Level 2.*

Rapid Regeneration. *(Passive) When below 10% health, regeneration is doubled.*

Nightvision. *(Passive) Increased vision in darkness and low light.*

Thick Skin. *(Passive) Take 10% less damage from physical attacks.*

Savage. *(Passive) Ability to eat uncooked meat without consequences.*

Camouflage. *(Passive) When out of combat and not moving for 20 seconds, trolls blend in with their surroundings.*

Sweeping Slash. *Form a sweeping arc in front of you, dealing damage and knocking your opponent off balance. Cost: 5 rage.*

Conceal (Passive). *Hides level from anyone who is not a guard on city grounds.*

Summon Horror (Passive). *Ability to summon a horror. Each horror grants a unique ability. For every horror active, gain 1% increased damage and health points. Horrors decay 10% for every minute outside of combat.*

Horror of Power. *Summon a horror with 20% of your strength. Cost: 100 mana. Cooldown: 30 seconds. Bonus: Your next attack deals double damage.*

Horror of Vitality. *Summon a horror with 20% of your health points. Cost: 100 mana. Cooldown: 30 seconds. Bonus: Opponents near Horror of Vitality are slowed by 20%.*

Horror of Finesse. *Summon a horror with 20% of your attack speed. Cost: 100 mana. Cooldown: 30 seconds. Bonus: Your next attack heals you for damage dealt.*

Sacrifice. *Sacrifice X amount of horrors to receive a temporary buff. Horror of Power: +1 Strength. Horror of Vitality: +1 Constitution. Horror of Finesse: +1 Dexterity*

Kamikaze. *Sacrifice a horror to deal a burst of damage.*

Champion. *Summon a copy of the most recent enemy you have* *defeated. Decays 10% every minute out of combat. Cost: 50% of mana pool. Cooldown: 6 hours.*

Available Abilities *(1 ability point to unlock):*

Massive Bite. *Deals double damage. Cost: 20 rage.*

Claws. *Swipe at opponent with both hands, dealing extra damage. Cost: 10 rage.*

Multi Attack. *Bite and Claw at the same time. Cost: 20 rage.*

Iron Will. *Immune to slows and stuns for 30 seconds. Cost: 50 rage. 180 second cooldown.*

Perception. *For 10 minutes, gain increased awareness of your surroundings. Spot hidden objects, as well as unusual sounds, odors, and tastes. Cooldown: 6 hours.*

Cleave. *Your next attack causes bleed damage, dealing 1% of opponent's health per second for 5 seconds. Cost: 10 rage.*

Battle Cry. *You let out a ferocious roar, increasing rage by 20. No cost. 60 second cooldown.*

Current Items:

Item. Phoenix Feather. 10% resistance to fire-based attacks. *A very rare item, phoenix feathers can only be gathered if they are willingly given by the host. Feathers plucked from unwilling birds turn to ash.*

Item. Tiger's Eye Pendant. Removes one debuff. Cooldown: 10 minutes. *A rare stone believed to ward off evil and bring balance to life.*

Item. Petrified Staff. An enchanted staff capable of taking on the properties of up to 3 attached stones. +3 Intelligence. +3 Wisdom. Bonus: *While holding Petrified Staff, the user can cast ranged physical attacks once every 10 seconds.*

Item. Forlorn Scepter. +5 Intelligence. *Increases the range of summoned creatures by 50%.*

Item. Glouwseeker Venom. *When injected into the bloodstream, glouwseeker venom immobilizes target. Length of stun dependent on size of target, resistances, and amount injected.*

Item. Sea Scorpion. +3 Strength. *An enchanted trident capable of taking on the property of 1 enchanted stone. Bonus: deals splash damage.*

Legendary Item. Angel of Death Brandy. *When drinker falls below 1HP, a metaphysical event will occur, rewinding time for the user to two seconds prior to death.*

Item. Brimming Tankard. *A magical tankard that, once filled, will never go empty. Warning: Once filled, contents cannot be changed. Only works on beverages.*

Item. Expandable Satchel. *A bag capable of holding enormous content and only burdening the wearer with ten percent of its weight. Simply focus on the item inside and it will appear in your hand.*

Item. Destroyer. An enchanted warhammer capable of taking on the properties of up to three stones. +2 Strength, +3 Constitution. *This ancient warhammer was forged in the heart of a volcano.* ***Bonus Ability: Inferno.*** *With each consecutive hit, Destroyer grows hotter, allowing it to warp or pierce through even the hardest metals. Multiplier works when hits are less than five seconds apart. Cost: 10 mana per attack. Cooldown: 10 sec.*

Item. Spaulder of Swiftness. +1 Constitution, +1 Dexterity. *Lightweight, durable leather mail designed to protect the off-hand shoulder during battle.*

Item. Mysterious Green Egg. *???*

Item. Halite Shield. *A lightweight translucent shield capable of taking damage without reducing visibility.*

PROLOGUE

VALERY SAT ALONE STARING into Chad Johnson's pod. He looked peaceful laying there, despite the chaos happening on the monitor above. The technicians responsible for monitoring player health had either gone home for the day or were asleep in the on-call bunks.

For the past five years, she had devoted her life to the lab. This was her pet project, after all. And now it had morphed into something far beyond what she'd ever imagined.

The lab was quiet except for the gentle whir of the machines. Machines keeping twenty-five men alive while their consciousnesses were fully immersed in a virtual world.

That in itself was a miracle so far removed from the days where gaming was nothing more than hitting a ball between two lines. But this, *Isle of Mythos*, was far more than just gaming.

She'd been sitting there so long that the automatic lights overhead had switched to low-power mode. The glow from the monitors and the electric blue nanites gave the pristine white lab an ethereal feel.

It was fitting.

Nearly two months had passed since Chad had first logged in. Getting a gamer into the trial had been the goal—an easy way to work out the bugs so they could move up the timeline—but he had changed everything.

When they'd discovered that he was the reason the game was crashing, she couldn't believe it. Somehow, the AI believed that he was a part of the system. An integral part.

Looking at his body lying peacefully inside the pod, there was no doubt that this was only the beginning.

The system was designed to rehabilitate. It wasn't as simple as going in and rewiring someone's brain to make better choices. That was impossible. The AI that ran *Isle of Mythos* was one of the most advanced of its kind. It presented the user with choices, evolving the world around them based on actions and reactions. While most programs struggled to accomplish this with any real results for a single user, this AI evolved the world seamlessly for dozens of users at the same time.

Valery had known she would face obstacles in bringing her vision to life. She'd seen the writing on the wall. The only way she could have gotten the funding to pull this off was by appealing to a company with deep pockets. A company like Mythos Gaming.

She believed that this technology could change the world.

What she saw before her sent terror into the depths of her soul.

Chad Johnson had climbed into that pod weighing one-hundred and twenty pounds, skinny as a rail with acne and a sunken chest.

The clear skin and superficial changes had been expected. The nanites cleaned the body better than a hot shower and steel wool.

When they'd first pulled Chad from the pod, he had looked leaner, more defined. That happened to most of the users. The nanites provided them with a perfectly balanced, nutrient rich diet.

What had happened in the weeks since then was anything but normal. Thompson had pointed out the discrepancy when it first became noticeable, and Valery had checked the stats on everyone else to compare.

Whatever was happening, it was only happening to Chad. She had combed over every move he'd made since logging in. She had theories. Theories she wanted to test, but that meant finding more volunteers.

That was easier said than done—especially knowing what she knew now.

Pretty soon, she was going to have to answer some very tough questions.

Like how Chad Johnson's body had managed to put on twenty pounds of muscle while in stasis.

CHAPTER I
READY TO RUN

"Are you sure this is going to work?" Taryn squints as he peers through the foliage, brushing several dreadlocks behind his ear. "It's the middle of the day. This still seems kind of reckless."

I duck a little lower, concealing myself behind a leafy frond that drapes across one of the canals carrying water to the bathhouses.

"It's not like we have a choice. The only time this guy comes out is during the day." My gaze shifts from Limery to the beastkin he's tailing. "It'll work. Limery is the best pickpocket I know. He'll be in and out before we know it."

I focus back on Limery as he hovers along the crowded street several meters behind his target. Massive beastkin walk leisurely through the stone streets of the market, furry humanoids with the heads of lions, tigers, bears, and a myriad of other creatures that occupy the city of Goldspire.

The center of the city is rife with activity, from shops to entertainment. Despite being closed off to lower-level NPCs and players, the city forum is thriving. Taryn, Limery, and I are some of the few foreigners currently on the continent, but my troll appearance doesn't stick out as much here as in Vanaria or Seascape.

Limery comes to a stop behind a beastkin with the head of a hippo.

Cornix Coinbearer

Hand of the Emperor
Level: ???
Monk
Beastkin

He wears a white canvas toga draped across his oily, slate-colored skin, and several amulets dangle from his neck. For his position, his clothing is surprisingly modest. Except for a golden key hidden among the amulets.

A key that will grant us access to the emperor's villa on the edge of town.

For the past three days, the emperor has been absent from the royal palace. Rumor has it he's indulging in his very own saturnalia of debauchery at his villa overlooking the Sapphire Channel. But time is of the essence, and we need to deliver King Orso's message so that we can be on our way.

The hippo leans forward, the necklaces dangling as he admires a selection of bright yellow fruit on a cart. In the shuffle, the golden key catches the light. Cornix lifts one of the melon-sized citruses to examine it, and Limery moves in.

Limery's hand burns a molten orange as he reaches for the chain holding the key. The golden chain melts against his long spindly finger and it slips off the hippo's neck, slinking into Limery's other hand.

The imp flashes me a demonic smile and zips through the air. The chain catches against one of the other amulets, jerking Limery back and tearing the hippo from his focus on the fruit.

There's a moment of startling realization on both their faces as the wide-eyed hippo stares at the bulbous-eyed imp.

Cornix shouts something, and I launch myself across the trickling channel, landing with a thud in the stone courtyard of the forum.

"Some pickpocket he turned out to be." Taryn grunts as he lands behind me. "He's going to get us all killed."

Limery darts through Cornix's legs. The hippo turns in a flash, extending a ki-powered punch at Limery. His impish speed saves him, but the force of the punch explodes the fruit cart, sending wood and pulp raining through the streets.

Limery speeds down a flight of wide, shallow stairs toward Taryn and I.

He hovers for a second, inches from my face. "We's needs to goes, Chods." He glances over his shoulder just as Cornix leaps through the air, nearly covering the distance in a single bound.

We don't waste any time putting our feet to the stone-covered streets of Goldspire. The fruit market empties into the main court-yard of the forum, where a beautiful mosaic depicts a colorful battle. Musicians and street performers cover the courtyard, playing for tips. Beastkin sit around fountains, and tall Corinthian columns rise into the air, their floral embellishments topped with statues of great warriors.

Cornix runs with surprising speed for a being so large. His big round eyes are slits of anger as he chases us down the city streets. I summon a Horror of Vitality, hoping for its passive slow to give us some breathing room. Cornix's fist moves in a blur, exploding the horror with a single strike without slowing even a fraction.

Damn, he's fast.

Goldspire citizens step back as we run, watching the chase unfold. In the center of the forum, Goldspire's namesake—a towering golden obelisk—juts into the sky.

Taryn casts Strong Wind, buffing our movement speed, but it offers little advantage. Cornix's stout legs take on a golden aura and he matches our speed once again.

"We need to lose him!" I point at a temple with ornate columns at the edge of the forum. "Through there."

I take the stairs into the temple several at a time. Taryn avoids the stairs entirely by transforming into his bird form, then returning to his dwarven form at the top. The temple is filled with statues of Goldspire's multi-limbed gods and goddesses. Scenes of divine magic plaster the vaulted ceiling, and even more detailed mosaics cover the floor.

I summon more horrors and send them toward the entrance to block our pursuer, but they meet the same fate as their predecessor, destroyed by the hippo monk's lightning reflexes.

We exit into another wide street that's littered with carts and merchants. Limery tosses a fireball at Cornix as he exits the temple, but the monk dashes to the right in a blur and the fireball leaves a scorch mark against the marble as it explodes.

I point to a bathhouse, and Limery darts ahead. As I pass through the wide, green marble arch, I bump into a tiger beastkin with a towel wrapped around his waist, nearly knocking him into one of the many rectangular bathing pools. All around us, dozens of beastkin soak in the water or sit on the tiered edges as attendants groom them and comb through their fur with lavish oils. The vaulted ceiling gives the bathhouse a spacious elegance as water drips and bubbles all around.

At the back of the bathhouse, I climb a spiral staircase that empties into a veranda overlooking a lush garden. Limery and Taryn once again take to the air.

A long crystal blue pool stretches the length of the garden, with two elephant beastkin fountains shooting streams of water from one to the other. Ornate topiaries run along the edge, forming their own menagerie of fantastical creatures. Large trees offer shade among the many patios scattered throughout.

The thud of hooves announces that Cornix is catching up, so I jump from the veranda, landing hard against the stone pathway. Another burst of Strong Wind sends me speeding down the garden path.

Cornix leaps from the veranda without hesitation, landing at a full sprint without so much as slowing.

Damn his monk abilities!

At the end of the garden, we pass through a set of triumphal arches, the entablature on top carved with gilded runes, and exit into another street lined with apartments.

Taryn summons a cluster of poison mushrooms under the arch, and I follow Limery as he takes to the right. A few seconds later, the monk passes through the mushrooms, setting off their poisonous gasses. Purple clouds waft through the arch, and a silver sheen covers Cornix's body, mitigating the poison entirely.

At the end of the row of apartments, we cut through an open-air theatre. Boos swarm us as we disrupt the performance of a plum-colored minotaur. He shakes his fist overhead in the throes of despair, replaying some tragedy for the crowd. A tomato splats against my face from some disappointed spectator.

We pass another row of buildings before the city wall looms before us.

"End of the line." For the first time since our chase began, Cornix slows to a walk.

I summon a round of horrors in front of me while I try to find us a way out of this. There's no way we can fight him, and I'd rather not spend the next few days locked away in the Goldspire dungeon. Cornix takes another step toward us, and Limery summons a fire wall in front of him.

Cornix smirks, revealing his massive cinderblock teeth. "Fire doesn't scare me." He steps into the flame wall and a dense silver sheen covers his lower body, reflecting the flames like he is made of metal. "My body is an unbreakable temple, crafted through years of discipline. Now, give me my key and be on your way. No one need get hurt. I'll chalk it up to the folly of heroes."

Taryn and I glance at each other. It's nice that he is offering us a way out, but to meet with the emperor, we need this key. It's the only way we'll be able to gain access to him. We can't wait however many days it takes for the emperor to decide to return to the palace.

Incoming Message (Taryn): *I've got a plan. When I give the signal, we run down the alleyway adjacent to the wall and cut through the basilica.*

Taryn steps forward, one hand raised in surrender with the other on his Sapling Staff. "You're right. It was a stupid mistake. If you'll just allow us to—"

The earth cracks and a stone wall rises between the buildings, Taryn's newest ability separating us from the Hand of the Emperor.

"Run!" Taryn shouts and we race down the alley, Strong Wind giving us added speed.

There's a loud crash of what I can only assume is Cornix smashing through Taryn's Stonewall with his mighty fists.

"I hope that wasn't your entire plan."

We pass the blacksmith, whose hammer and anvil echo down

the alley, and I jump through an open window into the basilica, where two long rows of spiraled columns run under the vaulted ceilings.

The elegant hall is filled with merchants selling spices, wool, clothing, and ancient books. We don't have time to appreciate the beauty of the art or architecture of the building before we exit the other side into another crowded street.

A door slams behind us as Cornix bursts out of the basilica. Steam shoots out of his nose just before we turn another corner and I lose visual. A moment later, he's right on us again.

"Taryn…" There's only a matter of seconds before we are about to be pulverized by this not-so-gentle giant.

He lifts his staff into the air once more, summoning a twenty-foot wall along the width of the alley. There's a crash as Cornix barrels into it at full speed. It won't be long before he tears through it as well.

"Quick, in here." Taryn pulls open the door, ushering us inside.

I'm about to chastise Taryn for thinking we can hide from a city official when a welcoming voice calls from over my shoulder.

"Welcome to The Wilty Rose Inn. Would you like a room for the evening?" A falcon beastkin wearing a purple silk toga bows slightly to us from behind the bar.

I reach in my pouch, pull out a gold coin, and slam it on the counter. "Yes!"

Taryn, you bloody genius.

CHAPTER 2

THE WILTY ROSE INN

QUEST ALERT. You have completed the quest "Sneaky Sneak Key." Reward: Imperial Key. This key opens the enchanted locks protecting all imperial estates, including the emperor's villa overlooking the Sapphire Channel.

I hold the small, golden skeleton key between my fingers. The handle is composed of elaborate metal knotwork with an encrusted ruby in the center. Funny how something so small caused us so much trouble. This key will give us access to the emperor, where we can plead our case on behalf of King Orso. With the power scale of those in Goldspire, having them on our side when the time comes could be the difference between victory and defeat.

"Close call." I hand the key to Taryn.

He lifts it and grins. "No kidding. I was not expecting him to move that fast. Or be that powerful. I thought monks just sat in silence all day." He flips the key over in his palm. "Talk about subverting expectations. Good job getting out of Dodge, Limery."

Limery peeks through the shutters, examining the streets below. "Limmy is too fasts for the hippo mans."

"But not fast enough to not get caught." Taryn takes a pillow off the bed and hurls it at the tiny red imp.

Limery dodges the pillow with ease, sticking his tongue out at Taryn. "Nobodies is perfect. Right, Chods?"

I can't help but laugh. Maybe my words are starting to sink in. "Right you are. It all worked out in the end, though. Thanks to Taryn's quick thinking."

Coming up with a plan to block off the road was a brilliant idea—especially considering we were running for our lives. One of the amazing things about inn rooms is that they are magically protected. While renting a room, heroes can set their spawn points inside. Even if Cornix had seen us enter the inn, we'd be safe inside our room until we decided to leave.

Thanks to Taryn's wall, we were able to disappear inside The Wilty Rose Inn, leaving the Hand of the Emperor none the wiser. No doubt he is scouring the streets of Goldspire looking for us.

Let's just hope we can make it to the villa without being spotted.

We spend the rest of the evening in our room, waiting for the sun to set while Taryn complains about us not taking his pets on our adventure.

He crosses his arms and frowns. "I just don't see why we can't ride them across the city. It's a long walk. And you know how Berry gets when he doesn't see me."

"Once we talk to the emperor, you can parade them through the city for all I care. But for now, we're trying to keep a low profile. They're well taken care of at the stables. Besides, they have each other."

Taryn lays back on the bed and pulls a pillow over his face. "It's like you're taking away my children."

"That's a little dramatic. But who knows, maybe after two days, Stompy will show you a little affection." I smirk.

He tosses the pillow at me. "Now, you're just being mean."

When the streets are dark except for the torches that light the stony corridors, we venture out into the inn.

There's a dull roar of chatter as we descend the stairs. Glass clinks as two satyrs toast one another, their glasses brimming with golden wine. Platters of grapes, cheese, and toasted breads cover the tables.

Compared to the raucous taverns of the dwarves, this inn has a certain sophistication to it.

"They're quite refined to be so brutish looking, don't you think?" asks Taryn.

I nod. "Everything does seem much more laidback here."

Since arriving in the city, it has seemed to move at its own pace. No one is in a hurry. The beastkin take time to enjoy the moment, and their fondness for sports and the arts is unrivaled.

"Fancy a glass of spiced wine?" a gentle voice asks from behind the bar.

The elegant falcon from earlier has been replaced with a slender fox beastkin who flutters her eyelashes in our direction. She wears a teal sash around her head, just below her pointy ears, and a yellow tunic embroidered with a wilted red rose. Several small golden hoops dangle from her left ear. When she steps out from behind the bar, her silky teal pants flow with her movements, and an ornate dagger hangs from her waist.

She picks up an empty glass off a nearby table and returns to the bar. There's something oddly alluring about her presence. I focus on her stats and am surprised to discover that the Goldspire bartender is level twenty.

We are so out of our league here.

"What's it gonna be, big blue?" She winks.

Limery flies over to the bar, reaching for a wine glass. "Limmy wants wines."

"When we get back," I manage to get out. "We have business to attend first."

She smiles. "I'll be here all night."

I force my eyes away and examine the rest of the inn. A brawny, bluish-black bear sits in the corner smoking a pipe. A lioness and minotaura lean in close at a nearby table, playing a game with black and white marbles.

Limery swoops in and snatches a piece of cured meat off the satyrs' platter without being noticed.

"Now he can pickpocket," Taryn mumbles under his breath.

"Ready to get this show on the road?" I ask.

Taryn pulls his hood over his head, concealing his features in shadow. "Let's do it."

I take the white-and-green shawl I purchased in Sandholde from my satchel and drape it over my shoulders, doing my best to conceal my identity. "Limery, it's probably best if you hide in here. You are a wanted man, after all."

Limery climbs onto my shoulder and nestles himself within the fabric.

I open the door and we step out into the cobbled streets. The moon shines bright overhead, casting the skyline in a silver glow. Every so often a torch crackles, illuminating the gray stone with hints of orange. From where we're standing, the golden obelisk of the forum towers above all, as if drawing in the light of the moon itself.

Further still, the royal palace, gladiatorial arena, numerous temples, and other structures look down from the hilltop.

A black minotaur comes lumbering down the street, a pike slung over his shoulder. Limery grows warm against my skin, and Taryn and I both lower our heads, avoiding eye contact. When he passes by, I let out the breath I've been holding.

"Where do you think Pressley is?" Taryn asks as we continue down the street.

We haven't seen the death knight since leaving the arena. I doubt we would be here now without him. He's a solo adventurer by nature, but when the time comes, I know we'll be able to count on him. "No idea. I'm sure he's around here somewhere, looking for gold and glory."

"Well, he certainly came to the right place. Marble buildings, golden statues. This entire city is a work of art."

We enter the forum, where braziers blaze all around, bathing the mosaics and sculptures in flickering light. The gentle gurgle of the canals puts me at ease.

Compared to most cities, Goldspire is surprisingly alive at night. With so many people still out, we easily lose ourselves in the crowd. Music carries through the open windows of the inns and taverns, and the open-air theatres are filled with crowds watching the evening shows.

The royal palace sits at the top of the hill overlooking the forum, but the imperial villa is located on the other side of the city with views of the channel.

We stop for a moment to admire a fire-breathing performance where a silver-furred wolf beastkin spews flames in a cone above the crowd. It reminds me of Hawkin and the Underground Circus.

I wonder what they're up to these days.

Two lion beastkin approach from across the way. Their eyes are piercing and alert as they scan their surroundings. Massive manes rest on segmented armor composed of metal strips that are tied at the front. A red sash drapes across their shoulders: imperial armor.

Gaurus Bladefur
Imperial Guard
Level: 34

Caius Timbertongue
Imperial Guard
Level: 35

I grab Taryn by the arm and pull him into an alleyway before they spot us.

"What the hell, Chod?" Taryn snaps.

I can tell by his stiff posture that he's scowling at me beneath his hood.

"Put your head down and just keep walking."

His shoulders relax, and he does what I say. Limery's claws dig into my shoulders, but the imp doesn't speak.

Once we pass through the alleyway onto another street, I finally breathe again.

"Want to tell me what that was all about?" Taryn lifts his hood and his eyes bore into me.

"Those two lions were imperial guards, both leveled in the mid-thirties. If they chose to focus on us, there would have been no hiding our identities."

He lets his hood drop, once again hiding his eyes. "Good looking out, but maybe be a little more gentle next time. We need to get to the imperial villa ASAP."

Taryn raises his staff and there's a lightness in my feet as Strong Wind takes effect. We move at a brisk walk that's more akin to a run. Before I know it, we're at the edge of the city where the high-walled estates conceal the rich and powerful from prying eyes.

The edge of the city along the channel has no walls, just a steep and unscalable drop-off into the roaring currents below. The views are splendid, but no one is going for a dip in those waters.

As the houses get bigger, we see fewer and fewer travelers on the roads. By the time we reach the stretch with the imperial villa, Taryn and I are the only ones on the street.

Fortune favors us as the moon disappears behind a thick layer of clouds, shrouding the streets in darkness. The rich and powerful prefer their privacy and keep the torches that light the streets to a minimum, leaving us with plenty of shadows to cling to.

Elegant villas with sweeping vistas of the Sapphire Channel surround us. The grandest among them is the imperial villa. A golden gate with two ornamental Fs back-to-back is all that stands between us and our mission.

I come to a stop in front of the gate. "Kind of eerie that it's so empty, don't you think?"

"These are the summer homes of the elite. Most of them are probably living it up at their mansions in the city's center."

"But we haven't even seen any guards." That's the part that concerns me.

Taryn shrugs. "Maybe the Hand pulled them all to the palace. At our levels, it's not like he's worried about us attacking the emperor. They're so powerful around here that I bet their stable-boys could kill us. He's probably more concerned with us stealing some rare artifact."

He makes a fair point. I take the key from my inventory and insert it into the lock. As I twist the key, the keyhole glows a bright white and energy flares along the metal of the gate.

The gate opens at the middle, and the facade of an empty villa fades. Lively music comes to an abrupt halt, and dozens of eyes stare in our direction.

CHAPTER 3

THE ROGUE EMPEROR

So much for not causing a scene.

My first instinct is to run, but it doesn't take more than a quick glance to know that if hands start flying, we'll be respawning back at the inn before we have time to blink. Except for Limery.

If nothing else, I have to play this cool for his sake.

My heartbeat pounds in my ears, and for the longest time, no one moves. The many beastkin stare at us with curious expressions. Some hold glasses of champagne, and others dip their feet into a pool with a vibrant purple glow emanating beneath its surface. Olive trees sway gently in the breeze. Many torches flicker around the edges of the property. A band, consisting of two foxes and a deer beastkin with massive antlers, play stringed instruments on a raised platform to the left.

The clank of metal cuts through the silence as two imperial guards, one a black-maned lion and the other a golden-skinned rhinoceros, step out from the back of the crowd. Their hands grip the gladius strapped to their waists as they walk with purpose.

"There's no need for that," a sultry voice speaks up from the back.

Several beastkin step out of the way, revealing a tiger beastkin sprawled on a daybed draped with furs. Two servants fan the tiger with massive leaves, and another holds a platter of grapes. In spite of the severity of our situation, I suppress a grin when I realize that all of the servants are mice beastkin.

I focus on the tiger.

Festa Forgetooth

Emperor of Goldspire.

Level: ???

Rogue

Beastkin

I don't know why, but I wasn't expecting the emperor to be a woman. But even more interesting is the fact that she has a class. A rogue emperor. Neither King Orso nor King Favian had a class listed when I focused on their stats. Was it because they chose to conceal it?

Festa doesn't move from her position as she lifts a paw, stopping the guards in their tracks. Her fur is a deep black, with orange stripes that match her fiery eyes. She wears a single golden necklace, and a golden laurel crown that glitters even against the night sky.

She extends a claw, pointing it in our direction. "It's not often we get outsiders in Goldspire. Even rarer that outsiders would be of such a low level." She pauses, and it feels as though she is looking into my very being. "But most strange is not the fact that they have a key to my private estate, but that two of them are heroes."

Gasps travel through the group, followed by hushed whispers.

"Heroes—"

"Is it true?"

"It's been ages. What could heroes be doing in Goldspire?"

The emperor raises her paw, and we stand in silence once more. "Leave us be."

There are more whispers as guests begin moving inside. The band exits the stage, taking their instruments with them.

The black-maned guard turns toward the emperor. "Your Majesty, it is unwise—"

"Choose your next words carefully, Cinnius," she cuts him off. "Do I not command the wisdom to lead Goldspire?"

The lion bows. "You do, Your Majesty."

"And have you met anyone who could best your emperor in combat, armed or otherwise?"

"I have not, Your Majesty."

"Then you would do well to remember your place and leave the decision-making to me. Now, inside with the others, for I do not fear two heroes and an imp, curious as they may be."

The lion nods. He takes one last glance at us over his shoulder before following the trail of whispers into the villa.

The emperor sits up on the daybed, waving away her servants except for the two fanning her.

"Come, I wish to look upon your faces."

Taryn removes his hood, and Limery burns uncomfortably hot against my shoulder as I remove the shawl.

"You have nothing to fear, little one. At least not yet." She flashes us a dangerous smile, her fangs a brilliant white against her obsidian fur.

We approach with caution. I keep mana at my fingertips, ready to summon a horror at a moment's notice. Not that it would do me any good. I could use Champion to summon Dakota, the minotaur gladiator we defeated in the arena. Perhaps he could buy us time to escape.

"Have a seat." She motions toward a second daybed nearby. "I have a feeling this story is going to take a while."

We do as she says, and once again, we find ourselves sitting in silence.

The emperor lets out a sigh. "Is my presence that all-consuming or are the lot of you mutes?"

Limery is the first to speak. "Chods saids Limmy should be quiet when we comes to the emperor's house. He saids we don't want to get caughts." The words spew out like a waterfall.

A grin forms at the edge of her mouth. "Is that so? I take it you are Limmy. Now which one of you would be Chod?"

I raise a hand. "That would be me. I am Chod, hero of the forest trolls of the Isle of Mythos."

The emperor can see our levels and the wanted marks placed on us by Cornix, but she must not be able to see our names unless we are identified. Or is she toying with us?

"A blue forest troll, that's a first. And who would that make you, Mr. Dwarf?"

Taryn proudly puffs out his chest. "I am Taryn, hero of the dwarves of Seascape."

Gentle music resumes inside the villa. Festa glances over her shoulder and her eyes narrow slightly.

"Never mind them." She places her paws on the daybed as she leans forward, and several ebony claws protract with the movement. Claws that could rip us to shreds. "Now, tell me..." Her voice has a gentle purr to it as she speaks. "How did you get this key, and what are two under-leveled heroes doing in my city?"

For less than a second, Festa's orange stripes turn black, her entire being a shroud of darkness. A cold breeze passes over me, sending a chill down my spine, and the next thing I know, Festa is holding the imperial key. She moved so fast that I didn't even feel her take it from my hand. I get the feeling that that ability is only a glimpse into what she is capable of.

Her eyes linger on Limery.

The small imp squirms next to me. "We stole its."

Sometimes I wish I could tape his demonic little mouth shut.

He scoots closer to me, as if I can shield him from her impenetrable gaze. Little does he know of my own inner turmoil. Because if this goes south, I'm not going to be able to protect anyone.

"Curious. You know, Cornix is renowned for—"

I interrupt her before she decides on a punishment to fit the crime. "We had no choice. King Orso asked us to deliver a message. You haven't been at the imperial palace since we arrived in Goldspire, and we didn't know when you would return. We were tipped off that you would be at the villa, and that your Hand had a key to all imperial estates. We didn't mean any harm, but we did what we had to do."

Her eyes turn to slits, and for a moment, my body tenses and I worry she is about to pounce. "Interrupt me again, and you will regret the day you ever set foot in Goldspire, hero or not." She sighs. "As flippant as you may seem to the hierarchy and rules of my empire, I am not without understanding. Like all Goldspirians, I too was raised on the legends of the Age of Heroes. I find it strange that only the Isle of Mythos has heroes, but more may reveal themselves in time. If you are here, it is because a change is coming. Now, tell me, what is the message from your king?"

Taryn gulps before speaking. He tells the emperor of the portals, of the king's fears, his council with the other leaders, and the behemoth that came through Seascape's portal. When he finishes, I receive a quest notification.

Quest Alert. You have completed the quest "First Contact: Gold-spire." You have traveled into the lands of Goldspire and delivered King Orso Brightgaze's message to its leader.

Reward: Increased favor with Seascape, potential allies in Goldspire.

The quest notification must boost Taryn's confidence, because he continues, "So, will you join us when the time comes?"

"I think not," she says matter-of-factly, as if the rise of the dark wizard is nothing more than a passing problem that can be shrugged off.

"B-but—" Taryn's eyes are wide. "—are you not worried about the dark wizard, about the safety of your people?"

A cool breeze washes over us once again, and Limery grows hot against my side. Festa returns to a shadow once more, and all around us, the torch lights go out one by one until only the soft purple glow of the pool and the moon overhead give us light.

When she speaks, even my night vision can't see the features of her face. "I do not fault a king who has only just gained access to the portals for being afraid, but Goldspire has nothing to fear. We have fought off invaders time and time again. The gladiators you faced in the arena were merely a test. A test to determine if you were worthy to even walk our streets. When our best enter the arena, we leave no opponent standing."

She may talk a big talk, but our fight with the warlock outside of Lynchton is proof enough that something bigger is at play. Something we all need to prepare for.

In the darkness, the shrouded emperor exudes power, but Taryn didn't get this far by cowering away. "Valmar Worren conquered the lands of Mythos once before. Who is to say he can't do it again?"

She scoffs. "Is that name supposed to frighten me? Do you know the history of Mythos, the history of Goldspire? I battled

Valmar on the sands of the arena when he thought my empire would be a worthy addition to his cause. He left the same way he entered: a would-be conqueror. Goldspire has never been conquered, and it never will be."

"You fought the dark wizard?" I stumble to my feet at the knowledge. This is a game-changer! Someone who actually knows how the dark wizard operates. "Then you can help us with the knowledge to defeat him. Not many were alive at that—"

"I have heard enough. Tell your king that I wish him well, but Goldspire will stand as it always has—alone. He is welcome to come and plead his case himself if it suits him, but my decision is firm."

"Festa, please," I plead.

I know my mistake instantly. Her shroud fades and the orange stripes along her body blaze with energy. She's in front of me in an instant, her long, lithe legs making her nearly as tall as me.

Her whiskers brush against my cheek as she whispers in my ear. "Leave now, and I will forgive this insolence. You delivered your message. You have your response. I do not advise you to test my patience."

I want to stay, to try one last time to win her over, but Taryn tugs at my arm, telling me it's time to go. We completed the quest, but we failed in the end. Goldspire will not be joining our cause.

CHAPTER 4
POUR ME ANOTHER

THE ONLY GOOD that came out of that meeting is that our wanted marks are gone. As we walk in silence from the villa to the inn, I'm sure we're all feeling the same thing.

Failure.

"I just don't get it." Taryn's voice is strained. "She's fought Valmar before. Not only that, they were able to keep him from marching on Goldspire. How can she just keep that information to herself? What if he's more powerful this time?"

I place my hand on his shoulder, offering what little comfort I can. "I know, buddy. We tried and we failed. Now, we have no choice but to move on."

"Yeah." Limery hops from my shoulder to Taryn's and pats him on the head. "It's like Chods says. It's ain't overs til it's overs."

He gives us a half-smile. "So what now?"

"Now, we continue on. We level up, and we get stronger. We explore new cities and keep trying to win people to the cause. With so many portals open, it will be a lot harder to find other heroes, but that doesn't mean we can stop trying. Who knows what else is waiting for us out there?"

He nods. "You're right. Only a handful of leaders came to the king's council. Our work is far from over, but I can't help but feel like we are leaving a lot on the table here. I mean, if Dakota and the others aren't even their strongest fighters, can you imagine what having them on our side would mean?"

"I do. But who knows what the future holds? For now, I say we're lucky we get to live to fight another day."

Taryn looks over his shoulder in the direction of the villa and shakes his head. "Ain't that the truth."

We spend the next while speculating on the emperor's power. The way she moved was like nothing I've ever seen.

The streets are much quieter on our return. By the time we reach the forum, only stragglers remain. A handful of imperial guards patrol the area, but we walk with our faces revealed, no longer having to worry about being arrested.

True to her word, the fox beastkin is still tending bar when we arrive at the inn. The lioness and minotaura continue their game of marbles, but the rest of the guests have cleared out.

"You boys look like you could use a drink." She gestures at three barstools in front of her.

"You have no idea." Taryn plops down on the stool. "I don't care what it is but make it strong."

I analyze the bartender a little more closely this time.

Portia Swiftwill

Level: 22

Beastkin

Limery stands on his stool and leans against the bar. Portia takes three glasses from the overhead rack and places them on the bar, filling them with a golden wine.

She slides the glasses in front of us. "I know a rough day when I see it. Here, these are on the house."

"Thanks." I tilt my glass to her before taking a swig.

The wine is cool and refreshing. It's crisp as it goes down, dry and minerally, like licking a wet stone, but the aroma is floral and vibrant.

Limery cups the wine glass in both hands and guzzles it, wine streaking down his chin. "Yums."

Taryn downs his and asks for another. "What can I say? Goldspire knows how to make a fine drink."

"That we do." She winks, her green eyes mesmerizing against her orange fur. "So, tell me, what has a group of travelers like yourselves in such a fuss?"

Taryn takes a chug of his new drink, then sighs. "We were on a quest for the King of Seascape. We failed."

She reaches out and taps Taryn on the hand. "That's unfortunate. Still, it must be pretty exciting to live the life of a hero."

Limery sways back and forth, the wine already hitting him. "They's the bestest heroes."

"Have a seat before you fall on the floor." I laugh as I help Limery sit on the stool before turning to Portia. "Do you have anything he's less likely to spill?"

She hands me a regular glass, and I pour the wine into it. Sometimes, having Limery around is like babysitting a toddler. If that toddler could burn you alive without so much as straining a muscle.

I take a seat between Limery and Taryn, finishing off my first glass. My head begins to buzz at the edges, and I suddenly feel much more talkative. "Being a hero is exciting. There's always something to do and someone to save, but there's a lot of pressure that comes with the territory. People look to us for answers, and we don't always have them. There's a lot more to being a hero than just adventuring."

Taryn gently pounds his fist against the bar. "That's the truth of it. And now that the portals are open, there's more to do than ever."

"What do you mean?" Portia leans forward, her green eyes vibrant with interest.

Taryn's eyes meet mine for a moment, and I can tell he's wondering the same thing I am. How much should we tell her?

I nod to him to go on. If we can't sway the emperor, we can at least spread word among the people of what we're dealing with.

"A war is coming…" he begins, recounting everything that has happened since the portal opened.

By the time he finishes, not only is Portia leaning against the edge of the bar, but the lioness and minotaura have quit playing their game. They both are turned toward us, enthralled like children at story time.

For the longest time, the only sounds in the inn are Limery's slurps as he drinks his wine.

"You are certain he has returned?" Portia's face is set in stone.

I shrug. "Nothing is certain, but everything points in that direction. The portals flaring to life on the Isle of Mythos, the only place where heroes have appeared. The warlock and his beings from the shadowlands. The behemoth. Something is definitely up."

She bites her lip and exchanges looks with the other two beastkin. "The emperor's battle with Valmar is one of the most famous tales in Goldspire. I was not yet born at the time, but we beastkin live long lives and there are many who can still vouch for its accuracy. It is said that the battle shook the heavens. That it was the only time in Goldspire's history where it was feared the city might fall."

"Tell us about it." Taryn slides his glass forward for another refill.

She shakes her head as she empties a bottle of wine into Taryn's glass. "I fear I do not have the skill to do it justice. We have talked enough of dark matters for one night. What is next for you three?"

I finish off my own glass and the room starts to spin. "Somewhere far from here. We're not sure where, though. What do you know of the other portals?"

"Me? Not much. There's plenty of adventure in and around Goldspire for me. You know, there are ancient dungeons of great power outside the city walls. I'm sure they are a worthy challenge for heroes."

Taryn laughs. "That might be too worthy of a challenge. Goldspire is beautiful and full of adventure, but for now, we should set our sights on greener pastures."

"It is rare for beastkin to leave Goldspire. We take pride in our lands and our culture. But there are those, scholars mostly, who have explored distant lands for first-hand knowledge of other cultures. I know one who may help guide you on your adventures."

Limery's eyes grow heavy, and he slumps over. I catch him and his glass just before they tumble to the floor.

"I think it is bedtime for this one. When can we meet your friend?"

She takes our empty glasses and sets them aside. "Take the day to explore some of the beauty Goldspire has to offer. At sundown, meet me by the spire, and I will introduce you."

I pay our tab, and we head to our room. Looks like we'll be in town for at least one more day.

CHAPTER 5
THE PRICE OF FREEDOM

WE ENJOY A MORE leisurely walk through the basilica now that we aren't being chased by a hippo capable of swatting us like mosquitos. Dozens of small shops and vendors line both sides of the hall. A white owl beastkin stands behind a counter selling perfumes and other concoctions. His head twists at an awkward angle as he eyes our approach.

Dozens of exquisitely-crafted glass vials catch my eye, each one filled with a colorful liquid. One glass is in the shape of a teardrop, another a flame.

I pick up a yellow flower-shaped vial and uncork it. The essence is strong and floral. I hold it out for Limery to sniff. He scrunches his nose and coughs.

"Limmy no likes." He shakes his head vehemently, pushing the bottle away.

I place it back on the table and pick up another one in the shape of a pyramid. "Before Taryn came here, he used to smell like this all the time. You could smell him before you ever saw him."

Taryn elbows me in the side. "That is so not true. My cologne smelled good." He turns to the owner of the perfume stand and lifts his hands in front of him. "Not that yours doesn't smell good. What I'm saying is—"

I nudge him in the side. "You might want to quit while you're ahead. Unless you want to get beat up by a perfumer."

The owl beastkin clicks his beak and scowls at Taryn from behind the table. His feathered arms bulge as he crosses them across his chest. Taryn mumbles his apologies as we continue down the hall, the owl's eyes following us all the way.

Taryn comes to a stop in front of a massive pillar. Flowers and vines are carved into the stone all the way up to a beautiful bouquet at the top where the pillar morphs into the vaulted ceiling.

He runs his fingers along one of the stone flowers. "I bet the dwarves back at Seascape would love this. Not their style, but the craftsmanship is superb." He turns back to me. "Want to get out of here now? I'm ready to pick up my pets so that we can get Berry some armor."

I let out a long sigh before responding. "We literally have all day until we have to meet Portia. Don't you want to explore the city some more before we have to start worrying about Stompy trampling someone?"

"It's been two days since I visited the stables, and I miss them. I don't like leaving them alone that long. Besides, think of how awesome he is going to look covered in armor!" Taryn grins from ear to ear.

I can't help but laugh at him. "You're going to be one of those clingy parents, aren't you?"

He stands there and frowns at me with his arms crossed.

I wink at Limery. "Fine, fine. Let's get Taryn to his babies."

"Limmy will leads the ways!" He tucks his arms and prepares to bolt.

"Hold up." I spot a table covered in thin round stones and wave them over.

Each stone has a hole in the center, just like the one around my neck. There must be dozens of communication stones here. Back on the island, these would sell for a fortune.

"How do you have so many?" asks Taryn.

Limery picks one up, examining it. He seems confused that there are so many spread out upon the table.

The elephant beastkin behind the counter stands from her stool. "We speak the common tongue in Goldspire nowadays, there's not much use for communication stones among our people."

I pick one up and compare it to my own. There's nothing remarkable about them, nothing that would signify how powerful they truly are. Just a light gray stone with a hole through the middle. There aren't even any runes on them.

I set it back down. "How did you get so many? I thought communication stones could only be given away willingly? Otherwise, they wouldn't work."

The elephant glances at Limery before looking away. "There is another way."

"How?" A sense of dread runs through me when I realize I already know the answer.

Her eyes look like they are straining as she attempts to hold eye contact with me. "If the owner dies, then they may be activated by anyone."

Limery runs his tiny fingers over the stone like it is a precious artifact.

A lump forms in my throat. "So all of these came from dead imps?"

Dozens of Limerys, Leos, Lilliths, and Bazels cross my mind. My chest tightens at the thought.

She nods. "I'm afraid so."

I place the communication stone back on the table. "What happened?"

Her trunk twitches as her eyes drift to the ground. For a moment, I'm not sure if she is going to say anything, but then she takes a deep breath. "When Valmar invaded Goldspire many years ago, he did not come alone. His army was powerful, and many on both sides lost their lives that day. It wasn't until much later that we learned the imps had been tricked into doing his bidding." Her eyes drift back to Limery. "We were fighting to protect our way of life. I'm sorry."

Limery's eyes glisten as he lays the stone next to the others. "It's okays. You didn't knows."

We leave the basilica with heavy hearts. Seeing all those stones laid out like that only reinforces how important it is to raise a force powerful enough to fight whatever comes through those portals. It has been hundreds of years since that battle and yet they still have so many communication stones. How many more were sold over the years? How many innocent imps were tricked into their deaths?

It's best not to dwell on it, so I try to cheer Limery up. "Hey, Limmy, what do you say we go get something to eat?"

He perks up at the mention of food, and soon we gorge ourselves on exotic meat kabobs from a traveling food cart.

The stables are located near the gated entrance into Goldspire. A gray satyr with a scraggly goatee greets us as we arrive. He brushes the coat of a massive beast covered in long, white, dread-locked fur. Two short black horns poke through the fur on each side of its head, and the locs hide large black eyes.

Gloomsheep. *Level 24. While gloomsheep make formidable mounts and pack animals, their wool is highly prized for being soft yet extremely durable.*

Taryn stops in front of the satyr. "I'm here to pick up my pets."

The satyr looks back up from the beast. "One moment and I'll have someone bring them out." He motions to a slightly smaller satyr cleaning out one of the pens before returning his attention to Taryn. "That's a mighty fine beast you have, the big one with the horn. Never seen one in Goldspire. He's got quite the attitude, too."

Taryn grins. "You must be talking about Stompy. Has he been behaving himself?"

The satyr grins. "I'd say so. The other two were inseparable, but Stompy, is it, well, he would sunbathe for hours. We tried to get him in the stable at nightfall, but he wasn't having it, so we let him sleep under the stars."

"That's Stompy." Taryn laughs. "He's got a mind of his own."

There's a loud grunt from the back of the stables and then a pattering of feet as Berry and Ruby race toward Taryn. The small straw-colored jackal jumps into his arms, long pointy ears pinned back as she buries herself in his cloak. Berry nearly knocks Taryn to the ground as he nuzzles against his leg. Stompy trudges out, huffing as he comes to a stop in front of Taryn. He snorts before turning the other way.

"Looks like someone is salty." I laugh at Stompy's stubbornness.

Limery flies over and perches on the moulhaug's horn.

Stompy huffs but allows him to remain.

Taryn pays the bill, and we're on our way. We travel much slower since Stompy takes up a lot of room, especially when we pass carriages or carts. Eventually, we make it to a more spacious main road.

When we arrive at the armory, we're greeted by the rhythmic clank of the blacksmith in the forge next door. Taryn ties Stompy and Berry to a post out front, and Ruby darts between his legs with each step as we head inside. She's so elusive that even though it looks like she'll be stepped on at every turn, it never happens.

The armory is long, with stone arches that run from one end of the building to the other. There are shelves with shields of various shapes and sizes, and bins stocked with a variety of weapons. Swords, axes, pikes, and spears. An assortment of daggers and other smaller weapons line the shelves. Whenever a breeze passes through, the plate mail hanging on racks clank together like windchimes.

A tall beastkin with the head of a panther steps out from behind the counter. Sleek black fur covers his entire body, and a pink scar cuts through one milky white eye. His muscles ripple with each step, and he wears a yellow toga with a black rope cinched around his waist.

"Good day, sirs. How may I assist you today?" His voice is gravelly as the panther beastkin dips his head slightly.

Taryn steps to the front. "I'm actually looking to buy some armor for one of my mounts. He's out front if you want to take a look."

We descend the stairs to where Berry waits patiently. His eyes follow our every movement while Stompy lays on the stone street without a care in the world. Several beastkin gather around pointing at Stompy, but the moulhaug pays them no mind.

The panther places a large paw to his chin. "Will you be requiring armor for both mounts?"

Taryn shakes his head. "Just for the bear. Stompy's hide is pretty tough on its own. Plus, I can't imagine the cost of armor for something that big."

"Very well." The panther squints as he examines Berry. "Bring him to the rear entrance and I will show you some of our larger armor."

Taryn unties Berry and rides him around while Limery and I follow the panther back inside. We pass through the main armory and down another set of stairs into a second open-air hall on the street level. Stacks of massive armor and weapons for mounted combat lie on the ground. There's plate mail the size of car hoods, lances, shields, saddles, armored carts, chariots, and carriages. Some of the chariots even have spikes extending from the axles.

The selection is impressive—even Vanaria and Seascape didn't have items like this.

"Do you sell a lot of these?" I make small talk as we wait for Taryn, pointing to the various chariots and carriages.

"A fair amount. The chariot races are a big attraction during festivals."

"It sounds like living here is one big party." I laugh.

The panther's face goes even more serious. "We have paid the price for our peace."

I wonder if the scar on his face was part of the payment.

Limery flies over and grabs the reins of one of the chariots, whipping them as he hovers. "Limmy likes to race. Limmy likes to go fasts!"

The panther's demeanor softens and his lip curls at the edge, revealing a sharp tooth. "Imps are renowned for their speed all over Mythos. I do not doubt you could put on quite the show."

With his ego stroked, Limery releases the reins and displays his blazing speed as he coats himself in fire and zips back and forth across the courtyard like a meteor. He nearly barrels into Taryn, riding Berry, as he and Ruby turn the corner.

"Oh, wow!" Taryn's mouth hangs open as his eyes take in the rest of the armory. "This is even better than I hoped."

He climbs down and starts looking over all the items.

The panther straightens himself and walks over to a large collection of armor spread out on the ground. "As you can see, we have many options depending on your needs. We have basic brigandine armor, a leather outer layer with dozens of individual metal plates set into pockets on the inside. This is the cheapest and also easiest to repair, as any individual plate can be swapped out with ease." He moves over to a stack of polished plate mail. "Next, we have traditional plate armor. Leather straps will hold the armor in place. On a beast like your bear, I would recommend covering the back, shoulders, and belly, as well as the forelegs and head. Many of our beastkin helms will likely fit your bear as well. Plate mail of this size is incredibly heavy and cumbersome, but extremely effective at blocking damage. With such large pieces of armor, repair will be difficult if you are not near a city with a large forge."

Taryn nods along to each word, but his eyes are already focused on a different pile of armor. Ones with intricate engravings and colored metals.

"What's this?" Taryn asks as soon as the panther finishes speaking.

The panther grins. "That would be our enchanted armor. Pricey, but worth its weight in gold. All enchanted armor comes with the bonus effect of fitting securely to whatever mount they are equipped. You could essentially switch them between both bear and moulhaug with ease." He runs his paw over a pile of seafoam-green plate mail with gold accents. "This one offers increased attack speed when fighting in snow or water. And this one..." He taps a set of golden armor with a lion head engraved on the shoulder pieces. "This one grants increased Strength and Constitution to both mount and rider."

"Nice! What about this one?"

At the very back sits a stack of charcoal armor with blood-red trim. Compared to the others, it's very sleek and minimalistic, but there is something about it that's intimidating. Not waiting for the panther to describe it, I focus on its stats.

Item. Armor of Darkness (Complete set). *50% noise reduction. When all pieces of Armor of Darkness are equipped, both mount and rider gain 90% stealth from dusk until dawn.*

"Holy shit!" I blurt it out without realizing, and they all turn in my direction. "Sorry." I grimace at my outburst and the panther returns to his description of the armor.

I'm amazed that something like this exists. Ninety percent stealth is practically invisibility at night, and for it to work on something as big as Berry, that's quite an advantage, especially when attacking. And the fact that the effect doesn't disappear when they attack is seriously OP. That's not even taking into account the noise reduction on a beast as large as Berry or Stompy.

"I'll take it!" Taryn shouts as soon as the panther finishes.

"Excellent choice. That will be one hundred platinum."

In the silence that follows, I swear we could hear a pin drop.

Taryn's mouth hangs open. When he tries to speak, he croaks like a frog. After struggling to gulp, the words finally come out. "One...hundred...platinum. That's, like, ten thousand gold. Who in the hell has that kind of money to spend on armor? Hell, who has that kind of money?"

No shit. That's some serious change.

The panther bows his head. "I'm sorry for the inconvenience, sir, but surely you must understand the value of a piece this exquisite. It was crafted many years ago by the emperor's very own enchanter. You'll not find another piece like it in all of Mythos."

Taryn's shoulders slump, and Berry nudges him in the side with his snout. "I get it, but we don't have that kind of money."

"No worries, good sir. I'm sure we can find something within your budget that is worthy of a hero."

In the end, Taryn is able to afford enchanted armor, but just barely. The simple golden armor offers Berry a ten percent bonus to his Constitution, but nothing to Taryn.

As we leave the armory, Taryn looks over his shoulder and shakes his head. "Bro, why would he even show me armor that costs that much? It's like trying to buy a used car but test driving a Ferrari. Only I didn't even get to take it for a spin."

I laugh. "We're heroes. Maybe he thinks we're ballers."

Taryn scoffs. "Nobody balls that much. Not even Pressley."

"At least you got armor, though. And you were right, Berry does look badass."

The golden armor stands out prominently against the umber bear's reddish-brown fur. The giant pieces of plate armor make him look even more formidable, especially with the helm. Considering how often Berry is on the front lines, I think it will do nicely.

We still have an hour or so before we're supposed to meet Portia, so we meander around the forum, checking out some of the quainter vendors.

A long, sonorous horn bellows across the forum, drawing our attention from a cart selling flamingo tongues. A second horn joins in and we turn to find out they aren't horns at all, but a group of broad-shouldered minotaur and buffalo beastkin gathering around the spire. Their chests begin to rise and fall as more join in, forming a deep melody that resonates within my chest.

Each member of the musical group has a part to play. Some repeat the same hum over and over. Others only chime in every ten or twenty seconds. Pretty soon, a crowd has gathered, and we climb on Taryn's pets, allowing us to see over the congregation of beastkin.

I'm always amazed by these simple moments where the

action and adventure of Mythos fades away and we're able to experience something every bit as magical and beautiful as anything in the real world.

To my right, Taryn is enraptured by the performance as he strokes Ruby behind the ears. Even Limery has found a moment of calm. When the buffalo all come together for a deep hum that shakes the very streets, Stompy tilts his head back and lets out his own matching tune.

Pretty soon, the sun dips below the horizon, and the golden spire illuminates the forum with reflected moonlight.

And then a familiar voice calls over my shoulder, "You boys ready for an adventure?"

CHAPTER 6

FIGHT CLUB

WE FOLLOW Portia down a dark street at the edge of town. The tail of the fox beastkin swishes back and forth as she leads us to meet her mysterious scholar friend. Hopefully, he will have some insight on where Taryn and I should head next. Somewhere we can level up without getting our heads thumped in.

We're far enough away from the city's center that I can see the guards patrolling the perimeter wall with bows and crossbows tossed over their shoulders. It makes me wonder what lies outside of Goldspire. What threats are so dangerous that even these mighty beastkin require defenses from their attacks? Portia mentioned dungeons, and I fear what beasts lurk within their depths. The behemoth we battled in Seascape Square crosses my mind and I shudder at the memory.

Limery sits on my shoulder tossing a fireball from one hand to the other. "Is we theres yet?"

Portia looks back, grinning as the golden hoops in her fox ears catch the moonlight. "Almost, little one. It will be worth the wait, I assure you."

Taryn and I exchange glances. The way she says it makes it sound like this is more than just a simple meet-and-greet. Where could she be taking us?

A few minutes later, we come to a stop in front of a bath house. Atop many levels of stairs, a white marble building looms over us. Ornate columns form the arched entrance, and at this hour, the place is completely empty.

"I'd recommend you tie your pets out front. It'll be easier for us to travel inside without them."

Taryn ties Berry and Stompy to the posts outside, but Ruby follows us as we ascend the steps into the empty bathhouse. The floors are tiled with green marble. What little moonlight passes through the archways reflects off the gold veins running through the marble like tiny lightning bolts. Long fronds sway in the breeze and water trickles along the aqueducts, feeding the large, square bathing pools.

At the far back, one of the pools is drained and empty.

Portia stops in front of it. "Not many outsiders have the pleasure of seeing what you are about to witness. On the surface, Goldspire presents a face that is elegant and refined, but beneath that facade lies the true nature of the beastkin. While we are majestic and proud, the thrill of the hunt still pulses within our veins."

That sounds pretty ominous, doing little to ease my concerns.

She kneels beside the ledge of the pool and presses a slab of marble. It sinks in and grating stone echoes around us as the bottom of the pool transforms into a stairwell that leads into an underground tunnel.

Now I see why Berry and Stompy needed to wait outside. My head nearly scrapes the ceiling as we descend into the tunnel. Torches line the dusty walls, casting everything with tints of orange and yellow. As manicured as the aboveground is, this is the opposite. The walls and floors are uneven, and rubble crunches beneath our feet every so often.

Ruby runs ahead of the group and comes to an abrupt stop, her nose trailing against an invisible line along the wall and floor. If she's focusing on it, there must be something there. Her perception is so good that she was able to spot the entrance to the cave where Limery's father was trapped when none of us could see it.

"Perceptive," says Portia as she passes the jackal.

When I step past the spot where Ruby is investigating, it's like I've entered an arena. Shouts, laughter, and the clash of metal assault my ears from down the corridor.

"What is this place?" I pull mana to my fingertips just in case, ready to cast a horror at a moment's notice. Whatever this is, we're not the only ones here.

Portia must sense my concern. "No need to worry, all will be revealed soon enough." She winks. "Now, hurry up before we miss the show."

"Show?" asks Taryn. He taps his leg and Ruby abandons her investigation.

I shrug. This sounds like a far cry from meeting a scholar for information.

"Limmy wants to sees the shows." He takes off from my shoulder and hovers beside Portia.

As we travel further down the corridor, light begins to spill in from an opening at the other end. There are bodies with their fists raised, cheering at something. Whatever it is, massive frames block our view.

And then a body soars through the air like it was shot out of a cannon. A green-furred tiger with purple stripes hits the ceiling with a crash, and two daggers fall from his hands. I push my way through the crowd of beastkin to get a better line of sight, and Limery hovers beside me.

"What's going on?" Taryn jumps up and down next to me, trying to get a view. "I can't see."

"It's the monk who chased us. He's fighting."

Cornix Coinbearer, the Hand of the Emperor, is fighting in some underground fight club. He stands over the prone form of the tiger that just flew into the ceiling.

Cornix extends a massive hand and motions for the tiger to stand. "Get up! I was promised a challenge."

The tiger stands, spitting blood to the side, and clenches his fists as he settles into a boxing stance, having lost his weapons.

As the two square off, I scan the area. Dozens of beastkin surround a raised platform where the two beastkin battle. It's like a boxing ring, minus the posts and ropes. Tables line the walls of the cramped area, and a dog-like beastkin bartender pours drinks at the bar in the back. Torches offer plenty of light. Whatever this place is, it feels like a cross between a fight club and a speakeasy.

Taryn continues to jump in the air, moving between one beastkin and the other, but they take little notice of his antics.

"Dammit! Why do they all have to be so tall?"

"I'm only going to ask this once, but do you want me to pick you up?" I can see the disdain in his eyes before he even speaks.

After a few more failed attempts at getting a better view, his shoulders slump. "Fine."

I try to hold back the grin, but I can't. Grabbing Taryn around the waist, I lift him up and place him on my shoulder.

"If you speak about this to anyone," he whispers in my ear, "I'll smother you while you're sleeping."

I suppress my laughter. "Easy, killer. Just watch the show."

Cornix and the tiger circle around the platform. I'm kind of concerned that we are so close to the actual fighting. Cornix is strong enough that a wayward attack could probably do some real damage to any one of us. The beastkin surrounding me range anywhere from level fifteen to forty-two, and I'm confident Cornix out-levels them all.

He huffs and smoke billows out of his massive nostrils. The hippopotamus beastkin still wears the same canvas toga we originally saw him in. His oily slate-colored skin glistens in the torchlight, and amulets dangle from his neck—minus the imperial key.

I wonder if he's met with Festa since our encounter.

The tiger feigns a jab with his left hand and follows with a right cross. In half a second, Cornix deflects the punch to the side and his fist glows green as he counters with a punch of his own. The outline of an emerald dragon coats his hand, roaring as it connects with the tiger's chest and launches him across the ring directly toward us.

Both Taryn and I raise our hands to defend ourselves, and Limery darts out of the way, but there is a second crash as the tiger smashes against an invisible forcefield along the platform's edge.

He falls to the ground, breathing heavily before raising a hand. "I yield."

The air around the arena shimmers. Cornix bows to his opponent, then descends the platform. The crowd erupts into chatter, and Taryn slides off my shoulder like he was never there.

Portia turns around and raises her eyebrows suggestively. "That was the Emperor's Hand. There are not many who can last more than a minute with him in the pits."

"We've, uh, had the displeasure of meeting him before." I grimace at the memory.

"How curious." She cocks an eyebrow. "Let's grab a drink while we wait for my acquaintance."

Portia orders us all a glass of a rich red wine that is somehow both tangy and spicy. We take a seat at a table along the room's edge. After a few sips, my fingertips have an electric sizzle to them.

Item. Dragon's Wine. *-2 Intelligence for one hour. Bonus effect: Grants dragon aura, replicating the fiery buzz of dragon fire.*

Portia grins. "It'll wear off in an hour or so, but it feels pretty good. Especially after you've downed a few."

"Ooh." Limery casts a fireball in his palm and lets it roll down his arm. "Limmy likes Dragon's Wines."

"Limmy just likes to drink. Try not to set us all on fire, please." I laugh at Limery as he snuffs out the fireball and tilts the glass back. I return my attention to Portia. "So, what is this place?"

She takes a long swig and then releases a pleasurable sigh. "This is one of Goldspire's fighting pits. Where the great fighters come to test their mettle against one another."

"Is this how you all get so strong?" I once again look around at all the beastkin out-leveling my party. This group of random beastkin could give the kingsguard of both Orso and Favian a run for their money.

"For some, this is how they grow stronger. For the majority of Goldspire, our strength is formed in the trials while we are young."

"The trials?" Taryn chimes in, nearly finished with his first glass. "What's that?"

Portia leans forward, excitement bubbling in her green eyes. "The trials have been a tradition since the most ancient of days. When we come of age, the young beastkin are sent into several of the lower-level dungeons known as the Trial Dungeons, where we are forced to fight our way out as a team. The strong survive and the weak go on to the next life."

"That's brutal." I place my glass on the table to keep from crushing it in my hand. "You just send your young into dungeons to die?" Not even the mountain trolls would do that, and they value strength above all else.

Confusion passes across her face. "No, we send them to live. Without strength of body and character, Goldspire would surely crumble. Many of the bonds I formed in those dungeons carry with me even today."

I start to argue, but Taryn grabs my arm, shaking his head. I almost shrug him off, but then I realize he's right. This is their culture, who am I to critique it? This is a different society, hell, a different world. They probably have more in common with the ancient Spartans than they do with me. I might be a tough troll in Mythos, but I'm really just a soft kid from New York.

A gong sounds and beastkin begin to shuffle back to the platform.

Portia finishes her wine and stands.

I hold up my hand. "Aren't we going to meet your scholar friend?"

A wicked grin spreads across her face. "As soon as he's done fighting."

"Fighting?" I stand up, nearly knocking over the bench we were sitting on. "I thought you said he was a scholar?"

She nods. "He is, and a very good one at that, but knowledge is not always freely given. Sometimes, it must be taken. Now come, it is always a treat to watch Jegaar."

Taryn just shrugs before following Portia toward the platform, with Ruby narrowly avoiding being trampled with each step.

Limery is still at the table, extending his pointy demonic tongue into our leftover glasses as he tries to lap up any remaining wine.

"Come on, wino." I scoop him off the table and sit him on my shoulder. "We've got a fight to watch."

CHAPTER 7

OUTSMART,
OUTWIT, OUTLAST

I PUSH my way to the front of the crowd, where Taryn and Portia are already waiting. I guess Taryn had enough of sitting on my shoulder.

A magically-amplified voice echoes across the room, introducing the fighters, but I have no idea where the sound is coming from. "Our first contender's love for fighting is undying. He's battled in the arena as a gladiator and has cleared dungeons single handedly. He has strength, speed, and a never-ending desire to better himself. Let out a roar for Gladiator Bellator!"

A stout warthog beastkin steps out from the crowd, his powerful muscles rippling with each step up the platform. His neck is almost as thick as his shoulders and framed by a black leather vest covered in studs. Corded muscles contract as he surveys the crowd. Leathery, dark brown skin is covered with scars and scattered patches of rough hair. A thin black mohawk runs down the center of his large head, and his eyes are small and beady compared to the rest of his massive frame. Four dangerous-looking tusks protrude from his mouth. The two larger ones curl out from his upper mouth framing his snout, and two smaller, pointier tusks jut upward from his bottom jaw.

I'd hate to be on the business end of any one of those.

A silver nose-ring dangles from his pig-like snout, reflecting the crowd in distorted proportions. He wears a black leather loin-cloth that matches his vest, and two sleek vambraces that shield his forearms.

In each hand, he carries a gladius, spinning them twice alongside his body before dropping to one knee and sheathing both swords in a fluid motion. He clenches his fists, each one a wrecking ball of pure power, and steam shoots out of his nostrils to the applause of the crowd.

Bellator

Level 39

Gladiator

Beastkin

He extends his arms and paces across the stage before the mysterious voice begins again. "Our next challenger is no stranger to the pits. It is said that knowledge is power, and if so, then Jegaar has it in spades. 'Outsmart, outwit, outlast' is his motto. Back from his adventures abroad, he's ready to test his mettle once again in the pits."

Bellator moves to the far side of the stage as a wolf beastkin ascends the steps. Jegaar's fur is a dirty tan, like desert sand, but it's so thick and shaggy that he looks more suited for a land covered in snow and ice than the temperate climate of Goldspire. His eyes are bright blue and alert. A thick tail swishes behind him as he walks, and his ears are tipped black at the ends, as are his paws. He wears a brown gladiator skirt similar to Bellator's and carries a buckler shield in his left hand. In his right, he holds a morning star. The metal club is tipped with a spiked ball, a brutal weapon for delivering extreme punishment, capable of both punctures and blunt force with a single strike. His paws are wrapped around the knuckles, which leads me to believe he's a decent fighter as well.

He's unlike any scholar I've ever seen.

Jegaar

Level ???

Battle Scholar

Beastkin

Battle scholar? This will definitely be interesting. His level is concealed, no surprise considering he's a scholar, but I can't imagine he's a higher level than Bellator. He looks badass for a scholar, but his opponent is a gladiator. Bellator has dedicated his life to fighting.

Jegaar nods to Bellator and then falls back to the other side of the platform. Compared to the warthog, he's slender and lean, even with all the fur. I just hope Bellator doesn't rough him up too bad before we get some information out of him.

A gong sounds, and the fight begins.

The two circle around the arena, eyes fixed on one another. Bellator holds both swords at the ready. He positions himself sideways with one blade pointed straight at Jegaar. The second he holds overhead, his arm curved like a scorpion's tail, showcasing his training with every movement he makes.

Jegaar has the morning star tossed over his shoulder. He moves casually, as if he was taking a walk in the park.

The metal whistles as Bellator steps forward and brings the overhead blade down in a forward slash. Jegaar steps to the side, leaving the warthog swiping at air. The second blade follows a split-second later, but the wolf evades again. Bellator quickly pirouettes, and attacks with both blades in a simultaneous strike, faster than anyone that big should move.

Jegaar raises his buckler shield above him at the last second, and both blades deflect to separate sides. The deflected blows barely slow the warthog before he is on the attack again. He brings one sword down, and then another as Jegaar uses the small buckler to block attack after attack.

Bellator presses until Jegaar's back is at the edge of the platform. He slashes again, and the wolf rolls to the side without moving the morning star from his shoulder.

"What's he doing?" Taryn throws up his hands in frustration. "He's going to get himself killed before we learn anything."

"Just wait." Portia's green eyes radiate with excitement.

"Wait for what, Bellator to tire out?" If that's the plan, put me in the ring.

She laughs. "Bellator could fight for days without tiring."

Then what the hell is Jegaar doing? Because right now, Bellator clearly has the upper hand. I return my attention to the ring just as the warthog unleashes another flurry of attacks. He moves with the finesse of a dancer, despite being so big and broad-shouldered, his vest fluttering with each movement like a cape. But no matter how swift or powerful the attack, Jegaar finds a way to deflect the blow, sometimes moving so fast that I'm not sure how he's able to get in position. He's quick, but can he fight?

Finally, Bellator stops attacking. His chest heaves, and steam pours from his nostrils, coating the arena in a dense layer of fog.

The barrier keeps the steam from spilling over the edge and into the crowd, so it accumulates in the ring until both fighters are covered to their chests.

Jegaar sniffs at the air. "Smoked pork. Now, that's the stuff."

A few laughs trickle through the crowd.

Bellator grunts before launching himself across the stage. He leaps with enough power that he crests the fog, leaving a trail of smoke behind him, tucking both knees and holding his swords in a reverse grip as he falls toward Jegaar.

At the height of Bellator's jump, the wolf crouches in the fog and disappears. Bellator lands with a thud, sending smoke shooting out in dozens of wisps that begin to dissipate.

He twirls the twin blades vertically by his side, blowing the steam like a fan. It rises into the air, forming a cloud overhead and revealing Jegaar sitting cross-legged in the center of the ring. He scrapes the sharp claw of his index finger over his canine tooth as if cleaning it. The morning star still sits on his shoulder.

Maybe it's more for show than practicality.

Bellator grunts again and charges at the sitting wolf. He's halfway across the stage in the blink of an eye, and I'm certain there is no way that Jegaar can dodge this attack. The warthog raises his blades and brings them down with dangerous speed.

And just like that, our best lead since arriving in Goldspire is about to be dead.

The blades are inches from Jegaar's head when he decides to act. In a flash, he removes the claw from his tooth and places his palm on the floor. Both legs uncross in a fluid motion. He extends one and sweeps Bellator off his feet. The warthog crashes to the platform, his blades clanking against the stone.

Jegaar follows through with the momentum from his leg-sweep and launches himself into the air, somersaulting before he lands.

Bellator rolls over and climbs back to his feet. He crosses his blades over one another and grinds the flats together. The resulting screech causes me and most of the crowd to grimace. Limery tucks his fingers in his ears.

"Quit playing games and fight," Bellator rumbles.

"But where would the fun be in that?" Jegaar once again rests the morning star on his shoulder.

"I'll show you fun!" Bellator cocks his arm back and slashes with enough force to split Jegaar from head to foot.

Jegaar lifts the morning star and swings it like an underhand pitch. It hits the blade with enough power that sparks shoot out and Bellator loses his grip. The sword flips end over end like it was shot out of a cannon and lodges in the ceiling.

"You son of a—" Bellator grunts as he follows up with his second sword.

The blade cuts through the air so loudly that it whistles. Taking a step back, Jegaar winds up again. The sword lands between the spikes of the morning star and sparks rain down again, but the result is no different. A second sword lodges in the ceiling.

Jegaar snarls. "You leave my mother out of this."

Without looking up, he flicks his wrist. His weapon goes flying and the morning star's spikes bury several inches in the stone ceiling between the two swords. "You want to fight? Let's fight."

Maybe I underestimated this guy.

He crouches into a fighting stance and raises both wrapped paws. When he motions for Bellator to come and get some, I swear we could hear a pin drop.

"Hell yeah!" I shout without realizing it, my deep voice echoing across the cavern.

The energy in the crowd suddenly shifts as someone else

echoes my sentiment. Pretty soon, the roars and yells are thunderous as the two beastkin square off.

Now, we've got us a fight.

Bellator's fists are massive, easily twice the size of Jegaar's. The muscles in his forearms tense as he clenches them. His reach is shorter than his opponent's, but I've already seen that he is lightning quick to be so big. He holds each fist level with his face, right foot planted in the rear for power.

Jegaar is light on his feet, rocking from left to right. His long reach might give him an advantage, but are his hits as powerful?

A quick jab from Bellator starts the second round of action. The boulder of a fist moves in a blur and Jegaar leans to the side, evading the punch. Bellator follows up with a cross, which the wolf ducks beneath before landing a jab of his own to his opponent's gut.

Bellator grunts but goes on the attack again, just like he did with his swords. Jab, punch, jab, punch, jab. Each one misses Jegaar by a fraction of an inch. A cross nearly connects, but only grazes the tops of Jegaar's ears as he ducks again.

Every time there is an opening, Jegaar lands a blow of his own. Bellator grimaces for the briefest moment, but then quickly launches another onslaught.

So far, Jegaar is evading with razor-thin margins, but one hit could rock his world.

After another flurry of attacks leaves Bellator with nothing more than a bruised chest, he takes a step back, steam pouring from his nostrils.

"I've had enough of your games, Jegaar. Fight me like a beast."

Echoes of "Fight him" are chanted from the crowd.

Jegaar takes a step forward and raises his fists again. Satisfied, Bellator charges at the wolf, fist cocked back. An orange glow forms around his hand, distorting the air. He swings, but Jegaar steps to the side, extending his leg and tripping Bellator.

The warthog falls face-first onto the platform, sliding until he crashes into the invisible forcefield.

He stands up, eyes narrow with fury, and a silver glow surrounds his body. For a second, it looks like he's going into a barbarian rage. But instead of steam radiating from his body, his dark leathery skin takes on a metallic sheen. The mohawk running down his head and back forms into metal spikes, and soon his entire body looks like liquid mercury.

Except for his eyes. They burn a fiery red.

"There it is." Jegaar grins. "I knew you had it in you."

"What just happened?" I ask Portia.

She places her finger to her lips, silencing me. "Watch."

I'm dumbfounded. Somehow, he got so angry that his skin turned to metal. Now, he's more dangerous than ever. Why in the hell would Jegaar provoke him like this?

Bellator charges, now moving faster than before. When he punches, Jegaar's fur ripples as he barely evades. If he was toying with Bellator before, he's certainly not now. His blue eyes are focused. When he tries to counter, a hollow metallic ring reverberates from Bellator's body. Instead of grimacing as he takes the blow, he lifts his knee into Jegaar's chin. The clack of the wolf's jaws snapping shut is like a gunshot. The force of the attack sends him soaring across the platform, where he lands on his back at the far side of the ring.

He opens his mouth a few times, rubbing his jaw as he stands up. "I guess I had that coming."

The warthog runs at him like a raging bull. Surprisingly, Jegaar charges back. Bellator lowers himself, arms spread wide, and metal mohawk pointed forward as he prepares to spear the wolf, but Jegaar jumps at the last second, using Bellator's shoulders as a platform to launch himself into the air. He grabs the morning star stuck in the ceiling and pulls it free.

When he lands, his smile is full of mischief. Bellator charges with blind rage, and I can't distinguish his actions from a barbarian rage at all. He attacks with the power of a feral meteor, but Jegaar doesn't back down. He holds the morning star like a baseball bat and swings it with two hands at the charging warthog.

Sparks explode as the weapon makes contact, and a metallic gong reverberates within my chest. Bellator flips backward twice before crashing into the forcefield.

Unfazed, he crawls to his feet and charges again.

Jegaar examines the tip of his morning star, where several of the spikes have bent sideways. He adjusts his grip and swings for Bellator once again. The blow launches the warthog for a second time, but again he stands, red eyes full of hatred.

Half of the morning star's spikes are flat and useless, but Jegaar adjusts his grip and repeats the process.

It's like Bellator is in a blind rage, incapable of any cognizant thought other than mauling his opponent. I really want to know what his deal is.

By the end of fourth charge, the morning star is nothing more than a dull club. As soon as his attack sends Bellator flying, Jegaar turns and runs in the opposite direction. He leaps in the air toward the forcefield, digging his claws into the invisible wall and using it to launch himself toward the ceiling.

He grabs both swords and pulls them loose as he falls back to the ground.

Bellator's skin begins to lose its sheen as he lays on the ground, slowly fading to its normal dull brown. He props himself up on an elbow as he attempts to stand, but Jegaar places a foot on his chest, pressing him back to the floor. With a flourish, he tosses both swords at the ground and they cross in an X over Bellator's throat.

The gladiator raises two fingers into the air. "I yield."

The crowd erupts into applause. Taryn turns to me with eyes as wide as saucers, mouth hanging open.

Jegaar bows to the crowd before exiting the stage.

I'm still not sure what we just witnessed, but it was awesome.

CHAPTER 8
WARFORGED

Portia taps me on the arm and points to the far end of the room. "Let's go. Jegaar will be waiting for us in one of the fighter pods."

The crowd shuffles all around us. Some beastkin head for the bar, while others discuss the fight. Slashing his arms in an X, a jaguar beastkin replays Jegaar's final move with the twin swords in front of his friends. Limery starts to join a group heading toward the bar with empty mugs, but I stop the little drunk before he can disappear.

"What in the hell did we just watch?" I squint at the platform as if it might give me answers as to what happened to Bellator.

Portia holds up a slender hand. "Save your questions for once we're settled. Now, hurry, there is probably already a line."

She pushes her way through the crowd and around the fighting pit. Taryn follows in her wake, and somewhere under the mess of legs, Ruby solves her own personal obstacle course.

We enter a tunnel. At the far end, there's another arena that's less crowded. Along the tunnel, there are a handful of rooms carved into each side.

Inside one of them, Jegaar sits atop a picnic table with a tall glass of white wine surrounded by a dozen other beastkin. He's in the middle of a story, but his blue eyes light up when he sees Portia. When his gaze drifts to Taryn and then me, he narrows his eyes quizzically.

His mouth hangs open for a moment, then he gestures to Portia. "Gentlemen, I'm sure you all know Portia. She's the finest bartender in the city." He winks at her. "I didn't expect to see you here tonight."

She grins. "That was quite the show you put on. I have a few new friends who could use some of your scholarly advice."

"Oh, really." He returns the grin. "Consider me intrigued. Could you give us a moment, gentlemen?"

Portia's ears tilt backward. "Actually, this might take more than a moment."

He turns back to the other beastkin. "Ah, well, I'll have to regale you all with my tales from abroad some other time. I can't turn down an audience with someone who saved my life on more than one occasion, now can I?"

They all look at Portia with shocked expressions. After witnessing Jegaar fight, I'm also curious how she managed to save his life.

The group leaves, and Jegaar motions for us to take a seat. "Shall I order some wine for us?"

Before any of us have a second to process the question, Limery is hovering, hands pressed together in excitement. "Oh, yes! Limmy loves the wines."

Jegaar snaps his fingers and a mouse beastkin steps into the room.

"A bottle of your finest for my new friends," he orders.

"Right away, sir." The mouse bows and exits the room.

"That's very generous of you." Portia bows her head slightly.

"Anything for you. Besides, fighters get a pretty steep discount." He climbs down from the table and sits on one of the benches. "What'd you think of the show?" He smirks as he asks. The wolf beastkin knows what he did was an incredible feat.

I take a seat across from him, with Taryn and Limery beside me. "It was amazing. I've never seen anyone move like that."

The mouse beastkin returns with the wine and pours us all a glass.

Item. Ice Wine. *-2 Intelligence for one hour. Bonus Effect: Grants a cooling chill all over the body.*

I take a sip and a chill runs through me. The sweat on the back of my neck from the crowded underground lair crystalizes, and goosebumps erupt along my arms.

Limery lets out a long sigh. I can't even imagine the effect it is having on his naturally hot body.

"Feels good, right?" Jegaar takes a long drink. "Imagine how it feels after being kicked in the chest by a fluid steel warthog."

"Fluid steel?" So that's what Bellator was. "How was he able to do that?"

"He's a rarity. Long ago, many generations before our current emperor, Goldspire soldiers consisted of a subclass of barbarians called the Warforged. The process to attain the class was said to kill more than half who attempted it. Once the class had been attained, it could be passed on to one's offspring, so the Warforged were carefully bred and monitored. When they entered a rage, their bodies turned to fluid steel, making them all but unkillable. On the battlefield, they were unmatched. But after Goldspire's enemies had been conquered, the path of the Warforged became less and less. Many of the soldiers were castrated to prevent passing on their trait. They were pure destruction, but uncontrollable during a rage. Now, the Warforged trait is all but gone, only surfacing in the descendants of the original Warforged on occasion. Bellator is one of three that I know of in all of Goldspire."

Warforged. The chaos I could cause if I were able to turn into metal when I raged. I'd be unstoppable. "How does one become Warforged?"

Jegaar stares at me for a moment before speaking. "I'm not sure. No one has attempted the process in hundreds of years. There may be records of it in the archives, but if our ancestors found reason to fade them out of existence, then there must have been good reason. Bellator is a formidable gladiator and a worthy opponent, but comparing him to a true Warforged is like comparing a cat to a lion."

Damn. It sounds like one hell of a class.

Jegaar grabs the morning star and looks at its dented spikes. "I've fought a lot of monsters with this weapon. Never so much as dulled a tip." He shakes his head. "It won't be cheap to repair."

He places the weapon under the table before I have a chance to analyze it. If what he says is true, and Bellator really is that strong, then what Jegaar did is even more impressive.

But it makes me wonder how dangerous these fights actually are. "Do you not worry about killing or seriously injuring someone in a fight?"

"It's not a concern." He shrugs it off. "I assure you that one does not accidentally kill a beastkin. Occasionally, an injury may occur when someone is too proud to yield, but we are stocked with potions and elixirs on the rare chance that it happens."

Taryn takes a calming swig and then leans forward. "Alright, I've got to know. How did Portia save your life?"

Jegaar grins. "Let's just say that Portia doesn't carry around those daggers for show."

Portia's ears tilt back, and she looks at the floor. "Oh, stop it. It was a long time ago. Long before you were the mighty Jegaar you are now."

"She does herself a disservice. Portia and I completed the trials together when I was but a pup. I never would have survived without her. I may be strong now, but there was a time when I was the runt of the litter. And my dear friend Portia took pity on me. After a disastrous battle, due to my ineptitude, the third member of our party was ready to cast me aside, but Portia refused. I was battered and bruised, and she stuck by my side the entire way until we eventually made it out alive."

"Don't flatter me." She pushed Jegaar in the shoulder. "You had a lot of fight in you even then. If you'd waited a year, you would have been fine. Once you were out of the trials, you never looked back. The fact that you were the first beastkin in three hundred years to rise from Acolyte to Battle Scholar is a testament to that."

"Now who's flattering who?" Jegaar smirks. "But enough about us. What I want to know is what brings a dwarf and a troll to Goldspire?"

I set my glass down. Finally, we're jumping into business.

"We're searching for allies," answers Taryn as he strokes Ruby between the ears.

Jegaar leans forward. "Allies?"

Taryn tells the story of the attack on Seascape and King Orso's meeting with the other leaders.

"That is most interesting." He scratches his chin, running his black claws through the dense fur.

"How so?" asks Portia.

"It certainly makes Cornix's outlandish requests make a lot more sense."

The conversation briefly halts as Limery slurps at the last remaining droplets of his glass of wine.

"What does Cornix have to do with this?" I ask.

Jegaar sets his glass down before launching into a speech. "The Scholars Guild reports directly to the Hand of the Emperor. We're responsible for the reports and histories of Goldspire, keeping detailed records and archives, maintaining valuable tomes and artifacts, and in certain cases, administering foreign reconnaissance. For the most part, we govern ourselves, following whatever leads interest us most to uncover the histories of the past. We report to Cornix, but he is usually disinterested." He taps his claw against the table in a rhythmic pattern. "However, recently, he's been spending more time in the archives researching ancient items and spells that were lost to the ages. Powerful items even by Goldspire standards."

Now, I'm even more interested. Items like that could be invaluable in the war to come. "What items?"

"That I'm afraid I'm not at liberty to discuss. But I can say that I just returned from a fruitless journey to find one of them. I spent months searching through ancient letters and accounts, only to find that someone raided the tomb before me. I'll be leaving in a few days to embark on my next mission."

Taryn and I exchange glances. I'm willing to bet anything I know who is responsible. Valmar, the dark wizard.

"So you think that Cornix is preparing for the return of Valmar?" I look down and notice that my hands are gripping the bench rather hard.

"It certainly seems so," Jegaar says darkly.

"But the emperor, she didn't seem concerned at all."

Jegaar laughs. "Why would she? You're foreigners. If she were concerned, do you think she would reveal her hand to you? Have you met anyone since you have arrived in Goldspire that has displayed even an ounce of weakness to you? If I had to guess, I would say this is Cornix's concern and his alone. There is no one better suited to defend Goldspire than our emperor, but it is Cornix's responsibility to look into all matters whether the emperor is concerned or not. While most races do not remember Valmar's reign of terror, there are many beastkin who fought on that day. Cornix will do everything within his power to make sure that if war does come to Goldspire, we will be prepared."

Taryn shakes his head. "Then why not form an alliance with the other kingdoms? There is strength in numbers."

Jegaar sighs. "I do not disagree with you. But the emperor's decision is law. Goldspire will not interfere in the wars of foreigners unless they fall on Goldspire soil." We sit in silence for a moment before he speaks again. "What is it I can help you with? As friends of Portia, I will do everything within my power to assist you."

"We were sent to Goldspire to find allies. Even though the emperor denied us, our quest has been fulfilled, and we can once again return to our own adventures. Portia told us that you were one of the few from Goldspire who have traveled abroad, so we were hoping you may offer advice on where we should go next."

He nods. "I have traveled extensively across Mythos, so I should be able to shed some light. Though if your goal is to continue to gain allies while also gaining power, I can point you in that direction as well."

"That would be great!" Taryn drums his fingers against the table. "Kill two birds with one stone."

"Two birds with one stone." Jegaar laughs. "I like that."

"It's a saying from back home."

"Interesting. I did not know that the dwarves were known for their proficiency with slings."

Taryn gulps. "We're, uh, full of surprises."

"Tell me, which portals had representatives at your king's meeting?"

I think hard on King Orso's council meeting, trying to remember the lands of the races that were present. "Well, there were the three kingdoms from the isle: Seascape, Vanaria, and the forest trolls. There were also the catfolk from...Antadale, I believe."

Jegaar laughs. "Ah, Antadale. We refer to them as lesser beast-kin. They are cunning, small, and particularly skilled with the healing arts." He pauses, raising a hand. "Sorry for interrupting, please continue."

I look to Taryn. "Do you remember where the others were from?"

He runs his fingers through his beard. "The gnomes were from Pruxford, and then the centaurs from Wandermere. And what about the merfolk? It was a fitting name. Watertown? Waterville?"

"Mistville," answers Jegaar. "That's the only kingdom of merfolk I'm aware of."

"That's the one." Taryn nods. "The only other portals we know of are seafaring orcs of Blacktide and the dark elves of Mosstar, and I doubt we'll be going there any time soon. We could always go back to Seascape and learn more, but I'd like to return with some sort of good news."

"Very well. All of the above portals are certainly within your range and should offer you sufficient challenges. But if they have already allied themselves with your king, then I would advise you to go elsewhere. The lands of Ellynmylly are sprawling, perhaps the largest continent in all of Mythos. You will find it full of adventure with a myriad of races to match. Ellynmylly is known as the 'Melting Pot of Mythos,' where races from all other kingdoms used to come to trade with one another before the fall of the portals. Several kingdoms call the lands home, and vast forests separate their borders. There is a network of lesser portals for traveling among its kingdoms. If Ellynmylly is a melting pot,

Frostmoor is quite the opposite. It is a frigid land of snow and ice where the mountain tribes dwell."

"Hold up for a moment." I lift a finger for Jegaar to give us a moment, and whisper in Taryn's ear. "When I logged out, I saw Glenn and Jude in a cave. Snow was piling at the door, and they were covered in fur blankets. They could be in Frostmoor."

Taryn shrugs. "It's worth a shot."

I return my attention to Jegaar. "What can you tell us about Frostmoor?"

He takes another swig of the ice wine and sighs as the chill courses through his body. "Frostmoor is a brutal land. Those who dwell there are forged from the ice like iron is from fire. Proud and mighty, the ice tribes govern themselves, each one with its own customs and histories. They value strength the same as Goldspire, and you will find it hard to tread on their lands unless you can prove your worth."

That sounds ominous. "Is Frostmoor the only portal covered in snow and ice?"

"There are mountain ranges among many of the kingdoms, but Frostmoor is the only place where society flourishes in the icy embrace."

This has to be it then. With so many tribes there, Glenn and Jude could have easily slipped away into a cave in the mountains. By now, he could even be up to his old tricks again. If nothing else, we can warn the tribes and at least try to convince them to join Orso's cause.

I look Jegaar in his icy blue eyes. "Frostmoor it is then."

He stares back at me for an uncomfortable moment, not speaking. The crowd cheers from outside the door as the next challengers are announced, followed by clashing metal as the next fight begins.

Finally, the wolf speaks. "Chod, it is not a common request, but would you humor a curious scholar and remove your veil?"

Veil? I frown at him for a moment before I realize he means Conceal. I deactivate the passive ability that hides my level, and Jegaar's gaze buries into me.

"Interesting." He looks lost in his thoughts for a moment. "Thank you, Chod."

Portia places a hand on Jegaar's arm. "Now that we've got that out of the way, would you like to join us at the inn? Drinks are on me."

Limery, whose head had been drooping ever closer to the table, suddenly perks up.

Jegaar places his hand on top of Portia's, dwarfing it by comparison. "I wish I could, but there is much work to be done." He lifts his hand and then stands.

The old trial partners embrace and Jegaar heads for the exit.

He stops in front of us and bows. "I hope that I have been of service to you all."

"More than you know." I stand and extend my arm.

Jegaar's firm grip clenches around my forearm. He squeezes and pulls me in close, whispering in my ear. "When you reach level thirty, come and find me. We will put the trials of the Warforged to the test."

My arm aches when he releases it, and before I can say anything, he is out the door.

"What was that all about?" Taryn looks at me curiously.

"Nothing." I rub my fingers over my bruised forearm. "Ready to get out of here?"

We grab Taryn's pets and make our way back to the inn. Portia tells us stories of her time with Jegaar. She has Taryn's rapt attention, while Limery bobbles lazily on my shoulder.

I barely hear a word of it, my mind consumed with dreams of a shimmery metallic body. It's time to grind.

CHAPTER 9

NOTHING GOLD CAN STAY

DESPITE LIMERY'S PROTEST, we call it an early night once we return to the inn. We'll be leaving Goldspire first thing in the morning so that we have a full day to get our bearings in Frostmoor. From what Jegaar told us, getting to the villages will be the toughest part.

As we lay in our beds, Berry whines outside. Deep, sonorous groans come through the open window. Taryn elected not to take the pets to the stables to save time in the morning, but knowing that Taryn is so close has Berry acting especially petulant.

Taryn rolls his eyes. "He's an eight-hundred-pound baby."

"Says the guy who couldn't spend a day walking through Goldspire without him." I snicker. "You two were made for each other."

I can tell he's smiling when he speaks. "What can I say? I love them."

Limery nestles against my arm, resting peacefully from all the wine he drank. He's such a peculiar creature, and yet I care for him in the same way Taryn does his pets. How could anyone ever believe that he isn't real just because he doesn't exist outside of this world? Out of the corner of my eye, Taryn strokes Ruby as she perches on his chest, staring at him.

I roll over to face Taryn and the bed creaks under my weight. "Today was fun."

His mustache twitches. "Yeah, it was. It was nice to take it easy for once, but it's back to the grind tomorrow. How are you feeling about heading to Frostmoor?"

"I'm excited." I pull my mana to my fingertips, trying to remember the last time I summoned a horror. "It'll be nice to adventure again. I can't remember when we last had the freedom to roam around searching for monsters."

"You're right about that." Taryn stops petting Ruby and she paws at his hand. "It's been one fight after another since we left Lynchton."

A long, deep groan comes from outside and we both laugh.

Limery stirs against my arm, and I pop his snot bubble with one of my claws. "It's funny...If Limery had snatched Cornix's necklace without getting spotted, we never would have ended up at this inn. We never would have met Portia or Jegaar."

"Yeah, crazy how things work out. Speaking of Jegaar, what was it he whispered in your ear?"

I watch Taryn as he strokes Ruby and wonder how much I should tell him. Level thirty is a long way off. I'm only level twenty-four, and it will be a real grind to get there. Who knows how much the world might change between now and then? I could be forced to log out before I ever get the chance to meet up with Jegaar. It's probably better to focus on the things right in front of us, not lofty ambitions we might never reach.

Still, Taryn is my best friend. And as far as I'm concerned, this is my life now. I've felt more at home in Mythos than I ever have in the real world.

"Well?" Taryn interrupts me from my thoughts.

What the hell. "He told me that if I reached level thirty to come back here and we'd put the trials of the Warforged to the test."

Taryn sits up so fast that Ruby falls off his chest. "What?! Are you kidding me? He told you that you could not only be a barbarian summoner forest troll, but that you could take on an additional class and turn to metal when you rage, and you were going to keep it a secret?"

His eyes are so wide I think they might pop out of his head.

"I didn't think it was important. I mean, it's not like I'll be level thirty anytime soon. And you heard what he said, most of those that attempted failed. We've got bigger problems to deal with at the moment."

Taryn shakes his head. "You better believe that if somebody told me I even had a chance at a super rare and powerful class, I would be annoying the shit out of you about it day and night until I got it."

I laugh. "Then I pray that never happens."

He tosses a pillow and it hits me in the side of the head. "You've got to admit, you're pretty damned lucky. You sure you don't have a hidden luck stat or something?"

"Ha." I flash him a rude gesture. "I'll try to remember how lucky I am the next time I get my face stomped in."

"Seriously, though." His eyes focus on me, all playfulness gone. "As fun as all of this is, the fact that it feels so real means that we're going to have to deal with some heavy stuff from time to time. We can all feel that something is changing, and if history has taught me anything, it's that casualties are the price of war. When bad things happen, it'll be important to have things we can focus on outside of trying to save the world. Things we can look forward to."

His words hit me like a punch in the gut. Are these the thoughts that keep him up at night? But more importantly, he's right. Even if we win, not everyone will make it through what's coming. My gaze lingers on Limery. I'll need to be Warforged to protect him.

I do my best to deflect the sobering topic. "Like an impossibly difficult trial that could very well be the most painful thing I have ever endured?"

"I'm serious." He sighs.

I'm not sure where this is coming from, but I know he is. "And what about you? What are you looking forward to?"

He grins. "More pets." As if on cue, Ruby climbs back in his lap. "Even if they don't listen to me. Now, let's get some sleep. Tomorrow is going to be a long day."

I put out the candle, leaving the room in the silvery glow of moonlight. As I drift off to sleep, I imagine myself with a body of steel as blades and arrows bounce off me like they are made of plastic.

***

"Rise and shine!" Taryn shoves me in the shoulder, then he pokes Limery in the stomach. "You too, little guy."

Limery sits up, bulbous eyes crusty and full of sleep. He sways back and forth before he focuses on me. "Mornings."

"Morning, drunkie." I rub his head gently. "We're going to have to muzzle you the next time we go into a bar."

"Oh, Chods." He brushes my hand away. "Limmy is fines."

He shakes his head and rises into the air. He does a backflip with none of the sluggishness he showed only moments before. I wish I could shake off a hangover that easily.

We gather our belongings and head downstairs. The falcon

beastkin stands behind the bar, and I'm a little sad Portia isn't here to say good-bye.

"Good morning, gentlemen," Portia's seductive voice calls from the booth in the corner. "I figured I would see you off this morning. Make sure you don't get lost on the way to the portal." She winks.

"That's very generous of you." Taryn places his hands together and gives her a slight bow.

Portia looks at Limery with amusement. "This one doesn't miss a beat, does he? He was out like a candle last night."

Taryn laughs. "He drinks like a dwarf."

She stands up from the booth. "Ready to hit the road?"

"Ready," we all say in unison.

She opens the door, holding it ajar for us to begin our journey. "Enjoy the crisp Goldspire air while you still can. I'm sure Frost-moor will have a bit of a bite to it."

Berry nearly tackles Taryn to the ground once we're outside. Stompy sits in the center of the street paying us no mind, forcing pedestrians to pass him on either side.

Taryn wraps his arms around the bear's head. "Nobody forgot about you, you big goon."

"How could we, with all of that whining?" I mutter under my breath.

He hugs Stompy, but all he gets in response is a grunt.

In the early morning sun, the entire city takes on a golden luster. The spire in the forum glimmers against the blue sky, and carts rattle against the cobbled streets as the vendors from outside the city come to sell their produce.

When we make our way into the arena, I'm suddenly confused by the layout. If those entering Goldspire have to face off with the gladiators, then how are we getting out?

Portia must notice my confusion as I stop underneath the arched tunnel entering the stadium. "What's wrong, Big Blue?"

"Are we just going to stroll by a bunch of gladiators mid-fight to get out of here?"

She tilts her head back and laughs. "Oh, wouldn't that be funny? Gladiators battling for life and death, and we just walk by with a nod." Her grin stretches from ear to ear. "As great as that would be, Goldspire has two portals. The one you entered through is for newcomers. For native beastkin, or those who have survived the arena, there is a separate portal at the far end of the arena. When you return, you won't have to fight your way through unless you have newcomers in your party."

"That's convenient. But how does the portal know who's been here?"

She shrugs. "Magic."

We follow her up a stairwell into the stands. The seats are mostly empty and only two gladiators stand in the arena. I recognize one of them as Mordrir, the satyr we fought on our second attempt into Goldspire.

At the far end of the stands, we descend another set of stairs to the portal. From inside the floor of the arena, it can't be seen because of the high walls. The swirling portal sits at the back on a raised platform, with no walls obscuring its view overlooking the sea. Compared to Seascape and Vanaria's portals, it's practically empty. Only one beastkin stands on the platform sorting through a satchel in front of the portal.

Jegaar closes the satchel and notices us, but he doesn't stick around for small talk. He gives a mock salute. "To new adventures." He winks at us as he steps through the portal.

One of the runes flashes red and then he's gone. Probably off to face some challenge that could kill the rest of us with its eyes closed.

"Well." Portia gives us a warm smile. "This is it. I'd never met a hero before, but I'm happy to have made your acquaintances. Perhaps we will meet again one day."

I extend my arm, and Portia and I clasp one another around the wrist. "There's still one somewhere in Goldspire. If you hear word of a death knight walking the streets, he's one of us."

"Yeah." Taryn repeats the gesture with Portia. "Don't let his appearance scare you off. He's a decent enough guy once you get past the skull and dark energy."

Portia scrunches her face in confusion, and Limery flies over from my shoulder, embracing her. "Its was nice to meets you. Limmy loved the wines."

She beams as the tiny imp wraps his arms around her shoulder. "It was a pleasure to meet you too, Mr. Imp. Good luck on your journeys."

We ascend the platform and focus on the rune for Frostmoor. It glows red, and with a final glance at Portia, we step through the portal.

In an instant, everything goes white and an icy chill pierces me to my core.

CHAPTER 10

FROSTMOOR

A GUST of freezing wind assaults my face, and my trollberries shrink like raisins in the sun. In the bitter temperature, I'm keenly aware of Limery's warm body clinging tightly to my shoulder. Everywhere is blanketed in white, except for the nearby blotches of Berry and Stompy. Even their massive frames are concealed by the dense snowfall.

The icy wind is uncomfortable, but not painful. I hate to imagine what this would feel like without my troll hide. Even now, it feels like being stuck in a freezer, and I don't know why we didn't think to bundle up. Limery will be fine, I'm sure, but what about Taryn?

"Taryn!" I call in the direction of his pets, but the words get lost in the wind.

Behind me, snowflakes melt as they hit the portal's whirlpool of energy. It's the only thing in the area that isn't blurred and muted by the snowfall.

I take a step forward and my feet sink calf-deep into the snow.

How are we supposed to find our way out of here when everything is indistinguishable?

"Limery!" I have to shout for him to hear me over the roaring wind even though he's sitting on my shoulder. "Can you melt some of the snow around the platform?"

"Limmy's on it." His claws dig into me as he launches himself into the blizzard.

A second later, a bright ball of flame springs to life in front of me as Limery takes to his molten form. He hovers near the ground, flying in circles until the platform is cleared of snow. Puddles fill the stone surface and each new snowflake melts against the warmed rock. He summons a flame wall in the center of the platform. The wind whips at the fiery wall but it withstands the assault, keeping the snow at bay long enough for Taryn and I to reunite. The warmth from the flames takes away the bite from the wind for a moment.

Suddenly, the wind fades, and the blizzard of seconds before stills to a light flurry. Without the wind, the snowfall is calm and peaceful. Silence stretches for miles.

A roar shrieks from overhead, and an icy-blue, winged creature the size of a barn soars by. Its wings spread like sails, and its underbelly is shrouded in shadow.

White Dragon. *Unique Monster. Level 35. Perhaps the greatest hunters of all dragon species, white dragons dwell in harsh climates with even harsher prey. While preferring to feast on mammoths, nothing is off-limits to these apex predators. Capable of spewing ice-flames that can turn flesh to ice in seconds, their frigid core is said to affect the climate of their immediate vicinity.*

Damn. To have that kind of power.

A chill runs down my spine that has nothing to do with the temperature.

As the dragon flies further away, the snowfall fades until it stops entirely. The sun peeks out from behind the clouds, igniting the landscape, and suddenly, everything is so bright it burns my eyes. I lift my hand to shield my view, waiting for my eyes to slowly adjust to my surroundings.

The snowfall fades and I find Taryn with ice crystals clinging to his beard. He gapes at the fleeing dragon from atop Stompy.

"Are you sure we took the right portal?" Taryn's gaze is still fixed. "Because that was a dragon that controls the weather, and I don't think we can survive a fight with that."

I watch the dragon until its icy scales blend into the sky. "If that's the toughest thing this place has to offer, then I think we'll be okay."

A level thirty-five monster could kill us no problem, but if it's the top of the food chain then most of the monsters have to be in the twenties. At least I hope so.

There's a soft thunk as Limery plops headfirst into a snow-bank. Steam rises as the snow melts against his warm body.

Berry follows him, his golden armor glimmering in the sun as he stands at the edge of the platform eating mouthfuls of snow. Even Stompy seems intrigued by our surroundings.

"Let's hope you're right." Taryn shivers and pulls his cloak tighter. Ruby's ears poke out from underneath. "I thought we made a mistake for a minute there, but this isn't so bad." He looks around. "This is peaceful. Cold, but peaceful."

Towering mountain ranges surround us on all sides. Five trails spread out from the portal in different directions. Somehow, their pebbled paths are not covered in snow, and torches with blue flames mark each path every so often.

I'm surprised the torches still burn after the powerful gusts of the snowstorm. Whoever is in charge of keeping them lit must have quite the challenge on their hands, not that it looks like this place gets too many visitors. Maybe they're enchanted somehow.

I approach one of the torches, hoping to steal some of its warmth, but the fire is no warmer than the air surrounding it. I place my hand in the flame, but it radiates nothing but a dull energy.

"That's cool." Taryn climbs down from Stompy and sticks his hand into the blue fire. He jerks his hand back immediately. "Ouch! What the hell?" he yells, shaking his hand before shoving it in the snow.

He grimaces as he lifts his hand from the snow, his fingers red and inflamed.

Strange. I place my hand in the fire once more and feel the energy it produces. It doesn't burn, but it's a familiar sensation I've felt before. It takes me a moment before I remember where.

Back at the forest.

"These are mana flames." I run my hand across the fire, and my mind runs wild with questions. Who did this, and how were they able to infuse fire with mana?

"Yeah, well, they still burn like a bitch." Taryn kisses his tender skin. "How are you not affected?"

"Really?" I hold out my arms, displaying the obvious. "I used to be green. Not to mention that forest trolls are capable of touching raw mana without being burned."

"Right," Taryn says flatly. "You could have warned me."

"Sorry, I didn't connect the two until you decided to make dwarf sausages. The forest trolls don't have anything like this." Were the damage severe, I might be concerned, but it's only a minor burn. I reach in my satchel and pull out a health potion, removing the cork. "Here, drink this and you'll be good as new."

He downs the health potion and after a moment, the redness fades from his hand. "Much better." He sighs. "So which way are we going? I'd like to find an inn with a warm fire."

I pull up my map, but it offers me little to go off. Aside from the portal, there's nothing displayed other than the mountain ranges. There are no towns or paths marked, and they probably won't populate until we've made contact with the locals. We're flying blind.

"I don't know, but I'd like our chances a lot better away from the dragon. Maybe we start on the opposite side and work our way through each path until we find something useful?"

"Works for me." Taryn climbs on Berry's back. "You can ride the big guy if you want. I'd hate for your toes to freeze off."

I climb on the moulhaug's back even though my feet would be fine in the snow. The skin on my soles is so tough I could walk on a bed of coals and probably not feel it. But riding Stompy, I can sit back and enjoy the view as we head toward the mountain.

The amount of snow distorts my perception, making it difficult to gauge just how far away the mountains actually are. As we travel, trees become visible in the distance, scattered around the landscape and covered in a thick layer of snowfall. Limbs shake on one of them, and sheets of snow fall from the branches.

I immediately jump down from Stompy and summon three horrors while equipping Destroyer. I have all my weapons back since defeating Dakota in the arena, but Destroyer is by far the strongest for combat. The ancient warhammer fills me with excitement as I grip the shaft, feeling the weight of the enchanted weapon. It's been too long since we've had a real fight.

Berry growls as a dark snout protrudes from underneath the pine.

Frost Wolf. *Level 18. With a thick coat and a dense layer of blubber, the frost wolf has evolved to survive the frigid climate of Frostmoor.*

If not for its black nose, the wolf would be indistinguishable from its surroundings. Brilliant white and ice-blue fur blends against the snow seamlessly, making me wonder how many other dangers might be lurking within plain sight.

Its mouth curls into a snarl as it emerges from the trees, revealing its giant frame, far bigger than any of the wolves I faced on Isle of Mythos. At level eighteen, it shouldn't be a challenge at all. Not when I'm level twenty-four and Taryn and Limery are both level twenty-two. With Berry level eighteen and Stompy at level nineteen, Ruby is the only one under-leveled at sixteen, but she's not here to fight.

This will be a nice warm-up.

The wolf tilts its head back and unleashes a loud howl. It carries over the quiet landscape like a foghorn, echoing off the distant mountains.

Stompy grunts and shuffles his feet. He must be dying for a fight as well.

"Who wants to do the hon—"

Before I can finish the question, several resounding howls answer all around us. A moment later, we're surrounded by wolves on all sides, at least a dozen, with golden eyes and black snouts their only revealing features.

This just got a lot more interesting. I summon a second wave of horrors, and our narrow path starts to feel a bit crowded. The grumbling horrors respond to my command, venturing out into the snow, but I quickly realize they aren't suited for this terrain. The lightweight Horrors of Finesse have no problem traversing the snow, but both the Horrors of Power and Vitality struggle to move as they sink into its depths.

The wolves trek through the snow toward us, their long powerful legs propelling them forward.

"Limery, can you clear some of the snow around the path? We need room to fight."

Without hesitating, Limery bursts into flames, and soon we have a circle of muddy earth to each side of the gravel path.

"How do you want to play this?" I ask Taryn.

He glances at the wolf pack slowly encircling us. "Spread out. Try to fight them in bunches and not all at once."

He lifts his Sapling Staff and summons a line of poisonous mushrooms along the boundary where the snow melts. Bulbous brown mushrooms with purple spots sprout to life, and once the cooldown wears off, he summons more until the perimeter is covered with a ring of fungi.

He scratches Berry behind the ears. "Time to put that armor to use."

Taryn climbs down and mounts Stompy while Ruby paces nervously between the moulhaug's legs. Limery hovers in the air between us all, his eyes darting from one wolf to the next.

I summon a third round of horrors and position each group an equal distance apart. I should be able to get in one more round before the wolves make it to us, two if we're lucky.

We briefly go over our plan of attack, making sure we're all on the same page before battle.

The wolves wait at the border still camouflaged in the snow. At this distance, I can see the saliva as it streams from their mouths, their sharp teeth desperate for flesh. Several of them eye Stompy, sensing a meal for the taking.

Not today.

The first wolf leaps from the snow into the mud, setting off a chain reaction of poisonous mushrooms. Purple gas erupts, staining the wolf's fur. The beast wobbles as it lands, coughing out the toxic fumes.

Nearby horrors rush toward the wolf, but before they arrive, there's a crack of thunder that startles some of the other wolves. Lightning and fire hit the wolf simultaneously, and the lingering gas takes out the rest of its HP.

One down.

Several more wolves leap the border. Taryn casts Stonewall,

blocking the approach of two wolves, and Limery's flame wall halts another.

Berry doesn't hesitate, armor clinking as he charges the closest wolf, his jaws wide. His paw is raised for an attack when my attention is diverted by the two wolves in front of me. One pounces at me, and I swing Destroyer horizontally. There's a sickening crunch as the warhammer connects with the wolf's jaw. The wolf yelps as it slides across the muddy earth into the snowbank.

The warhammer flashes red as it gains a stack of Inferno, the enchantment from being crafted in the heart of a volcano allowing the metal to grow hotter with each consecutive hit.

The second wolf snaps at my ankle but I step out of the way, leaving it chomping at air. A Horror of Power buries its tusks into the wolf's hind leg, eliciting another yelp. The wolf turns back out of instinct, sinking its teeth into the horror until the muscled summon combusts in a puff of smoke.

The distraction gives me enough time to land a hit against the wolf's ribs and gain a second stack of Inferno.

To my right, Stompy slams his horn into a wolf like a wrecking ball, knocking it away, deep into the snow. Taryn casts Stonewall in front of the beast, giving us time to deal with the others.

All around me, thunder crashes, fire sizzles, and both Berry and the wolves roar. The white wolves are now a mixture of purple, red, and brown, their fur painted in a mixture of mud, blood, and mushroom gas.

My horrors attack where they are needed, and I gain two more charges of Inferno. Destroyer glows molten red with every hit, singeing fur and burning flesh. Each time the wolves return, their thick fur grows patchier.

Between strategically-placed walls and raw power, it doesn't take long before a mound of corpses surrounds us. My muscles burn with the excitement of battle, and steam radiates from my skin even though I didn't have to use my barbarian rage.

"That felt good." I lean against one of Taryn's remaining walls. "Good job, everyone."

The wall fades into ether, and I tumble into the snow. For the moment, its cold embrace feels good against my skin. I catch Taryn's laughter right before Limery plops in the snow beside me.

"Limmy loves the snows!"

I cup a snowball in my palm and pelt him in the face with it as soon as his head peaks out. His bulbous eyes go wide for a moment before he erupts in demonic laughter.

"Limmy will gets you." He attempts to make a snowball of his own, but the snow melts in his hands each time he tries to pack it together.

"Sorry, dude. You're just too hot for this climate." I make another snowball and hand it to him.

Limery admires the snowball like a priceless artifact before throwing it at my face. I let him have his fun and allow it to hit me between the tusks.

"Nice one!" cheers Taryn as he finishes casting Restoration on Berry, healing his minor wounds from the fight. "That was a good fight. It won't be long until I hit level twenty-three."

I check my own experience and realize I hit level twenty-five during the fight. I've kept my notifications muted to keep them from distracting me during fights and didn't even think to check after the battle.

Twenty-five. Five more and I can return to Jegaar. I pull up my stats and examine them. With my racial bonuses to Strength and Constitution per level, they dwarf all my other stats. I still have six stat points I've been saving, and two ability points I'm not ready to use. None of my current available abilities are beneficial enough to justify using a point on them.

Underneath the level alert, there's a second notification.

Class Advancements. *Upon reaching level twenty-five, you have unlocked a class advancement. You may only advance one class at a time. A second class may not be advanced until completion of primary advancement.*

Barbarian Advancement.
> *Spirit of the Beast. Unlock for further details.*

Summoner Advancement.
> *Dreadbeasts. Unlock for further details.*
> *Dual Subclass. Unlock for further details.*

I sit there in shock for a moment. This is big. I won't know how big until I make a choice, but I have a feeling that whichever route I take could seriously change my role in the group going forward.

For now, I forget about the Warforged. Spirit of the Beast sounds awesome. And Dreadbeasts, that sounds terrifying. I have a feeling it would upgrade my horror summoning in some way. Dual Subclass sounds good, too, and I'm pretty sure that one would allow me to take on an additional summoning class that I was offered when I first became a summoner.

I take a deep breath. This is too big of a decision to make right now. I'll need to—

A snowball hits me in the face, interrupting my thoughts.

"Earth to Chod." Taryn looks at me expectantly. "What's going on?"

I must have been pretty zoned out. I wipe the snow from my face and join Taryn back on the path.

"I got a notification for hitting level twenty-five. There's an option for class advancement and I have three choices." I go on to tell him about my options.

"Dude, that's awesome!" Taryn grins, and his genuine happiness for me makes me appreciate just how lucky I am to have him as a friend. "Do you think I'll get one when I hit twenty-five?"

"Considering I got one for both of my classes, I would think so."

"Nice! Let's get moving then. Maybe we'll run into some more wolves."

I lose myself in thought as we travel. Since gaining a second class, I've been able to balance my summoning and barbarian abilities pretty well together. They synergize in a way that's rare, with my race and barbarian abilities improving my horrors. But now it feels like I'll be forced to commit to advancing one class for the foreseeable future. Regardless of what I choose, my horrors will continue to improve as I level and grow stronger due to their passive buffs from my Strength and Constitution. I can't think of another class better suited to my stats as a troll. But if I invest in my summoning, whether it be furthering my horror class or taking on a second summoning technique, I'll have reached the peak of my barbarian abilities for now.

This is a big decision, one not to be taken lightly.

"Do you see that?" Taryn brings Berry to a halt, and Stompy stops as well.

Taryn points to a splotch in the snow up ahead, where an abandoned wagon is surrounded by bloodstained snow.

Stompy snorts, and I pat him on the side. "Yeah, let's approach with caution."

"I can take my bird form and investigate," Taryn offers.

I shake my head. "I don't like that. Not here. We don't know what we're dealing with, and you'll stick out like a sore thumb against all this white."

He strokes his beard. "I could use transform and turn into a frost wolf."

"Badass, but likely to get you killed if wolves caused this."

"Fair point. Let's take it slow then and hope it's not a trap."

The closer we get, the more this feels less like a trap and more like a crime scene. Whatever was pulling the wagon is gone, the reins broken and lying on the ground. Bloodstained snow surrounds the wagon, and a crimson trail leads across the snow and into the snow-covered forest.

Something moves behind the wagon, and I equip Petrified Staff. Its bonus ability allows me to cast ranged physical attacks. Taryn readies his own weapon, and Limery grows even hotter against my shoulder.

"Who's there?" I ask.

A broad-shouldered human with a dense blonde beard steps out from behind the wagon. He wears a thick layer of furs drenched in blood and holds a bow at the ready, arrow nocked and pointed in our direction. He grunts, and his eyes narrow. I can't tell if it's in anger or fear.

CHAPTER 11
THE FIVE PEAKS

"STAND BACK!" the bearded man growls, the arrowhead swaying back and forth between us as he assesses which one of us is the bigger threat. "Gods as my witnesses, I will take one of you with me before I fall!"

His blue eyes flare with intensity as they dart between me and Taryn. Ice speckles his dense blonde beard. A massive axe hangs from his hip, and his stance shifts repeatedly, no doubt due to the adrenaline pumping through his veins.

I quickly analyze him before we find ourselves outmatched again.

Archard the Precise

> _Level 22_
>
> _Human_
>
> _Ranger_

He's strong, but we could handle him. I'm more concerned about his moniker than his level, though. A well-placed arrow to the eye could send me respawning back at the portal before I know what's hit me.

I put away my staff and raise my hands, showing him I'm not a threat. "We're not here to fight. We're on our way up the mountain. What happened here?"

He loosens the tension on the bowstring slightly. "What business do you have in Whitgard?"

Whitgard must be the name of one of the villages. "We're looking for allies, and we bring news from abroad."

He lowers the bow a couple of inches and laughs darkly. "Allies. You must be a long way from home."

"Further than you could guess." Taryn lowers his staff. "What happened here? There's a lot of blood. Are you injured?"

He finally releases the tension on the bow and lowers the weapon entirely. "Only my pride. A pair of frost giants caught scent of my hunt and ambushed me. Took my oxen as well. They don't normally venture this far down the mountain until winter, so they caught me unaware."

I glance around at the snowy landscape. "You mean this isn't winter?"

He lets out a hearty laugh this time. "You are a long way from home," he says again. "This is a crisp spring morning."

Taryn pulls his cloak tighter, as if imagining colder weather. "If you'll guide us to the village, I'll have my moulhaug pull your wagon. Looks like you could use the help."

Archard kneels and picks up the reins that once held his oxen. His eyes follow the trail of blood that leads into the snow-covered forest. "I can't return empty-handed. You lot know how to hunt?"

Taryn nods. "We provide for ourselves. What's on the menu?"

After some convincing, Stompy lets us harness him to the

wagon. He doesn't take kindly to being restrained, and the loss of influence for having more than one pet makes this more difficult than it should be. After some sweet-talking, Taryn's able to persuade Stompy to get moving. The wagon isn't big enough for me to ride up front with Archard, so Limery and I sit in the back while Archard steers the wagon from the narrow driver's seat. Taryn follows us on Berry.

The wagon bumps along as we travel in silence.

I clear my throat to get Archard's attention. "You said frost giants took your hunt? Are they common here? I once fought a mountain giant."

He grunts. "More common than we'd like them to be. You see that peak over there, the one that curls into the shape of a dragon's mouth?" He points to the nearest mountain range. "That's Icemaw. The frost giants call it home."

The peak is imposing, with massive icicles that give the appearance of teeth.

"How many live there?"

"Anyone foolish enough to attempt a count never lived to tell the tale. Could be a few dozen. Could be much more." Even with his back turned, I can make out the scowl at the edge of his brow. "You'd be hard-pressed to call them a tribe. They're more like a group of abominations that choose to dwell near one another. Sometimes their clashes can be heard in Whitgard on a calm evening. Hardly ever do they travel in more than pairs, and each giant is worth twenty men in combat."

They sound more dangerous than the giant I fought. If two of them ambushed his wagon, it's a miracle he's not dead. "How did you manage to survive them attacking you?"

He turns around and his blue eyes bore into me. "Fighting a frost giant is not bravery, it is a death sentence. You'd be wise to remember that. We avoid them at all costs, appease them when we can, and fight when it is the only option. I survived because I did what any smart man would do. I hid." His death stare dares me to contradict him.

Were I in his shoes, I have no doubt I would do the same. Facing off against something that strong with only one life to live leaves no room for error.

Taryn urges Berry closer until he's right behind the wagon. "I don't blame you. What was it you were hunting anyway?"

Archard sighs. "I spent three days tracking a mammoth, slowly wearing it down until I was finally able to finish the beast. Spent another day dragging it on a makeshift sled back to the wagon. And all for what?" he scoffs. "The moment I start to butcher the mammoth, the giants show up. That amount of meat would have lasted the village for weeks. Not to mention the oxen. We keep them in short supply, and it'll be a year to raise up another pair to replace them."

"Damn, that sucks." Taryn opens his cloak and guides Ruby onto Berry's back. "I'll take to the air, see what I can scout."

Archard whips the reins, but it does nothing to increase Stompy's speed. "There's a forest up ahead. Deer prefer the safety of tree cover."

There's a soft flutter as Taryn transforms into his bird form. As he soars through the white landscape, he sticks out like a ripe berry.

Archard's mouth hangs open as he watches Taryn fly away. "It's been many years since I have seen one blessed by the gods. It seems the dwarves spoke the truth."

He must be referring to the emissaries King Orso sent for the council. "There are more of us."

"Us?" He squints at me.

I summon a horror in front of me, and Archard nearly jumps from the wagon at the sudden appearance. "Heroes."

"And here I thought you were nothing more than a troll. I would love to hear your story, but I imagine Gherhardt will more so. Save it for when we return to Whitgard."

He certainly has more patience than I do. Archard is a man of few words, so we travel in silence, the only sounds are the crunch of pebbles beneath the wagon wheels and Stompy's occasional grunts or Berry's whines.

As we pass another torch with blue flames, I finally speak. "Where do the torches come from? There was a snowstorm when we entered. I couldn't see a foot in front of me but somehow the flames didn't go out."

"They've been there since before I was born, but the torches can give light in even the most menacing of storms. Before the fall, all of Frostmoor traded with the other portals. We had some of the best tinkerers in all of Mythos. We were once two mighty tribes, the Frozen Ash Tribe of Whitgard and the Snowwalker Tribe of Greypeak, and both of our societies prospered. We spread across four of the five peaks and rivaled many kingdoms in size. As the portals closed, our societies slowly crumbled and the knowledge we used to raise our people to prominence was lost to time. Greypeak was overrun by hobgoblins and the Snowwalker Tribe was forced to relocate to the remains of Boneholde. Now, we are but a scattering of villages doing our best to survive." His gaze lingers on the torch as we pass it. "On a clear night you can see their faint glow from the village."

The trolls aren't the only ones who have fallen from grace. All the more reason for these people to join the cause.

My notifications flash and I pull up a message from Taryn.

Incoming Message (Taryn): _Bro, bird form is amazing in the snow. I_ *can pick out every little thing that sticks out. I found a herd of some weird deer. Follow my location on the map and I'll keep trailing them.*

I pull up my map and locate Taryn. He's in the center of a nearby forest. It's not too far, but it will definitely take us some time on foot.

Message (Chod): Alright, we'll be there as soon as we can.

I relay Taryn's message and Archard nods, though it's hard to make out his facial expression underneath the massive beard.

"That'll save us some time at least. Finding the trail is the toughest part." He whips the reins, but we move no faster.

Stompy tilts his head and huffs.

Eventually, Archard pulls the wagon to the side of the path. "We'll take the rest of the way on foot." He releases Stompy from the harness, but the moulhaug doesn't move. Archard looks him in the eye. "You're a mighty beast, I'll give you that, but I don't think even you would want to tussle with a frost giant on your own."

Stompy grunts, but then takes a few steps into the snow.

I'll be damned. "I think he likes you."

Archard pats Stompy on the hindquarters. "I've always had a way with animals, ever since I was a boy."

"Berry's the friendlier one." I scratch him behind the ears, and he nuzzles against my fingers. "But if you want to take your chances riding Stompy, be my guest."

To my surprise, Stompy kneels in the snow—something he

has only ever done for Taryn. I've had to leap onto his back every time I've needed to ride him.

Archard climbs on his back, and I mount Berry with Ruby curling up between my legs. Limery perches on my shoulders, and I'm certain we're a sight to behold.

I lead the way, guiding Berry through the forest toward Taryn's location. Under the cover of the trees, there's a surprising amount of life. Ruby leaps from my lap in pursuit of a rabbit. A fox dives in a snowbank after some unseen prey. Occasionally, a bird will chirp in a distant tree or movement will send snow falling from branches.

I turn to Archard. "I had no idea so many animals lived here. Everything looks quiet and peaceful from far away."

The edges of his blonde mustache twitch. "Frostmoor is full of life if you know where to look."

Limery's body temperature suddenly warms, and I catch him staring at a nearby tree. A blue bird sits perched on a branch, its tender chirps carrying across the snow.

Limery licks his lips and pounces. Flames flare to life as he soars at the bird with breakneck speed. His fingers clench around the poor creature, and feathers flutter through the air as he ends its song abruptly.

I look away as he enjoys his snack. When he returns, he wears a devious grin.

"Limmy loves the birds." He picks a feather from between his teeth with a claw.

"A fine hunt." Archard winks at Limery.

The small imp blushes.

We travel for another hour before we near Taryn's location.

Incoming Message (Taryn): *About time you showed up. The deer aren't too far ahead.*

I squint my eyes to look through the forest, but I don't see anything—neither the deer nor Taryn.

"Psst." I wave my hands until I get Archard's attention, then I whisper. "Taryn says the deer are up ahead."

Archard slides down Stompy's side, equipping his bow as he lands softly in the snow. "We will pursue on foot. It is best if the animals remain here."

Berry listens obediently, sitting in the snow next to Ruby as she devours a rabbit she has been carrying in her mouth for the past hour. Stompy does little to acknowledge he heard anything.

Archard spots something in the distance and draws his bow. His vision must be better than mine because I still can't see anything.

"What is its?" asks Limery.

Archard points to a tree. "They passed through here. See the markings?"

I focus on the tree he's pointing at. The bark is scraped raw in several areas.

"And here." He points to a path of pressed snow. "Now we follow the trail."

He leads the way as Limery and I follow quietly behind. Archard moves like a ninja, his fur-covered boots barely making a sound. It makes the gentle crunch of snow beneath my own feet sound like thunder in comparison.

He raises a hand, telling us to stop, and then nocks an arrow. I follow the trajectory of the arrow but can't see what he's aiming at. Limery lets out a low "ooh" next to me just before I spot the outline of a solid white deer with icy-blue antlers emerging from behind a pine.

Frost Deer. *Level 16. The elusive frost deer blends in naturally with the terrain, making them difficult to spot for even the most seasoned of hunters. Their icy blue antlers are used to make weapons and are highly valued as jewelry due to the starburst pattern when cut open.*

"Pretties," Limery whispers.

Archard is about to take the shot when a red bird lands on the tip of his arrow.

He nearly falls down when Taryn returns to his dwarven form in a burst of feathers. Limery cackles on my shoulder, and the deer bolts away.

"What in the icy hells of Mythos are you doing?" Archard's face is red as a tomato. "You've gone and scared it away."

Taryn smirks, taking little offense to Archard's harsh words. "That's not the prize. Follow me."

A few minutes later, we stand on the edge of a clearing. A half-dozen frost deer lay in the center, soaking up the sun's rays. Two large bucks sit at opposite sides, their massive blue antlers casting elaborate shadows. These deer are bigger than any I have ever seen. The tips of their ice-blue antlers are translucent and seem to glow in the sunlight. They are truly magnificent creatures.

"Well done," Archard whispers.

Taryn equips his staff. "What's the plan? I can stun them with Lightning Bolt while the rest of you finish them off."

Archard places his hand on Taryn's arm, lowering the staff. "No need."

He draws an arrow from the quiver on his back and nocks it. I don't know what he's playing at, because as soon as he shoots the first arrow, the herd is going to bolt and we'll be no better off than if he had shot the solo earlier.

"Are you sure you don't want to plan an attack? My Horrors of

Vitality can slow the deer and make it easier. The four of us can handle them no problem."

He ignores me, lifting the bow until the arrow is pulled right beside his ear. I have the urge to smack it out of his hand and talk some sense into him, but I hold my temper.

The arrow releases with a thwip, and before it connects, he's already nocked another and fires. He shoots two more arrows just as quickly without checking to see if the others hit.

The first four shots land with dull thunks, hitting each deer right behind the forelegs. The two does wobble for a second before their heads drop. Both bucks are hit as they rise to their feet, taking a few steps before collapsing.

The fifth arrow zips through the air, hitting a deer as it prances toward the tree line. Archard holds the sixth arrow, trailing the movement of the final deer as it bolts away.

I'm certain the deer will escape, its long strides propelling it across the clearing. Archard looses the arrow and the beast tumbles to the ground inches from freedom.

Wow. The entire scene unfolds in under ten seconds. Six well-placed shots and not a single one off-target.

"How did you do that?" I look on in astonishment. He doesn't even have any magical ranger abilities.

"Practice." Archard slings the bow over his shoulder and heads toward his prizes, checking each deer to make sure it's truly dead. When he's satisfied, he turns to me. "I hope you're as strong as you look."

We wait while Taryn flies back to gather his pets. When they arrive, we strap the two frost deer bucks to Stompy. With their massive antlers, they take up the majority of the moulhaug's back. We tie one of the does to Berry. Taryn and Archard pull one together on a makeshift sled, and I'm stuck carrying one on each shoulder. At four hundred pounds, the does are mighty in their own right and will provide a lot of meat for the village. Archard refuses to gut them in the forest so that the village can use the entire deer, letting nothing go to waste.

By the time we reach the wagon, I'm covered in blood and sweat as I sling the deer into the bed of the wagon. Without the bonus Strength and Constitution I've gained as I've leveled up, I doubt I would have been able to carry both for such a long distance. Once I've loaded the others, I use the snow to wash away the blood from my shoulders.

Taryn sits in the front of the wagon with Archard while I ride Berry.

He plays with the vines on his staff, making them grow and retract with ease. "That was some amazing marksmanship back there. How'd you learn to shoot like that?"

"My father was a great hunter and ranger." Archard stares straight ahead as he answers. "He taught me everything I know."

Taryn smiles. "He must be proud."

Archard shrugs. "I'll never know."

"Why not?" Taryn's brows scrunch in concern, a look I've seen many times.

"Frostmoor is not an easy place to live. Even more so for a ranger. He went on a hunt one day and never returned. I was still a year or two from being deemed a man, but I had the skills to do the job, so I filled his place, and I've been a ranger ever since."

I speak loudly so that my voice carries over the crunch of the wheels on the path. "I'm sorry to hear that. Do you know what happened to him?"

He shakes his head. "We never found the body, but that's how it usually goes when someone goes missing. Could have been giants, hobgoblins, or any number of creatures. Not that the land is any kinder."

The sun dips behind one of the peaks, and suddenly we're

covered in shadow. We pass the stone ruins of a village. With the way the rocks have crumbled, it's evident no one has called this place home for some time.

"What happened here?" I ask.

"You ask a lot of questions, you know that?" His gaze lingers on the ruins. "Before the fall of Frostmoor, the villages of the Frozen Ash Tribe stretched all the way down the mountain. These are a solemn reminder of how far our people have fallen."

I can't imagine what it's like being forced to look upon these every time he descends the mountain for a hunt. "Are there still villages on any of the other mountains? I know you said that Greypeak was overrun, but what about the others?"

He turns around and stares daggers at me. "You know the best part about being a ranger? The peace and quiet. I'm grateful for your help, so I'll tell you what I know of the other peaks, and then I don't want to hear a peep out of you. Sound good?"

I nod.

He turns to Taryn. "And you?"

Taryn nods, then mutters under his breath, "Somebody is a grumpy goose."

For a moment, I'm certain that Archard is going to toss Taryn from the wagon, but he just sighs. "Long ago, when the Frozen Ash and Snowwalkers were at their height, we settled four of the five peaks. The Frozen Ash also held Icemaw, and in those days, we had the manpower to keep the frost giants at bay. The Snowwalkers expanded to Boneholde, and villages were built in the skeleton of some ancient beast."

He takes a deep breath. "Many of our men were sent to battle the dark one. Most of them never returned. When the portals closed, those left outside were lost to us forever. Without the able-bodied men to defend the villages, Icemaw fell to the giants. Sensing weakness, the hobgoblins that resided in the deep caverns of Greypeak attacked, killing many and forcing the rest to abandon their ancestral homes and relocate to Boneholde. A hundred years passed before Frostmoor opened to the world again, but by then, we had little to offer. Our numbers have dwindled little by little into what they are today."

Taryn sits on the edge of his seat. "Why did the humans never settle the fifth peak?"

Archard turns toward the center mountain. It is the tallest of the five, with the peak disappearing above a ring of clouds. Even though the sun is on the other side of the mountains, it ignites the side in blazing white. "According to legend, it was already settled."

"By who?" Taryn asks.

There's a long pause, just as an icy breeze blows down the mountain side. The chill is nothing compared to the one I get when he answers.

"Trolls."

CHAPTER 12

LET SLEEPING TROLLS LIE

I LEAN FORWARD SO FAR that I nearly tumble off Berry. "What do you mean trolls?"

Archard shrugs. "It's a legend as far as I'm concerned. You're the first troll I've ever seen in Frostmoor, but you look nothing like the trolls from the old tales. If there ever were trolls on Hornryx, they're long gone."

I think back to my first day in game, trying to recall what the arctic troll looked like in the creation menu. The option to play an arctic troll was unavailable to me, but I remember that it was massive, rivaling the desert trolls in size. It had skin that was a muted black and thick white fur covering much of its body, reminiscent of a polar bear. If not for the tusks and pointy ears, it could have been easily confused with a yeti. Is it possible that there are still arctic trolls in Frostmoor?

"What did the legends say?" I urge Berry to stay as close to the wagon as possible. Any clue, no matter how small, could give me guidance. If the arctic trolls are here, then I need to find them.

He frowns. "They're old wives' tales, nothing more. Stories

created to scare children into behaving. The trolls were said to have been so strong that neither frost giants nor hobgoblins would set foot on the mountain. Even to this day, no one ventures beyond the base of Hornryx. My nan would tell us stories about how the trolls could tell when a child wasn't asleep, and that they would slip into our rooms and devour us whole. I spent many a night unable to sleep, watching the shadows on the wall with my furs pulled up to my chin."

Taryn laughs. "Some things never change. My mom used to scare me and my sisters into going to bed with stories of the Boogeyman."

Archard scrunches his brow. "I have not heard of this Boogeyman."

I ignore their conversation, still occupied with thoughts of arctic trolls. Something doesn't add up. "After all these years, why has no one climbed the mountain?"

"What do we have to gain from venturing into unknown lands?" Archard tugs on his beard. "We have enough problems in Whitgard without adding the threat of trolls. Say they are nothing more than myth, there is still a reason we never summited Hornryx, a reason even the frost giants or hobgoblins have not claimed it as their own. It's an unforgiving mountain with steep cliffs and narrow passes. Snow falls heavier on Hornryx than any of the other peaks. If we managed to survive the climb and find that trolls do still dwell there, would it be wise to disturb them when they have left us in peace for so long?" He shakes his head. "No, if they do exist, it is best to let sleeping trolls lie."

I pester Archard for more information, but what little he does know is based on tales passed down through the ages. No one has seen an arctic troll since before the portals closed hundreds of years ago. Maybe they were on the same path as the mountain trolls, slowly fading to extinction high in the clouds. Or maybe they are thriving, alone and undisturbed.

To know for certain, we'll have to climb Hornryx before we leave Frostmoor. But for now, my focus needs to be on Whitgard and making sure I can convince them that forming an alliance with King Orso is in their best interest.

We failed in Goldspire. I can't afford to let that happen again.

"Ooh, looks!" Limery points to a dark blob moving across the snow, far bigger than any deer or wolf.

"Is that…" Taryn's words trail off and his eyes fill with greed.

"A mammoth," Archard finishes the sentence. "It will be a while before I dare to hunt one alone again."

Taryn's gaze follows the mammoth until we lose sight.

The temperature drops the higher we climb, causing goosebumps to erupt all over my body like a dense new armor. My troll body is holding up, but I'll need to find warmer clothes once we make it to the village.

Before long, night shrouds the landscape, and the temperature drops again. Howls of distant frost wolves carry far across the empty night, and occasionally something stirs in the depths of the snow-covered trees and bushes. I can't fight back the occasional shiver that courses through me, and I'm thankful for both Berry's and Limery's warmth.

The landscape is coated in a silver hue as the moonlight reflects off the snow. We pass several more ruins before a faint blue glow welcomes us up the mountain.

The enchanted path ends at the entrance to the village, where two blue torches flicker next to the gate. A wooden palisade wraps around the village for protection, but it obscures very little as buildings with thatched roofs scale up the side of the mountain. A second trail, snow-covered and no longer infused with mana, winds around the outside of the palisade and higher up the mountainside.

Archard pulls a bell from within his fur cloak and shakes it. A moment later, the gate cracks open and a fur-clad man with a thick black beard stands in the way. He watches Stompy warily, and his eyes narrow as his gaze shifts from the moulhaug to Taryn and then to me and Limery.

His eyes lock with Archard. "Explain yourself."

Archard's shoulders stiffen. "Did Gherhardt die and make you Head of the Frozen Ash while I was gone? Because that is the only way you'll get an explanation out of me. Now, open the gate."

"Gherhardt will not like this." The man slams the butt of his spear into the packed snow and pushes the gate open. "There have been too many outsiders within our walls as of late. It is unsafe."

Archard huffs. "Then perhaps we should send them down the mountain with the six frost deer they helped kill. You can thank these outsiders when you have a full belly tomorrow night."

None of us correct the fact that Archard single-handedly killed all six deer.

The man grunts before stepping out of the way.

Archard scowls at the man as we pass. "Warley has always been a coward, afraid of anything he doesn't understand. And for all of his cowardice, he believes his word carries weight. We will deliver the deer to the butcher and then I will find accommodations for you and your pets for the evening."

I silently will Stompy to move faster as another shiver courses through me. The streets of Whitgard are not quite what I was expecting from a tribal village. The buildings are more rustic and many are windowless, but they aren't that different from some of the smaller towns on Isle of Mythos. There is an assortment of buildings, all constructed from stone in a similar fashion to the ruins we passed. Only some of them have windows, with shutters pulled closed. Smoke billows from many of the smaller huts, and light peeks between the cracks in the door frames. The streets are empty, not that I would expect anything else at this hour.

We come to a stop in front of a square, stone building. Archard jumps down from the wagon and bangs on the door.

After a long moment, he bangs again. "Bernd, wake up, you old sod."

There's movement behind the door, and then it cracks open. A burly old man with wild gray hair rubs his eyes. "Archard, what is so important that it can't wait until morning?"

"I've returned from the hunt with six frost deer." He gestures to the wagon. "I figured you'd want to get started before they freeze."

Bernd does a double-take when he sees the rest of us, and the sleep vanishes from his eyes. "By the gods. Strange times. Strange times, indeed. First dwarves, and now this." He turns to Archard. "Unload them out back."

I unload the deer while Bernd watches me with curious eyes. A light snow begins to fall, and he pulls up the hood of his cloak. He mumbles something under his breath about trolls, but there doesn't seem to be any malice toward me, so I carry on.

Archard says something to Bernd I can't quite make out. Bernd nods and then we're back in the wagon.

We come to a stop in front of a long two-story building that resembles a barn. It has an arched entryway with two massive wooden doors.

"Stompy will have plenty of room in the stables." Archard turns to Taryn. "These stables have been here since before the fall, back when Aubert the Mighty was known for his domesticated mammoths."

Greed flashes through Taryn's eyes again and I'm certain he's imagining adding a mammoth to his menagerie. With another animal that big, we might as well join the Underground Circus.

"They'll be plenty warm inside its walls." Archard hops down and leads Stompy into the stable by the reins.

I climb down from Berry, keenly aware of the lack of warmth as a chill hits me between the legs. He follows Archard into the stable, and a moment later, Taryn returns with only Ruby as she scurries between his legs.

Archard strokes his beard in front of the stable entrance. "We haven't had a working inn in ages—there's been no need—so you'll have to stay in someone's home. I'd let you stay with me, but I'm gone so much that my hut is on the smaller side."

"They can stay with me." A figure cloaked in white furs is almost invisible against the snowy backdrop. He removes the hood, revealing a weathered face and forked gray beard.

Gherhardt

Head of the Frozen Ash Tribe
Level 25
Human

"Warley wake you up?" Archard frowns in the direction of the gate.

Gherhardt nods. "Leave him be. He likes to feel useful."

"Little snake," Archard mutters.

Those two must have some deep animosity between them.

Gherhardt extends a hand. "It is not often we receive visitors in Whitgard, so most of the village doesn't know how to act around outsiders. However, the fault is with me. I should have known after the dwarves dared to travel to our gates that it was an omen of more to come. The Frozen Ash have been in dark times for many years, but we will offer what we can, starting with a warm meal and a strong mead."

Limery perks up at the mention of mead, wiping away a drop of drool that trails down his chin.

I clasp Gherhardt's hand in mine and am surprised by the firmness of his grip. "That's very gracious of you."

Taryn and Limery echo their thanks.

"We have always been the more welcoming tribe of Frostmoor. I trust you had a good hunt, Archard."

Archard's face goes stern. "I lost two oxen, and the mammoth I killed, but we did manage six frost deer. Would have come home late and empty handed if not for this lot."

"Perhaps it wasn't an omen after all…" His voice is barely audible. "Let's get inside. I can't tell if it's troll toughness or bravado that has this one nearly naked in the snow."

I offer up a grin that probably looks more like a snarl. "Maybe a little of both."

We follow Gherhardt back to his home, where he pours us all a mug of deep amber liquid.

Item. Arctic Mead. *-2 Intelligence for one hour. In harsh climates, it helps to dull the senses.*

We sit around a roaring fire, sipping arctic mead from clay mugs as stew boils in a metal pot over the flames. The mead is syrupy and sweet, not my preferred drink at all, but Taryn and Limery seem to enjoy it.

"Just a few more minutes." Gherhardt stirs the pot and returns to his seat, a large chair with a wide back and legs that appear to be made of mammoth tusks. A fur blanket drapes over his shoulders, revealing a broad chest covered in gray hair. His hair is short and curly, the color matching his beard and chest. Though his face is weathered, he exudes a youthfulness in his blue eyes.

He lifts his mug in our direction. "For your help with the hunt."

I tilt my drink back to him. "Thank you, but Archard brought the deer down without any of our help."

Taryn mumbles under his breath, "Not like I spent hours tracking the damn things."

Gherhardt grins. "Archard is the most skilled ranger Whitgard has known since his father before him. He's a force to be reckoned with, but not even he can pull a wagon loaded with six frost deer up the mountain."

Taryn takes a deep chug from his mug. "If it's so hard to find food, why don't you move further down the mountain? There are certainly enough ruins."

Gherhardt sets his mug down on a polished wooden table in front of him. "This is our ancestral home. It has been the heart of the Frozen Ash Tribe for as far back as our story goes. We would not abandon it unless we had no other choice. Gods know the Snowwalkers have paid dearly since abandoning their homes."

He walks over to a wicker basket hanging against the wall and removes a purple carrot, tossing it to Taryn. "We provide for ourselves. We farm. We raise snowhogs and chickens. We would survive without the hunt, but the meat from the wilds reminds us of who we are and where we must go."

"I'm sorry. I didn't mean any offense." He raises both hands, nearly spilling his mead.

Archard pats Taryn on the shoulder. "Don't worry. It had been so long since an outsider visited Whitgard prior to your brethren that I feared the world had forgotten us. I doubt many know of our ways abroad, but it is good to know we have not been entirely forgotten."

I hang on the words he doesn't say. If the dwarves are the only people to have visited Whitgard in some time, then Jude and

Glenn aren't here. Where could they be then? I'm certain they were in a cave with a snow-covered entrance. Could they still be in hiding, or are they on a different continent entirely?

Taryn takes a bite of the carrot. "Oh, wow. This is amazing. You grow these here? In the snow?"

Gherhardt smiles. "We have our ways. I will show you tomorrow. For now, I'm sure you are famished."

He ladles the three of us a healthy serving of stew, and even fishes out a few pieces of meat from the pot for Ruby. The warm bowl in my hands is a welcome feeling, and my stomach growls as the smell overtakes me. Limery doesn't hesitate, slurping away at the piping hot broth.

Item. Gherhardt's Famous Stew. *+3 Constitution for one hour.*

I don't know if it's because this is the first real meal I've had after a long day of traveling, but the stew is so delicious that for a moment, I lose focus on everything around me as I devour the entire bowl. I thought Kea's stew from the troll village was good, but this is on a different level. The meat is soft and flavorful, yet the carrots and other vegetables have a crunch that adds complexity to the dish. There's a spiciness to the broth that packs a punch but isn't overwhelming. The Constitution bonus has my body feeling rejuvenated in seconds.

I tilt the bowl, letting the last drops of broth pour into my mouth. "This was amazing."

"I'll let the cook know." Gherhardt winks. "He carefully cultivates the spices for many of our signature dishes. Would you like some more?"

I enthusiastically accept, taking more time to savor the next bowl. Gherhardt watches us as we eat, the sounds of slurping and the crackle of fire filling the silence before he speaks.

"The dwarves that came here, they mentioned a council

hosted by the dwarven king of Seascape. I'm assuming that's why you are here?"

I set my bowl down, ready to finally discuss important matters. "Partly. Many of the leaders have agreed to form an alliance. King Orso fears dark times are coming, and he wants us to be prepared."

"Dark times." He chuckles. "Times have been dark in Frostmoor for many years. Giants run free across the lowlands. The Snowwalkers have been displaced by hobgoblins. My ancestors sent our best to fight alongside the other portals once, and we pay the price for it now. Where was this alliance when Frostmoor suffered?"

I can't fault him for his views, but this is bigger than what happened in the past.

"A behemoth crossed the portal." Taryn sits up straight. "It took dozens of the strongest fighters in Seascape to bring it down. What happens if one comes to Frostmoor?"

Gherhardt crosses his arms. "All the more reason for our men to stay here."

Taryn huffs and leans forward, passion burning in his eyes. "I can't speak for what happened in the past. All I know is that King Orso is a good leader. The portal to Seascape was open for less than a day before he started making plans. If you need help in Frostmoor, he will send it. We can help with the giants and hobgoblins, so long as you aid us when the time comes. That is all we ask."

Gherhardt's joyous eyes are lost in thought for a moment. "He would do that?"

Taryn places a fist over his chest. "On my honor."

He nods. "Then I will consider your proposal. Now tell me, what other news do you bring?"

We spend over an hour telling Gherhardt about the other

heroes, how we came to be here, our suspected connections of certain events to the dark wizard, and finally Jude and Glenn.

Gherhardt strokes the forks of his beard. "They haven't been here, but who is to say they haven't traveled to one of the other peaks."

Limery unleashes a belch so deep that I can't believe it came out of something so tiny.

"Sorries." He covers his mouth with slender red fingers. "Limmy is fulls now."

"It's about time." I gently poke his bulging stomach before returning my attention to Gherhardt. "If there is a possibility they are on the other peaks, then we will have to investigate. I can't leave here unless we know for sure."

Gherhardt frowns. "The Snowwalkers are a shadow of their former glory, even compared to us. I cannot say if they will welcome you or not. They have lost a great deal. As for the others, that is unwise, even for heroes."

"We'll take our chances. For what's coming, we'll need to grow stronger. We need stronger enemies to do that." I grin. "And it seems you could use fewer frost giants stealing your hunts."

His frown vanishes. "There is a truth to that. If you'd be willing, I am sure we can find use of your services in Whitgard before you leave."

Taryn downs the rest of his mead. "Say no more. We love a good quest."

"Excellent." Gherhardt claps his hands together and stands. "Then let me show you to your quarters. My ancestors had large families, so there are plenty of rooms to go around."

"And what about you?" I ask. "Do you have a family?" There's no evidence of anyone else here, but we did arrive late. Perhaps they are sleeping.

"I have no wife or children of my own. Maybe one day. There

is enough for me to do in Whitgard without the added burden of a family. The village needs me." He leads us down a stone hallway and up a flight of stairs.

Taryn and I take adjacent rooms. We say our goodnights and I close the door. Wood knocks against stone as both Taryn and Gherhardt bar their doors. I follow suit. Better safe than sorry.

The room is simple, with a wood-framed bed covered in an assortment of furs. A table topped with a candle sits to one side and a dresser to another. A large hide covers the floor in front of the bed and a small fire crackles in a fireplace on the opposite wall.

The stone floor is cool against my feet, but at least the fire will keep us warm.

I crawl in bed, and Limery curls up underneath my arm like a small furnace. It's crazy to me how far he and I have come since my first days in Mythos.

"Did you ever think that after trying to steal my necklace that we would end up traveling together to other portals and seeing distant lands?"

He touches the Tiger's Eye Pendant hanging from my neck and lets out a demonic laugh. "Limmy never thoughts he would leave homes. But now he has traveled lots with Chods. Farther than Mommy or Leo or Daddy."

"Do you miss them?"

He scrunches his bulbous yellow eyes for a moment as he thinks. "Oh yes. Limmy miss thems all. But Limmy loves Chods and loves the adventures. Mommy and Daddy just wants Limmy to be happy."

My words catch in my throat as I think about my own family. I've lost count of how long I've been in Isle of Mythos, but I still haven't heard a word from them. I wonder if they've even checked in with Valery. Do they have any idea what I've been through?

They arranged this, saving me from actual jailtime, but have they put in the slightest effort to find out how I'm actually doing? Do they even know I'm still logged in weeks after my sentence was over?

I'm pulled from my thoughts when Limery climbs onto my chest, his gaze fixated on me.

"Is yous okays, Chods?" His eyes radiate concern.

I snap out of my pity party. It doesn't matter what they're doing. None of it matters. Because everything that's important to me is inside Mythos.

"Yeah, buddy, I'm okay. Let's get some sleep. I'm sure we've got a big day tomorrow."

I close my eyes and let the crackle of fire lure me to sleep.

CHAPTER 13

A DASH OF SPICE

A LOUD BANGING on the door wakes me. Limery groans as I roll over him to check who it is.

The room is chilly, the fire nothing more than embers as I lumber to the door. "Who is it?"

"Does it matter?" Taryn taunts me from the other side. "What do you have to be afraid of?"

He has a point. I'm a pretty scary-looking troll, so it's not like I'm going to get robbed at knifepoint while I'm half-asleep.

I lift the wooden beam from the door, where Taryn waits impatiently on the other side.

"Let's go. Breakfast is calling." Taryn turns to head downstairs, Ruby trailing at his heels.

Limery lands on my shoulder, suddenly wide awake and grinning. "Time for breakfasts!"

The smell of roasted meat wafts up the stairs as we descend to the first floor.

Gherhardt leans over the fire, prodding a pan filled with sausage and eggs. "We rise early around here." Ruby stands at his feet, nose sniffing at the pan. "Get your fill and then I'll show you around the village."

Once we finish eating, Gherhardt leads us outside. Frigid wind assaults us as we step out into a bright morning. The sky is cloudless overhead, and the sun ignites the landscape.

In the daylight, the town looks as rustic as ever. Dozens of slate-gray stone buildings pepper the landscape between the palisade and the mountain cliff. A handful of people move about, fur hoods concealing most of their faces. A few stop in their tracks as they see us. Several nod to Gherhardt as we pass. There are no signs detailing the function of each building, making it difficult to determine what services Whitgard actually offers.

"Follow me. In exchange for your services, we'll outfit you in clothing more suitable for these parts." Gherhardt leads us to a building with a bear head mounted on the door.

Inside, a middle-aged woman sits at a table sewing two fur pelts together. Several racks hold fur coats, and shelves have blankets in different colors and sizes.

Her eyes go wide when she sees us. "So it is true."

Gherhardt shakes his head, turning to us. "Word travels fast around here. I swear they all have one hand sewn to their ears trying to catch the next piece of gossip."

"Oh, Gherhardt, we're not that bad." She flicks her wrist at him. "What can I do for you?"

"These three will be helping out around the village. I'd like for them not to freeze to death in the process."

She abandons her project and steps closer, eyeing us up and down. She points to Taryn. "Some of the children's clothing should fit you nicely."

I cough to keep from laughing, but Taryn still glares at me.

"And for you..." She points to Limery. "Amara and Flint's

daughter has outgrown her last set of furs. They should be the perfect size."

"It's okays, Limmy doesn't needs furs." He conjures a fireball in his palm and the woman takes a step back.

"Hmm, I suppose not." She focuses on me, her eyes wide with a mixture of caution and wonder. "How about you?"

"I'd be grateful for something warmer." I smile, but it does nothing to ease her tension.

She pulls a rope from her pocket and uses it to measure from my waist to my ankles. Her hands shake slightly when I crouch for her to take the rest of my measurements.

She grabs a few pieces of fur from one of the shelves and places it on the table. "Give me a few hours and I should have something for you. I don't keep anything on hand for someone of your size."

"That will be fine." Gherhardt pats me on the shoulder. "I think he can survive a while longer. Our next stop is indoors. Thank you, Maud."

Taryn changes into his new fur cloak and fur-lined boots. He loses the effects of the enchanted boots and cloak that he acquired in King Orso's vault, but for the time being, the new items are more practical, especially if we're going to be actually working in the snow.

I wrap my arm around him as we exit the tailor's shop. "It's adorable that you can still shop in the little boys' section."

"Shut up, Chode." He whacks me in the knee with his staff.

Pain sparks through my knee, but the joke was worth it.

With the sun out, the chill isn't quite as bad except for when a gust of wind comes down the mountain. We pass a forge, where smoke pours out of a chimney on top. A stout man with a braided brown beard wears a sleeveless fur tunic. He pounds a hammer against a piece of metal sitting on an anvil, a rhythmic clank echoing with each hit. His arms are nothing but thick, corded muscle and steam shoots out of his mouth with each heave.

He glances at us as we pass but doesn't skip a beat.

At the end of the row of stone buildings, there's a greenhouse filled with plants. It's hidden in the depths of the village, nestled against the towering cliff. Water trickles from the roof as snow melts in the sun.

"You guys have a greenhouse?" Taryn stares at the building in astonishment.

Gherhardt looks around, confused. "None of our houses are green."

"No, this." He points at the glass building.

"Ah, this is our growing barn." Gherhardt beams with pride. "A gift from the gnomes of Pruxford many ages ago. It has served our people well. The enchanted glass not only keeps the heat inside at a suitable temperature, but it is also unbreakable."

"Really?" Taryn taps the glass with his finger. "Unbreakable glass?"

"Truly. Go ahead, give it a try."

Taryn looks uncertain for a moment before he swings his staff at the glass pane. The Sapling Staff clinks against the glass. "Impressive."

"Now, you try." Gherhardt gestures to me.

"Are you sure? No offense, but I'm a lot stronger than Taryn."

"Brains over brawn," Taryn mutters.

I resist the urge to taunt him about his small cloak.

"Our growing barn has survived far worse." Gherhardt takes a step back. "Give it your best."

Limery hops from my shoulder, and I equip Destroyer, taking position next to the greenhouse. I shake my head as I lift the warhammer. There's no way that the glass can withstand my enchanted weapon. It seems silly that Gherhardt would risk his people's food supply for a demonstration. But I can tell by the look in his eyes that he's not taking no for an answer.

I swing and close my eyes as the hammer makes impact. There's a loud clink and the force reverberates up my arm. I take a deep breath, thankful that Gherhardt's word was true.

He laughs. "I hear that the capital city of Pruxford is filled with so much glass that it looks like it was carved from ice. Now, come inside. This is where I do my finest work."

I allow Taryn to walk ahead of me. "That sounds beautiful. Maybe we will adventure there someday."

"Ah, to be a hero with the freedom to travel wherever adventure calls and your heart desires. I relished the tales of great heroes as a child. Perhaps someday, tales of your great deeds will entertain young ones as they lay down to sleep."

"I like the sound of that." Taryn grins. "Why don't you visit Pruxford yourself?"

Gherhardt's face goes somber. "Being the Head of the Frozen Ash Tribe comes with many responsibilities. I do not have the luxury to follow whims, but I do take joy in my work in the growing barn."

"Uncle Gher!" A young woman with straw-colored hair peeks out from behind a bush covered in red berries. "Oh!" She gasps when she notices the rest of us.

"Don't be alarmed, Liyah. I'm just showing our guests around town. Everyone, this is my niece Liyah. She is one of our best growers."

She steps out from behind the bush, her gray tunic stained with dirt. "Don't listen to him. Uncle Gher loves the growing barn more than anything. If he didn't have to run the village, he'd never leave this place. His spice plants are like children to him."

"Spices?" I remember him making a comment about the spices in the stew last night. "Are you the spice master?"

He gives us a wide grin. "Guilty. Come take a look."

I activate my herbalism skill as he points out a variety of plants, and the skill quickly advances a level.

Congratulations! You have leveled up the skill 'Herbalism.' You are now a level 7 Herbalist (Apprentice). Increase your skill and learn advanced techniques for herbalism by finding an advanced herbalist (journeyman or above). Ranks: Novice, Apprentice, Journeyman, Expert, Artisan, Master, Grandmaster.

"These over here are strictly for flavor. The growing barn has been in use for ages, but the art of growing exotic spices and herbs were lost to our people. Until one day, many years ago, we found a bag of old seeds in one of our cellars, and Whitgard cuisine has never been the same. I've managed to harvest seeds from each crop and now provide enough spices for the entire village. Thanks to the power of the growing barn, we grow spices found all over Mythos."

He points from one plant to another, giving us details about the flavor profile of Desert Needle, Fire Mustard, Berry Pepper, Tartmint, and many more. He dishes out so much knowledge that my herbalism skill increases another level. If I were a chef or potion master, this knowledge would be invaluable.

He takes us to another section of the greenhouse where the produce grows. There's enough ripe fruits and vegetables to fill a farmers market.

"This is one of my favorites." He plucks a handful of red berries from the bush and hands one to each of us. "Torchberry."

I examine the berry. It's a vibrant red with streaks of orange running vertically.

Gherhardt pops one in his mouth and we all follow suit. Immediately, a warm sensation fills my throat, working its way down to my stomach. It's not spicy. The berry itself is quite sweet, but the warmth continues to expand inside of me.

"Whoa, that's intense." I hold up a hand as he offers another one.

Limery greedily accepts.

"They're the perfect cure for a cold day. They're also a key ingredient in Torchmead."

"This is amazing!" Taryn claps his hands together. "Your herbalism skill must be through the roof. What level are you?"

Gherhardt makes an attempt to be modest. "I'm sure you've seen many plants on your travels. I'm but a lowly artisan."

Artisan. That means his herbalism skill is somewhere between level thirty-one and forty. Only master and grandmaster are above him.

Taryn clasps his hands together. "I'm only a journeyman. If you will teach me, I'd love to learn more."

Gherhardt nods. "Help us around the village, and it shall be done."

He leads us deeper into the greenhouse when someone bursts through the door.

A young man with a patchy beard pants for breath. "Gherhardt! It's Alvyn. He's having a fit again."

Gherhardt brushes past me. "I'll be right there. Prepare the ice balm."

The young man's face goes a stark white. "We're out."

"What do you mean you're out?" Gherhardt grabs him by the tunic. "I told you to warn Archard when you were low and he would go acquire the necessary ingredients."

The young man's head sinks. "I thought we had more. I'm sorry."

Gherhardt slams his fist on the table, shaking several of the plants. "Sorry is not good enough. With no setbacks, it will take four days to summit Icemaw and return. That's with fair weather, little sleep, and no run-in with giants. Do you think Alvyn has four days?"

The young man shakes his head. "I don't know."

"Go and find Archard. I'll have him do what he can."

Under Gherhardt's stiff gaze, the young man looks more like a child. I'm certain he would vanish into thin air if he could.

"Now!"

The kid nearly bumps into a table of spices as he rushes out of the greenhouse.

"What's going on?" asks Taryn. "Is there anything we can do to help?"

Gherhardt sighs. "Alvyn is one of the village elders. He has a condition that requires a special elixir whenever he has a fit. One of the ingredients—arctic clove—only grows in one place in all of Frostmoor: Icemaw, the territory of the frost giants. It usually takes Archard a week to locate it in order to avoid detection. We'll do what we can, but I'm afraid we don't have that much time."

"Can you describe the plant to me?" asks Taryn, and I already know what he's thinking.

"I appreciate the offer." He grabs Taryn on the shoulder and squeezes. "But if Archard cannot make it in time, I fear no one can. He knows these mountains better than anyone."

"It's not about that." Taryn stares him down. "Describe the plant to me and give me a location. I'll fly there. I'll make it in a quarter of the time."

"Fly?" He scrunches his eyes. "Are dwarves made with wings now?"

Using Transform, Taryn turns into a red bird and sits on Gherhardt's shoulder. Liyah gasps, and her uncle curses under his breath. There's an explosion of feathers and Taryn returns to his dwarven form once more.

Taryn crosses his arms. "Now are you going to tell me what to do or not?"

Archard comes stomping through the door just as Gherhardt finishes describing the arctic clove to Taryn. "I've prepped the goat. I'll be back as quick as possible, but I doubt I'll be able to avoid detection. Things could get messy." He sighs. "One job. He had one job."

Gherhardt holds up a hand. "There's been a change of plans. Our dwarven hero will be flying to Icemaw in your stead. I've described the plant to him, but you'll have to tell him the rest."

Archard nods. "The arctic clove grows beyond the encampment of the frost giants, high in the peak. You will have to bypass the frost giants. But you must beware, there are other terrors beyond the giants. In your bird form, I fear for your safety."

"Limery will go with him," I interrupt, and they all turn to me. "If he wants to. I can't force him, but I remember what happened with the mountain trolls when you were shot down by goblins. If something happens, you need someone to look out for you."

Even though his bird form is small, he'll stick out like a beacon against the white landscape.

Limery grins. "Okays. I goes with Taryns."

My stomach feels uneasy at the thought of them both going into unknown territory. With me and Taryn's pets, I feel confident in our abilities, especially with my horrors. But the two of them against an angry group of frost giants that likely out-level them... I watched Taryn die once in Goldspire, and Limery... I would never forgive myself if something happened to him.

Taryn must sense my inner turmoil because he comes over and pats me on the arm. "Don't worry about it, big guy. We'll be back before you know it."

Archard fills them in on the rest of the details, and pretty soon, they're ready to go.

Limery wraps his warm arms around me as we stand at the gate.

"Take care of one another." I pull Taryn aside. "If it's too dangerous, promise me you'll turn back."

"Hey." His face is set in stone. "I'm not going to let anything happen to him. You just try not to let the place go to shit while we're gone."

I laugh at his poor attempt at a joke. "I'll do my best."

There's an explosion of feathers and then the two of them are soaring through the sky.

"Alright," Gherhardt calls from over my shoulder. "Time to put you to work."

CHAPTER 14

WORK, WORK, WORK, WORK

WE STOP BY MAUD'S, who has managed to sew a cloak capable of covering me from head to toe. With the hood pulled up, I look more like Bigfoot than a troll as I trek through the village, but I have to admit it does an amazing job of taking the chill from the wind. Maud even managed to sew me a pair of moccasins with slits for my claws to poke through. I much prefer the freedom of my loincloth, or battle skirt, and I'll be ditching these the moment we're in a warmer climate, but they do a lot for my quality of life at the moment.

I catch a few stares from the townsfolk after we drop Ruby off at the stables, but Gherhardt assures me they are all just confirming the gossip for themselves.

"There's not much to do in a village besides work and gossip. And the work is never done." He stops in front of a building at the edge of town. "You'll be working with Dando today. He's one of our village craftsmen. Don't let his age fool you, he's one of the best and brightest. Tomorrow is our annual goat race and we need the trail cleared. We had a heavy snowfall a few days ago, so it's probably tougher than usual. I'm sure he can use the extra help."

Quest alert. *You have been offered the quest 'Clear the Trail.' The Ascent is an ancient tradition of the Frozen Ash Tribe, and every spring, young men race frost goats along the mountain pass. Help remove snow from the trail and increase your standing with Whitgard.*

Reward. *Increased favor with the Frozen Ash Tribe.*

He knocks on the door before entering. Inside, a young man stuffs tools into a satchel. I'm surprised by how tall he is. He's well over six feet and lanky, with brown hair trimmed close, bright blue eyes, and a face as clean-shaven as a baby that only adds to his youthful appearance.

"Gherhardt, I was just heading ou—" He freezes in place when he sees me.

I should probably be used to that reaction by now.

"I brought you some help." Gherhardt gestures to me. "This is Chod. His companions are on another quest for the village. You might not tell it by looking at him, but he packs some muscle underneath these furs."

Dando lets out a nervous laugh at Gherhardt's joke. "Sorry for my rudeness, I've just... We don't get many outsiders around here. Nice to meet you. I'm Dando."

His honesty catches me by surprise. I forget that I'm not an alien to these people, just a foreigner. They are all well aware that other races exist even if they've never seen one in person.

"Don't worry about it. You can call me Chod." I extend my hand and we shake. "Ready to get to work?"

"The snow's certainly not going to shovel itself." He grins at Gherhardt. "Give Liyah my best, will you?"

"You gentlemen have fun." I'm not sure if Gherhardt intentionally disregards Dando's words for Liyah or not. "And, Chod, when you're finished, come find me. I'll have your next quest waiting."

Dando seems to loosen up once we are outside. "We'll stop by the stables to grab a pair of goats and then I'll show you the track."

"Sounds good. So, what's the deal with the race anyhow? And why goats?"

He laughs. "It's tradition. It's called the Ascent, and we do it every year to commemorate the tale of Umen the Steadfast's victory over Edrar Snowwalker. Legend says that Umen and Edrar were brothers born from the ice, and that when they cracked themselves free of its frozen embrace, they were tasked by the gods with settling the five peaks. Both of them wanted Whitgard as their home so they came to an agreement that the first one to climb the summit would claim the mountain for themselves."

We arrive at the stables, but Dando stops in front of the gate to continue his story. "Edrar had special boots that allowed him to walk on the snow without sinking, so he quickly outpaced Umen as they climbed the mountain. But Umen was cunning and had a way with beasts, so he captured a wild frost goat and mounted it. The goat ascended with ease, and by the time Edrar knew he was being overtaken, it was already too late.

"Edrar was a prideful man, and the thought of losing angered him. He nocked his arrow and fired upon the goat, piercing it several times. But frost goats are sturdy creatures, and the goat continued its ascent, leaving a trail of red in its wake."

Dando is so into the story that he begins acting out the scenes as they happen. "The goat collapsed as Umen reached the peak and claimed victory over his brother. He offered to roast the goat as a peace offering between the two. With his anger abated, Edrar agreed to settle one of the other peaks. No sooner had they taken their first bite when a shrill screech echoed from above and blue flames descended." Dando flaps his arms like wings. "A white dragon burned the trees they were using for cover and stole the goat for its own. And as Umen built the first home in the frozen ashes of that feast, so our tribe was named."

"Wow." I give him a round of applause for his storytelling. "Now that's a good story! Why didn't the other tribe get a cool name?"

He shrugs. "I guess Edrar was a sore loser."

As we enter the stable, a silver falcon swoops in to perch on top of the roof. It could probably pluck Taryn out of the air with no problem. I can't help but wonder what other dangerous creatures might be lurking outside the village walls.

Berry groans from the far end so I go and pay him a visit. He stands on his hind legs against the railing so that I can scratch him behind the ears.

"Don't worry. Taryn will be back before you know it. He's got Limery with him for protection."

Stompy leans against the stone wall of the barn, paying me no mind, with Ruby curled behind one of his massive legs. How she got here, I have no idea.

One of the stableboys ogles at me as he sweeps manure into a bucket.

"Are they behaving themselves?" I ask.

He gulps. "Yes, sir. They're well behaved, sir."

I leave the young man alone before he has a heart attack and go find Dando.

The young craftsman waits for me at the stable entrance with two goats unlike any I have ever seen. They have thick white fur, black faces with bright blue eyes, and black horns that curl around their heads. The horns fade from a deep black at the base to an icy blue at the tip.

Each goat is as big as a cow, and I can't think of any reason why Archard doesn't have them pulling his wagon. One of the goats steps closer to the other and there's a crack like a gunshot as the second goat rams its horns into the other's. The first goat rears on its back legs, and Dando grabs it by the reins, pulling it away.

"Hey!" His voice is stern and commanding. "Enough of that." He separates the two enraged goats like he's done it a million times and hands a pair of leather reins to me. "Here, take this one. Frost goats are powerful and graceful creatures, but they tend to butt heads, so to speak. They'll be the safest way to travel up the mountain, though."

I glance up at the peak that disappears among the clouds. "How far up the mountain are we going?"

He cocks an eyebrow. "To the top. How else are we going to properly honor the legend of Umen and Edrar if not by following in their ancient footsteps?"

Warley is on gate duty as we leave Whitgard. He stares at Dando with nearly as much hatred as he does me but says nothing as he slams the gate.

"What's his problem?" I ask as I climb onto my frost goat.

"Jealousy." Dando rolls his eyes. "We fancy the same girl."

I guess Liyah must be the catch of the town. "And Gherhardt, what does he think about all of this?"

"Gherhardt likes me well enough when I'm not making eyes at Liyah, but of course no one is good enough for his niece." Dando leans toward me, a bit of mischief in his eyes. "Warley would have better luck setting fire to a snowball. Liyah can't stand him." Dando laughs.

I grin at his antics. "I can see why. He certainly seems to have a chip on his shoulder."

Our goats are slow and steady as they move up the mountain. We make sure to give them plenty of space between one another to keep their bravado in check.

"I try not to hold it against him." Dando frowns as he looks out into the distance. "I'm sure he feels a lot of pressure to live up to his father's legacy. He manned the gate for thirty years."

Family issues are something I can definitely relate to. I'm sure I've done my fair share of dickish moves because of them, too. "What happened to his father?"

"A frost giant wandered up the mountain one night while the elder Warley was at the gate. The giant kicked in the gate. Elder Warley was able to sound the alarm, but at the cost of not being able to defend himself for a few seconds. Gherhardt and the others responded quickly, but it was too late for Warley's father. The giants haven't come to Whitgard since, but they give Archard hell every time he goes for a hunt."

"That's terrible. I'm sure he feels a lot of pressure to live up to his father."

Dando nods. "Archard and some of the others are less forgiving. I mean, he can be annoying as a hobgoblin, but I try to look past it."

I don't know why I'm so surprised by Dando's understanding, but I am. It's not often you find wisdom in someone so young.

It doesn't take long before the trail is obscured entirely by snow.

Dando climbs from his goat and opens the saddle bag. "We'll start here and work our way up." He tosses me a shovel. "Let's put those big blue muscles to use."

The work is slow going, shoveling snow off the side of the mountain. I can't help but think of how quickly Limery could have cleared this entire path if he was here, but I'm glad he's with Taryn. As long as they are smart, I doubt they'll get into trouble. Plus, Taryn can message me if something goes wrong.

After about five minutes of shoveling, I decide to work

smarter, not harder. "Don't freak out, but I'm going to bring in some reinforcements."

He gives me a questioning look, and I summon a Horror of Power. The muscled golden horror appears in a puff of smoke and Dando's mouth drops open. The horror's barbed tail swings back and forth as it paces through the snow, its black mane swaying in the breeze.

There's a huff nearby just before one of the goats charges the horror, ramming into it and snuffing out its life in an instant.

"What the hell was that about?" I shout as Dando reins in the crazed beast.

He pets the creature on the nose until the rage leaves its eyes. "What did you think was going to happen? The frost goats are here for our protection."

"Protection? I thought they were for carrying tools up the mountain."

He places a hand over his eyes. "No disrespect, but I could carry a shovel on my own. Frost goats are not work animals. They are natural protectors capable of punting anything that might attack us straight off the mountainside. With one above and one below, we can work in peace."

I'm a little embarrassed I didn't think of that. Most of the Frozen Ash tribe is so strong compared to those on Isle of Mythos that I didn't think they would need special protection. But just because they're high level doesn't mean they're all natural fighters.

I scratch my chin as I try to find a solution. "Well, is there any way we can tie them up behind us? I can make this go a lot faster if they aren't killing my horrors."

He rubs his baby smooth cheeks. "And what if something comes for us?"

A laugh escapes before I can stifle it. "If it gets past me and my horrors, then your goats never stood a chance."

"Are you really that strong?"

I flex my arms, but the effect isn't as impressive when I'm covered in fur. "These babies aren't for show."

With the frost goats tied up further down the trail, I summon as many horrors as I can. They work their way through the snow, scooping it and tossing it off the mountainside. The Horror of Power shovels mounds of snow between its legs like a dog digging through sand at the beach. As the time begins to expire on each horror, I move them further up the trail and cast Kamikaze, exploding them and removing even more snow.

Dando stabs his shovel into the snow and leans against the handle. "Wow, I've never cleared the trail this fast before! We'll be done before dinner at this rate."

We take a break for lunch while the horrors continue to work. Dando pulls out strips of jerky, bread, and a bright yellow melon.

I take the bread and jerky but leave the melon to Dando. "Where do you get the meat from? I find it hard to believe that Archard is hunting enough to feed a village the size of Whitgard."

"Gherhardt didn't show you the caves?" My look of confusion prompts him to continue. "We raise snowhogs and chickens in the caves at the base of Whitgard. There's a natural mana source that keeps the cave at a stable temperature even on the coldest of nights, and it provides a special grass that grows without sunlight. It's the main reason we don't starve."

That's fascinating. If there's a ley line running through the mountain, I wonder if that means there are dungeons in the area. What I would do for a map of Frostmoor with all the ley lines marked like the one Chief Rizza gave me.

"This place is full of surprises." I take a bite out of the jerky. It has a spicy flavor I can't quite place, no doubt from one of Gherhardt's spices.

I explode two horrors and then summon more to replace them while Dando packs away the leftover food. He starts to stand, but then sits down on the boulder again.

He hesitates for a moment before speaking. "You know, I've always wondered what drives heroes to risk their lives for adventure. Is there a big blue lady troll waiting for you back home? Is that why you are doing all this?"

The question comes so far out of left field that I laugh. Dando immediately frowns, and I do my best to get a hold of myself. I can't even remember the last time I had romantic feelings for someone. Probably my last train wreck of a date.

"I'm sorry, no, it's just that that's about the last thing on my mind. With all the adventuring and quests, my priorities have been elsewhere."

He gives me a questioning look. "If you're not doing this for a woman, then what's the point?"

I sit there for a moment gathering my words. I get what he's saying, but I don't buy it. I remember, a few summers ago, binge-watching a slew of superhero movies with Taryn. There was almost always a love interest that would drive the hero to be stronger or better than they would be on their own. In the hero's moment of weakness, they would think of this person and get the power to go on.

I believe that love has the power to make someone strive to be better, to fight against the dark when all hope seems lost, but it doesn't have to be romantic love. It can be the love of a friend or family. Or a community. Hell, it can be for no other reason than because someone refuses to have their future dictated for them. But for me, why do I do all this? Why am I still in this game when I could have logged out a long time ago?

"I do it for my people."

He nods, his face solemn. "There are rumors around the village that a darkness is coming. That the dwarves brought grave news from abroad. Is this true?"

I don't know if it's my place to tell him or not, but I do it anyway. "Something is happening. We don't know the full extent yet, but we're warning who we can, gathering allies for when the time comes."

He clenches his fist. "If there's anything I can do to make sure this darkness doesn't spread to Whitgard, sign me up."

I appreciate his enthusiasm. I'm certain that he's thinking about Liyah the same way I'm thinking about the forest trolls. He'll do anything to protect her. And at level seventeen, he's actually pretty formidable compared to a lot of NPCs I've met on Isle of Mythos.

Still, it's not my place to recruit individual soldiers. "You can talk to Gherhardt about it later."

It's not the answer he wants to hear, but he accepts it. We return to work, and within a few hours, the tip of the peak is within view. The trail ends and a hundred yards of steep rocky terrain is all that stands between us and a stone platform surrounded by a ring of trees. Dense firs grow on each side of the rocky path, framing the final ascent.

"Wow, I still can't believe we've cleared the trail so fast. The rest of this—" He points to the jagged rocks that lead up to the platform. "—is where the race takes place. Wait until you see the goats climb it. It's really something—"

A howl erupts from above, echoing off the surrounding mountains. Dando takes a step back and I instinctively equip Destroyer while recalling horrors to my side.

A level-twenty frost wolf peeks out from the tree line. It steps forward, carefully navigating the rocky incline. A moment later, four more wolves exit the wooded area. Their blue-and-white fur conceals them well against the snow-covered trees.

"This is why we bring the goats." Dando's voice is higher-pitched than normal.

"Go untie them. I'll hold off the wolves."

Dando takes off running down the trail. The biggest frost wolf, sensing its prey escaping, leaps over the rocks after him.

A Horror of Finesse greets the wolf, but it chomps off my horror's head, destroying it in one bite. A Horror of Vitality slows the wolf with its passive, and a Horror of Power gores its tusk into the wolf's hind leg. The wolf yelps, and the rest of the pack leaps down to protect their leader.

There's a mixture of snarls and growling as my horrors swarm in a frenzy, but the wolves hold their own. It took our entire party and my horrors to defeat twice this number at the base. Taking five on by myself might not have been the smartest idea.

The wolves' health bars trickle down, but their incredible Constitution means they'll outlast my horrors in a sustained fight. Eventually, I won't be able to summon horrors quick enough to attack in force.

Time for me to turn the tide while I still can.

I cast Champion, and a clone of the frost wolf I killed at the base of the mountain forms in front of me. It snarls at the other wolves, and I unleash its fury on them.

Hooves trample against the cleared path behind me as the cavalry arrives. With the frost goats, along with my champion wolf and horrors, we should be able to take care of this handily.

The first goat passes me by, head lowered as it charges into battle.

It collides with my champion like a battering ram, and the unexpected force launches the wolf off the edge of the mountain.

You have got to be shitting me.

The presence of the horror grows less and less as it tumbles down the cliff before fading entirely.

The second goat plows into a group of horrors clinging to a wolf. The horrors shoot through the air like confetti and the wolf is knocked back. Several horrors tumble off the mountainside and the other wolves chomp at more as they fall back to earth.

Dando apologizes frantically behind me, but I tune him out. The second goat elicits a shrill yelp as it rams into the shoulder of a frost wolf. It then kicks out with its hind legs, knocking more horrors away.

The goats attack in a blind rage, not caring if they hit wolves or horrors, or occasionally each other.

I grip my warhammer and activate Berserker Rage. Steam shoots out from underneath my cloak and it pulls tight against my skin as my muscles bulge. If I want this done right, it looks like I'm going to have to do it myself.

I rush into battle, grabbing the first goat by the horn and pulling it away. It tries to ram me when I let go, but it meets the head of my hammer. Red streaks through the weapon as Inferno activates and the goat charges again. A second hit knocks the goat back further and its knees buckle.

It stands up, woozy, and Dando grabs it by the reins.

Just as I turn around, a wolf lunges at me. I sidestep, dodging the attack and landing a hit to the ribs that sends the beast over the cliff.

One down, four to go.

The free goat runs rampant, kicking and ramming, hitting horrors and wolves. Two of the wolves have squared off with the goat, and the other two have turned their attention toward me.

"Bring it!" I roar, and they answer the call.

The two wolves leap over the small mound of horrors

standing between us. Steam rises from Destroyer like an erupting volcano as it grows hotter from each consecutive hit.

With the increased power from Berserker Rage, I hit the first wolf with enough force that it smashes into the second. The second wolf tumbles to the edge of the trail and rolls off without ever gaining its footing. The first wolf follows it, but rolls over at the last second, gripping the ledge with its front paws as it tries to climb up.

Three horrors tackle it off the ledge.

I'm down to a handful of horrors that do their best to avoid hurting the goat while also attacking the wolves. One wolf has pinned the goat to the ground and has its teeth sunk in the thick fur around the goat's neck. As far as I can tell, there's no blood.

Yet.

I leave them to their stalemate while I deal with wolf number four.

The wolf backs against the row of rocks that mark the beginning of the race. Icy blue fur arches in spikes across its shoulders reminiscent of icicles. I twist Destroyer's handle against my palm as I wait for the threatened creature to lunge.

When it does, I sidestep at the last second. It goes flying past me straight for Dando. His eyes go wide and he lets go of the frost goat. It rams into the wolf with pinpoint precision, propelling it off the ledge.

Berserker Rage ends, and there is only one wolf remaining. It still has the goat pinned to the ground, but no matter how much it adjusts its bite, the fur doesn't give. I can see now why they are such great protectors. Fast-twitch muscles for lightning-fast rams, hard heads, and fur that serves as natural armor and insulation.

The wolf eyes me as I approach, but it doesn't release. I switch to Forlorn Scepter and slide the end of the staff in the open space at the back of the wolf's teeth in order to pry its mouth open.

It releases, snapping at me before backing up defensively. The goat stumbles to its feet and shakes out its fur.

Our standoff only lasts a moment before the wolf bolts into the woods.

Dando runs past me, inspecting the goats matted fur for wounds. "That was nuts! You were... You were... That was crazy!"

I summon more horrors just in case something else shows up. "Are they okay?"

He pets one on the neck. "Oh yeah, these guys have saved my bacon more than once. Sorry about your pet wolf."

"Don't worry about it. The important thing is that we survived. With only one wolf left, I don't imagine it'll be causing problems anytime soon."

"Yeah, the wolves don't normally come up this high. I wonder what they were after."

I shrug. "Beats me. You ready to get out of here? I'm sure Gherhardt has more work waiting for me at the village."

After gathering up the tools and belongings that got tossed aside during the fight, we head down the mountain.

Ever since Taryn arrived, I've been more focused on fighting as a team than anything, but it's good to know I can still hold my own when I need to.

We're halfway back to the village when my notifications flash, telling me I have a new message.

Incoming Message (Taryn): Yo, Chod. Can you let Gherhardt know we're not making it back tonight? Things got a little wild. We're stuck in a cave, but we'll be back as soon as possible. I'll tell you all about it when we get back.

CHAPTER 15

A WING AND A PRAYER

Quest alert. You have been offered the quest 'A Wing and a Prayer.' Alvyn, one of the village elders, is in dire need of a special elixir, but they have exhausted their supply of arctic clove. Time is running out. Fly to Icemaw, acquire the arctic clove, and return to Whitgard with haste.

***Reward.** Increased favor with the Frozen Ash Tribe, and advanced herbalism training with Gherhardt.*

Taryn closed the quest notification for the tenth time since leaving the village. He'd been flush with quests after logging in at Seascape, but since grouping up with Chod and Limery, quests had been few and far between. He'd leveled up nicely fighting monsters and clearing dungeons, but there was something special about following a quest line to completion. At times, quest rewards were even greater than experience. Training with Gherhardt was an easy opportunity to dramatically increase his skillset. With a high enough herbalism skill, he could search for rare plants and either sell them at the market or use them for advanced potions and elixirs.

The latter sounded better. Their small group was pretty well-balanced, except for not having a healer. He had Restoration, but it only worked on his pets. If Taryn could level up his potion-making skill as well then that would be a major boost to their team composition.

For the third time since leaving, he and Limery stopped to rest on a tree limb. Unable to communicate with the imp in his bird form, he transformed back into a dwarf. Red feathers exploded around him, and the branch sank with the added weight. Snow fell, plopping against the ground.

His dwarven form was much warmer, and Taryn was thankful for the magical properties that allowed his clothing and items to remain on his body when switching between forms. Transforming from a bird to a naked dwarf in this weather would be a nightmare. The ability only allowed for Taryn to be in bird form for two hours at a time, so he was forced to return to his natural state before the countdown expired. His primary form didn't have a set cooldown, compared to an hour for other animal forms. This was the perfect opportunity to talk things over with the imp.

Limery wiped a bit of drool from his mouth and grinned. His bulbous yellow eyes watched Taryn intently.

Taryn was well-aware of Limery's fondness for birds, and he often wondered if the imp was imagining a dozen different ways to cook him up. Their first encounter often replayed through his mind—when Limery had pelted him with a fireball.

"Rest up, Taryns. We's still has a long ways to goes." He leaned forward, falling until he was hanging upside-down like a bat.

Taryn stretched his arms overhead, almost losing his balance.

"I know, I know. Red birds weren't meant to fly long distances non-stop. I'll be ready in a second."

Constant flying took a lot out of his stamina. In his bird form, he was great at covering short distance and had amazing agility. But long flights were more suited to birds of prey than songbirds. Taryn had never seen Limery so much as break a sweat.

He had second-guessed his decision to make his mother's favorite animal his avatar before, but for all the inconveniences it caused, he still smiled every time he saw those red wings out of the corner of his eye.

He was doing all of this for them. And Chod.

Who was he kidding? He was mostly doing it because this was the opportunity of a lifetime. No one had access to this kind of tech. If he won the lottery, he'd never be able to repay Chod for this experience.

What was a little homesickness when he could literally fly?

"Alright, let's do this!" Taryn transformed into his bird form and took to the air.

Limery let go of the branch and fell face-first into the snow, melting an imp-sized crater. He giggled to himself before joining Taryn in the air.

Bird-eating antics aside, it was easy for Taryn to see why Chod loved the little guy so much. He was endearing in his own special way, like a cute puppy that could burn down a house with a flick of its paw.

He was a troublemaker, that's for sure. A gifted pickpocket with a love for shiny things. Taryn often imagined this is how humans would behave if they abandoned the ego and superego, giving in to the primitive desires of the id.

Limery slowed down for Taryn to catch up. They both knew where they were going, relatively speaking. Somewhere above the mouth of Icemaw, the arctic clove would be growing. Limery could have undoubtedly made it faster than Taryn, but he had practically no herbalism skill to speak of. He could probably have flown straight across the gap between the two peaks, but Taryn needed to recharge periodically, so they followed above the mountain path, resting when they needed.

Even so, they were making way better time than they could have possibly done on foot.

The enchanted path wound its way up the mountain, mana-infused torches burning every so often, but there were no travelers. They passed a lone giant dragging the carcass of a frost deer through the snow, but otherwise, the ascent had been pretty boring and didn't seem that dangerous.

Halfway up Icemaw, a heavy snow began to fall, obscuring the path and the torches. Even with his bird-vision, navigating became increasingly difficult. With no clear destination, they didn't have to worry about getting lost. As long as they kept going upward, they were heading in the right direction.

After a couple of hours of flying blindly, the downfall abated, leaving the world freshly painted in white. A warm sensation enveloped Taryn as hands plucked him from the air and pulled him to the ground. The heat quickly became unbearable, forcing Taryn to transform back into a dwarf.

"Limmy, what the hell?" Taryn shouted, but a hot hand pressed against his mouth.

"Quiets." He pulled Taryn behind a tree, incredibly strong to be so small, and pointed at the clearing up ahead. "Giantses."

Taryn squinted but saw nothing until a large figure moved against the mountainside. The level twenty-four giant was nearly invisible against his surroundings, its slate-gray skin streaked with patches of blue. White hair covered his shoulders and arms, matching the dense beard that hung from his bald head. The giants were bigger than the one they had fought in the Greystone Mountains. Was everything bigger in Frostmoor?

The giant pushed a massive boulder across the snow. It grunted, thick muscles bulging with every movement.

The longer he looked, the more giants he was able to spot. They blended in well with the landscape and ranged from level eighteen to thirty. A chill ran down Taryn's spine. If he and Limery were spotted, they were toast. Dozens of giants were scattered around the maw of the mountain, which was easily the size of a football field. It resembled a cave without walls, and icicles and stalactites hung from the roof of the mountain like giant teeth.

If one happened to fall, it could crush them like ants.

Many of the giants were sleeping, only the rising and falling of their chests indicated they were more than errant boulders. Two larger giants fought over the bone of some large beast. Strips of meat and tendon still hung from one end. A mother sat against an old tree stump feeding a young giant.

If Chod were here, he'd make a comment about it being as big as Taryn. He pretended those type of comments offended him to keep the banter going, but they both knew that this was temporary. The day he logged out, he would be six-feet tall and two-hundred pounds again, back to where his mere presence caused people to keep their distance or eye him warily whenever he entered a store.

Being a dwarf, it was nice to just fit in. An ebony dwarf was treated no less than an ivory, and they both agreed that there was something strange about the blood dwarves. How he looked didn't define him. His abilities did. When he did stand out, it wasn't because of his size or his skin color, it was because he was a hero. This was the first time in his life that strangers had treated him like royalty.

He wanted to hang on to that feeling for as long as possible.

A loud crash pulled Taryn from his thoughts. The two giants skirmishing over the bone had erupted into an all-out fight. One held the bone over its head about to swing. The other held his jaw and blue blood trickled from his mouth to the snow.

The injured giant grabbed a stalagmite by the tip and pulled. The large spear of rock cracked like thunder as it snapped, and the giant wielded it like a club. He roared something, but the words were lost in the wind.

The two giants swung for one another, and the stalagmite club shattered the bone club on impact. The battle reminded him of Chod's fight with Kronan after their run-in with the mountain trolls. Pure power and rage. A third giant rushed in, gesturing wildly at the other two, but the stalagmite-wielder swung for him as well.

Taryn turned to Limery, who watched with interest. "That's our cue to go. We don't want to get caught in a giant brawl."

They used the distraction to slip out the backside of the maw and up the mountain. The enchanted path ended at the maw, but there was a well-trodden path that led higher up. There was a clear area of devastation around the trail. Tracks of moved boulders, broken trees, and animal carcasses littered the landscape.

The maw was only about three-fourths of the way to the peak, so they still had plenty of area to cover, but they were getting close to where Archard had predicted they would find the arctic clove.

The plant thrived in the highest altitudes, and only grew on Icemaw. Gherhardt had tried to grow some in the greenhouse, and even attempted to relocate some to the area above Whitgard, but it refused to grow. Instead, Archard was forced to go search for more whenever Alvyn was running low.

Taryn laughed to himself. Being a ranger seemed a lot like being a glorified errand boy.

The mountain was clear of wildlife in the immediate vicinity around the maw. Any creature smart enough would give the frost giants a wide berth, which explained why the giants had been down far enough to catch Archard on a hunt.

As they flew higher up the mountain, the trail grew less and less noticeable. If not for the slight indentation, the fresh snow would have blotted it out entirely.

It spiraled around the mountain until Taryn was certain they were above the maw. Several caves tunneled into the mountain, and a dangerous-looking platform stretched out from the mountain into the clouds.

The sun was beginning to dip closer to the horizon. They only had an hour or two of daylight before it disappeared behind the peaks.

Taryn transformed into his dwarven form and walked out onto the natural platform of the maw. There wasn't much time to waste, but he basked in the beauty of his surroundings. From this high up, there were clouds floating beneath them. The portal into Frostmoor was nothing more than a speck against the white wilderness.

He went to find Limery, who had disappeared inside one of the caves, and activated herbalism so that he could spot any plants in the area.

A faint glow surrounded the plants he had learned to identify, many from the brief visit in the Whitgard greenhouse. They grew along the side of the mountain, an occasional sprig fighting through the snow. None of them were arctic clove, but he'd expected as much. Nothing was ever that easy.

"What are you looking for?" he asked Limery when he found him in the cave.

The imp landed and picked up a rock, examining it. "Chods

saids that he found daddy in a caves. Limmy doesn't know what might be in the caves."

He rested a hand on the imp's shoulder. "Maybe we can explore some other time. Right now, we have a plant to locate."

Limery nodded and tossed the rock over his shoulder. It skipped along the cave, echoing several times over.

As they were about to exit, the ground shook and stone grated against stone from somewhere deep within the cavern.

Taryn equipped Sapling Staff and prepared for a fight. "What did you do?"

Had they awoken a giant sleeping in the depths of the cave?

Limery summoned two fireballs in his palms. "Limmy didn't do nothings."

Taryn pulled one of Jon the Enchanter's enchanted flashlight stones from his bag and activated it. Limery's fire was casting enough light to see by, but if he tossed them, they would be sitting in darkness. Taryn didn't have the night vision that Chod and Limery had.

He took the lead. "Let's check it out, but be cautious."

Part of him wanted to run up the mountain and get the quest over with, but he didn't want some unknown foe attacking them from behind. If they knew what they were dealing with, then at least they could prepare for it.

Taryn's heart raced. It was one thing to follow Chod and his horrors offering support. It was quite another thing entirely to be the front line of defense. Berry and Stompy usually had that covered, but they were a long way from helping. He had his mushrooms and Stonewall if they needed a quick exit, but he silently prayed whatever they had awoken would fall back to sleep.

Light played tricks on the eyes as they turned the corner, and the shadows of every rock or hanging strip of moss took on the appearance of an unknown threat.

His heart skipped a beat when Limery abruptly canceled his fireballs and bolted down the cavern.

Taryn rushed behind him as fast as his dwarven legs would carry him. Chod would never forgive him if something happened to the imp on his watch. He found Limery standing in front of an arch carved into the mountain. Fresh marks lined the floor where a door had opened, and runes glowed around the edge.

Icemaw Dungeon. *Would you like to enter?*

CHAPTER 16

DUNGEONS AND DRAGONS SECOND EDITION

"But Limmy wants to sees the dungeons," the imp begged, hands clasped together in prayer under his chin.

Taryn sighed. "For the third time, we can't right now. There's a man whose life depends on us finding this plant."

Limery crossed his arms and huffed. "Fines."

Other than moss, Taryn was unable to identify any plants in the cave using his herbalism skill. Limery was intrigued by the dungeon, but considering they had no backup and the levels of the frost giants below, it seemed like an unnecessary risk even if they weren't against the clock.

They had wasted precious minutes already and the sun dipped further with every moment they waited.

After Taryn returned to bird form, the duo took to the air to hunt for arctic clove once more. With his herbalism skill active, the white landscape became speckled with green outlines. Frozen and snow-covered plants dotted the landscape. There was more life here than Taryn had ever imagined.

They turned another bend and an icy roar stopped Taryn mid-flight. It was a roar he'd heard before. He tucked his wings and dove for the nearest tree, returning to his dwarven form. Limery's warm body hovered behind him.

"What is its?" He peeked around Taryn.

Taryn gulped. "Dragon."

The imp's eyes flushed with greed. "Ooh, Limmy likes dragons. They's strong."

"Yeah, well, I'd like to keep roasted dwarf off the menu tonight. Let's creep around and see what the situation is." He lifted his index finger to his mouth. "Stay quiet."

The untouched snow gave a muffled crunch with each step Taryn took. He clung close to the mountainside, careful not to accidentally reveal himself.

Another shriek cut through the thin air, and Taryn froze. This was stupid. Suicide.

If they were spotted, what chance did he have of escaping a dragon?

He peeked around the corner and all thoughts of running fled his mind. Less than twenty yards away, a radiant white dragon clung to the edge of the mountain, teeth ripping into a giant gray bird with white-tipped feathers. He tried to analyze the bird, but since it was dead, he got nothing.

Even in the fading sun, the dragon sparkled. It was truly breathtaking, the most beautiful destructive force he'd ever witnessed. As it ripped a piece of flesh from the creature, Taryn was content to watch it for hours. The dragon repositioned itself, pressing a clawed foot against the bird's neck, and a patch of green flashed across Taryn's vision.

His heart raced. "That's it. That's the arctic clove," he whispered.

Limery didn't respond, apparently just as enraptured.

Taryn took a step closer and his foot slipped. He fell into the snow with a grunt.

The dragon's head whipped in their direction, and it unleashed a powerful roar. Snow plummeted to earth, and a blizzard erupted out of nowhere.

"Run!" Taryn yelled.

Limery bolted like a bat out of hell, instantly disappearing among the dense snowfall.

Dammit! Taryn cursed to himself as he transformed into bird form. *I finally found what we're looking for, and it's under a feeding dragon.*

Everywhere he flew, more snow followed. He wasn't sure how far the dragon's abilities spread, but he didn't want to risk being eaten alive. They still needed the arctic clove though, and the dragon couldn't stay there forever. All they needed to do was wait it out somewhere safe.

He kept close to the mountain, careful not to fly into open air. He had to go slower than usual to make sense of his surroundings at all. When he finally located the entrance to the Icemaw Dungeon cave, Limery was already waiting.

Taryn activated Jon's flashlight rock and walked deeper into the cave. "I thought I might find you here."

He grinned at Taryn. "Can we goes in the dungeons now?"

Taryn shook his head. "There's a dragon out there that could wipe us out with one attack, and you want us to go into a dungeon that could probably do the same?"

Limery nodded. "Yes, Limmy wants."

"No way. Not going to happen. We just need to wait out the drag—"

Something landed outside of the cave entrance, and Taryn's blood turned to ice. Frost crept along the cave wall toward them, spreading like an infection.

Taryn grabbed Limery's shoulder and ushered him deeper

into the cave. The cave was spacious, but not big enough for the dragon to walk unimpeded.

Scales grated against the cave floor, and Taryn tried to walk faster without making noise. His feet pattered against the stone floor, and he wished desperately that he was wearing his cloak that concealed his movement right about now. Heavy breathing cut through the empty silence as the dragon sniffed at the air. It grunted and then its scales scraped against the floor once again as it crawled deeper into the cave.

Taryn tapped Limery on the shoulder and pointed to the entrance of the cave's dungeon. Limery nodded.

If they could enter the dungeon before the dragon saw them, maybe it would leave. But the dragon was getting closer, and they were almost out of time.

The prompt for the dungeon flashed across his vision.

Icemaw Dungeon. *Would you like to enter?*

Taryn accepted and everything turned black.

CHAPTER 17

CONTENDERS

I TRY to message Taryn several times over the course of the evening, but I don't hear back from him. I'm not too worried, though. He said they are stuck in a cave, but that could mean anything. Taryn has always been more tactical than me, planning things out and taking precautions instead of running in blindly. Since he didn't seem panicked or ask for help, I'm taking that as a good sign. If something bad had happened, I'm certain he would let me know.

Gherhardt must sense that something is up because he places a firm hand on my shoulder. "It's tradition to have a feast on the evening before the Ascent. Come and enjoy the delicious food and entertainment. There is nothing you can do for your friends from here."

I nod, knowing he's right. I have faith that Taryn and Limery can handle whatever they are up against, so I need to quit worrying. I force a smile and try to push the thoughts to the back of my mind.

The silver glow of night paints the town as I follow Gherhardt through the moonlight to a long stone building. He opens the door, and chatter and music spill into the cold, along with a slew of delicious smells, once again reminding me of my night at The Underground Circus.

Since I've been in Whitgard, I have only seen people occasionally as they walk through the streets, but there are easily a few hundred people filling this building. Their thick fur coats are hung along the walls, and most of them wear some sort of wool or leather tunic. Even without all the fur, the Frozen Ash Tribe are still a large people, not nearly as big as a troll, but much taller and broader than the humans in Vanaria.

The fireplace combined with the body heat of so many people has me removing my cloak.

My blue skin is a beacon among the pale humans. One thing I've noticed about the tribe is that they are not a colorful society. Everything from their clothing to their buildings come in shades of gray or dull brown.

Two long tables stretch the length of the room. At the front, there is a platform where a band plays music. I spot Dando playing a drum. He sits on a stool with a large bongo-type drum cradled between his legs, tapping it with his fingers. Next to him, Liyah strums a stringed instrument with a short neck and round body. They both grin from ear to ear and occasionally steal a glance at one another. A dark-haired lady plays a second stringed instrument behind Liyah, and a young man shakes a tambourine vigorously as he dances across the front of the platform.

A group dances in the space between the stage and the table, swaying back and forth.

This reminds me of my first night in the troll village. No matter what a society looks like from the outside, there are always moments like this where they are able to unwind. Even when clinging to survival, art and culture are a reminder of what they are surviving for.

The music fades and hundreds of eyes turn in our direction.

Gherhardt raises a hand to the onlookers. "Yes, the rumors are true. We do have a forest troll in the village. Chod here helped clear the trail up the mountain for the Ascent, and other members of his party are currently on a quest to gather arctic clove for Alvyn's elixir. We owe them our gratitude. While they are here, I trust that you will treat these heroes with the same respect you do me."

"And what if I don't respect you?" Archard shouts from the center of the left table and laughter snakes throughout the crowd. He holds a massive mug in his hand and foam coats his mustache.

Gherhardt grins. "Ah, yes. And let's not forget the man responsible for the roasted frost deer we are all about to enjoy, Archard the Precise. Humble as always."

Clapping and cheering fills the room. Archard climbs on the bench and takes a bow, mead sloshing onto the table.

The music resumes and people return to their business. I catch several glances as people try to conceal their interest in me, and others who are not so discreet and openly point in my direction. Their reactions don't bother me. I'm probably more out of place in their village than if I showed up as a blue-skinned troll in the middle of New York City.

"You're going to be the talk of the village for some time once you leave." Gherhardt winks at me. "Shall we grab a bite to eat? I spent all day roasting the frost deer. I'm sure it will be unlike anything you have eaten in Mythos."

There's a buffet-style table on the far wall loaded with food. Plenty of bread and vegetables, and in the center, giant slabs of meat.

I stick to the meat, grabbing myself a platter Limery would be envious of and a mug of arctic mead.

Taking the massive slab in both hands, I sink my teeth into it. Juices explode in my mouth and an uncontrollable grunt of pleasure escapes my lips. An array of spices battle for supremacy as the smokey, fatty meat melts in my mouth. It's so tender that the strips practically fall off the bone. I close my eyes and let the flavor profile wash over me.

When I open them, Gherhardt is grinning at me.

I analyze a piece of meat to see what deliciousness I just ingested.

Item. Frost Deer Chops. *Food coated in Gherhardt's Secret Dry Rub offer 50% reduction to cold weather effects for 1 hours.*

"How did you do this?" I ask as I wipe juices from my chin.

"If I told you, I'd have to kill you." He smirks. "I've done a lot of things that I'm proud of in this life, but perfecting my dry rub is at the top of the list."

I'm going to have to see about getting some of that for the road. Food is food, but this...this is an experience. And the effect from Gherhardt's dry rub will be incredibly useful while we're in Frostmoor. Too bad Taryn and Limery are missing out.

The music takes a break and Dando joins us at the table, Liyah close behind.

She wraps her arms around her uncle from behind. "The venison is delicious, Uncle Gher."

"Yes, perfectly seasoned," Dando agrees.

"Save your flattery for someone who needs it." Gherhardt stuffs a piece of bread in his mouth, but it does little to disguise his smile.

Dando takes a seat next to me with a mug of mead.

I clink my mug to his. "You're a man of many talents."

He blushes. "Ah, this is nothing. Liyah does the hard work. I just bang my hands."

I lean in closer, careful not to talk too loud. "I see you're getting some one-on-one time, where's your nemesis?"

"Warley?" He laughs. "He's on gate duty tonight."

"What are you two whispering about?" Liyah tilts her head and flashes a mischievous smile.

Dando stutters for a moment before I save him from his misery.

"I was trying to get him to reveal Gherhardt's eleven herbs and spices."

Dando breathes a sigh of relief.

She laughs. "Good luck with that. Uncle Gher keeps his roasting recipes a secret. It's probably the only reason he's still in charge." She pokes Gherhardt in the side.

After a few minutes of small talk, the duo returns to the stage, where they play something reminiscent of folk music.

I try my best to be a wingman for Dando. "Dando seems like a good kid. Smart, funny, hard worker."

Gherhardt glances up at the stage. "He's certainly an asset to the tribe."

"Seems to have caught Liyah's attention, too." I grin.

His brow scrunches. "She'll never have a thing to do with him if I have a say."

"Well, you are the head of the tribe." I cross my arms and lean back. "Why do you want to make it so hard on him, though?"

He sighs. "Bah. The writing is already in the stars. They are both good kids. Hell, don't you dare tell him I said this, but if I were a father, I'd be proud to call Dando my son. And I know Liyah's a woman now. I just want to keep her as the girl who used to stand on my shoulders for as long as possible."

I sit in silence for a moment. Gherhardt has an entire village to look after and yet here he is dealing with the same kind of family drama as anyone in the real world.

"You know there's nothing wrong with your relationship evolving. Just because she's not a little girl anymore doesn't mean you lose her."

His gaze drifts to the stage. He smiles at Liyah before returning his attention to me. "Yeah, I know. But unless I have children of my own, Liyah will be the next Head of the Frozen Ash Tribe. That is a lot of responsibility, and her partner will have a part to play in the future of Whitgard. I'm not ready for that yet."

The music stops and then a quick succession of drumming calls our attention.

"That's my cue." Gherhardt wipes the specks of food from his beard and stands.

All eyes fall upon him as he takes the stage. He strokes both ends of his forked beard before speaking.

"It's always good to see the Frozen Ash Tribe gathered together. Minus Alvyn, his caretakers, and the few who have other duties, this is it. This is who we are." He clears his throat. "As far back as I can remember, we have commemorated the ascent of Umen and Edrar every spring as a reminder of where we come from. Our people were born from the ice, and one day we will all return to its frozen embrace. But just like Umen before us, we will hold off that fate for as long as possible. The Ascent is a celebration of life, of overcoming the harsh reality of our surroundings, and a reminder that even our ancestors could not escape the calamity of Frostmoor. So without further ado, allow me to introduce our competitors.

"This year, we will have three new contenders. Though he is not here tonight, Warley has protected our gates tirelessly over the years. This will be his first time attempting the Ascent."

There are a few groans, mostly from around Archard, but a few claps are scattered throughout.

"Our second challenger has been begging me to compete since he was a child. Though he may look like a summer babe, he's assured me he is of age to compete."

Laughter erupts through the crowd before Gherhardt reveals Dando's name. With bright red cheeks, he salutes the crowd before returning to his drum.

"The final competitor holds a special place in my heart, so just know that if anything happens to her, you'll have to take it up with me." His gaze narrows on Dando. "My very own niece, Liyah."

The entire building cheers for Liyah, and she beams as she waves to the crowd. She winks at Dando, but his mouth hangs open in astonishment. Clearly, he had no idea she was planning to compete.

Gherhardt raises a hand, and everyone quiets down. "Enjoy the evening. Eat, drink, and be merry. Tomorrow, we will pay tribute to our people's beginnings."

He rejoins me at the table, and for the rest of the evening, we share stories as we down glass after glass of mead. I tell him of my adventures, the different troll tribes, and other societies. He shares the ins and outs of the Whitgard, along with their challenges and accomplishments over the years.

By the time the building begins to empty, my head is buzzing from the mead. We stumble our way back to Gherhardt's. Before I crawl in bed, I send Taryn a final message, wondering what on earth they have gotten themselves into.

CHAPTER 18
ON THIN ICE

"Shit. Shit. Shit. Shit. Shit." Taryn pressed his palms against his eyes, trying to clear his thoughts.

He'd panicked at the approaching dragon, and in a desperate attempt to make sure nothing happened to Limery, they were now in a dungeon with who-knew-what kind of monsters and traps.

Taryn opened his eyes to find Limery staring back at him. The imp's bulbous eyes were larger than normal as he watched Taryn.

He tried to reassure the imp. "Everything is fine. We'll just wait in here for a couple of hours and then go back into the cave. Then we'll get the arctic clove and fly back to Whitgard. Nothing else can enter as long as we are in here."

Limery frowned. "Limmy wants to see the dragons."

Taryn fought the urge to raise his voice, not letting the stress win. "We can see the dragon when it's not trying to eat us. Let's just chill out and rest for a bit while we can."

Now that he thought about it, Taryn couldn't recall the last time he'd really rested since entering Mythos. He leaned back against the cave wall and took in their surroundings.

The inside of the dungeon was vastly different from the outside cave. Where the cave had been formed out of rough gray stone, the dungeon had smooth, navy-blue walls with white veins that arced like lightning. The walls still had a natural look to them, unlike the intricately-detailed walls of the dwarven kingdom, but it was as if the room they were in had formed inside of some precious gemstone.

Straight ahead, a crack in the wall emanated a blue glow. It was big enough to walk through but cut sharply to the right, hiding what lay beyond. Ice crystals covered the ground beneath the chasm, similar to the frost that had formed inside the cave when the dragon entered.

Taryn didn't want to think about what kind of monsters might be lurking on the other side. This was a high-level zone after all. He pressed his ear to the door, but whether it was because the dragon had left or the door was magically sealed, he heard nothing from the other side.

When he turned around, Limery was gone. His chest grew tight as he rushed through the crevice in the wall. His feet slipped on the icy surface and he fell hard, pain shooting through his right shoulder as he crashed into the wall.

He tried to regain his footing, but it wasn't until he equipped Sapling Staff and used its viny appendages to form a support base that he could stand.

Taryn gasped when he saw the source of the glow. Translucent gemstones in a dozen shades of blue protruded from the ceiling and walls, each casting its own aura. The gems pulsed with a gentle energy. Some had a similar coloring to the flames burning along the enchanted pathway up the mountain, so he assumed they were mana-infused.

In front of him, a bridge of ice stretched across a deep pit to a wooden door on the other side. Light blue runes glowed dully on the door, but there were no handles for opening it. The reflective gleam from the surrounding gems gave the bridge an ethereal appearance.

Carefully, Taryn peered over the edge of the cliff into the depths below. Limery was nowhere to be seen, furthering his worry, but there were many more bridges that led to similar doors as far down as he could see. From what he could tell, the runes were different on each door. If only his communication stone translated written language as well, but reading runes was a skill in itself. The pit descended deep into the mountain, and hundreds of mana-infused gemstones protruded from the walls, pulsing like some alien hive.

The blue glow seemed to go on forever. Did this dungeon descend the entirety of the mountain? And more importantly, where was Limery?

A struggling grunt caught Taryn's attention just above the crevice he was standing in. Very carefully, he stepped onto the ice bridge to look above the pit, where he found Limery struggling to pull a mana crystal from the wall. Above him, a slew of dangerous icicles and stalactites descended ominously from the ceiling.

Taryn let out a sigh of relief. "You can't disappear on me like that. You nearly gave me a heart attack."

Limery let go of the gem and tilted his head. "You's heart attacks you?"

Taryn placed his hands on his hips. "It's an expression. It means you worried me. I didn't know where you were."

"Sorries." Limery flashed a demonic smile. "Limmy found the shinies."

The apology was clearly fake, but Taryn still appreciated it. "Let's get back to the entrance."

Limery frowned. "Waiting is boring. Limmy wants to explore."

Taryn understood his frustration. Waiting around was boring, but Taryn was trying to be responsible and put them in the least amount of risk as possible. They had been sent here to find the arctic clove, not to adventure. There would be plenty of time for that once they had returned.

But there was nothing they could do about the arctic clove until the dragon left, and they were in a dungeon filled with opportunity. With so many closed doors, this place was practically a gold mine if they played it right. He'd been fantasizing about the new classes he might be offered at level twenty-five, and he wasn't getting any closer by sitting around.

Every minute they wasted was a minute their enemies were growing stronger. Taryn wasn't an offensive juggernaut by any means, especially without his pets, but Limery was pure destruction and especially suited to wreak havoc on an area like this.

Limery hovered in front of Taryn with his long, spindly fingers clasped together. "Please."

Taryn relented. "Fine, but give me a few minutes to prepare. And the first sign that we are out of our league, we're coming back. Deal?"

Limery gave the gemstone another tug and grinned. "Deals."

If they were going deeper into the dungeon, Taryn needed to make sure his stats were properly allocated. He pulled up his character sheet.

Taryn, Level 23 Ebony Dwarf Druid
   HP: 4592/4592
   Mana: 3210/3210
   XP: 485,679/525,000

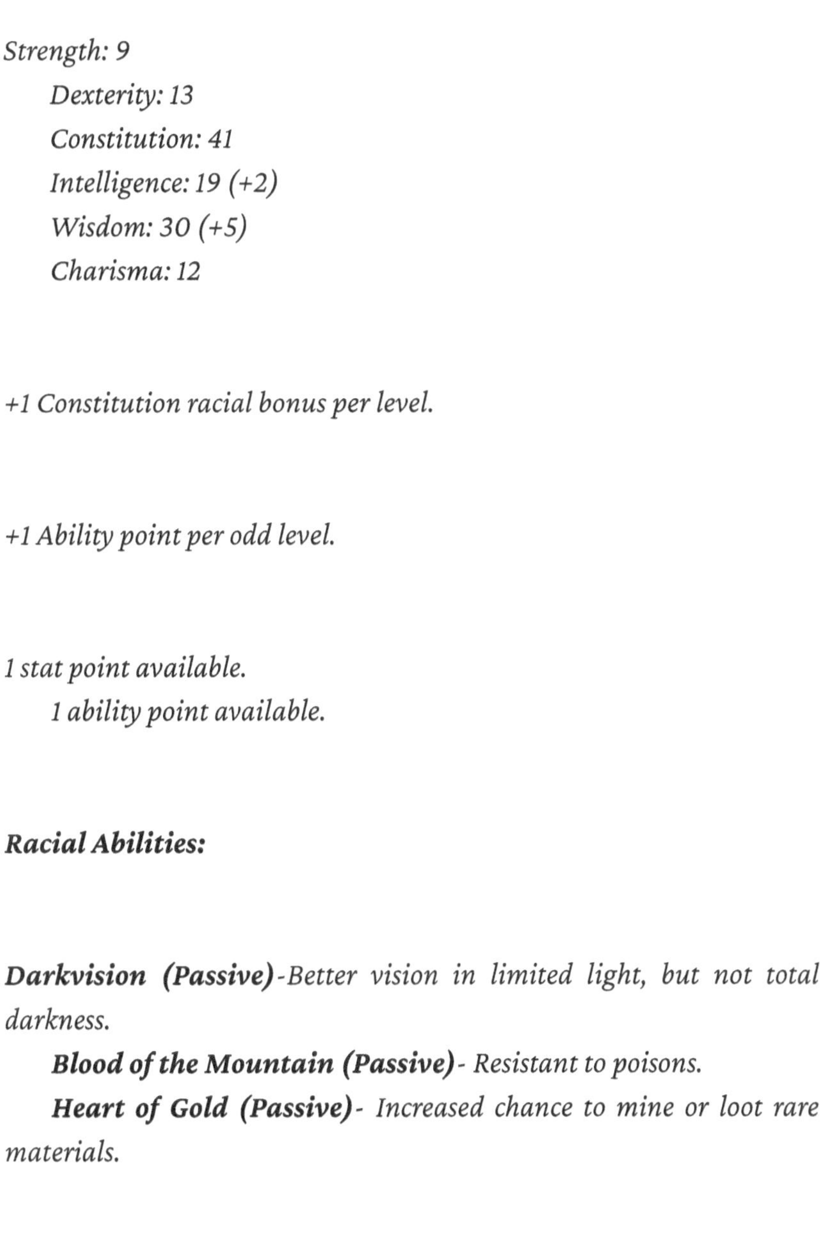

Strength: 9
Dexterity: 13
Constitution: 41
Intelligence: 19 (+2)
Wisdom: 30 (+5)
Charisma: 12

+1 Constitution racial bonus per level.

+1 Ability point per odd level.

1 stat point available.
1 ability point available.

Racial Abilities:

Darkvision (Passive)-Better vision in limited light, but not total darkness.

Blood of the Mountain (Passive)- Resistant to poisons.

Heart of Gold (Passive)- Increased chance to mine or loot rare materials.

Abilities:

Transform- Transform into an animal you have seen for up to two hours. Primary animal: Red bird. Upgrade for additional time. Cost: 100 mana. Cooldown: 1 hour for non-primary transformations. No cooldown for primary transformations.

Lightning Bolt (Level-2)- Deals a massive burst of damage with a 50% chance to stun. Cost: 200 mana. Cooldown: 10 seconds.

Strong Wind- Increases movement speed of those in your party by 50%. Cost: 100 mana. Cooldown: 60 seconds.

Imbue- Increases the size of a summoned monster or pet by 100% for 10 minutes. Cost: 200 mana. Cooldown: 5 minutes.

Restoration (Level 2)- Restores 100 HP to a pet or summon every 10 seconds while communing with nature. Cost: 10 mana per second. Cooldown: None.

Nature's Aegis (Passive)- You are immune to elemental effects.

Nature's Bulwark (Passive)- Animals will only attack you if they are provoked.

Tame (Available at level 10)- Form a pet from any beast brought to 5% HP and within 5 levels. Cannot be used on Unique Monsters. For each additional pet tamed, tamer loses 5% influence over each creature. Cost: 500 mana. Cooldown: 24 hours.

Current Pets (10% influence loss):

Berry- Level 19. Umber Bear.

Stompy- Level 19. Moulhaug.

Ruby- Level 16. Jackal.

Summon Fungus- Summon a troop of poisonous mushrooms. Cost: 200 mana. Cooldown: 30 seconds.

Stonewall- Summon a wall up to 20' x 20'. Cost: 200 mana. Cooldown: 1 minute.

Available Abilities *(1 ability point to unlock)***:**

***Barkskin*-** *Strengthens skin as if it were made of wood, offering damage reduction. Cost: 100 mana. Cooldown: 60 seconds.*

***Stoneskin*-** *Strengthens skin as if it were made of stone, offering additional damage reduction. Cost: 200 mana. Cooldown: 120 seconds.*

***Insect Plague*-** *Summon insects within a 50-yard radius to attack a target. Cost: 200 mana. Cooldown: 5 minutes.*

Conceal (Passive). *Hides level from anyone who is not a guard on city grounds.*

Perception. *For 10 minutes, gain increased awareness of your surroundings. Spot hidden objects, as well as unusual sounds, odors, and tastes. Cooldown: 6 hours.*

Current Items:

Item. Boar's Tusk Staff. +2 Intelligence, +2 Wisdom. *A staff fitted with an enchanted boar's tusk.*

Item. Druidic Helm. +2 Constitution, +2 Wisdom.

Item. Sapling Staff. +3 Intelligence, +3 Wisdom. *A living staff capable of sending out whip-like vines.*

Item. Shadow Dagger (x2). *With blades of shadow energy, this dagger bypasses armor and drains mana and life force directly without leaving physical wounds. Drains mana equal to user's Wisdom and HP equal to user's Intelligence with each attack.*

Item. Cloak of Silence. *A cloak capable of concealing sounds associated with movement.*

Item. Smuggler's Boots. *Boots that leave no tracks no matter the substance or terrain they step through.*

*Item. **Enchanted Rock Light.** This enchanted rock emits light for a limited distance. 92% power remaining.*

*Item. **Ring of Insight.** +1 Wisdom.*

*Item. **Ring of Understanding.** +1 Intelligence.*

*Item. **Ring of Judgement.** +1 Wisdom.*

*Item. **Sage Amulet.** +1 Wisdom, +1 Intelligence.*

*Item. **Expandable Satchel.** A bag capable of holding enormous content and only burdening the wearer with ten percent of its weight. Simply focus on the item inside and it will appear in your hand.*

*Item. **Fur Cloak.** Protects wearer from the effects of frigid temperatures.*

*Item. **Fur Boots.** Protects wearer from the effects of frigid temperatures.*

He also had a fair amount of health and mana potions that they'd purchased in Goldspire.

Taryn had wanted to save his most recent stat point and ability point for when he unlocked his new class, but there was no point in hoarding it. He added a stat point to Intelligence. It would help increase the damage on the few offensive abilities he had.

So far, he'd sunk all his points into Intelligence or Wisdom, with the majority in the latter. Points in Wisdom increased his mana pool and decreased his cooldowns, allowing him to better support the group, but Lightning Bolt and Summon Fungus both drew power from Intelligence.

He'd relied more on the potential stun from Lightning Bolt than its damage, but sinking another point into Intelligence could mean the difference between life and death. With his natural dwarven Constitution, he was a far cry from a glass cannon and could still outlast a lot of opponents at his level even with minimal damage output—especially with his pets around.

Taryn stared at the five available abilities. Neither Barkskin or Stoneskin appealed to him. He wasn't a front-row fighter, and putting an ability point into either of those felt like a waste. Casting it on Chod or one of his pets could make them tougher, but they weren't here right now to benefit. Insect Plague could be useful, but not currently. There had to be insects in the area to use it and the frigid temperatures meant that was unlikely. Conceal had little appeal since he didn't really care about concealing his level from strangers. Chod had invested in that ability because he had needed to when he was traveling solo, but now that they were traveling together, it seemed trivial. Perception was useful, but when they were able to craft perception potions, it really felt like a waste of a good point, especially when Ruby was around to investigate.

There was still the option to further upgrade Lightning Bolt or one of the other abilities, but he was so close to level twenty-five that it made more sense to save it. A new class with new abilities meant he would be able to unlock two instead of one. That could be a game-changer.

Though Perception seemed like a good option, the six-hour cooldown steered him away. He doubted they would still be in the dungeon in six hours, so a ten-minute window of increased perception was all but useless. He made peace with the risks and rewards of holding onto the ability point and closed his character sheet.

The message icon pulsed slightly, and Taryn opened it to see he had three messages from Chod.

Incoming Message (Chod): *Hey, haven't heard from you. Figured I would check in. They've got me clearing snow for some race they are doing tomorrow.*

Incoming Message (Chod): *It's me again. Just checking in to see how things were going.*

Incoming Message (Chod): *I'm sure you guys are fine. Just check in when you get a chance.*

Taryn smiled as he read through all the messages. It was a side of Chod not many people got to see, the complete opposite of the sarcastic, rage-fueled gamer he portrayed online. He'd really found a place for himself in this world. Somewhere he could finally be his best self.

He knew that if he told Chod that he and Limery were in a high-level dungeon by themselves, it would only make him worry more, so he kept it simple, letting him know they wouldn't be back tonight, but everything was okay.

After sending the message, Taryn equipped his old cloak and boots and returned to Limery, who had finally given up on the gemstone he was trying to remove.

"We play this smart." He tossed his satchel over his shoulder and stepped out onto the ice bridge. "We're already on thin ice as it is, and we can't afford to make any mist—"

Limery pulled on a different gemstone and it moved as if it was a switch. The ice cracked beneath Taryn's feet, chilling him to the bone. Tiny fractures spread out beneath his boots, turning the transparent ice into a fragmented kaleidoscope.

He froze in place. Cracks snaked along the bridge, spreading further as the ice fractures battled for supremacy against Taryn's thundering heartbeat.

Limery's eyes looked like they might pop out of his head as he hovered helplessly.

Finally, the cracks stopped spreading, leaving them in uncomfortable silence.

Taryn released the breath he was holding, and the entire bridge shattered. Limery let out a yelp of surprise, and Taryn extended the vines of his staff toward the wall. They wrapped around a three-pronged gemstone, but the prongs broke and Taryn continued to fall.

His HP dropped a fraction as he shattered through a second bridge. Splintered ice rained down, clinking and bouncing off the walls and other bridges. Taryn crashed through three more bridges before he had the wherewithal to use Transform.

Feathers exploded and ice speckled him as he flew to one of the glowing gemstones and perched on top. Even in bird form, his tiny heart pounded quicker than usual. He waited a moment before moving, letting his heart rate slow and trying to comprehend what had just happened.

Limery hovered in front of him. "Is yous okays?"

Taryn tweeted his affirmation, then he extended a wing, pointing up top. He couldn't talk to Limery in his current form, and he didn't trust any of the other bridges to support his weight.

Limery nodded. "Okay. We goes up!"

Once safely back at the entrance to the dungeon, Taryn returned to dwarven form. "Man, that was scary as hell. I was so shocked by the bridge falling it took me a minute to transform."

"How did yous break the bridges?" Limery put a clawed finger over his lips.

Taryn crossed his arms and scowled. "Me? You triggered a

trap. I think the different colored gemstones are our key to opening the doors. Pull the wrong one and something bad happens."

Limery grimaced. "Limmy didn't knows."

He couldn't blame Limery for being enthralled by the gemstones. Chod did a good job of keeping the imp's baser instincts in check most of the time, but he was still like a small child in a lot of ways, always chasing the shiny object.

His younger sister had been the same way when she was a toddler. At age twelve, Taryn was the de facto evening babysitter while his parents worked multiple jobs to make sure he and his siblings all got the educations they deserved. So from four to eight every night, Taryn was in charge of cooking, homework, and baths. By the time he had been old enough to work an actual job, he'd gladly shirked those responsibilities to the next in line.

He'd need to recall some of those skills to keep Limery from killing them both.

Triggering the gemstone had reduced the integrity of the bridge, or possibly all the bridges, since his weight had been enough to shatter the others. They would need to carefully test what other traps might be waiting for them.

"Okay, here's the deal." Taryn snapped his fingers to gather Limery's attention. "I have a theory that there's a connection between the gems in the walls and what happens in the dungeon. We're going to need to test them out to see what happens. We're lucky that we have an advantage others don't. Do you know what that is?"

Limery scratched his chin with a clawed finger. "Limmy makes fires?"

"Not quite what I was thinking, but that's definitely in our favor. What I was thinking is that we can fly. So, here's the plan."

Taryn explained his theory on how the gems worked and then

transformed into his bird form. The gemstone Limery had triggered had returned to its place in the wall. He landed on it, and sure enough, his weight wasn't enough to trigger the effect.

He chirped at Limery, and the imp carved a mark into the wall next to the light blue gem. Next, Taryn perched on a gemstone the color of a deep blue sky. It pulsed with energy. The gem next to it, a vibrant turquoise, did not. Taryn chirped once again and Limery pulled on the cerulean stone. It triggered and the dungeon shuddered. Cracks echoed above them, and icicles broke free from the ceiling, falling like missiles. One shattered an ice bridge that had reformed, and several others plunged into the depths below. They crashed like a bull in a china shop until eventually fading to a trickle, and then silence.

With the icicles gone, there were gaps between the stalactites that remained, but the icicles were already reforming. Taryn was certain a separate stone triggered those.

Next, Taryn had Limery pull the turquoise gem, and just as he expected, nothing happened. While all the gemstones produced light, only the ones that pulsed seemed to have an effect on the dungeon. After marking both stones, they moved on to the next.

Limery pulled on an indigo stone. It moved, but it appeared to have no effect. Taryn was prepared to chalk it up as a decoy when a door unlocked somewhere beneath them.

The bridges and icicles began to recrystallize, and if not for his increased eyesight in bird form, he wouldn't have noticed the dozens of tiny creatures emerging from an open doorway several floors below.

The humanoid creatures were smaller than Limery, with light blue skin and sapphire hair. They reminded him of the salt fairies from the dungeon outside of Seascape. Crystalized armor coated their bodies and snowflake wings fluttered behind them. Each one had horns made of icicles and blue orbs for eyes.

Ice Fairy. *Level 25. The most fragile of all fairies, what they lack in durability they make up for in elemental power.*

The fairies had set their eyes on Limery, snarling with an icy vengeance, and each of their hands glowed with white light. Frost formed in the air around them as they powered up attacks.

Taryn tried to yell, to warn Limery, but all that came out was a peep.

The fairies unleashed their attacks, streams of ice shooting in their direction.

Limery looked intrigued, but wasn't alarmed by the tiny creatures.

Taryn panicked. No matter how fragile they were, dozens of level-twenty-five fairies would be the death of both of them if they didn't act fast.

Not knowing what else to do, Taryn perched on the cerulean gem and returned to his dwarven form.

An ice blast hit him in the shoulder, numbing it on impact and dropping his health by ten percent.

"Kill them!" he shouted as he held on for dear life to the gem, his increased weight triggering the effect.

Spells exploded on the wall around him as half-formed icicles plunged from the ceiling. Limery sent a maelstrom of fireballs as the icicles fell. The heat from the fireballs was enough to melt several fairy wings, sending them falling to their doom or spiraling into the wall. The ones he hit directly turned to water instantly. Icicles impaled others, and a molten Limery finished the rest.

"Good job," Taryn grunted as he hung on for dear life, feeling slowly returning to his arm. "Going back to bird form now."

He let go and used Transform as he fell, flying down to inspect the door the fairies had come out of. It was still open, and Taryn was surprised to discover that the runes engraved in the door were the same shade as the gemstone that had opened it. He glanced at the doors above and below, and each one had a slightly different shade of runes.

Inside of the doorway, the room was small, barely ten-by-ten feet. In the center, a shimmering chest made of ice rested on a platform.

Taryn transformed back and called Limery to join him.

"Ooh, shinies." Limery licked his lips as he approached the chest.

"Easy." Taryn extended an arm to stop the imp. "We need to make sure it's not a trap."

He equipped Sapling Staff and spread the vines out across the room, making sure there weren't any hidden tiles or trip wires. Once the room seemed safe, they knelt in front of the chest.

The chest was made of thick pieces of translucent ice. Intricate patterns were carved into each side, with a thin snowflake-shaped latch over the center. Something silver gleamed inside, but the translucent ice distorted whatever it was.

The latch was cold to the touch, sending a shiver through Taryn as he flipped the lid. Inside, a small buckler shield with a snowflake engraved in the center gleamed in the dull light.

Item. Frosted Buckler. +2 Constitution. *A lightweight and small shield capable of deflecting blows as well as being used offensively.* ***Bonus Ability:*** *Physical attacks blocked with Frosted Buckler cut the attacker's Dexterity in half for ten seconds.*

Taryn picked up the shield. It was lightweight and cool to the touch. His first thought was of Jegaar, the battle scholar from Goldspire who wielded a buckler. Having a shield that could slow an opponent would only further increase his power.

He handed the shield to Limery for him to inspect. If the imp sat in it, he could practically use it as a sled. Taryn didn't want to give him any ideas, so he kept that part to himself.

Taryn strapped the shield to his arm for the time being, though he doubted he could use it to its full potential. Of their group, Chod was the only one who specialized in hand-to-hand combat. But if he didn't want it, maybe they could sell it for a good price in the next city.

Still, this was a great item even if it didn't fit their needs. Was it possible there was a chest behind each door? If so, this dungeon was even better than Taryn thought.

After returning to the top floor, they quickly discovered that gems of the same color triggered an identical effect if it occurred in the pit, but once a door had been unlocked there was no replicating the action. Which was unfortunate, because Limery could have destroyed the ice fairies a hundred times over.

The cyan gemstones caused one end of the bridges to lower, creating a slippery ice slide. The cerulean gems had been particularly troublesome, as they were actually the protruding abdomens of frost wasps. They'd had to barricade themselves in the entrance behind Stonewall and wait for the wasps to return to their positions.

Taryn had nearly run out of the dungeon when an ice spider had emerged from one of the doors. Its frozen abdomen was bigger than him, and it grated against the wall as it climbed with grotesque movements. He had triggered falling icicles, stalactites, and summoned poisonous mushrooms along the wall, all while begging Limery to burn it faster.

It eventually died, legs curling up as it fell into the abyss.

Taryn was hesitant to enter the web-shrouded room until Limery had sufficiently burned the webbing, leaving nothing but another ice chest in the center.

After opening the chest, they found a white pelt inside.

Item. Winter's Might. +2 Wisdom. *The pelt of the elusive snow fox grants the wearer immunity to the effects of frigid temperatures* *while also casting an illusory aura that blends them into snowy landscapes.* **Bonus Effect:** *Druids or shapeshifters in animal form are granted a winter coat while in sub-freezing temperatures.*

Taryn snatched the pelt out of the chest, equipping it over his shoulders. Now he could wear his own clothing and not the hand-me-downs of some overgrown child.

"You okay if I take this?" he asked Limery after the fact.

"You takes." Limery grinned.

To further test out the pelt, Taryn transformed into his bird form. Instead of the vibrant red feathers, he was covered in stark white. He'd be practically invisible while flying in Frostmoor. This alone had made it worth entering the dungeon, and there were still dozens of rooms they had yet to unlock.

But time was ticking by. They had already been here for a few hours at least—plenty of time for the dragon to have moved on if it was going to. Strangest of all was the fact that they hadn't found a gemstone that matched the color of the top door.

Was it possible that there were multiple entrances into the dungeon? Or were they missing the obvious?

They needed to leave soon. A man's life was hanging in the balance, after all. And maybe they could return with Chod once they were done in Whitgard. A long venture through the Icemaw Dungeon could put them both closer to their goals.

But one more room wouldn't hurt.

CHAPTER 19
WORK SMARTER, NOT HARDER

W_HEN_ I _WAKE UP_, the first thing I do is check my notifications. Still nothing from Taryn since yesterday evening. We've always been different in that regard. Back in the real world, I'm the type of person to respond to a message straight away, where Taryn might not pick up his phone for hours at a time.

I wonder if this was what life was like before location tracking and instant messaging, back when people had to leave messages on answering machines and wait to get a call back.

No offense to Taryn, but waiting for responses is for the birds.

For now, I'll take no news as good news.

Downstairs, Gherhardt once again greets me with a delicious breakfast. "The race won't be until later in the afternoon, and I believe Dando can manage the final touches, so I'll be putting you back to work if that's alright with you."

I stuff a boiled egg in my mouth, enjoying the delicious spices sprinkled on top. "I live to serve."

After breakfast, I'm introduced to a man named Oakley. He's

more broad-shouldered than either Archard or Gherhardt and sports a cropped red-beard.

We load tools into a cart pulled by a single ox. Oakley drives while I sit in the back alongside various axes, saws, and pickaxes.

He eyes me suspiciously before returning his attention to the path. "Never met a troll before." His voice is deep and gravelly. "Always thought the lot of you were monsters. You don't seem so bad."

I'm not entirely sure how to respond. "I mean, we are monsters. That doesn't mean we're evil."

He grunts. "I suppose. You ever eaten a child?"

"What? No! Of course not. We're not that kind of monster."

He shrugs. "What do I know? Like I said, never met a troll before."

"Well, I can assure you we don't eat children." I lean a little closer. "Not even when we're especially hungry."

He glances over his shoulder, one eyebrow raised, and I can't contain my grin.

"So, what are we working on today?" I ask, even though I have a pretty good idea based on the tools.

"We need wood and ore. Gherhardt assures me you are worth ten men, so I aim to put it to the test while my men work on other projects."

"I see. So, I get to work hard so they don't have to." This must be how Taryn feels in the real world, always being asked to do the heavy lifting.

He laughs. "Smarter than you look."

"Same to you." I chuckle to myself as I lean back against the cart, feeling each bump as we roll along.

After about an hour, we detour from the main path, following a non-enchanted trail that leads through abandoned ruins. We travel until we come upon a grove of trees growing in the shadow of the mountain. A dark cave disappears inside.

"You'll be working over here." Oakley hands me a pickaxe and points to the cave. "Once you fill up two carts of ore, come find me. The cart is inside the cave."

Quest Alert: *You have been offered the quest "Working for the Man." Fill two carts of ore and load them into the wagon.*
Reward: *Increased favor with Whitgard and the Frozen Ash Tribe.*

Oakley's not one for detailed instruction, but I'm sure mining can't be that hard, so I toss the pickaxe over my shoulder and get to work. Just past the snowbank at the entrance to the cave, a small wooden wheelbarrow rests against the wall. I lay the pickaxe inside and push it down the well-trodden path. My eyes adjust to the dark, and pretty soon, only the faintest amount of light spills in from outside.

The cave goes deeper than I imagined, and before long, I'm in complete darkness. My night vision allows me to see unimpeded as broken axe shafts and rubble litter the cave, making it difficult to navigate the wheelbarrow.

I park the wheelbarrow at the end of the cave and equip the pickaxe. It's a little small compared to many of my weapons, but it feels natural in my hand. The Frozen Ash Tribe are a hearty people, so their tools are larger than most I've seen on Isle of Mythos. I'm not sure what I'm supposed to be doing, so I take my first swing at the cave wall.

A chunk of stone explodes from the impact, revealing a vein of rusty ore underneath. I swing again, further revealing the chunk of ore until I'm eventually able to pry it free.

Item. Iron Ore. *A mixture of raw iron and minerals, which can be smelted and further enhanced for use in tools and weapons.*

Congratulations! You have learned the skill 'Mining.' You are now a level 1 miner (Novice). Increase your skill and learn advanced techniques for mining by finding an advanced miner (apprentice or above). Ranks: Novice, Apprentice, Journeyman, Expert, Artisan, Master, Grandmaster.

As soon as I dismiss the notification, the cave is filled with translucent outlines marking iron ore veins along the wall. After half an hour, my mining skill reaches level two and the outlines become more detailed, now able to reveal iron ore that is a few inches beneath the surface. Before long, I have the wheelbarrow filled with ore.

A rhythmic clack echoes from outside the cave as I deliver my first load. Oakley grunts as he swings his axe, leaving a nice size gash in a towering pine.

He looks over as I dump the ore into the wagon and does a double-take. "Gods be good, you are a strong son of a dragon. It would take my men hours to mine that much ore."

"This is nothing." I finish dumping the wheelbarrow and stretch my arms overhead. "With an army of horrors, I could probably do it twice as fast."

He lets his axe fall in the snow. "You don't say."

"I do say. Promise not to piss your pants and I'll show you."

After lighting a torch, Oakley follows me into the cave. I can feel his eyes boring into me from behind. I'm sure a lifetime of stories where trolls are the boogeyman is hard to shake, but he seems open-minded enough.

We reach the end of the mine and I tell Oakley to stand back. "Wouldn't want you to get hit by any rogue projectiles."

He takes a few steps back. "You forgot the cart."

I wink at him. "We'll be running an assembly line for this next part. Now, try not to freak out."

I summon one of each of my horrors, and Oakley's eyes go so wide he almost looks like Limery.

"What madness is this?" His hand rests on the dagger strapped to his side. "Do you summon these beasts from the gates of hell?"

His question flusters me for a moment. I've never given it a second thought to where the horrors actually come from. They're not as intelligent as Limery, but they do have a sense of where-withal about them, even if they do respond to my every thought. The shadow demons that Ethan the Warlock summoned outside of Lynchton cross my mind and I wonder if my horrors come from the same place or if they are nothing more than mindless creations.

"Uh, you know, that is a good question." I watch the horrors grumble about for a moment, lost in thought. "I'll have to get back to you on that."

Over the next ten minutes, I summon a total of sixty horrors, separating them in a single file line down the length of the cavern. They grumble and shuffle their feet as I wait to get started. It might just be Oakley watching, but I have every intention of putting on a show.

As the first horrors expire, I summon three more to replace them, positioning them at the beginning of the line and forcing the others to shuffle their way to the end.

I take off the thick fur cloak and lay it to the side. I flex for Oakley and get to work. With sixty horrors active, I have a one percent increase in damage and health for each one active. Each swing digs deeper than before and chunks of stone and ore fill the ground around me. My horrors sort through the rubble, tossing rocks aside and sending ore down the assembly line toward the wagon.

As soon as horrors expire, I summon more, never missing a swing or slowing. Sweat trickles down my arms and back as the cavern grows warm from my body heat.

Then I activate Berserker Rage. Steam radiates from my skin as my muscles bulge and increased power flows through my body. My swings grow easier, and the pickaxe snaps from the force. I quickly replace it with another propped against the cave wall and carry on. Dust and debris fill the air as I break through the cave wall like a troll possessed. Ore notifications fill my vision and each hit lands with power and precision, knocking more and more ore free.

After thirty seconds, Berserker Rage ends and I take a step back, admiring my devastation.

Oakley looks on in awe, eyes blinking rapidly and mouth hanging open. "Do you have any brethren?"

I pat him on the shoulder. "I do, but we have bigger fish to fry at the moment."

With more ore mined in two hours than he had expected for the day, I lend my talents to chopping trees. I level up my logging skill, becoming a level-three lumberjack, and by midday, the wagon is loaded to the brim with ore and lumber.

"Looks like we're going home early." Oakley rolls his shoulders and they audibly crack. "You surprised me, troll. Not only are you strong, but your work ethic is admirable. I dare say you have what it takes to survive in Frostmoor."

"Now that is a compliment I'm proud to take." I walk beside the wagon as it trundles up the mountain, since there is no room to fit in the back. "Are you excited for the race?"

He nods. "The Ascent is always full of surprises. I competed myself when I was younger, though I never won."

After making short work of the day's tasks, Oakley is more talkative on the ride back. He asks a lot of questions about the world outside of Frostmoor. Even though their portal has reopened, no one from the Frozen Ash Tribe has passed through since it began functioning again. With the harsh terrain and climate, they don't worry about invaders, but they have surprisingly little interest in venturing to lands on the other side.

The return to Whitgard takes much longer with a full wagon, but we arrive with plenty of daylight remaining. Even though it's cold out, the village is more alive than I would ever have imagined. Music echoes from the mountainside and villagers stroll through the streets with steaming-hot beverages like this is some sort of winter wonderland.

As we enter, Gherhardt greets us with a shocked expression.

He picks up a piece of iron ore and examines it. "The two of you managed all of this?"

"You were wrong." Oakley slaps him firmly on the shoulder. "This troll is worth more than ten men. Any chance we can convince him to stay?"

Gherhardt smiles. "I fear there's no amount of gold that could keep him here. His sights are set far beyond Frostmoor. Isn't that right, Chod?"

"As much as I would love to mine ore and chop wood all day every day, there are a great deal of people counting on us back home. I'll have to leave the skilled labor to the professionals."

"Well, if you change your mind, I'm sure my men would love a chance to rest their backs." Oakley extends a hand to me and we shake. "It was an honor to see what trolls are made of. You've earned a drink. Enjoy the festivities, and I'll unload the cart."

He leads the ox through the crowded street.

"You must have made quite the impression. Oakley's not one to offer unearned compliments." Gherhardt places a hand on my shoulder. "Come, let's get you a drink. I've worked you enough for the day."

In the village center, a large bonfire blazes. People stand around with steaming cups, while Dando and Liyah play music. A rowdy group of men, who I assume had the day off, sway back and forth singing a song about a great battle. Dando and Liyah wave when they see us. Warley stands alone nearby, a mug in his hand and eyes fixed on Liyah. He frowns when he turns to see who they are waving at.

I lean in closer to Gherhardt so I don't have to yell over the music. "You think Dando will give it his all against your niece?"

"I'd prefer if he didn't so she wouldn't be interested anymore." He laughs. "She'd lose respect if he held back even the smallest amount."

Nearby, there's a smaller fire under a large pot full of steaming liquid. Gherhardt fills a mug and hands it to me.

A scream echoes from down the street and a crowd rushes in our direction.

"Demon!" someone shouts. "Demons in Whitgard!"

My body tenses and I turn my gaze toward the screaming. The last thing we need is a demon attack right now.

Gherhardt drops both mugs and grabs the woman by the arms. His gaze is piercing. "What's going on?"

She looks over her shoulder with wide eyes. "There's a demon at the gate."

I equip Destroyer and summon horrors, eliciting more screams from the unsuspecting crowd.

"Calm down, everyone. I'll get to the bottom of this." Gherhardt tries to maintain order as he unsheathes the dagger strapped to his waist.

We rush down the street to find a crowd gathered around the gate. I push my way through and find Limery pressed against the wall like a scared dog, with a fireball in his hand as the villagers point weapons at him.

"Stays back," he whimpers. "Limmy doesn't wants to hurts yous."

The fear in his voice breaks my heart, and I unleash a powerful roar, startling everyone. "Back away, all of you!"

I know they are scared of what they don't understand, but anger floods my being. If one of them so much as lays a finger on him...

Archard pries his way through the crowd, pushing weapons down as he does. "Lower your weapons, you fools. He's not here to hurt you."

"It's okay, everyone." Gherhardt sheathes his dagger. "He's an imp, not a demon. And he's a friend of the tribe."

There's uncertainty in their eyes, but they lower their weapons.

Limery's eyes glisten as he wraps his arms around me. "I sorries, Chods. Limmy didn't mean to scares them."

I gently pet his back. "Don't worry, buddy. You didn't do anything wrong."

Gherhardt addresses the crowd. "Alright, everyone, back to the festivities. There's nothing to see here. Give them some space."

Once the villagers begin to disperse, he and Archard come over.

"Is he okay?" asks Archard.

"Just a little shaken up."

Archard wipes his face, holding a hand over his eyes for a moment in frustration. "Bloody dolts. The lot of them wouldn't know a demon if it smacked them in the face."

My anger subsides a little. It makes sense to me that they

wouldn't recognize an imp, especially if he wasn't with me. Luckily, no one was hurt.

I'm suddenly aware that Limery is here alone, and my heart leaps into my throat. "Where's Taryn?" I blurt out.

"Taryns will be heres soon. He tolds Limmy to fly ahead."

I take a deep breath and some of the tension leaves my shoulders.

There's a flutter of wings and then a whistle as a small white bird lands on one of the posts of the palisade. The bird winks at me right before there's an explosion of white feathers and it transforms into an ebony dwarf.

Taryn reaches into his satchel and hands a bushel of herbs to Gherhardt. "Sorry it took so long, but here's your arctic clove. We had a bit of a run-in with a dragon." He looks around at the awkward situation. "What's going on here?"

Gherhardt takes the herbs. "Just a misunderstanding. I'd love to hear the story of your adventure, but right now, I need to visit Alvyn."

I turn to Taryn, wide-eyed. This was supposed to be a simple fetch quest. "Dragon?"

He grins. "And a dungeon. I'd love to tell you all about it, but what's a dwarf got to do to get a drink around here?"

"A man after my own heart." Archard claps him on the back. "Follow me."

CHAPTER 20

THE ASCENT

Taryn downs the warm mead in a single gulp, and some of it lingers on his mustache. "That's the good stuff."

Limery watches everyone with suspicion from my right shoulder. He's still a bit shaken up by what happened. He could have easily fought the villagers off or escaped, but this was the first time in all our adventures that townspeople had outright attacked him. Imps weren't well-liked back on Isle of Mythos, but I don't think he ever experienced anything quite like this.

Archard returns carrying a massive stump on each shoulder and plops them on the ground next to the bonfire. He gestures for Taryn and I to sit. "So, you had a run-in with Nessie?"

"Nessie?" Taryn cocks an eyebrow.

He glances in the direction of Icemaw. "That's what I call the white dragon. Nesira means 'snow' in the old tongue."

I take a seat on one of the stumps. "Fitting. We saw one when we first came through the portal. How many dragons are there?"

"Just the one as far as I can tell, and she's plenty to deal with. Nessie flies all over Frostmoor, and a blizzard usually follows in her wake. She likes the three center peaks most, but it's smart to give her a wide berth."

"Has she ever attacked the village?" I ask.

Archard shakes his head. "Dragons are intelligent creatures. They usually don't attack settlements unless provoked. I've seen her fly off with a mammoth clutched between her talons, so I'd rather not see what she can do to Whitgard."

"She was something else." Taryn looks longingly back at the mountain. "What I would give for a pet like that."

I scoff at his idea of a pet. "I think we're all better off without a giant snowstorm following us around. So, what took you guys so long?"

Taryn tells us of their journey, of the frost giants and the dragon, and how they hid in a cave until the dragon found them and they were forced to hide inside the dungeon. "It was like one giant puzzle. Each of the gemstones activated an effect corresponding to the color. Had Limery and I not been able to fly, we never would have gotten anywhere."

"Speaking of flying, why was your bird form white?" I ask.

Taryn frowns. "Bro, I don't interrupt you when you go on one of your long monologues. Can you let me tell the story?"

I scowl at him. "You interrupt me all the time when I'm talking."

He clasps his hands over his heart. "I would never."

I have half a mind to throw a snowball at him, but I'm more interested in what he has to say. "Whatever. Finish your story."

He continues, telling us how Limery's fire attacks were especially effective on the enemies they came across. About fairies, and spiders, and other ice-themed monsters. "There were dozens of rooms to explore. I'm pretty sure the dungeon extended to the base of the mountain, but we were only able to open a few chests in the time we had. I got a pelt that mitigates the effects of cold weather, while also making me camouflage in snowy environments. And we got this for you."

He reaches in his satchel and pulls out a small shield with a snowflake engraved in the center. He hands the shield to me. "I know you don't normally use a shield, but with this one, it's small enough that you can use it offensively as well. I haven't tested it out, but hitting someone with the shield might also trigger the bonus ability."

Item. Frosted Buckler. +2 Constitution. *A lightweight and small shield capable of deflecting blows as well as being used offensively.* **Bonus Ability:** *Physical attacks blocked with Frosted Buckler cut the attacker's Dexterity in half for ten seconds.*

The shield is lightweight, with a strap that moves easily up my arm, so I could still wield Destroyer with both hands if I needed to. After watching Jegaar fight with a similar shield, I'm well aware of how dangerous a small buckler can be.

"Not bad. What else did you get?"

He grins, and there's mischief in his eyes. "We were running low on time, but we decided to check one more room before leaving. Honestly, I don't want to tell you what we went through to get it, but the loot was worth it. Don't you think so, Limery?"

For the first time since we sat down, Limery is aware that we're having a conversation. He looks to Taryn, confused.

"Never mind. Here." Taryn pulls a frozen orb out of his satchel and tosses it to me.

The orb feels delicate to the touch, like it's made from a thin layer of pure ice, but my warm hands do nothing to melt the frosty exterior. It radiates a cold chill, and as I wipe away the frost from the outer layer, several snowflakes flutter inside.

Item. Frost Bomb. *Frost bomb explodes upon impact, freezing an enemy in place for five seconds.*

"That's sick! How many do we have?"

He holds up five fingers. "You can have two, but you better use them wisely."

I don't know if it's possible to activate them accidentally, but I'm extra careful as I place them in my satchel. Crowd control abilities are what help turn the tide of battle, so these little orbs could save our lives one day.

"So what now?" Taryn asks.

Archard claps his hands together. "I'd say you two have earned some relaxation. We'll start heading up the mountain in an hour or so for the race."

"Race?" Taryn looks confused.

Archard fills him in on the history of the Ascent, albeit with a lot less enthusiasm than Dando.

When Archard finishes the story, Taryn makes a pit stop by the stables to check on his pets. While he checks in, I watch the stableboys prepare the goats for the ascent. They cinch the saddles and check the shoes tacked to each hoof. Limery clings to my shoulder, unusually quiet and observant.

As we leave the stables, Berry's whines carry through the town.

I shake my head. "You know taking Ruby is only going to make him more jealous."

Ruby winds herself between Taryn's footsteps, narrowly avoiding being stepped on as if she is one move ahead of him.

Taryn sighs. "I know, but I hate to leave Stompy alone. And Berry isn't the most compact. There's no way Gherhardt is letting me bring a bear into his house." His eyes light up. "But I can't wait for him to help me advance my herbalism. I told you my story, but what have you been up to while we were gone?"

We follow the procession of people exiting the town, and I fill in Taryn on all the work I've done around the village.

He laughs. "Talk about grunt work. I'm sure you're ready for a little excitement."

I open the cloak I'm wearing, revealing my chest and posing suggestively. "Even with this beautiful blue body, I was not born for manual labor. I'll take fighting monsters any day of the week."

Taryn snickers before mumbling, "Beautiful, my ass."

The climb is slow, but eventually, we make it to the top of the mountain. Villagers line the wooded mountainside above the path before the trail cuts inward straight to the peak. No one stands on the path itself. I'm sure they are all well aware of the risks that are posed by the frost goats.

Where the trail diverges, it becomes rocky terrain and trees grow along both sides all the way to the summit. Villagers are more densely packed in the second stretch, and some have even perched themselves in the trees.

A firm hand clasps me on the shoulder, and I turn to find Gherhardt slightly behind me and Taryn, a hand on both of us.

His shoulders relax. "I mixed the elixir and Alvyn is in better shape already. He doesn't have the energy to climb the mountain yet, but I owe you a great debt for your heroism."

Taryn puffs his chest out, and the clasps in his beard jingle. "It was nothing. We were happy to help."

Gherhardt smiles. "We'll discuss your reward later this evening."

Taryn and I take a spot midway up the raceway, where we can see both the beginning and the finish line. Gherhardt trudges up the rocky trail, taking his position at the finish line.

Several minutes pass as the last of the stragglers make their way up. Pulling up the rear are the goats and their handlers. Even though they are wearing blinders, the stableboys give each goat plenty of space, and so far, they remain calm. Three goats are about all I would be willing to risk on the path considering the width and the treacherous fall from the embankment. After seeing my horror head-butted off the side, I do not envy those racing. It would be a painful fall down the mountainside. The contenders will definitely have their work cut out for them.

Warley, Dando, and Liyah wait behind the stableboys as they wrangle the unruly goats to the starting line. Even with the blinders, the goats can somehow sense one another. Steam shoots out of their nostrils as they struggle and huff.

Warley stands to the side of the group, an outsider as Dando and Liyah joke around. Liyah pushes Dando in the shoulder, and he tilts his head back in laughter. I'd almost feel sorry for Warley if he wasn't such an insufferable prick. But I'm sure many people have said the same thing about me in the past.

Taryn leans in closer. "Who's your money on?"

I shrug. "I've never seen any of them race, so I don't really know. Dando spends a lot of time working with the goats, so that may give him an advantage, but they are so unpredictable that I'd say they all have a shot. Warley has a chip on his shoulder, so that makes him dangerous, and Liyah seems the type who has something to prove."

"Hmm, I'll take your word for it. Should be an interesting race."

A long, bellowing horn resounds from atop the mountain. Gherhardt stands tall with the last rays of sunlight setting him aglow from behind.

He clears his throat and the crowd quiets. "For many years now, we have celebrated our forebearers and their famous ascent up Whitgard alongside the return of spring. As the frigid winter becomes slightly less cold, it is a chance for the young and hearty to test themselves in the same way as Umen and Edrar did many years ago. For Umen, his prize was the very land on which you stand, a land we still defend and call home. For our contenders today, victory comes with the respect of the tribe, and in the ancient tradition, this ice wreath."

He holds up a crystal wreath that sparkles in the fading sun like a chandelier. As the sunlight hits the wreath from behind, rainbows sparkle on the trail below.

"This wreath has been with our tribe for many years, created by the last mage to be born in Whitgard, Proma of the Frozen Heart. Her beauty was said to enthrall the hearts of men and women alike, but her magic was known all over Mythos. She left in the great battle against the dark one, arming our warriors with precious enchanted weapons and emptying the troves. All that remains is this exquisite wreath, which is said to bring luck to those who wear it. May it serve the champion well." He pauses and lets the sparkles of the wreath fall over the crowd. "Riders, take your positions."

Warley, Dando, and Liyah climb onto their goats and take the reins. They each have about two feet of space between one another, but I don't know if that is enough to keep the goats in check. Each rider wears metal armor over their legs, probably to prevent them from being broken in the event that a goat rams them.

The stableboys remove the blinders, and Dando's goat rears back, nearly throwing him off. Warley's goat tries to headbutt Dando's in the hindquarter, but a quick tug by the stableboy avoids catastrophe.

A horn erupts from overhead. "Begin!" Gherhardt's voice echoes off the mountains.

The frost goats dart forward, thick white fur whipping around as they are spurred on by their riders. Warley clearly has the most aggressive goat, because it swings its horns at Dando anytime he gets close. After a few failed attempts, it charges Dando. Dando tugs the reins to avoid being hit off the mountain, narrowly dodging the charge as his goat spins in a quick circle.

Warley's goat speeds toward the edge from the momentum of the attack, but it regains its balance before toppling off, setting his sights on Liyah. Is he the type of person that would let her win to try and gain her favor, or does he see her for the feisty person she is? Her goat gallops up the mountain, putting distance between her and the others.

Dando is several paces behind after the spin, but he whips the reins and his goat moves faster.

Warley catches up to Liyah, his goat chomping at the bit as it tries to bite the other goat's stubby tail. Liyah steers closer to the mountain, and Warley closes the distance until they are side by side. The two goats crack their massive black horns against one another, and the impact echoes like a gunshot. Each goat stumbles, and they square off in the center of the path.

Warley tries to lead his goat away toward the finish, but it's a mistake. Liyah's goat rams Warley in the leg, denting his armor. He unleashes a pain-fueled groan that echoes time and again.

Their standoff allows Dando to catch back up, and he charges in at full speed. He steers his goat toward the mountain, but there's not enough space between the embankment and Liyah. He's going to plow right into her.

Her goat turns and lowers its head, ready for a fight, but Dando guides his goat toward the embankment. He whips the reins and his goat jumps.

The goat leaps at the embankment, hooves landing inches from crushing a villager's dangling feet. The goat springs forward, bypassing Liyah without incident as he takes the lead.

Liyah and Warley both abandon their scrap to chase Dando, but it's too late. He doesn't slow down as he enters the final stretch. The goat hops from one boulder to another, ascending the rocky finish to where Gherhardt waits.

Warley and Liyah are only halfway up the final stretch when Gherhardt blows his horn. Dando crosses the finish with his hands raised overhead.

"We have a victor! Dando is this year's champion of the Ascent!"

Dando takes the wreath and holds it over his head. It catches the final rays of light and looks like a glowing beacon as he pumps it in the air.

Cheers erupt from all around. I join in because I'm happy for the kid. He ran a good race, and that jump over Liyah was executed to perfection.

The stableboys, who have run along the trail following the race from start to finish, retake the reins. With heaving breaths, they lead the frost goats back down the mountain. Now that the entertainment is over, the villagers begin the journey back to Whitgard, but I keep my eyes focused at the top.

Warley extends a hand to Dando and the two young men shake. As Warley begins his long walk home, Dando hands the wreath to Liyah. She smiles for a moment before placing the wreath around Dando's neck, and they both laugh.

Looks like he won more than just the race.

"Chod?" Taryn pokes me in the ribs.

I'm startled back to the company at hand. "Huh?"

"I said that was wild. Those goats seem like a terrible choice to domesticate." He shakes his head in disbelief.

"They're actually really good guardians when they are alone, but I get what you're saying. Pretty cool tradition, though."

He grins. "Is it even a tradition if it doesn't have the threat of imminent death?"

The sun descends on the hike down the mountain, and every-thing is once again shrouded in a silver glow.

Limery hasn't made a peep on my shoulder since we got here. He watches everyone from my shoulder as if they are out to get him.

"You okay, buddy?" I tap Limery on the toe to get his attention.

He crosses his arms, brow furrowed in frustration. "Limmy doesn't likes it here."

I lift him from my shoulder and hold his small body in my palms so that I can look him in the eye. "That's okay. I know it was scary for you, but they didn't know who you were. They thought you were coming to hurt them."

"But Limmy doesn't hurt nobodies."

"I know." I stop walking and take a seat on an old tree stump. Taryn nods to me as he waits a few feet away. "Do you remember when you and I first got together, how we had to hide from all the humans because they wanted to hurt me?"

He nods.

"It's like that. They were scared of me because they didn't know me. But once they saw that I wasn't going to hurt them, they stopped attacking us."

That's a simple way of putting it. It's more like once they saw that I could destroy them but wasn't going to, they saw it was better to treat the trolls with respect than to anger them. But I'm trying to ease Limery's worry, not have him scare the villagers.

"We'll be leaving soon, so if you don't want to get to know them, that's fine. But you're a funny, loving imp, and I bet they would really like you if you gave them the chance. What do you say?"

He lifts a finger to his chin as he considers my proposition. "Limmy will thinks about it."

"That's more than enough."

CHAPTER 21

LEAVE THE WORLD BETTER THAN YOU FOUND IT

After we arrive back in Whitgard, everyone gathers in the communal building where we'd eaten the previous night. Music blares and I immediately spot Dando on the stage with the ice wreath around his neck. He holds a mug in both hands and dances with Liyah to the folksy music.

Good for him.

Ruby darts beneath the long table on the left to scavenge for scraps of food that may have fallen.

"Might as well enjoy the mead while we can. There's no telling when we'll have access to more. Want me to grab you a drink?" asks Taryn.

"Yeah, sure. Give me a minute, though, I want to talk to Warley."

Taryn tilts his head, but then shrugs and walks away. Limery joins Taryn at the table brimming with food and mead. He seems to slowly be coming out of his funk.

Warley sits alone at the far end of the table staring into his mug. I'm surprised by how big he looks sitting there all alone. His shoulders are broad even without the fur coat, and his beard is full and thick, and yet he's around the same age as Liyah and Dando. Where Dando is youthful in appearance and attitude, Warley looks haggard and aged.

I tap my claws on the table, stirring Warley from his thoughts. "Mind if I take a seat?"

"Sure," he mumbles before taking a long swig of his drink.

I sit across from him. "Hell of a race today. I wasn't sure who was going to win."

"Pretty boy Dando wins again." He stares back into his mug. "Not that anyone is surprised."

I don't know why, but I suddenly recall a memory from my childhood. We were at a family gathering, back when they still happened. My mother's sister, Aunt Susan, was there. She'd never had children, and from what I recall, she worked as a park ranger upstate.

I'd just tossed a soda can on the lawn like I'd seen my father do many times when she picked it up. When I'd told her the maid would clean it, she knelt in front of me and said, "Always leave the world better than you found it."

Man, that was so long ago. Those words meant little to me at the time, and I can't even remember the last time I saw Aunt Susan.

I tap my finger against the table until Warley looks at me with annoyance. "You know it's not always about winning, right?"

He looks me in the eye, searching for anything to tell him I'm messing with him. The way his fingers clench around the mug doesn't escape me. "What's it about then?"

Before I logged into Mythos, I doubt I could have given him this talk. I honestly don't even think I ever understood what Aunt Susan meant until now. But here I am, in a position to maybe do some good not just for Whitgard or the trolls, but for all of

Mythos. I've been in Warley's shoes way too many times—angry about losing and blaming it all on someone else.

"Sometimes, it's just about showing up."

He scoffs. "What does a troll know?"

"More than you could possibly imagine. Look around, there are a lot of people in this village, and you were one of three who were chosen to compete. That's an accomplishment. Tell me, did your dad ever compete?"

His face softens, and he lets go of the mug. "What do you know about my father?"

"From what I can tell, he's pretty famous around these parts. Sounds like growing up in his shadow, especially with him not around, was a lot to live up to."

"He was a great man. Before he passed, he was my best friend. Taught me so much. He actually won the Ascent three times." Warley smiles for the first time since I've known him. "Probably could have won a few more if he were still around."

"Hey, I get it. We all live in our parents' shadows. The difference between mine and yours is that it sounds like your dad was a decent person. I'm sure he'd be proud of you."

"Are you saying there's truth to the tales of trolls eating children?"

"No, I'm not saying that." I laugh. "I'm saying that you don't have to live up to his image to be a good man. You didn't win. So what? You protect the gates of the village. You do your part. And you never know what part you may have to play in the future."

He sits in silence for a long moment. Music and chatter fill the room, but I can tell that his mind is elsewhere.

"It's really going to happen, isn't it?" He stares at the table.

"What's going to happen?" I ask.

"I've heard the rumors. No one has shown up in Whitgard for

many years, and now dwarves, and then you. Whatever it is you're trying to prepare for, it will find its way to Whitgard."

I sigh. This conversation has taken an abrupt turn. "I hope not. I pray that Gherhardt will—"

"Excuse me," a young woman interrupts us, eyes locked onto Warley. "Sorry to intrude, but I was hoping you might want to dance. You did a great job in the race today."

Warley looks around, making sure someone isn't playing a joke on him, before he finally returns her smile. "Uh..." he stammers.

"Go on," I encourage him. "Show the lady a good time."

He takes her by the hand, and they disappear to the front of the building.

Even though I can't picture Aunt Susan's face, the words still resonate with me. *Always leave the world better than you found it.*

Maybe being a hero is more than just killing monsters and finishing quests after all.

After having a heart-to-heart with Limery and Warley, I think I've done enough good for one day. I can't help but wonder if I've really grown this much as a person since entering Mythos, or if the AI is partly responsible. Valery did say that it would have an effect on us. The hair on my neck stands up just thinking about it.

I close my eyes and take a deep breath. Those are concerns for another time. For now, it's time to find Taryn and get that drink.

The evening passes in a blur of delicious food, strong drinks, and laughter. The villagers sing and dance, and even Taryn and I join in for a few songs. Limery makes friends with a young girl, and soon he has his own crowd as he juggles fireballs in the corner. Warley's spirits lift immensely, and by the end of the night, he has his arm wrapped around the young woman who whisked him away.

Everyone is cheerful as we stumble back to Gherhardt's,

except for Limery, who is passed out on my shoulder. A gentle snowfall muffles the sounds of the night.

"What a day!" Gherhardt wraps an arm around me, and I feel the brunt of his weight. "It's a good thing it only comes around once a year."

"I'd say. You drink like a dwarf." Taryn chuckles.

We turn the corner, where Dando has his arms wrapped around Liyah as they make out.

I abruptly change course, taking the next street over before Gherhardt has a chance to see what's happening.

We make it back to his place, and Ruby darts past us as we shuffle through the door frame, taking several attempts before unlocking our arms so that Gherhardt can enter first.

He plops down on a chair in front of the fire. "I'm just gonna... stay down...here...tonight."

His eyes flutter before he falls asleep. I toss a few more logs on the fire and cover him with a fur blanket. As we're going up the stairs, he calls out.

"Taryn...I...teach herbalism...mornin'." His words are jumbled, but we get the gist of what he's saying.

Upstairs, I lay Limery in bed and he starts snoring immediately.

Taryn joins me in the bedroom by the fireplace. "Once we're done with herbalism training, what's next?"

"We? That's your reward. I doubt I'll get in on it."

He laughs. "Don't be silly, I'm sure he'll let you join."

"We'll see. I'm sure it's more beneficial to you anyways. Herbalism probably goes a lot farther with being a druid. I've only got a handful of potions in my arsenal as it is."

He shrugs. "You never know what might be useful down the line. But seriously though, what's next for us? I was thinking that dungeon could be pretty lucrative."

"Maybe, but with me, Stompy, and Berry, I don't see us sneaking past the frost giants like you did. Not to mention if the dragon actually lives at the top of the mountain."

He strokes his beard. "Hmmm. I hadn't thought of that. Maybe there's a lower entrance."

"We need to go to Boneholde so that we can warn the others, but first, I'd like to take our chances with Hornryx. Even if nothing is there, there might be clues as to what happened to the arctic trolls."

"Yeah, strange that they just disappeared. Who knows, maybe they went through the portal when no one was looking."

We say good night, and I try my best to get some sleep. Tomorrow will be a long day of learning and traveling.

CHAPTER 22
HERBAL T

GHERHARDT MOVES AROUND SLOWLY the next morning, and the curtains are pulled when we head downstairs.

As usual, Taryn has no effects from the previous night's shenanigans, and compared to Gherhardt's, my hangover is minor.

"Morning, Sunshine." Taryn plops on the couch.

"Mornings, Sunshines!" Limery giggles as he joins the dwarf.

Gherhardt tosses a piece of sausage to Ruby and the jackal snatches it out of the air. "Old age has its pitfalls, let me tell you. In my youth, I could drink from dusk till dawn and still fit in the day's work. I hope I didn't embarrass myself too much last night."

"You were a drunken gentleman," I tease.

He laughs. "I don't doubt it. You'll have to serve yourselves this morning." He points to the bowls and takes a seat by the fire. "It's a good thing you were around to help Archard bring the frost deer up the mountain. The village devoured all of the venison in two days. The celebrations wouldn't have been the same without it, though."

Taryn enthusiastically scarfs down his meal.

"In such a hurry to be out of Whitgard?" asks Gherhardt.

"Not at all." Taryn picks a piece of egg from his beard and tosses it in his mouth. "I'm excited to learn enough herbalism that people will start calling me Herbal T."

"Oh, that." Gherhardt sighs, oblivious to the terrible pun. "What do I have if not my honor? A reward is a reward. Let me know when you're ready, and I'll brave the brightness."

After breakfast, we return to the greenhouse. Dando is leaving just as we arrive. I wink at him as he exchanges pleasantries with Gherhardt, and he returns a mischievous grin.

When they are done talking, he shakes my hand. "It was nice to meet you, Chod. Maybe our paths will cross again someday."

I grip his hand firmly. "No one knows what awaits any of our futures."

Taryn elbows me in the side. "Okay, Confucius." He shakes Dando's hand. "Congrats on the race." He leans in closer. "And the girl," he whispers.

Dando turns bright red as he heads to work.

"No one knows what awaits any of our futures," Taryn mocks me, moving his hands through the air like a mystic.

"Oh, shut up." I roll my eyes. "What would you have said?"

"Uh, something normal. Like, I don't know, 'I look forward to it,' or 'I hope so'."

I shove him into the snowbank. "Nah, doesn't have the same ring to it."

Taryn pulls himself up, snow covering his beard.

Limery bursts out laughing and dives into the snow next to Taryn.

Inside, Gherhardt leads us to the far end of the greenhouse. After a quick hello to Liyah, we get to work.

Gherhardt leans against the table. "I'm sure you already know this, but there is more than one way to increase your herbalism skill. Learning and identifying plants is the easiest way. You gain a certain amount of experience when you learn a new plant, and less and less each time you identify it in the wild. It will gain you quick levels and it is as far as most herbalists will go with their skills." He presses his hands together. "Why do you think that is?"

Suddenly, it feels like I'm back in school.

Taryn answers. "Because most people are only using their herbalism to find food or ingredients."

Gherhardt nods. "Exactly. But there is so much more to herbalism. To be a great farmer, gardener, florist, or proficient in any profession or skill where you will be growing your own plants, you will need to know advanced techniques. I have heard tales of druids capable of enhancing plants with deadly power and energy. Those skills are well beyond me, but I will teach you what I can today. To start with, I'll have you identify every plant within this growing barn. Thanks to me, we have quite the supply."

We spend over an hour with Gherhardt identifying plants. While we learn, Liyah harvests crops all around us, filling wooden boxes to be divvied up among the villagers. Limery helps, using his tiny fingers to pluck hard-to-reach fruits and vegetables. Ruby investigates the greenhouse, occasionally returning to check on us.

Gherhardt goes into great detail about each plant. Most are standard fruits or vegetables for feeding the village, but there is a good amount that have special effects. Fever grass is used in several potions and elixirs for various illnesses. A pinch of golden thorn will give any drink a metallic sheen, but at the cost of breath that reeks like death. Many of the plants do nothing on their own, but have profound effects when mixed.

By the time we are done, my herbalism skill is up to level ten.

"It is quite possible to reach beyond apprentice solely by identifying plants—many wanderers and scholars have done just that —but the further one levels, the longer it takes to see results from this method alone. To truly gain insight into what it means to be an herbalist, one must not only learn to identify plants but to tend them and cultivate them.

"Each plant is different. Some need direct sunlight and lots of water. Others—" He lifts a curtain beneath the table where clusters of vibrant mushrooms grow. "—can survive in the depths of caves without ever seeing the sun. To propagate, some plants bear seeds, some must be severed at the root, and some only need to be plucked from the source and are able to sprout roots." He leads us to a thick bush with waxy leaves shaped like teardrops.

Taryn listens with wonder. "This is fascinating."

Maybe for him. I can see the use of identifying as many plants as possible, but I doubt I'll ever be growing my own. My skillset lies elsewhere.

Gherhardt looks at Taryn like a proud father. "For this next part, you won't see any noticeable increase in your level, but if you use this knowledge in the future, it will be invaluable. Cultivating plants takes time, but its possibilities are endless. Advanced herbalists are capable of breeding vastly different varieties, sometimes creating new species altogether." He grabs a pair of small shears off the table. "A pair of quality pruning shears are an herbalist's best friend."

For the next few hours, he instructs us on techniques for pruning plants for optimal growth, cutting off diseased areas, and how to tell if a plant is thriving or dying. We break for lunch before continuing our education, learning about repotting, splicing, and so much that I'm sure I could probably work at a greenhouse in the real world with the knowledge I've gained.

True to his word, my herbalism skill only goes up if I'm

putting this knowledge to use on actual plants. While I find it mostly boring, Taryn is absolutely enthralled, asking questions and doing as much hands-on learning as possible.

I'm sure we could spend days here, doing nothing more than increasing our herbalism skill, but by early afternoon, it's time to leave. Gherhardt gives Taryn a large box filled with carrots for Stompy, and a vial of his dry rub to me. I'm sure it'll be gone in no time.

This herbalism knowledge may prove valuable one day, especially for Taryn, but being able to grow and identify plants will do little in the battle against Valmar and his dark forces. My time would be better spent leveling my mana infusion skill, if anything, not that there's easy access to raw mana anywhere outside of the troll forest.

What we need are warriors, and people willing to fight for what they believe in.

Gherhardt accompanies us to the stables to pick up Berry and Stompy and I make one last pitch for him to join the cause. "I appreciate your hospitality. As outsiders, we weren't expecting to be welcomed like this. I hope you will consider our offer. If nothing else, go to Seascape and meet the king in person."

He nods. "We offer hospitality to all who venture this far up the mountain. You are no longer outsiders to the Frozen Ash Tribe. I dare say you are friends." He turns to Limery. "I'm sorry for the confusion at the gate. I hope that you have seen that we mean you no harm."

Limery smiles. "It's okays. Limmy knows theys was scareds."

At the gate, Archard waits alongside Warley. The ranger has his axe strapped to his side, a pack on his back, and a bow on his shoulder. A surly frost goat stands behind him.

"Going out for a hunt?" I ask.

He taps the bow. "Not as far as last time, but we'll see what I can find. I'll accompany you a short way at least. Find out what you really think about Gherhardt when he's not listening." He winks.

"Nothing but kind words, I'm sure. Stay safe out there." Gherhardt gives us each a final pat on the back.

Warley opens the gate. As we're leaving, he steps outside. "Thank you. For the talk." He looks down and shuffles his feet. "I've been living in the past for far too long, holding on to what's gone, and blaming everyone else for not being stuck there with me." He lifts his gaze, meeting my eyes. "I can see that now. I've got big plans, and I'm certain our paths will cross again someday. Take care until they do."

I'm speechless. Last night, I spoke from the heart, but I never thought my words could have such an effect on him.

Warley extends his hand and when I move in to shake, he clasps me around the forearm, a gesture usually reserved for those considered brothers.

"Now that's how you say good-bye." Taryn grins as he climbs atop Berry.

I straddle Stompy, and we descend the mountain. Archard stays a healthy distance ahead of us. As powerful as that frost goat may be, I'll put my money on Stompy or Berry any day of the week.

The gate snaps shut behind us, and a fresh snowflake melts against my nose as we head to our next adventure.

CHAPTER 23

PIGS AND A BLANKET

THE SNOWFALL CONTINUES as we descend Whitgard, covering the sprigs and patches of escaping greenery until the world is blanketed in white once again—everything except for the enchanted path that guides us down the mountain. Snowflakes melt as soon as they touch the trail.

Every so often, a mana-infused flame burns continuously, and I'm once again curious if ley lines run underneath the pathway or if they are pulling mana from some other source. Maybe the enchantment that keeps them burning is just that strong.

Up ahead, Archard pulls his fur coat tighter. "Every year, you think spring is finally here and then another snowfall turns it all upside-down. At least this isn't Nessie's doing."

"Does the snow ever truly melt away?" asks Taryn.

Archard grunts. "It clears around the portal and about halfway up the peaks. Summer comes and goes within weeks, but it's a beautiful sight while it lasts. Whitgard is rarely snow-free, but the trees and bushes shed their snowy coats."

I don't think I could handle a climate as unforgiving as this. Even in New York, I preferred the warmth of the indoors during the winter.

Whitgard is lucky to have the greenhouse. I wonder if the Snowwalker Tribe has something similar.

We pass the ruins where I helped Oakley mine and chop wood. Archard leads the frost goat off the path.

"This is where I leave you be. There's usually a fair amount of smaller game around these parts." He climbs down from the frost goat and adjusts the pack on his shoulders. "Time to see what beasts are lurking nearby. I wish you safe travels. Wherever you go, keep an eye out for frost giants."

We continue down the mountain, but I doubt we'll reach the base before nightfall. The sun is already slipping across the sky, and we got a late start.

Snow falls from the branch of a nearby tree, and Limery darts off in pursuit of whatever small creature made the disturbance.

"They were a nice group of people." The clasps in Taryn's beard jingle with each of Berry's steps. "More civilized than I expected."

"You mean aside from wanting to kill Limery?" I laugh half-heartedly. "No, they weren't half-bad."

"Yeah, but can you blame them? He can be a scary little bugger." He gestures toward Limery, who has feathers clinging to his cheek and fingers as he returns with a devilish grin.

Poor bird.

Truthfully, the Frozen Ash Tribe treated us better than I imagined they would. When Jegaar described them as mountain tribes, I expected something more along the lines of the mountain trolls. But these were salt of the earth people who kept to themselves. They are only a generation or two removed from trading with the outside world.

As good as this experience was, we must remember not to let our guards down. While they still held onto the civility of days past, that doesn't mean the Snowwalkers have done the same. We are outsiders. And that is always dangerous.

"I'm concerned if we'll be welcomed quite the same in Boneholde. Gherhardt says they're a more barbaric tribe. Especially since they were displaced."

"At least you're worried about something." Taryn rolls his eyes. "I'd say you should be more concerned with what lies up the mountain you're so intent on climbing."

"If there was anything worth worrying about, someone would have seen it by now. Even the frost giants come down from their mountain from time to time."

He sighs. "I hope you're right."

An hour later, we come across more ruins of Whitgard's past. Many of the houses are dilapidated, with roofs or walls long crumbled, but some of them still seem habitable. Stompy grunts as I force him to stop.

"Want to camp here for the night? I'm not sure where the next ruins are, and we don't want to be traveling at night."

Taryn looks around, frowning. "I'm going to miss that warm bed tonight." He rubs Berry behind the ears. "I hope you're ready to cuddle."

We find the ruins of an old barn and make camp. The walls are made of thick stone, but even so, there are gaps where the wind seeps through. It's the only place we find that's big enough to fit Stompy and still has four walls and a decent roof. This may be considered springtime for Frostmoor, but we're going to need all the warmth we can get during the night.

I gather logs, and Limery starts a fire, which eases some of the chill. After a quick dinner, I sleep against the wall, bundled up in my fur clothing and an extra blanket Gherhardt gave us. Limery's warm body curls up in the crook of my arm.

"Wake up!" Taryn shakes me. Even though he's whispering, urgency coats his voice.

"What is it?" I wipe the sleep from my eyes, but immediately discover what has him so alarmed.

Something grunts outside of the barn, and feet crunch through the frozen snow. A second later, another grunt answers.

Berry stands snarling in front of the door, hair raised. His growl is low and sonorous. I nudge Limery, and he frowns as he wakes.

Outside, it's still dark, and the dull glow of the night seeps in through the cracks in the slatted roof. A shadow passes across the gap in the door frame and the creature on the other side sniffs at the door. Dust shoots across the floor as it snorts again.

A wooden beam holds the old barn doors in place, but I don't trust it to keep whatever's on the other side out if it really wants to get in. It was more for peace of mind than anything. The hinges are rusted from years of disuse and are likely to break with the least amount of pressure.

"I'm going to check it out," Taryn whispers.

Without waiting for my response, he transforms into his bird form. Thanks to his new item, he's a brilliant white in the cold climate. He flutters up to the ceiling and disappears between a crack barely wider than he is.

More shadows pass over the door, and the snorting continues. Limery climbs onto my shoulder, and his hot claws dig into my muscles. Whatever's outside, they know we're in here.

Mana rages at my fingertips, and I summon my horrors. If

whatever's outside breaks down the door, they're in for a rude awakening.

Incoming Message (Taryn): *This could definitely be worse, but there are four iceback warthogs outside the door. They're pretty big, with nasty tusks, some kind of frozen armor on their backs. All level twenty.*

Four level-twenty warthogs. I'm positive we can take them, but we'll probably tear down our shelter doing so.

Message (Chod): *Get back inside. I say we wait it out. Maybe they'll leave, and if not, we fight them at daybreak.*

Tiny claws scratch against the roof as Taryn squeezes back through the crack. He transforms into a dwarf just as I summon another round of horrors.

The sniffing gets louder as what I assume is all four of the warthogs pressing their snouts to the bottom of the door. Berry continues to snarl, but Stompy rests against the back of the barn like he doesn't have a care in the world. Ruby stares silently at the door.

"I don't think they're going anywhere." Taryn strokes Berry on the shoulder in an attempt to calm him.

"Yeah, well, neither are we."

Taryn fills me in on a more detailed description of the warthogs as we wait, and over the next hour, I keep a steady supply of horrors. With sixty of them crammed into the barn, there's enough body heat that it actually feels warm.

We use the time to come up with a plan, and once the first rays of sunlight pass through the slits in the roof, all hell breaks loose.

We cram against the back wall, using Stompy as a shield while Taryn casts Stonewall inside the barn, pinning my horrors between his wall and the door. My horrors are crammed together like stuffed animals in a claw machine.

Taryn hands me his Sapling Staff and flies through the crack in the roof to ready the next stage of our plan. The vines from the staff crawl through the slim space between the top of Taryn's wall and the roof, descending and wrapping around the wooden beam that bars the doors in place.

Footsteps thud overhead, and the wood groans as Taryn returns to his dwarven form.

I adjust the grip on the staff and turn to Limery. "Ready?"

"Readies!" He grins.

Taryn stomps twice, giving the signal that the cooldown for Stonewall is up.

With a heave, I pull on the staff, removing the beam from the door. There's a crash as the warthogs trample into the barn. If this works, then he should be summoning a second wall where the doors used to be, pinning the warthogs inside.

"Now!" Taryn shouts.

I cast Kamikaze, exploding all sixty of my horrors in a single blow. The explosion is so powerful that it shatters Taryn's wall. Stompy's massive hide shields us from the blast, and he bellows as he loses a chunk of health to the debris.

Limery summons a wall of fire in the wreckage, and warthog squeals pierce through the dawn. With the doors blown off, light floods into the barn.

The warthogs, gashed and bleeding, are the most ferocious-looking pigs I've ever laid eyes on. Their skin is a light blue with stripes of white that are stained red. Where a normal warthog would have a strip of coarse hair running down its back, these have shards of jagged ice. Two piercing icicle tusks jut up from their lower jaws, though some look to have been broken or chipped in the blast.

They thrash around in slow-motion as their health ticks down in the fiery rubble. Then one locks its eyes on us.

The passive slows from the Horrors of Vitality fade and one warthog squeals as it charges.

I toss the staff aside and equip Destroyer as I vault over Stompy. As soon as I land, I swing at the charging beast, and Destroyer connects just above the front shoulder. Red flashes through the weapon as the warthog spins, flying into the barn wall with a thud, and Berry pounces on the downed creature.

I hit the second warthog with an upward swing. Its jaws clack and a tusk breaks at the base as it flips backward into the third warthog.

I can't get my weapon down in time before the final warthog buries a tusk into my leg. The tusk pierces my flesh like a toothpick through warm butter, and shooting pain is all I can focus on as I'm bulldozed into Stompy.

There's a flash of bright light as the roof explodes and a deafening thunder rattles my bones. The pressure vanishes from my leg, and I'm launched against the wall. Somewhere, Limery's voice calls out to me, but it's quickly drowned out by the ringing in my ears.

I attempt to stand, but my left leg doesn't support my weight and I collapse against the wall. It's been a while since I felt this kind of pain. Without thinking, I pull a health potion from my inventory and down it. Immediately, the world comes back into focus.

Limery's warm hands press against my cheeks and two bulbous eyes blot out my vision. "Chods, is yous okays?"

I'm suddenly aware of the smell of roasted pork, and my mouth waters involuntarily. "Yeah, I'm okay."

His tiny shoulders relax.

Next to me, Taryn kneels over Stompy, casting Restoration, and the two are shrouded in a golden glow. The potion slowly stitches the wound in my leg back together and I'm able to stand by the time he is finished. Four warthogs lay scattered around the barn among rubble and smoking wood.

I take a deep breath. That was a lot harder than I expected.

Taryn presses his boot against one of the warthogs, checking to make sure it's dead. "That went well."

I stretch my neck from side to side. "Easy for you to say. You didn't have a foot-long tusk stabbed into your leg. I don't even know what happened at the end there."

He grimaces. "Yeah, that looked rough. Once I saw they were making Chod kabobs, I figured it was time to step in. You and Limery took out about three-fourths of their health in those first few seconds. My lightning bolt finished off the one you smacked in the face and stunned the other for Limery to take out. Stompy sideswiped you with his horn. It got the beast off of you, but it looked like it hurt."

I walk over and pat Stompy on the shoulder. "Thanks for looking out, big guy. You hit like a sledgehammer."

He huffs in response.

Taryn offers him one of Whitgard's carrots and he chomps it with vigor.

I kneel by one of the warthogs and slice off some of the meat with my claw. It's fatty, with a smoky flavor. "Loot what we can, but we need to get moving. We caused quite a commotion and we don't want any big scaries getting scent of this roasted meat while we're around."

Most of what we loot is meat for our journey. Gherhardt gave us eggs, bread, and vegetables, but meat was in short supply. I also manage a few warthog tusks. If we had time, I would have skinned them for their armored hide, but we want to be as far away from this place as we can.

I don't know how far a frost giant can smell, but I most certainly do not want to find out.

CHAPTER 24

AIN'T NO MOUNTAIN HIGH ENOUGH

OUR JOURNEY back to the portal is uneventful. Even though I'm sure we pass the areas where Archard lost his hunt and where we battled the frost wolves, all evidence has been hidden by the snow.

When we arrive at the fork where the five paths meet, the view is daunting. Hornryx towers above the other peaks. A ring of clouds surround it where most of the other mountains reach their summit, obscuring its apex. The mountain is still wide at that point, so there's no telling how much further up it goes.

"You sure you want to do this?" Taryn squints as he stares up at Hornryx. "We could travel to Boneholde in the time it would take us to reach halfway up this one."

"I need to go. It's going to suck, but I need answers. There's no way I can go back to Chief Rizza and the others knowing I was this close to the home of one of our people and didn't at least check it out, you know?"

"I know." He sighs. "Damn it to hell."

"Damns it to hells." Limery scowls up at the mountain.

I push Limery off my shoulder, and he falls into the snow. "You two have been spending too much alone time together."

He pokes his head up from the snow, giggling. I think the little devil has discovered that copying Taryn is a good way to annoy me. I hope he hasn't just entered the annoying teenager phase of imphood.

We carry on traveling, and by twilight, we've only just reached the base of Hornryx. There are no ruins or caves for us to make camp, so we have to get creative.

"We could try to make shelter between those two trees." Taryn points to two massive pines not too far from the trail.

I'm all for sleeping outdoors, but not in freezing temperatures. "How long does one of your walls last?"

He shrugs. "No idea. I've never actually tested it. The ones from our battle with the wolves were gone, so I'm guessing they decay at some point. Either that or something destroyed them."

"I guess there's only one way to find out."

I summon enough horrors to clear a large patch of snow. Once the area is cleared down to the frozen grass, Limery summons several flame walls, drying away the moisture. His attacks leave the ground barren and charred, but that's better than wet and cold.

Once a big enough space is cleared, Taryn casts Stonewall. After each cooldown, he summons another wall. Before boxing us in with the final wall, we gather wood for a fire.

The opening above us is too big to tie any of our blankets together for a roof, so the cold air still creeps in, but with a roaring fire and tall walls, the frigid breeze is kept at bay.

Stompy lays against one wall, and Taryn bribes him with more carrots so that we can use his broad belly as a pillow. Taryn cuddles against Berry as Ruby curls up in his lap. Limery nestles in my arm.

The moulhaug's chest rises and falls with each boisterous breath, and the wind whirls overhead. It's kind of comforting.

"This was a good idea." Taryn gently strokes Ruby from head to tail. "You're not such a dumb brute after all."

"You know it." I laugh. "I've got brains and brawn."

"You must have learned from the best." He smirks.

"Maybe once upon a time, but now you're more like brains and scrawny."

"Pssh, it's called being stout." He crosses his arms.

"Okay, Mrs. Teapot." I put one hand on my hip and extend the other like a spout.

He shows me a rude gesture. "Either way, we're a pretty good team. Good night, guys."

"Good night, bro."

"Good nights, bros." Limery tosses a final flame at the fire before tuckering out.

From where I'm lying, the mountain takes up the entirety of my view of the outside world. The clouds have a silver glow as they hug the mountain, and I can't help but wonder what lies within their depths. Trolls? Dungeons? Monsters? Or nothing?

It could very well be that the first race of trolls has gone extinct from the world. All the more reason why we must fight like hell to protect what we have.

A cold gust of wind wakes me up as one of Taryn's walls disappears. Stompy stirs, agitated, before Taryn calms him.

"On it!" He sounds half-asleep as he summons a new wall to replace it. Over the next few minutes, the other walls fade from existence, and he immediately replaces them. Once our new fortress is in place, Limery stokes the fire and we're back to sleep.

In the morning, we roast some of the boar meat over the fire. When we're ready to leave, I use the water from Brimming Tankard to douse the fire. Even though Taryn can cancel Stonewall himself, I equip Destroyer to break through just to test it. While it has the strength of stone, the wall itself has no magical properties and it breaks easily enough under the enchanted weapon.

We load up the animals and begin the slow crawl up the mountain. Snow falls all around us, concealing everything but the enchanted path. Occasionally, we pass frost deer and even a few wild frost goats as we ascend. The higher we climb, the more dangerous the monsters become. We do our best to avoid them when we can.

At one point, an icy blue spider with spiked crystalline legs clatters out from a cave, but a well-placed flame wall from Limery sends it skittering back inside.

"Never going in a cave again." Taryn shivers, shaking his head in disgust. "Nope."

Wolves howl nearby, but we're unable to see them. With their white fur, they could be anywhere and with the way the wind is blowing, it's hard to tell the direction the howls are coming from. I'm not sure if they are following us or not, but I summon horrors just in case.

We'll need to keep watch tonight.

By nightfall, we can't be more than a few hours from the ring of clouds. The closer we get, the heavier the snowfall.

Now that we're near the ring, I notice that the clouds are actually rotating around the mountain at a pretty fast pace. I watch them, mesmerized. "I'm excited to see what's beyond the clouds."

"Just please don't let it be spiders." Taryn grimaces. "That's all I ask."

He summons his walls and we make camp for the night. Tomorrow morning, we'll know if this was all worth it.

The high walls obscure the light from our fire, but I still don't feel safe without one of us keeping watch, especially after our encounter with the spider. Who knows what else could be creeping around the mountain at night?

I take the first watch, staring up at the sky as snores erupt all around me. The fire crackles, basking my toes in warmth and sending the occasional ember drifting through the air.

Sitting against the wall, I wonder how this space compares to a prison cell. It's not lost on me that this could have been my fate had I not been able to log into Isle of Mythos. As shitty as the situation feels knowing I haven't heard from my parents, I still owe them for getting me here. I could have been stuck in a cell with a less-promising view.

I can't even imagine how I would have dealt with that, with people like Glenn or Jude. Pressley and Jon seemed normal enough, but even they are from worlds vastly different than my own.

A chill runs down my spine.

Something taps against the other side of the wall, startling me, and I fight the urge to scream. In a flash, I'm on my feet with Destroyer clenched tightly in my grip. Ruby shuffles in Taryn's lap at my sudden movement. Her ears twitch, and she's wide awake staring at the same spot on the wall where I heard the sound.

Wind whooshes overhead like a whirlpool, making it impossible to hear anything on the other side of the walls for that moment, but I know something is out there. I heard it through the stone.

I wait for another scratch or tap, but it doesn't come.

My heart pounds in my chest, the fear of the unknown running wild in my mind. Spiders, wolves, it could be anything on the other side. I take solace in the fact that if it was Nessie, she would have destroyed us by now.

Maybe this was a bad idea.

After several long minutes, Ruby rests again. That puts me at ease a little. Her perception is incredibly high after all, but I keep a hold on Destroyer just in case.

The hours pass slowly before it's Taryn's turn to take watch. I tell him about the noise as I settle down against Stompy.

"Maybe it was a tree branch?" His gaze drifts upward, toward our only view of the outside world. "Or it could have been the antlers of a frost deer passing by."

I shrug. Whatever it was, I pray it's long gone by now.

I wake briefly in a couple of hours to a chill as Taryn's walls fade and he summons more. Luckily, there's no monstrous beast waiting to kill us on the other side, and I'm able to return to sleep with only the vaguest recollection of being awakened.

Once morning comes, we pack up and I summon a full army of horrors as we journey toward the clouds that bar our view of the top. I don't know what waits beyond, but I'd rather be safe than sorry.

A silver falcon perches in a tree, watching us as we gather our belongings. Limery eyes it greedily, but then it disappears into the clouds.

The snowfall steadily increases the closer we get until eventually, we can't see more than a dozen yards in either direction. It's like when Nessie passed over the portal, only never-ending. The only warmth comes from Stompy's hide between my legs, and Limery clinging tight against my shoulder. His heat permeates the fur cloak.

I send half of my horrors to lead the way and have the other half bring up the rear, using them as bumpers against the fog of snow. If something happens to them or their presence goes missing, I'll be able to tell right away.

Taryn pulls Berry to a halt and turns around. Ice crystals cling to his beard. "How are we supposed to find anything in this blizzard? It's only getting worse."

Shivers run through my body as cold wind seeps into every open crevice of my fur clothing. "I don't know. I'm hoping it clears up once we get high enough."

He squints in my direction. "We can barely see the trail as is. If we leave it, we're screwed."

"I know. So, don't leave the trail."

A half-hour later, Taryn stops again. A thick layer of snow has gathered on both Berry's and Stompy's backs. The snow comes down faster than it can melt away. My breath comes out as thick steam, causing a layer of ice to coat my tusks. Limery is the only one not covered in ice and snow.

"What is it this time?" I shout above the wind.

"End of the line!" His voice is soft in the snowfall.

I climb down from Stompy to see what Taryn is talking about. Sure enough, the enchanted trail ends abruptly against a mound of snow. A single mana-infused torch crackles against the wind.

Fuck.

Berry groans beside me, his displeasure mirroring my own.

"What now?" Taryn calls from the bear's back. "Should I scout ahead?"

I shake my head. "Too dangerous. I don't want to risk getting separated. We've made it this far. Let's push a little farther."

He stares at me intently. "If we push much farther, we're not escaping this blizzard tonight."

Icy dread rests on my shoulders. I hope like hell we make it to the other side.

Stompy and I take the lead, using his massive horn to bull-doze a path for Taryn and Berry to follow. My horrors pick up the rear, no longer able to scout ahead without slowing us down.

With every step, I'm more and more certain this was a bad decision. The reason nothing comes down from Hornryx is because nothing can survive this type of environment. This was nothing more than a fool's errand. I should have listened to Taryn. Now, I've wasted precious time that could have been spent else-where. We could be in Boneholde by now, presenting our cause to their leaders. Then we'd be off to somewhere new, some place where my ass cheeks wouldn't be frozen together.

One of my horror's presences vanish.

I turn around, but I can't see past Taryn in the snow, much less to any of my horrors. In these conditions, it could have fallen off a cliff for all I know.

"One of my horrors went—"

Taryn's black eyes go wide, and he points a stumpy finger over my shoulder. As I turn around, I'm keenly aware as several more horrors vanish.

Frost spreads across Stompy's hide. There's a loud crack as it thickens and forms into ice. His body freezes in place.

The frost spreads, creeping up my legs. I try to move but I'm stuck. It inches up my body, rapidly freezing me in place before I can escape.

"Chods!" Limery yells as he presses warm fingers against my neck.

For the first time, his touch feels anything but warm. The ice crawls up his arm and his bulbous eyes bulge with panic.

I try to tell him it's going to be okay, but my jaw locks in place.

For the longest time, the world is a swirl of snow. My eyes lock with Limery. He's scared, and it's all my fault.

As we look upon one another, I try not to think about the fact that this might be the last time I'll see him alive.

I've fucked us all. And for what?

I struggle against the ice, but it doesn't budge.

I'm a second away from activating Berserker Rage when a hulking white figure steps into view. My hesitation dooms us all because before I can activate my ability, my eyes freeze shut, and everything goes dark.

CHAPTER 25

ARCTIC STROLLS

I'VE NEVER BEEN SO cold. Not even the time I locked myself inside the freezer at one of my parents' business galas. I was only eight or nine, and so bored out of my mind that I wandered around the event space. I ended up in the kitchen because it seemed more exciting. After shutting myself inside the walk-in freezer, I panicked, not knowing that the doors opened from the inside as well. I had frosted tears on my cheeks by the time a server came in to retrieve the desserts.

Everything is dark and hazy. I can't move, but uncontrollable shivers still somehow manage to snake through my frozen body.

Figures move across my blurred vision. I have no idea what's happening, where I am, or who or what is responsible. The last thing I remember is the hulking figure and everything going dark as ice covered my eyes. I pull up my notifications.

Alert! You have been frozen. You are unable to move for the next thirty seconds.

More than thirty seconds has passed but I still can't move. I might not be technically frozen by whatever ability hit me, but I'm guessing I'm stuck in a block of ice.

The ice cracks around my forehead and shards break away from my eyes. The rush of sunlight is blinding, but all I can do is squint.

I have access to my abilities, but I don't want to waste Berserker Rage without knowing what the situation is. Even though it makes me immune to stuns, slows, and effects, I don't know if being stuck in a block of ice counts as an effect. Or if it just means I'm trapped. The heat that accompanies my bulging muscles might be enough to break through, but I can't be certain. If it was enough to freeze Limery, then I doubt I have any chance of breaking out. Whatever did this is more powerful than we are.

So I'll need to be smarter.

My eyes finally adjust to the daylight, and two large bright blue eyes stare back at me. My heart jumps, but the ice keeps me in place. Even my startled scream stays constrained within my chest. The eyes are so close to my face that I can't see beyond them.

I attempt to look around, but my neck and jaw is still frozen. I have no idea if Taryn, Limery, or the others are with me or not.

"You are either incredibly brave or incredibly stupid." The voice is deep, even with layers of ice muffling my hearing. "It has been a long time since someone attempted to climb Mount Hornryx. We normally kill those that make it to the ring. Usually, it's an adventurous hobgoblin, or a frost giant that has forgotten its place in the world, occasionally, a greedy tribesman, but imagine my surprise when I find a troll leading a party of misfits onto my lands."

He leans back, revealing black skin the color of a faded charcoal. Two short tusks poke through the hair of his thick white beard. White fur covers the majority of his body. All except for his hands and a large patch on his stomach, both areas are the same faded charcoal black as his face. I take a second to analyze him.

Chief Laojin
Level: ???
Druid
Arctic Troll

My chest tightens, and it feels like it could crack through this frozen prison. An arctic troll! I was right. I found one, and now it's about to be the death of me. I struggle against the ice, but it is unforgiving.

"What I really want to know…" He leans in again, blocking my view. "Is why there's a lone forest troll on my mountain?"

There's a long pause before he speaks again. "Senzala, can you do something about this ice? I'd like to talk to him before we decide whether or not to kill them."

Chief Laojin slides off the side of Stompy's neck and lands in the snow, revealing a second troll that was standing behind him.

Senzala
Level: ???
Shaman
Arctic Troll

Another troll shaman. She's the only one I've seen besides Jira. She's more slender, almost half the width of the male troll. She doesn't have a beard, but she does have an ample amount of fur-covered bosom above a patch of hairless black skin on her midsection.

She waves her hand in my direction and ice falls from my face.

"Where's my party?" I shout. "If you hurt them, I swear I'll—"

As quickly as it disappeared, ice reforms over my mouth.

"You'll do what, exactly?" Senzala laughs mockingly.

Laojin climbs back atop Stompy, a frown plastered on his ugly face as he sits backwards in front of me. "You have no power here. Look at me." He presses a thick finger against my forehead, and rage boils inside of me.

Once I break out of this ice, I'm going to show him what real power is. I bring my eyes to meet his.

"That's better." His mouth curls into a snarl. "You're only alive because I am a curious troll. Let that sink in for a minute. We could have killed you in the ring. We could have left you there to die slowly and painfully. We could have pushed your frozen bodies off the cliff and watched you break into a thousand pieces as you fell down the mountain. We could have fed you to the dragon. There is no end to the number of ways we could have caused you to suffer, ways we can still make you suffer. Make no mistake, you came into our lands and you will deal with the consequences of those actions. We live in peace because we stay hidden. Because one cannot bother what they don't know exists. But now here you are, so I will ask you one time and one time only. Why?"

He nods to Senzala, and she removes the ice from my mouth once again.

They both stare at me with a bone-chilling intensity.

I choose my next words carefully. If there's a chance Limery and the others are still alive, I need to talk my way out of this.

"We—no, I—I was looking for you."

He places his hands together, and his blue eyes fill with mischief. "Continue."

"It's a long story."

He holds up a finger, telling me to wait a second as he slides off Stompy's ice-covered hide and disappears from my view. Senzala watches me with cold eyes.

A moment later, I can barely see him out of the corner of my eye as Laojin pushes Berry's frozen body. It's like the bear is sliding on a conveyor belt as his stiff legs glide across the snow. Taryn sits atop him, face petrified mid-yell, his right arm outstretched with the Sapling Staff still frozen in his grip. Ruby's snarl is carved in ice.

If I weren't a troll ice cube, I'm certain I would collapse from relief. They're still alive, which must mean Limery is still on my shoulder. I don't know how they were able to freeze his hot imp body, but at least I have a shot at saving them.

Laojin lifts Taryn's frozen body from Berry and tosses him into the snow like he's nothing more than a toy. I clench my jaw, fighting the urge to yell as he does the same to Ruby before he climbs on Berry's back and faces me. If I lose my cool, we're all dead.

He leans forward. "I've got nothing but time."

I take a deep breath, and recount my adventures since entering Mythos. "It all started when I woke up in the forest..."

Laojin listens with rapt attention, hanging on to every word as I tell him of my adventures since arriving in Isle of Mythos. Aside from the times I logged out, I tell him everything. He doesn't interrupt, but he does make comments to himself as I tell the story, mumbling "interesting" or "curious" all the way until I get to us reaching the ring around Hornryx.

Telling the story, my origin story, reminds me of all the people and places I have experienced in this world. From my first encounter with Gord until right now, this world has shaped me, and continues to shape me, into the hero I am. That in itself is worth fighting for.

By the time I finish, the sun has set and we sit in a silver glow. There's been no snowfall since the ice was removed from my eyes, and this high up, the moonlight seems to shine brighter. Or maybe it's because there are no clouds blocking its reflection.

"This has been a fascinating tale. I am glad we didn't kill you on sight. It is good to know our brother and sister tribes have not yet perished." He runs clawed fingers through his beard. "You have told us how you came to Hornryx, but you haven't answered my question. Why are you here? You didn't know what awaited you past the ring, so what were you hoping to find?"

I sit in silence for a long moment, not sure that I have an answer. "I don't know. Hope, maybe. I've gone from one society to another, having to convince everyone but the dwarves at Seascape that this world is worth fighting for. I guess just once I was hoping to find someone who didn't need convincing, a troll society that wasn't on the brink of collapse or afraid of the outside world."

"I am sorry, but you will find none of that here." He turns to Senzala, and she nods. "While I do not agree with your path, you are a troll after all, and I believe that Chief Rizza was correct in supporting you. A troll hero still means something; therefore, I will allow you and your party to stay in Hornryx for the time being, and we will help you with what knowledge we have. After that, I will send you on your way and you will forget you ever saw this place. We will have no part in the wars that plague men, dwarves, elves, and the like. Understood?"

I nod. It might not be what I hoped for, but it's something. "Understood."

"Release them."

A white aura surrounds Senzala as she slashes her hand through the air. Ice cakes off my body like I stepped out of a mud bath, and everything devolves into chaos as my companions unfreeze all at once.

Stompy bellows and thrashes his horn. Limery yells, and ice sizzles and turns to steam as he goes molten. Taryn looks up from the snow, confused while Ruby rushes to him, licking his hand. Berry thrashes about, tossing Laojin from his back.

The druid chieftain lands with one knee pressed to the snow and extends his arm as a shield of ice materializes just as Berry swipes at him.

"Everyone, calm down!" I roar.

Taryn crawls to his feet. "What the hell is going on? Where are we?" He holds his staff ready to attack the two arctic trolls. "Who are they?"

"Later!" I shout. "Call off your pets. Limery, back to me."

Limery's flames fade and he lands on my shoulder. He stares at the two new trolls with uncertainty. Berry returns to Taryn's side, still snarling, and Stompy huffs in agitation.

Taryn stabs his staff into the snow. "Will someone tell me what the hell is going on here?" His gaze shifts between me and the other trolls. "Where are we? And who are they?"

Laojin smiles as he looks at Taryn. "It has been too long since I have met another druid. And a feisty one at that." He motions up the mountain. "Come, follow us to the village and all will be explained."

"Another druid?" Taryn's eyes light up as he analyzes Laojin. "You're a troll druid! I am so confused. The last thing I remember, we were being attacked in the blizzard."

Laojin nods toward the shaman. "You can thank Senzala for that. Her totem grants her the ability to cast the ring."

I stop in my tracks. "The entire ring? You have the power to cast a spell that strong constantly?"

Her level must be through the roof.

Senzala gives me a blank expression. "The closer I am to my totem, the more powerful my magic."

Just like Jira. His attacks were powerful in the forest, but when the phoenix was nearby, they took on another level.

I fall back in line and follow them up the mountain. "What's your totem?"

She smirks. "Nesira, the guardian of Frostmoor."

"Nesira." I stop in my tracks as the realization seeps in. "Do you mean Nessie? Your totem is a white dragon?"

"Nessie?" She laughs. "You've seen her around?"

"You could say that." My mind runs wild for a moment. With the arctic trolls having a dragon, Jira's phoenix, and the three wyrms the forest trolls have, troll society isn't looking as fragile as it once was.

But everything feels like it's resting on a razor's edge. The difference between a thriving kingdom and extinction rests on the fate of impending war.

It rests on my shoulders and the rest of the heroes.

Laojin leads us up the mountain, while Senzala brings up the rear. Taryn and I walk on foot with his pets following us.

Limery sits on my shoulder complaining. "Limmy was colds. So colds. Limmy never knows what the colds is like, but now he knows. No likey."

"Now you know what it's like for the rest of us," I tease. "We don't all have a furnace inside of us."

"Are you sure we can trust them?" Taryn leans in close and whispers. "They literally froze us."

"I don't think we have much of a choice. If Senzala really does control the entire ring, there's no telling how strong she is. She has the power of a white dragon behind her, and there's no way we're making it back down without them. Besides, if they wanted us dead, then we wouldn't be here right now. They want to help us, and where else are you going to get one-on-one training with a high-level druid?"

Taryn tilts his head forward, eyebrows raised. "Uh, seriously? How about Seascape?"

I cock an eyebrow. "If that were the case, then why did King Orso send us away to train? Why not train us at the castle?"

Taryn purses his lips. "Hmmm. Good point."

"I know it's a good point. It's because he wants allies more than just two strong heroes. This might be a way for us to get both."

"Yeah, yeah. I guess your instincts were right after all, but I wouldn't count your chickens just yet. Our track record has been pretty shitty for gathering allies."

He's right, but that doesn't mean we have to give up.

As we climb the mountain, I can't help but notice how quiet it is. We haven't seen any other trolls or animals since coming out of the ring. Are the arctic trolls barely holding on to life this far up?

I catch up to Laojin, who seems unconcerned with whether or not we can keep pace. Ahead of him, there are only two sets of tracks in the snow, both leading down, so they obviously don't come down this far very often, and they must have been confident enough that the two of them could take on whatever threat we presented.

Or they were the only two capable of fighting.

Laojin comes to a stop and raises his right arm for us to halt. "Welcome to Hornryx, home of the arctic trolls. While you are here, you will be treated as honored guests."

Taryn and I exchange glances. Has Laojin been living alone in the mountains for so long that he considers the wild terrain his village?

"Uh, it's beautiful..." Taryn lets the words trail off as he looks around.

And then I see it: a faint shimmer in the air. One that I've seen before.

"You have a protective barrier." Now that I've spotted it, I can see more ripples in the air. The same type of forcefield that kept strangers from approaching the forest troll village.

Laojin puffs out his chest. "Remnants of a different time, but you can never have too many defenses."

"What's he talking about?" Taryn scrunches his eyes in confusion.

Ruby passes through Taryn's legs, stepping through the barrier. For a second, her body is distorted, until it vanishes entirely.

CHAPTER 26
HORNRYX

"Ruby!" Taryn chases her through the barrier, the frozen clasps in his beard jingling like a cat with a bell around its neck.

I call for Taryn but it's too late. He's already stepped through.

Laojin makes a noise that's somewhere between a grunt and a deep chuckle. He steps through, and I follow him. On the other side, Taryn stands frozen, Ruby squirming in his grip.

My chest tightens for a moment before I realize Taryn isn't actually frozen. My jaw drops wide open as I take in the surroundings, just as awestruck as he is.

Before me, a frozen jungle spreads up the mountain, a fusion of plant and ice. There's more greenery here than I've seen in every other part of Frostmoor combined. Yet at the same time, there's so much ice that the entire place shimmers in the moonlight, like a garden carved from colored glass. Plants grow tall and vibrant even though many are encased in ice.

The sun has already set but I don't need my night vision to see. This high up above the clouds, the sky is filled with streaks of green and purple, reminiscent of the Northern Lights. This must be what it's like to live in Alaska during the summer when it never goes completely dark.

Trees and vines form the foundation of a handful of buildings, while thick, translucent ice blocks make up the walls—like a cross between an igloo and a treehouse. Vines cross over one another, forming windowpanes with ice so thin they appear as clear as glass. Frozen flowers cover many of the roofs, and some of the trees grow frozen fruit.

Pathways wind through the village. Vines run along the edge of the paths like a sidewalk, and the ground between is free from snow just like the enchanted paths from the portal. The land where the village is located is relatively flat and recesses back into a deep crag in the mountain. Each path leads to a different cave in its depths. Some are small, while others are tall enough to drive a semi through. To the left and right of the village, trails disappear higher up the mountain.

"You infused all of this?" I kneel and examine the vine-work of one of the structures.

Laojin nods. "The mountain provides all we need."

Through the window of the nearest building, salted meat rests on several racks. A large cauldron filled with some sort of stew bubbles over a low fire, reminding me of Kea's delicious stew in the forest. Steam rises out of a small chimney made of ice.

I'm impressed. This place is even more beautiful than the forest troll village.

As I continue to survey the area, I notice two guardian trolls standing sentry beyond the buildings where the paths lead to the caves. Their bodies are translucent from using Camouflage while not moving. Unlike the forest troll guardians, who normally crouch while on watch, these stand like soldiers, and each one holds a massive sword made from ice, each one taller than Taryn. Serrated edges cover one side and sharp ice the other. The sword tip sticks in the snow, and the trolls rest their hands at chest-height on the pommels. The guardians watch us with interest, but neither move. Aside from them, the village is eerily empty.

"Where is everyone?" I ask.

"It is late." Laojin glances at the moon. "I am sure you are tired. We will find you a place to sleep and introduce you to everyone in the morning. Then we will begin training."

"This place is crazy," whispers Taryn. "No offense, but it's way cooler than the forest."

As we approach the caves, the guardian trolls step back, canceling Camouflage and revealing their location to the non-trolls. Taryn jumps back, nearly falling into me.

"Tits on a pig!" He takes a fighting position, looking around for more trolls. "Where the hell did they come from?"

I laugh to myself before nudging him in the back. "Camouflage. It's a troll passive, remember?"

He stands up straight, relaxing his shoulders. "Right." He nods to the two guardian trolls as we pass, but they are stoic as ever in their new positions.

They must be incredibly disciplined, because it's unlikely they have ever seen a dwarf or forest troll, yet they show no reaction to our presence. The only explanation I can imagine is that they have absolute trust in Laojin and Senzala.

That's one thing I appreciate about trolls—not just here, but everywhere I've encountered them. When they believe in a leader, they will follow them to the ends of the earth.

Laojin pulls Taryn aside as we continue along the path. "Do you prefer your pets to stay with you or with the others?"

"Wait, you have pets?" Taryn looks at him incredulously.

"Am I not a druid? While I may have focused on the elemental path of druidism, we are all called by the wild. Come." He gestures for us to follow him.

He leads us to the first cave on the left, where a massive chasm disappears into the mountain, big enough for even Stompy to follow. A rumbling sound grows louder as we step inside, and Limery's claws dig into my cloak.

The cave is cast in a dull blue from mana-infused torches that burn along the walls. This sparks more questions, but for now, I'm interested in what Laojin is about to show us.

We follow the cave a short way before it opens into a wide cavern, tiered with natural formations and indentations along the floor and walls. Dozens of animals are scattered about, all sleeping. Snores rumble like a gentle thunder. A gargantuan mammoth rests against the far wall, its belly heaving with each bellowing snore erupting from its snout like a trumpet.

"Bro." Taryn elbows me in the side. "They have a freaking mammoth."

"Don't get any wild ideas." I grab him by the shoulder and force him to look elsewhere.

In the far back, several white bears lay huddled together. There are wolves, foxes, and a few snowy owls perched near the ceiling.

Little white creatures hanging from the ceiling catch my eye.

Frost Bats. *Level 18. These small, winged creatures are prized for their ability to scout without light. Native to Frostmoor, in the past, many were trained as guides to adventurers exploring the shadow lands. Their blood is a key ingredient in advanced Intelligence and Wisdom potions.*

"This is amazing," Taryn whispers. "How do you control them all?"

Laojin lifts his arm, and one of the owls flies down from its perch. "They are not all pets. I have bonded with many, but others have arrived of their own accord. This is a sanctuary of sorts."

Taryn's eyes widen. "Wait, you can do that?"

"You have only touched on what druids are capable of. Here, raise your arm." Laojin nudges the owl to hop over.

Berry grunts and moves in closer, prodding Taryn in the leg with his snout.

Taryn leans into Berry. "Oh hush, you'll always be my first."

The owl twists its head backward, watching Taryn with golden eyes. The owl is pristine white except for speckles of black along its legs and wings.

Limery's body grows warm against my shoulder and he smacks his lips.

"Don't even think about it," I order before he gets any wild ideas.

Taryn gently strokes the owl. "So, where's Nessie?"

"Nesira is not a pet!" Senzala snaps. "She is my totem, and she possesses powers you could only dream of."

"Sorry." Taryn raises his free hand in apology. "I didn't mean any offense. Nessie—I mean, Nesira—is an amazing creature. Beautiful, powerful. She has my respect."

The scowl fades from Senzala's face. "Nesira goes where she pleases. As my totem, I borrow from her power, but I have no influence over her."

Laojin extends his arm, and the owl jumps back onto his forearm. "I'm sure you are aware that there is a limit to the creatures we can tame. Unique monsters can only be bonded with under special circumstances, they cannot be tamed as pets."

Taryn instructs his pets to stay in the cave for the night. Berry is reluctant, but eventually curls up against the wall with Ruby. Stompy leaves them to go deeper into the cave, where he sits beside the mammoth.

Taryn shrugs. "He has a mind of his own."

After leaving the pet cave, we go deeper into the gorge to a cave in the far back. Two more guardian trolls wait outside the entry.

With only four guardian trolls watching over the village while the others sleep, either they are very confident in their protections, or their society is on the brink of collapse, perhaps even worse than the mountain trolls.

Compared to the human and dwarven cities on Isle of Mythos, the entirety of troll society barely rivals a town. I don't know why I expected one of the harshest climates to be any different.

Briefly, the lone desert troll we came across outside of Sandholde crosses my mind. How many of them are left? Or was it a lone survivor?

Laojin leads us past the guardian trolls, and Taryn remains oblivious to their presence. This cave is more narrow, but it has the same mana-infused torches along the wall.

At the end of the long tunnel, the cave opens into a cavern once again. It looks like the cavern is covered in shag carpet before I realize that the white carpet is hundreds of arctic trolls sleeping together. Since camouflage only works when a troll is awake and purposefully standing still, their bodies are all visible. There must be three or four hundred trolls scattered about.

I stand there for a moment, taking it all in. Maybe I was wrong. Maybe the best thing for trolls is for them to hide away and rebuild their numbers. Whatever the arctic trolls have been doing seems to be working.

"That's a lot of trolls," Taryn whispers. "This is like a bear cave."

Laojin steps between us. "We still keep to the old ways. Every night, we all gather in the cave to sleep."

"Maybe you're used to sleeping in castles where you're from —" Senzala walks past, kneeling between two large trolls. "—but in Hornryx, everything we do is for the tribe, for its safety."

Laojin gestures toward the mess of trolls before us. "Go ahead, make yourself comfortable."

Taryn takes a deep breath and navigates his way through, careful not to step on any outstretched arms. "I just hope they don't stink."

I follow him, and we find an open spot in the back against the wall. At least this way, we're only surrounded on three sides.

I take off the fur cloak and use it as a pillow. With so many trolls, their body heat keeps the cave warm enough that I don't need the furs. I lean against the wall, and Limery takes his usual spot in the crook of my arm.

As I lay there counting the white-furred trolls like sheep, I eventually drift off to sleep.

CHAPTER 27

KNOWLEDGE IS POWER

I WAKE up surrounded by trolls. They hover around us, a wall of white with icy blue eyes that watch us with curiosity. A young troll, no more than two feet tall, grabs my toe with its small fingers.

"Hey, there." I raise my hand slightly to wave.

The small troll jumps and hides behind the leg of an adult female.

"Hellos." Limery waves at the young troll and grins.

The young troll peeks her head between the adult's legs and gurgles, not the least bit terrified of the imp's demonic smile.

Another young troll, this one slightly taller than Taryn, tugs on the adult's fur from behind. "Are you sure he's not a mountain troll? Grago said forest trolls were green." The voice is surprisingly childlike.

"He's a special troll." Taryn sits up, rubbing the sleep from his eyes, and they all gasp. "One of a kind."

"Doesn't look special to me." A tall, broad-shouldered, level-twenty-five troll with a deep voice crosses his arms. "What's he doing here anyhow?"

A female troll answers, "Chief Laojin and Shaman Senzala brought them here. Says they are heroes."

They continue their conversation like we're not even present.

"Very strange." The tall one scowls at us.

"I agree. In all my years, they have never brought an outsider to the village. Something is up."

"And what about the two little ones? Are we supposed to eat them?"

"Whoa, whoa, whoa." Taryn backs against the wall, extending his arms. "Nobody is eating anybody. We're here to train."

The large troll scratches his chin. "Hmm. Never had dwarf before. Or imp."

I rise to my feet. All the trolls take a step back except for the big guy. He's several inches taller than me, but I look him straight in the eyes.

"They're not food. They're my companions."

He frowns. "If you say so."

"Rhaz, that's enough." Laojin makes his way through the group, and they all step out of his path. "How many times must I explain we don't eat the other races?"

"But you said—"

"What I said was that many races fear us because they believe we will eat them. We're nothing more than monsters to them."

Rhaz stomps his foot. "But they don't even know we exist. How do they fear us?"

I answer. "People fear what they don't know. But they are learning."

Laojin rests a hand on Rhaz's shoulder. "That's enough questions for now. You all have work to do, and I would like to speak to Chod and his companions with the council."

The trolls disperse. A few of the young ones crane their necks in our direction as they walk away.

I wave at the young girl who pulled my toe, and she waves back. "There are so many of you. How?"

"So many?" Laojin snarls. "How far have we fallen that filling a cave with our people is seen as some great accomplishment? There was a time when trolls roamed all of Frostmoor. A time when we may not have been respected, but we were feared. That fear still runs deep, even if we are nothing more than legends."

I understand his frustration. I've felt it myself during my time in Mythos. It's not easy being a troll. "The world is changing. There is a place for trolls once more."

He shakes his head. "Maybe for a hero. But I will not risk the fate of my people because there is something out there more scary than a troll. Now come."

Taryn leans in close. "Who peed in his cereal this morning?"

I narrow my eyes at Taryn. The last thing we need is to piss off the chief.

We follow Laojin out of the cave. In the daylight, the village is even more resplendent. The ice-covered buildings and trees sparkle in the morning sunlight.

Trolls are on the move all about, some heading out toward the buildings, others disappearing into various caves, a few carrying weapons. Laojin leads us into a smaller cave without speaking.

After a short walk, it empties into an oval room with a rectangular stone table in the center. Four trolls sit at the table in stone chairs, a male and female on each of the longer sides. One of the males is overweight, with a potbelly. If not for his broad shoulders and chest, he could pass for a pregnant female. The other male is the prototypical arctic troll, muscled underneath a mound of fur. One of the females is much older, at least according to her withered face and saggy bosom, but that is all that gives away her age. The second female has longer fur and hair than any of the other trolls, nearly concealing her charcoal features. They all have shorter tusks than any of the other troll races.

A throne-like chair sits at the far end and there's an empty seat closest to us.

Laojin sits at the head of the table. A moment later, Senzala arrives and takes the final seat, leaving Taryn and me standing.

The chief clears his throat. "In all the years since the ring of Hornryx was forged, our council has gathered in this cave to discuss the fate of our tribe. We make the difficult decisions that keep our tribe safe. I have already informed them of your position, that you would have us risk our lives to join our brothers and sisters in battle. That will not be happening." He pauses, locking eyes with me.

I clench my fist, not allowing my face to show the disappointment washing over me.

Laojin continues, "However, we respect the path of the hero. A path often imperiled with difficult choices. It is no coincidence that you have found your way to Hornryx just as you have the other tribes. We do not fault you for fighting against darkness. As a hero, we recognize your duty is greater than one tribe. You fight for all trolls. While stories of troll heroes are rare, there have been a few in our history. You may check our library if you are inclined to learn of their deeds. But for now, we are here to discuss what we can offer you."

Typical speech, and nothing I haven't heard before. At this rate, I'd be more surprised if someone actually decided to join us. Whether trolls, humans, or beastkin, it's always the same. Everyone feels betrayed and let down by the other kingdoms. They have all suffered in the past and are reluctant to risk their people for a cause when those old wounds still sting.

But the fact that my own people turned me down is somehow

more disappointing. Still, I can't say that I don't understand it. We'll take what help we can get, and then we'll travel to the next village.

I meet the chief's eyes. "And what is it you can offer?"

He shrugs. "You tell us. If you have questions, we will answer what we can. Our library is yours while you are here. We are strong believers that what you know is as important as what you can lift. Our dungeon is yours to train in. Show us your weapons and abilities and we will share what knowledge we have of them."

Taryn raises his hand before speaking. "Hold up, you have a dungeon? And a library? None of the other tribes have libraries. And what's the deal with the frozen plants? And what can you teach me about being a druid?"

"Easy there." Laojin laughs. "One question at a time. Tzane maintains our dungeon. He can enlighten you."

The pot-bellied troll huffs before speaking. "We have one of three known dungeons on Frostmoor. Hornryx Dungeon provides us with enough food to feed the village and keeps our bodies strong. It is an ancient dungeon, so while it does not provide loot, it is rich in mana and provides a steady supply of spawn."

Interesting...so it's like a hack-and-slash dungeon. Now, that sounds like fun.

"And the library?" I ask. "Why do none of the other tribes have them?"

Laojin gestures to the older female troll. "Oyana."

She taps her clawed, black fingers against the table. "It doesn't surprise me that none of the other tribes have chosen to preserve our histories. The forest trolls were always too proud for such things, thinking their kingdom would live on the lips of men forever. The mountain trolls were too brutish, caring for strength above all else. And the seaside trolls, I always feared that a stiff breeze could blow them across the ocean. Here in Hornryx, we value knowledge. Knowledge is in itself a power. I am saddened that we have not added to our collection since removing ourselves from the world, though your news from abroad will be added soon."

"What about the desert trolls?" I interrupt. "You didn't mention them."

"Theirs is a sad story for another time. You may find it in the library if you wish, but it will not help you on your journey. To answer your question, why do we have a library when the others do not, we must go back many ages. Before the fight with the dark wizard and the closing of the portals, before our retreat into the mountain and the forging of the ring, we had a chief by the name of Titamora. She was a sorcerer troll, the only one known to have ever existed, and she prized knowledge for the powers it could grant her. Heroes roamed Mythos during this time, and her power rivaled the strongest among them. She traveled far and wide, gathering tomes from different kingdoms and creating a vast library for us to use."

Limery leans forward on my shoulder, enraptured by the story. "What happeneds to hers?"

"She perished. It turns out there is some knowledge too great for even a sorceress."

That sounds like a fascinating tale for another time. For now, we need to take advantage of the situation we find ourselves in.

"How can you help us get stronger?" I get right to the point. Libraries and frozen villages are nice, but we need to get stronger. No matter how many kingdoms we gather, the heroes will be the ones on the front lines. We can make the biggest impact. At level thirty, I hope to unlock the Warforged class. And right now, I have the option to further advance my summoner or barbarian class.

"That depends on what you are after." Laojin taps his claws against the stone table. "If you only want to grow stronger, the dungeon will provide. If you are looking to make the most of your class and abilities, then that will require a more specialized approach."

I pull up the notification that I received for class advancement after hitting level twenty-five.

Class Advancements. Upon reaching level twenty-five, you have unlocked a class advancement. You may only advance one class at a time. A second class may not be advanced until completion of primary advancement.

Barbarian Advancement.

Spirit of the Beast. Unlock for further details.

Summoner Advancement.

Dreadbeasts. Unlock for further details.
Dual Subclass. Unlock for further details.

I've been letting it marinate in the back of my mind for days, but I still have no clue which one to choose. I'll take all the advice I can get on my class options.

"What do you know about class advancements and multiple classes?" I ask.

The group exchanges a look before Oyana speaks. "Class advancements are common once someone with a class reaches a certain threshold. It seems heroes are always blessed with a magical class. For the rest of us, it comes down to the will of the gods. Laojin and Senzala are the only ones with magical classes within our tribe. Having multiple classes is known to have happened occasionally among heroes, but it is very rare among the rest of us. Many who are blessed with a class never reach the level of advancement. Why do you ask?"

"I was granted a second class after the mana explosion, but now I am being offered the choice of three class advancements."

Taryn eagerly steps in front of me. "And I'm only two levels away from my own class advancement."

"Wait your turn." I playfully shove him out of the way. "I was hoping you could give me some insight on what to pick."

"You two are heroes from different cultures, yet you bicker like brothers," Laojin laughs. "There is no need to worry. While it is our duty to help a hero of the trolls, I have taken a special interest in you, young druid."

Taryn blushes before stepping back beside me. "Thank you."

"What abouts Limmy?" The imp bats his eyelashes.

"It seems these two would not be where they are without your help. We will do what we can for you as well." Laojin winks. "But perhaps we should nourish our bodies before we begin planning your futures."

Limery offers him a grotesque grin in appreciation.

After checking on Taryn's pets, we follow the council to the buildings out front. The door is open to one of the buildings, where an elderly male troll stirs the massive pot of stew. I make a comment about how Kea has a similar pot boiling in the forest troll village.

Tzane rubs his potbelly like a pregnant woman. "I am glad to hear the forest trolls have kept something of the past."

"I'm not sure what stories you have heard, but the forest village is not that different from your own." I take the bowl of stew that is offered to me and say my thanks.

He frowns. "Maybe so. Too much time has passed since the

troll tribes last gathered. I doubt any living troll was alive at the last grand council."

We all take a seat at an overlook near the entrance to the village. From this high up, we can see over the clouds, over the ring around Hornryx, and even the peaks of some of the other mountains. It's like we're looking out from a plane window.

The stew is meaty and delicious. There's a gaminess to it I haven't tasted before, probably from some animal they hunted in the dungeon. It has less spice than the food from Whitgard, but there's something about it that nourishes me on a deeper level.

Taryn bites into a bright-red fruit that he plucked from one of the ice-covered trees. "Oh god, this is so good. It's like biting into a slushy."

Laojin smiles. "The fruits are a favorite among the young. They are not so appetizing once our tastes shift."

"More for me," Taryn mumbles between bites.

Limery slurps down his stew between us.

"Can I ask you something?" I say to none of the council in particular.

Oyana answers. "You have a thirst for knowledge rare among your people. Go ahead."

"Why are there arctic trolls in Frostmoor and not on Isle of Mythos?"

Oyanna looks around at our surroundings, as if taking it all in for the first time. "The answer to that lies in our first story, the origin story of all trolls."

Two female trolls lead a group of young ones from the caves to the stew building, but Oyanna waves them over.

"Have a seat." She gestures. "It is important that the young ones remember where we come from."

One of the young trolls crosses her arms. "But Gran, we've heard this story a hundred times. I'm hungry."

"Our people's history is food for the soul." Loajin's voice booms as he displays his authority. "And you will hear it a hundred more times if it pleases your gran."

The young troll takes a seat quietly, pouting.

Oyanna clears her throat. "In the beginning, when all of Mythos was still one land, the mother of Mythos birthed five troll sisters from the earth. With gray skin and short tusks, they were sent out into the world as a blank canvas. The first of the sisters was playful and quiet, so she made her home by the sea. As time passed, her skin began to mirror the ocean she loved, and her hands and feet formed webs so that she could be as nimble in the sea as on land. The second sister took to the mountains, for she loved the thrill of the climb. Her skin took on the purple hue of the mountains at dusk, and muscles formed from her hearty adventures. The third sister was bold and reckless, and she set out to travel far away to the volcanoes on the coast to view their power and destruction. The mother warned her of the dangers, and that if she crossed the desert she would never return."

Several of the young trolls gasp at the revelations, and I find myself equally enthralled by the origin of my people.

"But the third sister wouldn't listen. The journey was long and perilous, and after days of travel, she thought she would die to the sands. However, the mother was not without mercy, so she granted the sister salvation in the form of an oasis. The sister made her home in graceful defeat, and her body adapted to the harshness of the sand.

Oyanna locks eyes with me. "The fourth sister traveled to the forest, for she loved the frenzy of the hunt. Under the trees, she grew fast and wild, a deadly blend of speed and strength, and soon all of the forest bowed before her. The fifth sister watched as the others traveled and waited for their return, but they never did. She waited until her heart grew cold. Her cold spirit spread like wildfire until the ground was frosted and mountains rose from the earth, fracturing a piece of Mythos into the sea. As her sisters floated away, she climbed the mountain. The world around her grew colder, and fur erupted along her body as she climbed higher and higher to catch a glimpse of the others as they drifted across the sea." She offers me a sad smile. "And that is why there are no arctic trolls on the Isle of Mythos. Now, go on, children. Have your stew."

"And fruits," her grandtroll says excitedly.

A genuine smile returns as Oyanna turns to the young trolls. "Yes, and your fruits."

Listening to Dando describe the history of the Frozen Ash Tribe, and now this. I'm once again amazed by the depth of this world. Every race, every kingdom, every person has their own history. And now I am a part of it.

I tilt the bowl, finishing the last of my stew. "That was quite the story. It's the first time I've heard it."

She slurps at her own stew now that the story is over. "I'm not surprised. The forest trolls lost a great deal when their kingdom fell. I can only wonder what we could have achieved with our tribes together."

"You can still find out. The mountain troll tribe has already relocated to the forest."

"Enough of that." Laojin's voice is stern but not angry. "Our decision is final on the matter."

I can make another push before we leave, but for now, we need to make the most of our time here. If I anger them, they could cancel all of this and send us packing.

I nod. "Understood."

The chief stands. "Good. Now, if you would like to follow me, your training can begin."

CHAPTER 28
CHOOSE YOUR OWN ADVENTURE

A Horror of Vitality sits in the center of the library, a furry finger stuck up its nose. Chief Laojin, Senzala, Tzane, and Oyanna watch it with great interest, poking and prodding it and observing it from every angle.

After lunch, the other two council members had matters to attend to while the rest of us go to the library. Taryn and I have been describing our abilities to the council so that they can help us decide where to go from here.

For a troll village high in the mountains, the library looks like it belongs in a castle. There are hundreds of leather-bound books, rolled parchments, and scrolls stacked from floor to ceiling. The shelves are carved into the walls and the cave stretches deep into the mountain. Cobwebs coat many of the nooks and crannies. Some of the books are so old that the leather binding is barely holding the pages together.

Blue mana flames light the room in an ethereal glow. Half a dozen intricately-carved chairs are spread around the cave, and several stone tables with matching stools are scattered throughout. Ladders are propped against the wall for reaching items on the higher shelves. Limery perches on the top rung of one of the ladders.

Laojin taps on one of the horror's horns with his claw. "You are a special troll, indeed. With enough of these, you're practically a tribe all by yourself."

"Maybe, if they didn't puff out of existence whenever I'm not in combat." I summon a Horror of Power and it prowls around the library like a lion. "They get stronger as I do, but they don't last nearly long enough in an extended fight."

"Then you need to be stronger," he says matter-of-factly.

Senzala scratches the Horror of Power behind the ear and its leg twitches in pleasure. She offers it a rare smile.

"Don't get too attached. It'll be gone in ten minutes," I chuckle.

She gives the horror another scratch and then takes a seat in one of the leather chairs. "So tell us, what are your options for class advancements?"

I pull up the notifications again. "I have one path for my barbarian class and two for my summoner class. Is it strange that I only get one for barbarian?"

Laojin answers, "It depends on the advancement. No two classes are guaranteed the same advancement path. Some are offered multiple path options because each path is rigid. Others are offered a single path capable of multiple branches. What is your barbarian path?"

"It is called Spirit of the Beast."

The other council members nod approvingly.

The chief grins. "And the two summoner paths?"

"One is called Dreadbeasts, and the other is Dual Subclass."

Oyanna disappears deeper into the cave. A minute later, she comes back with a thick book and places it on the table. The cover is a deep black with a golden inlay of runes and geometric shapes.

She blows the cover and a thick layer of dust puffs into the air. "This may be of use."

Taryn stands on his tiptoes to try and get a view. I can't read the words as Oyanna flips through the book, but there are plenty of pictures. I spot images of imps and goblins, and many creatures I've never seen or heard of. Finally, she comes to a stop.

A grotesque monster snarls out from the page. Even on paper, the creature looks dangerous with its powerful muscles, barb-covered joints, and jagged teeth. She flips the page to a second monster, this one with barbed ram horns. It has thick hooves on all four legs and tusks that jut upward from the lower jaw.

"Look familiar?" she asks, flipping to the next page.

This one is tall and slender, with sharp claws and pointy ears. It walks on two feet and a shadow trails behind it.

"Are these horrors?" I lean in closer, examining the details of each image.

"They are similar. These are dreadbeasts. They come from the same plane of existence as your horrors, but where your horrors might be the cub, these are the mother bears."

I gulp at the thought. My horrors are scary, but these are the creatures of nightmares. No one would ever come near me with an army of dreadbeasts.

"So you're telling me that if I choose the dreadbeast path, I can summon them? Will I still be able to summon my current horrors?"

She shrugs. "I can't answer that for you. This is one of our oldest tomes. Even before the fall, summoners of horrors and dreadbeasts were a rarity. I'm sure you can imagine why. If I had to guess, judging by their appearance and since it is an advancement, choosing this path would improve your current horrors by turning them into dreadbeasts." She closes the book. "I'm sorry I don't have more info, but I can tell you how the Dual Subclass works."

"I think I have a pretty good idea on that one, but go ahead."

She nods. "It's pretty simple. Many classes have it as an advancement option, allowing for a wider array of spells and abilities. For summoning, whatever option you had when you picked your class, you will be able to choose a second. What are your options?"

I pull up my notifications from when I first unlocked the summoner class.

Class:

Summoner. *Magic users capable of summoning magical beings to fight on their behalf.*

Subclass:

Elemental. *Summon golems created from the elements.*

Brood. *Summon insects that evolve.*

Horror. *Summon monstrous creatures. Requires 20+ Strength and Constitution.*

Techno. *Summon robotic beings. Requires 20+ Intelligence.*

Undead. *Summon undead creatures from nearby bones.*

Champion. *Summon one powerful creature at a time.*

I tell her each of the classes that were available to me, and then add, "I have something similar to Champion already, but it only allows me to summon a copy of the most recent monster I killed. I imagine the Champion subclass works differently?"

"That is correct. Champion summoners were well-known among the elite in ancient times. Upon killing a beast, a champion summoner could choose to have it as a member of their stable, calling it to battle whenever they wished. A champion summoner could claim three champions at a time. This led to grand adventures with massive parties designed to procure the strongest champions for the kingdom. One of the Pruxford gnomes was said to have claimed three dragons as champions. But those days are long gone." She watches my horrors as they puff out of existence. "You made the right choice. While the other classes are worthy for certain races, the horror class is especially suited for trolls. If only more of us were blessed with mana in our bodies." She sighs. "Nonetheless, if you choose to embark further down the summoner path, I would advise you to stick to what you know."

"That makes sense. I'd like to hear about the Spirit of the Beast path. My summoner abilities have made up for our lack of allies, but it has always been my barbarian abilities that have proved the difference. So, if this is a barbarian path, it should be well suited for trolls, right?"

She smiles, looking at the other members of the council. "He is smart for a forest troll."

At least she has a sense of humor for an old bag of bones.

Taryn snickers behind me, but I pay him no mind.

Laojin rests a heavy hand on my shoulder. "You are in luck. As it happens, my predecessor walked the Spirit of the Beast path. He was a true barbarian, meaning he could go into a rage at will, not under intense situations like the rest of us."

My hands practically tingle with excitement. "What can you tell me?"

He gestures for me to take a seat at the table. "The Spirit of the Beast advancement is rooted in nature, just like trolls themselves.

It's not that different from the shaman and druid classes. This path blends nature with magic."

I tap my foot as I wait for him to get to the point. Just tell me what awesome abilities it unlocks, already.

"Embarking down this path will change your body—" He looks at my blue skin. "—but that is nothing new for you. There are five stages to the Spirit of the Beast path. First is the Spirit Inquiry. To achieve this you must locate your spirit animal."

I furrow my brow. "Uh, how do I do that?"

"That is for you to discover. A spirit animal is similar to a totem, but vastly different. While a totem is a singular creature that grants power to the shaman, a spirit animal is not one particular animal. It is an animal that resonates with you, that feeds your spirit. My predecessor went on a pilgrimage for weeks to discover his spirit beast."

I clench my fist, wishing I had something to smash. "There's a war coming. I don't have time to get lost in the woods."

"You put too much pressure on yourself." He sighs. "The war is unlikely to start tomorrow. But even if it did, you are not the only one who will be fighting. You are a piece of the greater puzzle. Not everything will always line up as you wish, but if this is the path you choose to take, then you must embrace it."

I take a deep breath to calm my raging hands. "I know you're right, but there are a lot of people counting on me."

He rests his massive hand on top of my own. "That is the burden of the hero. But it is still your choice. Nothing comes easy."

I nod. "What else can you tell me about this path?"

"Once you locate your spirit beast, it will influence what comes next, but the path remains the same regardless of the beast. After Spirit Inquiry comes Spirit Embodiment. You will need to find an amulet that connects you to your beast. Once you have done so, a change will happen in your body that connects you to your spirit beast. Then comes Spirit Enhancement, where you will gain a passive ability based on the animal. Fourth is the Spirit Guide, where you will be able to summon a spirit version of the animal for guidance. Lastly is the Spirit Power. Here, you will gain a powerful active ability from your spirit beast."

So essentially, I'll gain three new abilities, the same as the dreadbeast path. While it would be useful to have some abilities that weren't directly related to smashing shit, there's no way to tell what those abilities might be, especially since I don't know my spirit beast.

I close my eyes and massage my temples, hoping the answer might present itself, but I'm still not sure which to pick. Stronger horrors would be nice, but they already grow stronger with each level I gain. Even though Oyanna advised against it, having a second summoner class could be beneficial, but considering how low my Intelligence and Wisdom are compared to the rest of my stats, would they be anything better than cannon fodder?

I open my eyes to find Laojin watching me with amusement. "Your predecessor, what was his spirit animal?"

Laojin grins. "Erato was a fierce warrior from a young age, but to find his spirit beast, he had to learn patience. For the first two weeks of his pilgrimage, he searched high and low for a spirit to connect to. It wasn't until he gave up searching that the spirit came to him. After three days of waiting in the snow at the peak of Mount Hornryx, a lone frost wolf sat down in front of him."

Taryn's eyes light up at the mention of the wolf. "Dude, we could be beast brothers."

I roll my eyes. Taryn's enthusiasm is a major knock on the Spirit of the Beast path. I don't think I can handle any more animal puns than we already have.

I ignore the comment, returning my attention to Laojin. "What abilities did he gain?"

"Once he found his amulet, his fur took on a blueish-white color, matching the frost wolves. For his passive ability, his senses were heightened and he could move twice as fast while tracking the scent of an enemy. His active ability was a howl that confused enemies and rallied allies. They were all fitting attributes for a leader of the tribe."

"I'm going to need time to think," I confess. This is a big decision, and with how slow levels are coming now, who knows when or if I'll be able to do another advancement.

He nods. "I've often found that a walk through the snow does wonders for the mind. Go, clear your head. I have much to discuss with the dwarf."

CHAPTER 29
BIRD PEOPLE

TARYN LICKED his lips at the prospect of actual alone time with the chief. Well, the chief and three-fifths of the council.

Druids were not common in Seascape. Most dwarves blessed with a class were either clerics, paladins, or warriors. Mages were rare, druids rarer. And now not only did he have a powerful druid to learn from, but also a library that spanned ages. Not just the history of trolls, but the history of Mythos. Taryn had a million questions.

"What kind of class advancement do you think I'm going to get? What's yours? What abilities do you have? I saw the ice shield thing, but what else can you do? Can you transform into an animal? Which one? Did you use your druid abilities to make the ice plants? Can I do that? What about—"

"Easy there," Laojin laughed. "Slow down and take a breath. I can only answer one question at a time."

Taryn bowed his head. "Sorry. I know I still need two levels, but I can't wait to see what happens."

"Do not worry. I have a plan for you, but first we must wait for Chod to make a decision."

"You have a plan for me?" Taryn blushed. He'd known the chief was planning to help him, but he'd assumed Chod was the featured artist on this track.

"You are a special dwarf to have allied yourself with a troll. Most dwarves care only for the material things of the world. I sense that you give much of yourself to those you care for."

Taryn found himself at a loss for words. Were the NPCs of this world that perceptive or was the AI feeding the chief these lines based on what it knew of Taryn? He very rarely put himself first, in life or in this game. That was just how he was built, a natural caretaker. A pillar of support. He'd taken on one responsibility after another since he was a child. Whether it was watching his siblings while his parents worked or picking up a part-time job to help his mom and dad make ends meet so that he and his sisters could have a quality education, he did what needed to be done. Even with Chod, while they had a ton of fun together, it was always Taryn helping to put things in perspective for his best friend. If there had not been pay involved, Taryn wasn't sure he would have taken the time off from school to play this game. There's no way he would have put the added stress on his family.

He put a lot of himself out there, but it was also what kept him fulfilled. That was just how it was.

"You're right. I do."

Laojin's icy blue eyes bored into Taryn. "That is the nature of the druid, to nurture and protect, but that doesn't mean always putting yourself second. Making yourself a priority at times allows you to better support those that you care for."

Once again, Taryn was speechless. He felt more like he was in a therapist's office than a troll library.

He scratched his chin. "How do you do that?"

The chief grinned. "Follow me." He turned to the other council members. "If Chod returns before we do, entertain him with a story."

Taryn waddled behind the chief, his short legs practically jogging to keep up with Laojin's long strides. They left the library cave and entered a smaller tunnel barely wide enough to fit the massive troll.

After walking a long way down the narrow hall lit by mana torches, they came upon a spiral staircase carved into the mountain. Chief Laojin took the stairs up three at a time while Taryn's heart raced as he hurried behind. Riding his pets everywhere had been terrible for his cardio. His breathing was so ragged he couldn't even manage to ask where they were going.

They climbed for what felt like an hour before the chief stopped. If not for his discomfort, Taryn might have been amazed that a stairwell was buried this deep in the mountain. Architecturally, it was something even the dwarves of Seascape could respect. Instead, he grimaced as he sucked in air.

"How...much...further?" he asked between breaths.

With the way the staircase spiraled, it was impossible to tell how far they'd come or how much further they still had to go. He didn't even want to think about the climb back down.

If this was Laojin's idea of taking care of himself, Taryn wanted no part. A strong ale in a crowded tavern suited the dwarf just fine.

The chief reached back and patted him on the shoulder. "The journey will be worth it. Not much further now."

Sure enough, after about a dozen more stairs, bright light flooded the stairwell. The stairs emptied into a long hallway where white light spilled through an open doorway.

Taryn squinted as a cold wind blew past him, jingling the clasps in his beard. Once he stepped through the doorway, his eyes adjusted to the brightness, revealing a stone platform that extended from the side of the mountain. There were no walls or railings, just a flat platform floating in the air.

Cold wind whistled around them. Chief Laojin walked to the edge and Taryn joined him. As he looked down, the summit of the other mountains seemed small, barely peeking above the clouds.

The view was beautiful, but Taryn was more confused than ever. Was this where the chief came for alone time? To meditate? It was peaceful, but how was this making anyone a priority?

The chief sat, letting his legs dangle from the edge. He patted on the ground next to him for Taryn to join.

Taryn scooted toward the edge, keenly aware of how high they were. This would be a hell of a fall.

"Who made this?" asked Taryn.

As far as he could tell, the trolls weren't well known for their craftsmanship and this stairwell had to have taken a lot of time to carve into the stone.

"My ancestors, long before I was born. They used to force their prisoners to make the climb and then toss them from the ledge." Chief Laojin leaned forward, looking into the depths below.

Taryn instinctively scooted back. Had Chief Laojin brought him all the way up here just to toss him off the edge? Maybe he'd misread the whole situation. Clearly, the arctic trolls had no love for the outside world. If the chief killed him, there was no way he was making it back past the ring without them knowing. Senzala had been able to sense their presence the first time. His pets and Limery would be at the arctic trolls' mercy. Chod would do his best, but what could he do against an entire village?

Laojin stood, and Taryn's heart threatened to burst from his chest. If Senzala was capable of forming the ring, there was no telling how powerful the chief was. What could Taryn do against that kind of power?

"I use it for a different purpose now."

Taryn let out a sigh of relief just before the chief grabbed him by the cloak and tossed him from the ledge. He flew high into the air like he had been launched from a cannon. There was a moment of panic before he remembered his bird form.

He could fly down and find Chod before the chief could descend the stairs. But first, he would need to sell the fall.

As gravity took hold of Taryn, Chief Laojin exploded into feathers, his troll form replaced by a silver falcon that quickly dove past him.

No fucking way. He's a bird guy, too!

Taryn laughed as he used his own ability, transforming into a small white bird.

Chief Laojin dove through the air, and if not for Taryn's heightened eyesight, he might not have seen the bird of prey barreling toward the clouds below.

He dove after the chief.

Tucking his wings, Taryn darted toward the clouds. He'd never been interested in sky-diving, but if the rush felt like this, he'd leap out of a plane the first chance he had. This was the fastest he had ever flown, and he still wasn't catching the chief.

The silver falcon dove like a missile. He spiraled, doing barrel-rolls with unimaginable grace for something so fast.

Just when Taryn was certain the chief would leave him in the dust, the falcon's wings extended and he soared up, doing a massive loop that brought him closer to Taryn.

Taryn flapped his own wings, and the two slowed until they were floating on an air current. Laojin's falcon form was beautiful. His silver feathers were tipped with navy, and black slits cut through the icy blue eyes. The falcon outsized

Taryn's bird form by nearly the same ratio as the troll did the dwarf.

The falcon unleashed a piercing screech and dove once more. Taryn followed. Laojin was clearly holding back, occasionally extending his wings to slow his acceleration.

This was a hell of a way to unwind.

They barreled through a layer of clouds and all of Frostmoor became visible once again. The ring circled Hornryx, hiding the majestic village above its cloudy depths.

Laojin shifted course, flying back to the mountain and perching on the limb of a snow-covered pine. He hopped to a few lower branches before landing in the snow and returning to his troll form.

Taryn changed forms as well, electing to remain on the tree branch. It sagged with his new weight and snow plopped against Laojin's shoulder.

He expected a reprimand, but the chief gave him a mischievous smile. "What did you think?"

"That was amazing." Taryn beamed with delight. "I don't know if I've ever felt so free."

The chief wiped the snow from his fur. "Protecting a village is a great responsibility. The council is invaluable, and they each have their own responsibilities, but there is still enough trouble to drive one mad. This is how I take care of myself and clear my mind. Plummeting through the clouds has a way of putting things in perspective."

"I bet." Taryn narrowed his eyes. "But did you really have to throw me off the mountain?"

Laojin's laughter echoed off the mountain. "Your face was priceless. I will carry it with me for all my days."

Taryn joined in. He had always found it amusing when something so big and scary showed its playful side. Like watching lions play like kittens, or Berry's obsessive need for attention. The trolls had their quirks, but underneath it all, they weren't that different from the other races.

"So, what now?" he asked.

"The flight up will not be as quick with those tiny wings of yours."

CHAPTER 30
SPIRIT INQUIRY

COLD WIND ASSAULTS MY FACE, and I pull my cloak tighter. I've narrowed my decision down from three to two, but I still have no clue what class advancement to pick.

With the dreadbeasts, I know what I'm getting, and I already have experience with summoning horrors. It seems like the smart choice.

Spirit of the Beast is more like a lotto ticket. It could pay off big time with the right abilities, but if I end up with a snow bunny as my spirit animal, I could be screwing all of us over.

Still, something about it calls to me. I lucked into being a summoner when I fell into the ley line. My horrors have saved my ass more times than I can count, but I came into this world as a barbarian. The Spirit of the Beast path has a place among the history of trolls. It feels fitting. Natural.

As far as I know, I'm the first troll summoner to ever exist. But does that mean I shouldn't pursue summoning to its highest power?

I sigh as I kick the trunk of a pine tree. Its branches whisper as snow collapses on my head.

I could walk this entire mountain and I'd have no better understanding of what I should choose. Closing my eyes, I kneel and rest my back against the trunk.

Maybe I'm making all of this unnecessarily complicated. I'm not alone here anymore. I don't have to be a one-man army, and all of this isn't resting solely on my shoulders. We might not have had luck abroad, but King Favian and King Orso are doing everything within their power to unite as many people as possible. There were at least half a dozen kingdoms at his council meeting. The forest trolls and mountain trolls have joined forces. They have wyrms and goblins on their side. We're not alone.

Hope isn't lost.

I don't need to overthink this. I can be a piece of the puzzle and let everyone else play their part. That's how we will win this war. I've made it far with the abilities I have right now. Abilities that will continue to gain power as I do. Dreadbeasts are awesome, and I'm sure that one day I'll witness their power. But for now, the best thing I can do for myself is to unleash my inner beast.

As I return to the village, I'm nearly clobbered by two birds speeding toward the caves. A silver falcon explodes in front of me, and I equip Destroyer out of instinct before I realize it's the chief. A moment later, Taryn appears in a flutter of white feathers.

I narrow my eyes. "What have you two been up to?"

Taryn grins. "You wouldn't believe me if I told you."

Considering all the weird stuff that's happened to me in this game, I doubt that.

A loud groan echoes from a nearby cave, followed by the patter of footsteps. Berry comes tottering out of the cave like an excited puppy followed by Ruby, two foxes, and a turtle with a translucent shell that looks like ice.

Stompy slowly brings up the rear next to a massive mammoth, proof that the big guy loves Taryn just as much as the others even if he doesn't show it.

Berry tackles Taryn to the ground and he licks him vigorously.

"Did you miss me?" Taryn talks to him like a baby as he wraps his stubby arms around the bear.

"Looks like they've made friends. Even Stompy." I laugh as the moulhaug huffs over Taryn, blowing his dreadlocks aside.

Chief Laojin strokes the mammoth behind the ear and the beast wraps its long trunk around his arm. Each of the mammoth's tusks rivals Taryn in size.

Watching a troll ride a mammoth into battle would put fear in anyone.

The chief turns to me. "I take it you have found some clarity?"

I nod. "I have."

"Good." He pats the mammoth on the side. "Let us return to the council."

After escorting the pets back to their cave, we find ourselves in the dimly-lit library where three of the council members are already waiting. Limery has curled up on one of the highest shelves and snores loudly. Laojin stares at me expectantly, and Taryn sits on the edge of his seat.

I feel like I'm about to give a press conference. *Tune in for the latest on Chod's Decision.*

I clear my throat. "I've decided to take the Spirit of the Beast class advancement."

"A worthy choice of a hero." Laojin walks over and extends a hand. "But there is no time to waste. Bonding with a spirit beast is different for everyone. It could take days or weeks, so it's best to have you on your journey at once. Now, remove all of your items and hand them to me."

He nods to Tzane, and the pot-bellied troll disappears out of the cave.

I unhook my satchel and give it to Laojin. Nearly everything I own is in that tiny bag. I remove the phoenix feather from my hair and the Tiger's Eye Pendant around my neck.

"And that." He points at the communication stone hanging from my neck. "You won't need it where you're going." He stares at the fur cloak from Whitgard and grunts. "Keep it. This is all for nothing if you freeze to death."

It suddenly feels like I might have bitten off more than I can chew.

Laojin grabs me by the arm. "Come." He turns as we exit the cave. "Have the others ready upon my return."

Everything is suddenly happening so fast. I stop walking, pulling my arm from Laojin's grip. "What in the hell is going on?"

He raises an eyebrow. "You have chosen to embark on the Spirit of the Beast path."

I stand firm. "I don't know what that means. Or why you're having the others get ready. What are they getting ready for?"

"You do ask a lot of questions." He sighs. "I am glad you have chosen the advancement you did. It is fitting for a troll, but your path is yours alone. Once you embark, there will be nothing I can do for you until you return. You must find your own way. For the others, there is still much we can offer but it will take time. Which is all the more reason for you to be on your way. Do this right and you will all leave here stronger than you came."

That still doesn't answer any of my questions, but I suppose it's better than nothing. I give a final wave to Taryn as we leave. I want to say good bye to Limery, but he looks so peaceful with his closed eyes and expanding snot bubble that I leave him be.

Outside, we travel up a snow-covered path that winds higher up the mountain. Laojin stops once we can no longer see the village.

"This is where I leave you. Travel far and lose yourself. Once you are ready, select your class advancement. It will give you all the information you need to find your spirit beast."

I clasp him around the forearm. "And what about you?"

He winks. "The dwarf and I have a dungeon to clear."

Stupid. Stupid. Stupid.

This idea was so fucking stupid. I could be summoning dread-beasts right now, but instead, I'm knee deep in snow, freezing my balls off, with no idea of where to go.

I've been walking for at least a few hours now. Far enough that there is nothing reminiscent of troll society out here. No fancy ice plants, no broken trees from troll antics. This high up, there isn't even a trail to follow. Nothing but wilderness.

Cold wilderness.

The sun is nearly below the horizon, but there is still plenty of light to see by. Not that I need it with my night vision.

I pick up a handful of snow and toss it in my mouth, letting it melt into water. With my satchel gone, there's no more Brimming Tankard, no jerky. Everything that I'll need to survive, I'll have to find out here.

This far from the village, I should be good to choose my advancement, but before I do, I need to eat. Once I start the search for my spirit beast, I don't want to have to slow down to hunt.

I find an open area between two pine trees. Tiny tracks trail across the snow, so I'm certain there are animals around here.

I sit down, waiting for Camouflage to take effect. When it does, the reaction is worlds different from the troll forest, where it would spring to life with birds and insects the moment I was no longer visible. For the longest time, all I hear is the wind.

But then suddenly, there's a crunch. If not for the overwhelming silence, it would normally go unheard, but in this climate, it sounds like an iceberg breaking into the sea.

There's movement beneath the snow at the base of the pine tree as something burrows out from underneath. A tiny pink nose breaks through, followed by a white head.

Snow Bunny. *Level 15. Maddeningly quick. Although small, their hind legs pack a ferocious kick.*

The bunny crawls from the snow and hops around, sniffing at the cool air. It hesitates for a moment, cocking its head to the side and looking in my direction.

Too late.

I use Intimidation, roaring at the bunny and confusing it for two seconds. It stumbles back and forth, eyes glazed over. With a quick snap of its neck, I have my dinner before it knows what's happening.

Thanks to my Savage passive ability, I don't need to cook the meat before eating. I skin the bunny with my claws, tossing the pelt aside since I don't have my satchel. The meat is not nearly as enjoyable as something roasted over an open fire and covered in spices, but it gets the job done.

Once I'm done eating, I pull up my notifications and select the class advancement for Spirit of the Beast.

Alert! You have selected to advance the Barbarian class. New class option available.

Barbarian. *Savage warriors capable of using basic weapons and entering into a berserker rage.*

Subclass:

   Spirit of the Beast. *Bond with a spirit animal to gain new abilities. The Spirit of the Beast path is composed of five phases.*

Phase 1: Spirit Inquiry. *A spirit animal is a guide from the spirit world, possessing traits similar to those of the individual. Unlocking one's spirit animal leads to a better understanding of the self and one's place within the world.*

   Completion: Locate your spirit animal. Further phases will become available upon completion.

That's it? Talk about finding a needle in a haystack. There are no instructions, no guide points, just "go and find the damn thing."

I sure hope Taryn is faring better than I am.

I ball up the bunny's pelt and toss it as far as I can down the mountain to keep whatever predators are lurking at bay. Without my weapons, it's just me and my horrors against whatever is out here.

For someone supposedly helping me, Chief Laojin has done a shit job at preparing me for this. He practically kicked me out of the village with an attaboy. I spend several hours walking through the snow. Not knowing what I'm looking for, my frustration builds with every step. I don't even know how I'm supposed to bond with an animal. Do I have to kill it? Tame it? Blow it a kiss? Laojin acted like it was simple, but this is anything but.

Compared to Whitgard, Hornryx is severely lacking in

monsters. I imagine it takes a lot of food to feed so many trolls, so it makes sense, but I remember the chief saying they hunted their food in the dungeons. Why couldn't I find my spirit animal in there?

An owl swoops down nearby, plucking a small rodent from beneath the snow. I take off running as it flies to a nearby tree.

The owl watches me with large round eyes as the rodent squirms within its beak. A leg twitches and a long white tail jerks back and forth.

"Are you my spirit animal?" I feel like an idiot even asking. Like the owl is going to magically start talking.

The owl crunches the rodent in its beak and the twitching stops. With a few quick motions, the rodent slides down the owl's throat until only the tail is remaining. A second later, the tail disappears in the owl's beak like a spaghetti noodle. The owl extends its wings and puffs out its chest, hooting softly before flying higher up the mountain.

"I guess not."

I continue my search over the next few hours, coming across bears, a lone wolf, and even a sleeping mammoth. I sit near the mammoth for a while, hoping that it will become my spirit animal, but nothing happens.

Eventually, tiredness wins out and I carve myself a makeshift cave in the snow. I take one last look at the beautiful streaks of blue and green across the sky before settling in my cave. Before I fall asleep, I send Taryn a quick message.

Message (Chod): *I hope you're having better luck than me. It feels like I'm walking blind out here.*

I wait a few minutes for him to respond, but he doesn't. Leaning against the cold packed snow, I'm more aware than ever of Limery's absence as I drift off to sleep.

I wake up screaming as something cold and wet presses against my cheek. A small, white, cat-like creature hisses at me from the corner of my snow cave. I summon a Horror of Power and it pounces on the cat, pinning it to the ground. I quickly summon two more horrors to help.

Arctic Bobcat. *Level 18. Smallest of the Frostmoor predators, the arctic bobcat is fast and agile while packing a dangerous bite. Solitary creatures, they are known to have fought off predators three to four times their size.*

The bobcat screeches so loud that I wince as my Horror of Power latches its jaws around the bobcat's neck. The cat kicks out, hitting the Horror of Finesse and launching the blue, gangly horror at me. It rakes its back claws across the Horror of Power, ripping into its flesh. After a flurry of quick kicks, the horror dissipates. The bobcat is on its feet in an instant, lunging for the Horror of Vitality.

The cat buries its sharp claws into the horror before biting it on the nose with enough force to kill it. The bobcat's hair stands on end as it arches its back. The Horror of Finesse runs in, but a quick swipe across the face ends it.

The bobcat hisses at me and makes a noise like a demon caught in a blender before bolting out of my snow cave like a rocket.

I rush out behind it, shouting. "Wait! Are you my spirit animal?"

CHAPTER 31
DUNGEONS AND DRUIDS

TARYN KEPT to himself as several more trolls entered the library. From the looks of it, these were the biggest and strongest trolls in the village. With Chod gone, what were they up to?

Taryn gravitated toward Limery, leaning against the cave wall next to the bookshelf. The imp's snores were like a dull saw cutting through wood. A bubble of snot expanded to the brink of bursting with each breath.

Tzane, the pot-bellied council member, barked orders at Rhaz, the troll who had expressed an interest in eating Taryn and Limery earlier in the day. Rhaz carried a bag over his shoulder that was filled with weapons.

Taryn gripped his staff a little tighter. He wanted to know what was going on, but the less attention he drew to himself the better, at least until the chief returned. It wasn't that he didn't trust the arctic trolls, but he was still a level-twenty-three dwarf, and he didn't quite feel he could call these trolls friends yet.

When the chief finally returned, his eyes flared with excitement.

He knelt before Taryn. "Do you wish to advance before Chod returns?"

Taryn nodded. "I want to advance as soon as possible."

"Good." He flashed Taryn a smile. "It will be difficult. It will be exhausting. You will be pushed to your limits. But it can be done. Shall we begin?"

Taryn stood. There was no point waiting around while Chod was already out on his quest. "Let's do it."

Laojin's gaze fell on Limery, who was oblivious to the world. "Wake the imp."

With Limery awakened, and extra grumpy because Chod didn't say good-bye before leaving, they all gathered around Chief Laojin.

The chief raised his hand and all eyes fell upon him. "It has been a long time since the thrill of adventure has swept over Hornryx. Many lifetimes have passed since heroes and outsiders have set foot in these caves. We have worked hard to keep ourselves hidden, yet Chod still felt the call of our tribe. I, for one, am glad he came. While he travels through the wilderness searching for his spirit beast, we are tasked with a quest of our own." He gestured to Taryn and Limery. "The world below Hornryx is dangerous, and dark tidings whisper from abroad. While we have fortified ourselves behind the safety of the ring, these two heroes and their companions aim to meet the darkness head-on. I'd like to see them stand worthy of the challenge."

He looked from Rhaz to Tzane and the others before continuing. It felt as if the speech was as much for the other trolls as it was for Taryn.

"I've gathered our strongest trolls here for one purpose: to delve deeper into the dungeon than we have gone in many years. We have used the higher levels for food and sustenance since the days of old, but it has been too long since we tested our bodies against the threats that lurk deeper. Our guests are not strong enough to face these threats alone, so we must accompany them so that they may grow stronger. Now, who's ready to rage?"

Rhaz beat a fist against his chest. A second later, Tzane joined in, then another troll and another, until all of them, even the elderly Oyanna, sounded like they were ready to tear the mountain down.

Chief Laojin tapped a fist to his own chest. "Good. Choose your weapons."

The trolls riffled through the bag, picking out all manner of brute-force weapons: axes, warhammers, maces, and more. The weapons were fine quality. Some had runes carved into the handles, and others had settings for stones. It was clear the trolls knew how to do one thing.

Smash.

Chief Laojin held a silver staff made of a sleek metal that was tipped with a clear blue gemstone. Wherever the weapon was from, it wasn't troll-made, that was for sure.

He tapped it on the ground three times to gather their attention. "Rhaz, Tzane, you will accompany me alongside the dwarf and imp on the first team. Senzala, Machu, and Fiero will be second team. When the three of us tire, you will support our guests."

They all nodded in affirmation.

"Why can't we all go in?" Taryn asked.

"Too many of us will cut into your experience. We need enough in the party to survive, but not so many to where you gain nothing."

"Do I get to bring my pets?"

The chief frowned. "Normally, yes. But by splitting the experience further, it will only prolong the process."

Taryn crossed his arms. "But they are going to be with me in every battle going forward. Shouldn't they be as strong as possible?"

Laojin sighed. "Yes and no. I know you can't stay here forever. The hero's journey is far from stationary, and as soon as Chod returns, you will be on to your next adventure. There are many paths for a druid, and wherever you are when you choose to advance will determine the paths you are offered. If you advance here, you will be offered paths not available through the other portals. The choice is yours. If you want your pets to level with you, we will still help, but there is no guarantee you will advance in time."

Taryn racked his brain. There had to be a solution that would help keep Berry and Stompy on pace with him. The bigger the gap in their levels, the more danger he put them in in every fight.

"What if we took in one less troll. Stompy and Berry can make up the difference, and I can fight in my natural style, using my pets."

The chief ran his fingers through his beard before nodding. "Spoken like a true druid." He looked around the room. "We will make it work."

***

"Will Limery get a class advancement?" asked Taryn as they waited outside of the entrance to the dungeon.

The group had to wait for the trolls currently hunting for food inside the dungeon to exit before it would allow anyone else to enter. Only one party was allowed in the dungeon at a time.

Chief Laojin shook his head. "Imps do not progress in the same manner as other races. They are beings of raw power and do not take on classes. Limery is a special case, though."

Limery sat on Stompy's snout with his back against the moulhaug's horn, but he perked up at the mention of his name. "Limmy is?"

"You are. Imps were never known as great adventurers or for their ambition. Most were messengers. Others took jobs as servants or apprentices. They did not need to reach high levels to unlock their power or speed. You—" He tapped Limery on the foot, eliciting a giggle. "—you are one of a kind."

"I don't think we could handle two of him." Taryn laughed to himself.

Limery had never spoken about his class or his abilities to Taryn. Maybe Chod knew more, but Taryn had no idea if Limery had an interface or not. It was clear that many of the NPCs could access their stats and abilities, at least the ones with classes, but whether they could allocate points and choose their abilities, or received predetermined stats, he had no idea.

Either way, Limery was pure offensive firepower, and ridiculously strong for his size. He didn't need a second class to make his presence known. He was a pint-sized wrecking ball, and Taryn knew he could count on the imp in any situation.

Stone grated against stone as the dungeon entrance opened. Five male trolls, levels twenty-five to twenty-eight, exited carrying dead animals over their shoulders. One carried a boar. Two others held opposite ends of a giant frost deer. The other two carried large rabbits with unicorn horns.

As they left, the dungeon entrance closed. Taryn was greeted with a prompt.

Hornryx Dungeon. *Would you like to enter?*

Taryn glanced around at his party. Rhaz held a massive axe across his shoulder. He looked ready for a fight. Chief Laojin spoke a few words to the troll hunters as they exited the cave. Limery mesmerized Stompy with a fireball that he kept tossing from one hand to another. And then there was Berry, his oldest and most loyal pet.

Ruby wasn't a fighter, so she didn't need the levels like the rest of them. She would wait with the council until their dungeon run was over.

Taryn took a deep breath. "What are you chumps waiting for? Let's go."

Chief Laojin tapped his staff on the ground. "You heard the dwarf."

The entrance to the dungeon groaned as it closed behind them. With both Berry and Stompy, the tunnel felt extremely tight. This dungeon was a more natural formation than any other Taryn had been in. The walls were rocky cave walls, nothing was polished or carved. It was no different than any other cave aside from the mana torches that continuously blazed along the walls.

Rhaz led the way with Laojin not far behind.

The chief turned to Taryn. "The first few levels are not difficult. They can be cleared once per day, but they provide more than enough to feed the village. Today, we'll be going deeper."

The first level was empty. Several corpses of the unicorn bunnies lay scattered around the room. Rhaz walked past them without stopping, entering a crude stairwell with uneven and misshapen steps. Stompy barely fit through the spiraling tunnel. On level two, blood covered the floor. Skid marks, from where corpses had been dragged across the dungeon, painted a gruesome picture on the floor. Only a lone warthog remained, its thick body gashed along the side with claw marks. Taryn finally understood how they could feed so many trolls this high up the mountain.

Judging by the scene, the dungeon may have provided for the arctic trolls, but that didn't mean it was easy pickings. The stronger trolls had been forged inside this dungeon.

Taryn hoped the same would happen to him.

The third floor was not much different, with the warthogs replaced by frost deer. A couple of detached antlers lay on the ground. They clattered as Rhaz kicked them aside.

He stopped at the next stairwell, looking to the chief for instructions.

Laojin stepped forward to where he could face them all. "This is the boundary for our hunts. Those empty rooms we passed have taken our hunters all day to clear. The next few levels offer no sustenance, so it's normally not worth the energy or danger to press forward. But today, we will go as far as we can."

"Whats is downs there?" Limery hung onto Stompy's horn like a pirate in the crow's nest.

The chief smirked. "You're about to find out. Follow me."

Laojin took point, with Rhaz close behind. He held his axe firmly with both hands, ready for action. Taryn followed next on Berry, and Limery and Stompy pulled up the rear.

As they descended the next stairwell, frost clung to the walls reflecting the light of the torches in a glimmering sheen. Laojin tore through a spiderweb that blocked the entrance to the next level.

Taryn stopped Berry in his tracks. "Not spiders," he whispered to himself. "Please, not spiders."

The room only had a single torch burning. Stalactites hung from the ceiling and much of the room was hidden in shadow. Webbing draped across the cave, and something chittered up above, raising the hair on Taryn's neck.

"Limmy no likes." The imp conjured a fireball in his hand.

More chittering erupted, drowning out all other sounds. It

was like a swarm of cicadas had descended on them. Laojin shouted something and pointed at Taryn, but the words fell mute.

Prickly legs wrapped around Taryn like a straightjacket, pinning his arms to his sides and ripping him from Berry's back. Stompy bellowed nearby. Taryn struggled against their embrace, but the long legs were unforgiving. Their sharp barbs penetrated his cloak, slowly dropping his HP. Several spiders descended from the ceiling like this was some sort of Halloween spectacle. Rhaz split one in half with his axe, the force of the blow spraying a line of green ichor across the wall.

Laojin raised his staff, and a spike of ice shot up from the ground, impaling another spider on a frozen skewer.

Limery tossed a fireball in Taryn's direction, and he suddenly plummeted to the floor. His chin smacked against the hard ground. Stars danced across his vision, but the legs still held firm around his midsection. His body jostled as someone or something fought the spider holding him in place.

There was a loud crunch, and then cool slime dripped down Taryn's back and neck. Berry nuzzled him, his face covered in green goo from his attack on the spider. Taryn crawled to his feet as battle continued to rage all around him.

A spider lunged for Taryn, but Stompy's massive hoof squashed it inches from his face. Green guts exploded into his beard and eyes.

He didn't have time to be grossed out by spider guts. More arachnids appeared by the second.

Laojin formed an ice spike on the end of his staff, using it as a spear to pierce the barbed abdomens of spiders as they lowered themselves from the ceiling or skittered across the floor. A half-dozen butchered spiders lay around Rhaz. Limery tossed fireballs, severing webs so that Stompy could crush the fallen spiders with his hooves.

"Alright, boy, let's do this." Taryn climbed on Berry's back and joined the fray.

He extended the vines from Sapling Staff, forming a makeshift cage around his body to keep any spiders from prying him off again. If there was an opportunity, he cast Lightning Bolt, but with how crowded the room was, those chances were few and far between.

A spider landed on top of the viny cage and it pressed its head against the bars, its mandible clacking as a toxic substance dripped from the pincers. The spider pried at the vines, desperate for Taryn's flesh.

He equipped one of the Shadow Daggers in his off-hand, and a blade of shadow energy erupted from the hilt. He stabbed the spider's face through the cage. The dark shadowy blade bypassed its tough exterior, depleting the spider's life and mana directly.

The spider shrieked as it recoiled, right into Laojin's ice spear.

One by one, they finished off the spiders until the chittering was replaced by the group's heavy breathing.

"I see why you don't come down here." Taryn retracted the vines back into his staff, freeing himself once again.

Laojin snapped off the green-tinted ice from the end of his staff. "This is only the beginning."

CHAPTER 32

THAT'S THE SPIRIT

INCOMING MESSAGE (TARYN): Bro, I hope you're having fun out there, because you are missing out. This dungeon is legit! I hit level twenty-four earlier today. The chief thinks I might hit twenty-five tomorrow morning.

I close the message. Two days freezing my ass off in the wilderness is not what I would call fun, but I'm glad Taryn is leveling up while I'm away. They must be really grinding to get those kind of results so quickly. Hopefully, when we meet up again, we'll both be stronger than ever.

Having a high-level druid showing him the ropes can't hurt. Then we can make a quick stop by Boneholde and be off to warmer climates.

After searching for tracks, I sit down and wait for dinner to appear. Snow bunnies have been easy enough to catch once I'm in Camouflage. I've eaten so many that I'm ready to give up the hunt for my spirit beast just so I can have a real meal again.

Swallowing the last of the stringy raw meat, I climb higher up the mountain to make camp for the night.

A snow fox scurries away in the distance, but I pay it no mind. I assume I'll receive some kind of alert or notification once I've found my spirit beast. If that's the case, I've eliminated a majority of the wildlife on Hornryx already: snow fox, snow bunny, arctic bobcat, frost deer, mammoth, various owls, wolves, and bears. I've seen a lot of animals while I've been sitting around waiting.

Waiting and freezing. My tough troll skin and cloak have kept me from suffering any damage from the cold, but I've been in discomfort almost non-stop.

With my luck, my spirit animal is something either incredibly rare or incredibly stupid. I swear if my spirit animal is some kind of arctic skunk, I will log out before I go around blasting stink gas out of my ass.

As I prepare for my second night alone on the mountain, my horrors and I dig a large burrow in the snow. When we're done, I hunker down in my snow cave wrapped in the cloak from Whitgard.

I decide not to message Taryn back. I'm in a grumpy mood from finding no leads, and hearing about his awesome adventures will only make me more jealous that I'm not there.

I close my eyes and wait for sleep to come.

A clack like a gunshot wakes me. I reach for my weapon before remembering that all my items are back at the village. Instead, I summon a round of horrors and peek my head out of the entrance to my cave.

The mountain basks in the light of early morning, the one part of the day where birds can be heard actively chirping. Another gunshot echoes from higher up the mountain, and I shift my gaze upward.

Two glowing frost goats lower their heads, pawing at the ground with their hooves. These two are much bigger than the goats in Whitgard. Their thick white fur isn't as clean and groomed as the domesticated versions, and the horns that curl around each side of their heads are much larger, fading from deep black at the base to icy blue at the tip. Blue eyes stand out predominantly from their black faces.

A smaller female with nubs for horns stands to the side watching the battle unfold.

The two rams rise onto their back legs, almost hovering in the air for a moment before charging one another with concussive force. Their horns clash, the violent collision echoing off the mountain. The force separates them, where they paw at the ground before charging again.

The brutality of their collisions is awe-inspiring, but I'm drawn to the orange aura that surrounds the males. I never saw anything similar on the goats in Whitgard. Are they in some kind of goat rage, or are they—

A notification alert flashes in the corner of my vision.

Alert! *Spirit beast located. Subdue the beast in order to bond and unlock phase two.*

As lame as saying my spirit beast is a goat sounds, the creatures before me are impressive. Raw power and stubbornness rolled into one. Not all that different from me. The goat's muscles ripple as they crash into one another again.

I'm far from disappointed, but how in the hell am I supposed to subdue an angry goat without killing it? It's not like I can tame it like Taryn. I've seen what these things can do in Whitgard, and those were domesticated. How much more dangerous are wild ones? Judging by the sound of their collisions, these hit like a wrecking ball.

Both male frost goats are level twenty-five, and the female is twenty-three. I'm sure I could take them one on one, but if I run in guns blazing, they could forget about their beef with each other and focus on me. Without my items, I'm not a hundred percent certain I could win that fight. Especially if the female joins in.

I summon more horrors into the back of my cave just in case. Then, I watch.

I've been searching for my spirit beast for two days. What's a little more time?

The goats ram each other for what feels like hours, and their health barely drops. They're fighting in a display of dominance, not to actually kill one another. Still, their health trickles down with each collision, but the Constitution it takes to endure such repetitive attacks means their health recovers just as quickly. There can't be an animal on the mountain who hasn't heard their ruckus.

The orange outline covers their bodies like someone sketched over them with a watercolor. If my instincts are correct, then I should be able to subdue either one of them. This gives me an idea.

I watch and wait as the goats square off again and again, wondering if they are ever going to stop fighting. When one of the goats takes a hard fall upon impact, he's slow to get up. The other ram looms over him, steam pouring from his nostrils. He lands a few hard kicks against the downed goat before leaving with the female.

The loser eventually stands, and after a few agitated huffs and angry paws at the ground, he stalks away in defeat.

Sixty of my horrors and I set off in pursuit. To anyone below, I'm sure we look like a blotch on the mountainside.

The frost goat quickly ascends the rough, snow-covered terrain, and if I don't make my move quickly, he'll be gone before I have a chance to subdue him. So, I grab a Horror of Vitality by the horn and chuck it at the goat with all my might. It tumbles through the air, screaming its disapproval, and I activate Berserker Rage.

My legs move faster through the snow as my body flexes with rage. The horror hits the goat, its passive ability slowing the creature momentarily. The frost goat headbutts my horror, obliterating it with one hit, but I already have a second horror flying through the air.

After three horrors descend on him from the sky, the goat finally notices our approach and charges in for a fight. I run toward him at full speed, and the goat lowers his head.

At the last second, I jump, twisting in the air as the goat barrels into my army of horrors, turning a handful into smoke instantly. The others swarm the beast as I land on his back, hands gripping firmly around his horns. I pull back with all my strength as my ultimate ability continues to pump through my veins.

My horrors attack the goat's legs, dropping him to his knees. Horrors of Finesse claw while the Horrors of Power gore the goat with their sharp tusks. His health ticks down more rapidly than it ever did in the fight with the other ram. My muscles burn as I continue to pull back on the horns, giving the goat nothing more than his legs to attack with.

The goat falls to his side with ten percent health, each breath ragged as he kicks out. My horrors are depleted by half, but I have them pile on the goat thirty strong.

Berserker Rage ends, but the goat has given up the fight. The orange glow fades around his body, and I receive a new notification.

I release the goat and take in a deep, cooling breath. Phase one complete. The creature kicks out and then stumbles to his feet. I stand, ready to fight if I have to, but the goat lowers his head, huffs, and then runs up the mountain as his health begins to recover.

Once I'm out of combat, more horrors fade away as their timers expire. I pull up my new notification.

Alert! *Spirit of the Beast Phase One: Spirit Inquiry complete. New class option available.*

Phase 2: Spirit Embodiment. *Bonding with a spirit beast is only the beginning of the Spirit of the Beast path. By finding an amulet that connects you to your beast, the bond between the two will grow stronger, unlocking further advancements.*

Completion: Find an amulet that connects you to your spirit beast. Further phases will become available upon completion.

I gather myself and set off after the frost goat once again. If I'm going to find an amulet, it has to be connected to the goats somehow.

But at least I don't have to subdue it again.

The black specks of the frost goat's horns grow smaller and smaller as he climbs the mountain. I wish Taryn was around to cast Strong Wind right about now.

With each step, my anger continues to simmer. The goat is now so far away that I can't even hit him with a horror if I tried. It took three days to find my spirit beast and now I'm about to lose the only clue I have.

I'm about ready to scream when I pass a cave emitting a

familiar orange glow—the same shade of orange that the goats had when they were fighting.

I summon more horrors and step inside the cave. If this isn't a clue to finding the amulet, then I just fucked myself over big time. But it can't be a coincidence that they are giving off the same aura.

The cave is long, and the glow grows denser the further in I go. When the tunnel empties into a large cavern, it's practically a sea of orange. Bones litter the cavern floor. Hundreds of them.

This is a graveyard.

A frail frost goat lays against a pile of bones in the far corner. When he sees me, he fights to stand. His legs tremble and then he collapses to the ground, rattling the bones and stirring up a layer of dust. His horns are bigger than either of the goats that were fighting earlier, and his eyes are a faded gray.

Poor guy. He must have been a hell of a fighter in his prime.

I carefully approach. Even though the goat is on his deathbed, his eyes burn with the same intensity as his brethren. He huffs, stirring up bone dust before resting his head on the cavern floor.

The bones surrounding the dying goat are coated in the same orange watercolor outline that the goats had earlier. I pick up one of the skulls and the aura of the cavern instantly fades.

My head pounds with a splitting headache and stars dance across my vision. The ram's skull dissipates in my palm, and orange energy floods into my chest. Skin tears at the side of my head and I fall to my knees in intense pain. It feels like someone is drilling into my head for about five seconds straight before the pain stops and the tip of two blue ram's horns appear in my peripheral vision.

I receive a new notification, but I ignore it for now. The giant horns sprouting from my head have all my attention. I trace my fingers from the tip of each horn as they widen, curling around and connecting to the side of my head. The tips are the same translucent blue as the frost goats, so I'm certain that they fade to black at the base as well.

Holy shit! I'm a troll with ram's horns.

I rap my knuckles against the horns but feel nothing. Giving them a firm tug, they don't budge. They're literally fused to my skull. If they are a fraction of the strength of the real thing, then I just got a hell of a lot tougher. I quickly pull up my notification.

Alert! Spirit of the Beast Phase Two: Spirit Embodiment complete. New class option available.

Phase 3: Spirit Enhancement. *Just as your body has undergone a change reflective of your spirit beast, your spirit may be enhanced in the same manner. Gain a new passive ability based on your spirit beast.*

Completion: Unlock using one ability point. Further phases will become available upon completion.

That's it? All I have to do is use an ability point and I gain a new passive? I knew I was hanging on to the ability points for something great and this is exactly it. I don't hesitate, using my ability point on Spirit Enhancement. Immediately, I'm flooded with new notifications.

Alert! Spirit of the Beast Phase Three: Spirit Enhancement complete. New ability and class option available.

Ability: (New)

Ram Rage: *Barbarian rage now lasts twice as long. Physical attacks deal splash damage.*

Phase 4: Spirit Guide. *Your body and spirit have undergone great changes, but your bond with the spirit world is only beginning. Summon your spirit beast as a guide. Spirit guides are capable of leading you through darkness and guiding you to locations you have previously visited, even if you do not know the way. Spirit guides may be absorbed for a 50% increase to Wisdom for 10 minutes. A spirit guide may not be summoned for 24 hours after absorption.*

Completion: Unlock using one ability point. Further phases will become available upon completion.

I could do without the darkness guide thanks to my night vision, but the other part is pretty cool. It's like I'll have my own personal GPS.

I use my final ability point to unlock phase four and more notifications appear.

Alert! *Spirit of the Beast Phase Four: Spirit Guide complete. New ability and class option available.*

Ability: (New)

Spirit Guide: *Summon a frost goat spirit guide. The spirit guide may lead you through darkness and guide you to locations you have previously visited, even if you do not know the way. Spirit guides may be absorbed for a 50% increase to Wisdom for 10 minutes. Cooldown: 24 hours after absorption.*

Phase 5: Spirit Power. *The path of the beast is not for the faint of heart, and those who complete all five stages are blessed with a mighty power from their spirit beast. Gain a new active ability based on your spirit beast.*

Completion: Unlock using one ability point and the Spirit of the Beast path will be complete.

Of course they save the best for last. A new active ability. My mind races with possibilities of headbutts with my new horns, powerful kicks, or the ability to climb mountains with ease. Whatever it is, I'm sure it'll be awesome. But I won't know the real ability until I hit level twenty-seven. Talk about anticipation.

I can't be mad, though. I've unlocked two new abilities and went through a transformation over the span of a few minutes. I doubt even Taryn is having that kind of luck right now.

The frost goat groans, drawing my attention away from my interface. He rests his head on the cave floor and looks up at me with knowing eyes, the fire all but gone. This is it. He came here to die, and it will all be over soon.

I kneel and rest my hand on his head. Surprisingly, he doesn't fight me. Gently, I stroke the patch of rough white hair between his horns. If only Taryn were here, he could cast Restoration and maybe buy the goat some more time.

Taryn might not be here, but maybe there's still a way to help this goat. It's not like he'll be any worse off if I fail.

I scratch the goat behind the ear. "What do you say, big guy, want to go on an adventure?"

The goat groans as I struggle to lift him onto my shoulder. He must weigh two or three hundred pounds, but nothing I can't handle. The bigger issue will be making it down the mountain in time. I've been wandering for three days and have no idea what the quickest route is.

Luckily, I have just the answer. I cast Spirit Guide and a ghostly frost goat appears in front of me, its body made of an ethereal white-and-orange aura. The spirit goat puffs out its chest and paws at the ground, head raised high.

"Lead us to the village."

CHAPTER 33
THE GRIND

Taryn brushed a chunk of ice from between Berry's ears and it clattered against the floor. The remains of shattered ice golems littered the dungeon. Nearby, steam radiated from Fiero's fur as he pulled his spiked mace from a block of ice that had once been the head of a golem.

Watching the arctic trolls rage felt different than when it happened to Chod. His was a controlled burn, devastating but directed, while theirs was like an all-consuming wildfire.

True to the chief's words, Taryn was exhausted. He'd barely slept for the past three days, rotating between the three groups of trolls. Loading up on potions and elixirs, he kept going with one group while the others rested, and Restoration kept his pets in good health. The first team was Chief Laojin and Rhaz. Second team consisted of Senzala and Tzane. The third and his current team was Machu and Fiero.

Machu took in deep breaths as he leaned on his warhammer like a crutch. They'd been clearing levels for a few hours now, and it was almost time to switch teams again.

He'd reached level twenty-four early in the morning the previous day. With a little luck, he could hit level twenty-five before the day was out.

Taryn put away his staff for the moment. "You two can go on and rotate. I'll wait here for the next team."

Fiero patted Stompy on the side. "This one is formidable. I have enjoyed witnessing his power."

Stompy huffed as he leaned his weight against the large troll while he munched on a carrot. The moulhaug had stomped and smashed his fair share of monsters the past few days.

"Good fortune with the bats." Machu nodded as he and Fiero left the room.

"Thank you for your help!" Taryn shouted after them.

He knew what was coming for the next few levels. They'd made it further on day two than day one, and they were on schedule to go even deeper into the dungeon today. Knowing what to expect meant they could go in with a game plan. After the ice golems, frost bats awaited.

Limery splashed around in a puddle that had once been an ice golem before he'd melted it like ice cream on a hot summer day. His fire abilities were especially effective against anything ice-related. He was now level twenty-three and part of the reason they had cleared so many levels already.

Taryn healed his pets and popped a mana potion as he waited for Laojin and Rhaz to arrive. While Laojin and Senzala were the only members of the tribe that had mana in their bodies, the trolls were rather adept at making mana potions. Their access to the mana well and the potion recipes in the library allowed them to concoct enough potions to keep Taryn going until he advanced.

If they had any left over, he'd make sure to pack some for the road. The ones in Hornryx felt more potent than any he had purchased in other cities. Perhaps it was the proximity to the source.

Taryn lay on Stompy's back while he waited, making shapes with the vines of the Sapling Staff until he heard footsteps approaching.

Chief Laojin grinned as he entered the room. "No time to waste, young dwarf. No time to waste."

A change had come over the trolls as they cleared the lower levels of the dungeon. Even though it was dangerous work, they seemed more relaxed between battles. They laughed. Occasionally, they even joked. After so many years of only clearing the upper levels for food, it had to feel good for them to really test themselves.

The chief held up a hand just outside the entryway to the next level. "Same plan as before."

Taryn and Rhaz nodded. Limery cackled.

Laojin rushed into the room and raised his staff, the tip flashing with a blue aura. Dozens of large bats, each one two to three feet tall with an even wider wingspan, hung from the ceiling. As soon as the group entered, the bats began to stir.

The chief's attack took hold, and a thick layer of frost formed across the ceiling. It spread over the feet of the hanging bats, down their legs, and across their bodies until they were frozen in place like icicles.

The group didn't have much time, so Taryn rushed into action, casting Stonewall beneath a row of frozen bats. The wall erupted from the cave floor, stretching all the way to the ceiling and crushing five bats in one go.

Limery zoomed through the air, flames coating his hands as he melted the ice around the feet of the others one by one. The frozen bats crashed against the floor, ice shattering from their bodies upon impact. The beasts stumbled around like they had just woken up from a deep sleep.

Rhaz's axe hit one with so much force that it split the bat in half and sparks flew as the blade gashed the cave floor. Stompy's massive hooves flattened two bats into pancakes, and Berry mauled a third. Chief Laojin took out the rest with some well-placed ice spikes.

Taryn's experience bar shot up once again. It wouldn't be much longer before he was finally the same level as Chod, then he could give him a hard time for the foreseeable future. He already had a few jokes brewing.

After a short wait, they readied themselves for the next floor. It had nearly done them in the previous evening, leaving their party battered and bruised.

From the entrance, they counted six gargoyles statues around the room. The surprise of them coming to life had been part of their near-downfall. These were not as intricately carved as some that might be spotted in Seascape or other cities with great architecture. Instead, they had the look of a statue that had endured the elements for many years. They had the appearance of some winged creature, but the features were hard to define. They could have been carved from the cave itself, whittled away by someone with only the most primitive tools.

Six on six should have been a fair fight, but the gargoyles were nearly impossible to kill. They had tough stone skin, and when not moving, they received an additional buff making them near invulnerable. They'd learned that the hard way.

The group entered the room and twelve orange eyes suddenly opened. The gargoyles stood silent, waiting for the intruders to make the first move.

Taryn cast Stonewall, summoning a wall that divided the cavern in two, keeping three of the gargoyles at bay temporarily.

He'd talked it over with Laojin, and they thought they had a better plan for this second attempt. Divide and conquer.

He equipped Sapling Staff in one hand and a Shadow Dagger in the other. Vines extended from the staff, wrapping around the closest gargoyle. The monster didn't struggle against the binding, not until Taryn plunged the Shadow Dagger into its heart.

The weapon bypassed the gargoyle's natural stone armor, its formless blade of energy depleting health and mana directly. Vital areas like the heart and head drained HP and mana more quickly. The gargoyle convulsed from the sudden disturbance like its heart had been jolted with electricity. Its health dropped rapidly as it struggled against the entangling vines.

The gargoyle roared, stretching the vines to their limits, and the other two gargoyles stirred. Thuds echoed from the other side of Taryn's stone wall.

The vines snapped from the tension, and a stone fist punched Taryn in the chest, knocking him across the room. Taryn collided with the wall, losing only a sliver of health due to his high Constitution, but he felt every bit of it. He sucked in air and his vision flared in and out of focus as all hell broke loose.

Frost spread across the ground as Laojin froze the other two gargoyles in place. Rhaz chopped at one of the stone beasts with his axe and sparks exploded from the impact. Meanwhile, Stompy pinned the third gargoyle to the ground with a massive hoof while Berry mauled it and Limery pressed molten hands against the gargoyle's head, slowly draining more HP.

That's it. If Stompy can pin them down, I can drain their health.

Taryn grimaced as he crawled to his feet. His staff and dagger were scattered somewhere around the room, but he still had a second Shadow Dagger.

The two nearest gargoyles broke free from their ice prison, keeping the two trolls' attention.

Taryn shouted at Laojin as he ran past. "New plan! Keep the others busy while Stompy holds one in place and I drain its life."

Limery and Berry had whittled the gargoyle down to a quarter-health by the time Taryn arrived. He plunged the dagger into the monster's head. Its health dropped more rapidly than ever, and a few seconds later, it lay still.

"One down, five to go."

Stonewall exploded as the other gargoyles broke through, sending rubble across the cavern.

Chief Laojin cast an ice wall, but the gargoyles smashed through it in seconds. A blue aura surrounded his staff as he raised it in the air. When he slammed the butt of the staff against the floor, ice spread out like a shockwave, turning the cavern into an ice rink.

Rhaz slipped and fell, his axe clattering against the floor. The gargoyles slid across like butter on a hot pan, unable to gain their footing. Taryn dropped to all fours to keep from falling. Only Stompy seemed to have no trouble standing.

A gargoyle slid into the moulhaug, and he swung his horn like a wrecking ball, knocking the monster against the back wall.

One of the gargoyles punched the ground, splintering the ice. The others followed suit and soon the ice was nothing more than slick gravel.

Taryn cast Lightning Bolt. The accompanying thunder was deafening in the packed cavern as it stunned the closest gargoyle in place. Laojin seized the opportunity, summoning a stalagmite-like spear of ice that pierced the monster from underneath. Taryn leapt for the gargoyle while it was still stunned, plunging the Shadow Dagger into its face. The critical hit drained health rapidly, and there was only a sliver left when the stun faded.

A sliver too much.

A powerful fist launched him across the room for the second

time, dropping his health once again. His entire body ached as he struggled to stand.

"Twos downs!" Limery's voice carried above the chaos while he hovered over a downed gargoyle.

Rhaz took a beating as he traded blows with one of the former statues. Blue blood trickled down his nose, staining his fur. Laojin held his left arm out, a shield of ice protecting him as he stabbed with his staff, an icy spear on its end. One of the gargoyles glowed red as Limery summoned a flame wall underneath it. When the flames faded, Laojin hit it with an ice blast, slowing the gargoyle. A powerful strike from Berry sent cracks forming all along the stone creature before it crumbled.

"Hit them with fire and then ice!" Taryn shouted. "It weakens them."

He grabbed a Shadow Dagger laying on the ground as he ran toward Stompy, who had another gargoyle pinned to the ground under his massive weight. The gargoyle swung its arms desperately, but it was no match for the moulhaug's weight. Taryn effortlessly drained the creature's health with the Shadow Dagger he'd recovered.

They made short work of the final three, taking two out with a fire-and-ice combo, and draining the last as Stompy sat on it.

Laojin leaned against his staff, breathing heavily. "Gargoyles: strong, slow, and difficult to kill."

Rhaz puffed out his chest. His white fur was stained blue in several areas. "We showed them." He grimaced as he raised his axe overhead.

Taryn took a deep breath as he cast Restoration, healing the lacerations across Berry's snout before moving on to Stompy. Even with the chief on their side, that had been a difficult fight. But he was so close to leveling up.

With the pets healed, the rest of the party downed potions to restore their health, minus Limery, who had escaped unscathed. The gash on Rhaz's nose rapidly sealed itself, leaving only crusty blue blood in its place.

Taryn gathered the dagger and staff he had lost during the battle and placed them back in his inventory.

He paced with nervous energy. The final grind was upon them.

Taryn lay on his back, the soft corpse of a shadow fox draped across his face. His heart pounded as he pushed the body to the side and sat up. Notifications flared in the corner of his vision, but they would have to wait.

Berry groaned as he collapsed to the floor. His claws and snout were coated in a thick layer of blood. Rhaz leaned against the wall, a chunk of fur completely missing from his forearm. Laojin leaned over Stompy, who had taken the brunt of the damage, whispering encouragement.

Limery lay on the ground, his arms and legs splayed in an X formation. "Limmy is tireds," he whispered.

Taryn gathered the last of his strength and huddled over Berry. Energy from the mountain passed through him and into the bear as he cast Restoration. Once finished, he moved on to Stompy.

Since Taryn had been so close to hitting level twenty-five, Laojin had wanted to stay for one more battle even though they were low on potions and scheduled for a team switch.

They ran out of potions in the middle of the fight. In addition to being lightning quick with sharp teeth and claws, the shadow foxes left a trail of dark energy in their wake that drained health and mana from anyone who stepped into the shadows. The foxes could also hide and travel in the shadows, attacking the group from multiple angles without warning. Stompy had been too big to avoid the shadows, but in the end, they'd scraped by.

Barely.

With his pets healed, Taryn pulled up his notifications. He'd have to tend to his own health once they were back aboveground.

Congratulations! You have reached level 25. +1 stat point to distribute. +1 Constitution racial bonus. +1 ability point to distribute.

Class Advancements. *Upon reaching level twenty-five, you have unlocked a class advancement. You may only advance one class at a time. A second class may not be advanced until completion of primary advancement.*

Druid Advancement. *(Choose one)*
Shadow Druid. Unlock for further details.
Druid of the Dawn. Unlock for further details.
Ice Druid. Unlock for further details.

Taryn was so lost in the notifications that he didn't notice Laojin standing over him until a firm hand squeezed his shoulder.

"I see you have succeeded." There was a look of pride on the elder troll's face. "You have the heart of a troll within you. What advancements have you unlocked?"

Taryn couldn't quite explain it, but he suddenly felt overcome with emotion. His cheeks grew hot, and he blinked rapidly to fight back the tears. The way Chief Laojin looked upon him with a sense of pride reminded him of his own father.

His father had been a star athlete in high school. He'd even gotten a scholarship to play for a small college in upstate New York, but a knee injury his freshmen year and lingering medical bills had put an end to any dreams beyond that. He'd always been proud of Taryn for choosing academics over sports, even though Taryn had inherited his father's physique and work ethic.

He took a deep breath and recentered himself, pulling up the notifications again and reading them aloud to the chief.

"Interesting." Laojin stroked his beard. "You have been blessed with quality selections. The Shadow Druid draws his power from the night, with spells that harness the moon and darkness. Druid of the Dawn is quite the opposite, harnessing the power of the sun. And then there is the Ice Druid—" He grinned "—which you may have guessed is my own path."

Taryn scratched his head. They all sounded like good options. "Which one should I choose?"

Laojin frowned. "That is not for me to decide, but I can offer you some guidance. The path of the Ice Druid has favorable crowd control. Slows, freezes, and the ability to make the terrain slick and difficult to battle on are only some of its benefits. It also possesses a fair number of offensive abilities with bonus effects. The path of the Druid of the Dawn is more common, using the sun for light-based attacks and healing. The Shadow Druid is a rare path, powered by the moon, it is devastating at night and in the shadow realms. It offers a balance of offense, defense, and subterfuge. Each has its strengths, but you must decide which one is right for you."

Taryn nodded, and Berry nudged a blood-stained snout against his hand. He had a lot to think about.

Each advancement sounded awesome in its own right. He'd seen firsthand the power that an ice druid had. The ability to freeze enemies in place was advantageous, especially considering the synergy it could have with Chod and his horrors, and not to mention the fire-and-ice combo with Limery.

Then there was the Druid of the Dawn. If Taryn could offer more healing to the rest of the party, and not just his pets, he'd be even more valuable as a support, especially once their party grew. They did most of their fighting during the day, so that would lend to making the most of the source of his druid powers. It seemed like a no-brainer.

But something about the Shadow Druid called to him. Maybe it was what Chief Laojin had said about it being more powerful at night and in the shadow realms. They'd gone head-to-head with demons and behemoths from the shadowlands already. And unless the dark wizard attacked them first, at some point they would be doing battle there. Wouldn't Taryn want to be at his best when it mattered most?

He sighed. Maybe it was possible to have too much of a good thing.

Who was he kidding? There were worse things than having to decide between three awesome class advancements in the most fully-immersive game on the planet. He thought deeper about his choices and what Laojin had said. The word 'devastating' kept replaying in his mind. Taryn loved being the support of the group, but there might come a time when he needed to be more. When that time came, he wanted to be devastating.

Taryn stood straight and spoke with confidence. "I'm going to advance Shadow Druid."

Laojin nodded his approval.

Taryn selected the class advancement, and a flurry of notifications appeared.

Alert! You have selected to advance the Druid class. New class option available.

Druid. *One with the natural world and the elements, druids take their power from nature itself.*

Subclass:

Shadow Druid. *Blessed by the moon, shadow druids draw power from its light and the darkness.*

Available Abilities *(1 ability point to unlock)***:**

Moonbeam: *Cast a beam of radiant energy. 50% increased damage at night. 100% increased damage against the undead. Cost: 100 mana. Cooldown: 60 seconds.*

Scry: *Using a personal item of your intended target, channel the power of the moon to locate their presence on your map. Cost: None. Cooldown: 24 hours.*

Mind Warp: *Corrupted by the darkness, a targeted enemy will attack its allies for 30 seconds. Cost: 200 mana. Cooldown: 30 minutes.*

Tidal Wave: *By harnessing the pull of the moon, cast a tidal wave from a nearby body of water. Cost: 200 mana. Cooldown: 120 seconds.*

Shooting Stars: *A celestial barrage of stars falls from the heavens, dealing damage. 50% increased damage at night. 100% increased damage against the undead. Cost: 100 mana. Cooldown: 60 seconds.*

Shadow Cloak (Passive): *While enabled, shadow druids have increased stealth at night or in the shadows.*

Endless Night: *For 30 seconds, shroud an area in a veil of impenetrable darkness, obscuring the sight and smell of those within. Cost: 200 mana. Cooldown: 1 hour.*

Taryn rubbed his hands together, giddy with excitement. "Oh, this is good! This is really good."

He had his ability point from reaching level twenty-five, but he also had the point he had saved from level twenty-three. He knew he was saving it for something great, and this was it. The only problem was choosing which two to spend his points on.

There were three active abilities: Moonbeam, Shooting Stars, and Tidal Wave. Tidal Wave was cool, but since it had to be near a body of water, it was best to put it on hold for now. Moonbeam and Shooting stars were similar abilities, and their bonus damage against the undead would likely be a huge benefit in the future. Moonbeam was more of a directed attack, while Shooting Stars covered a larger area and was capable of hitting more enemies. He would be choosing one of those, for sure, but would it be better to hit one enemy with a powerful attack or to spread that damage over several enemies?

The choice between the final four would be tough. The ability to locate someone as long as he had one of their items seemed extremely powerful, especially with the portals opened. But how often would that situation arise?

Mind Warp could offer some interesting possibilities, effectively giving them another party member for thirty seconds.

Shadow Cloak would be great for recon and stealth, but Taryn could accomplish most of those feats while in his bird form, so he eliminated that one for now.

That left Endless Night. It reminded him of a better version of the Infernal Darkness Potion, which they had wasted during their first fight with Dakota upon entering Goldspire. While Endless Night only lasted half as long as the potion, it could be cast every hour.

Taryn took a moment to describe the abilities to Laojin.

The troll ran his fingers through his beard. "You have quite the decision ahead of you."

Taryn nodded. With seven available abilities and only two ability points, it would take him ten more levels to unlock them all. He'd been lucky with power-leveling the Hornryx dungeon, but once they left the village, he'd have to earn the upcoming levels the hard way.

All the more reason to get this right.

He'd pick an offensive ability for now, and then discuss the other options with Chod once he returned. Who knew, if he took much longer, maybe Taryn could grind out another level or two.

After careful deliberation, he placed his first ability point into Moonbeam. It added more direct firepower to their arsenal.

Taryn raised his staff and activated the ability toward the center of the room. Shimmering silver light blasted from the ceiling, momentarily casting back the darkness. The beam sizzled for a second against the cave floor before fading away. Aside from that, it was completely silent, a far cry from the accompanying thunder of Lightning Bolt. This attack could kill without ever making a sound.

"Shinies." Limery stared at the area the moonbeam had hit, where a silvery residue coated the ground.

Rhaz looked impressed as he crossed his arms.

Chief Laojin slightly raised his eyebrows. "Very nice. Now, let us return to the village. If you wish, we may continue tomorrow."

Taryn laughed. "I'll take all the free levels I can get."

"Free?" Rhaz frowned, lifting his hairless, blood-covered arm. "Your levels were paid for with my blood."

Laojin laughed.

"You're right, Rhaz," Taryn conceded. "I couldn't have done it without you."

Rhaz stood a little taller after receiving the compliment.

They made the long journey up to the dungeon entrance, bypassing their carnage from previous fights along the way. Having completely cleared the food levels three days in a row, the village was well stocked on meat for the next few weeks.

As they exited the dungeon, a group of people had gathered in the crag. It was far later than Taryn thought, and darkness reigned overhead. Taryn thought maybe they had heard he'd advanced somehow, but they were all facing the opposite direction.

The group parted in front of the chief, revealing a ghostly image of a frost goat that approached from outside the village. The beast's body looked to be formed completely from some ethereal energy, and a hazy orange outline surrounded it whichever way it moved. The goat stopped, turning sideways and looking over its shoulder.

There was a grunt as a large figure emerged from the night. Everyone was suddenly silent, and Taryn could hear the heavy breathing of the creature even from so far away. The figure was as tall as a troll, but with much broader shoulders and black horns that curled around its face. A large fur cloak covered its shoulders.

Taryn stared at it for a minute, sensing something familiar but unable to place it. Suddenly, all the pieces came together. "Chod? What the hell happened to your head?"

Chod fell to his knees. He struggled to remove the fur cloak, and Taryn realized it wasn't a cloak at all. It was a frost goat he'd been carrying on his shoulders. How far had he traveled like this?

Chod leaned over the frost goat's body. "Please, I need your help."

CHAPTER 34
GREATEST OF ALL TIME

WITH MY LAST bit of energy, I lift the dying frost goat from my shoulders and collapse to the ground. A multitude of arctic trolls watch with shocked expressions. Some stare at my spirit guide, its glowing body a beacon against the night. Others look at me warily, no doubt unsure of what to make of a blue forest troll with horns sprouting from his head.

I search for a friendly face, anyone to ask for help, but find no one. When the crowd parts, Taryn and Chief Laojin step through. Taryn shouts something, but I can't hear him over my thundering pulse.

My hands rest on the frost goat as it struggles for breath. "Please, I need your help."

Limery closes the distance in an instant, his warm hands clutching my shoulder. His bulbous eyes are ripe with worry. "Is you's okays, Chods?"

"Yes...need...Taryn."

"Taryns!" Limery yells, but the dwarf is already running in our direction.

He and the chief kneel beside me when they arrive.

I meet their eyes. "I'm fine, just heal the goat."

Taryn exchanges looks with Laojin as he places his hand on the goat. I wait for the familiar glow of Restoration, but it never comes.

He curses. "I'm sorry, but I can't heal animals that aren't my pets." He turns to Laojin. "Can you?"

The chief shakes his head. "I'm afraid I reached my limit for pets long ago."

"Then make him your pet, Taryn," I snap—whether from panic or exhaustion, I'm not sure. All I know is that I didn't carry him all the way down the mountain just to watch him die.

He frowns. "I don't know. I can't just—"

I grab Taryn firmly by the arm with what little strength I have left. "Please. I'll explain everything later, but for now...just, please, help him."

I don't know why this goat means so much to me. He was going to die anyway through no fault of my own. Maybe it was finding the connection to my spirit beast, and the stubbornness that frost goats represent. If I can't save my own spirit beast, what chance do I have against the dark wizard?

He nods. "Okay."

Taryn places both hands on the goat, and a green aura surrounds him. The creature is so weak that he's practically ripe for taming. Taryn's hands glow yellow, and energy spreads out from his palms, coating the frost goat in a similar aura. After a moment, the goat's breathing steadies, and then his health begins to trickle in the other direction.

When the aura fades, Taryn takes a step back. The goat rolls over, his hooves clacking against the ground as he stands. He lowers his head, and I wonder if I've made a mistake, but then the goat slowly steps forward, pressing his horns gently against Taryn's chest.

Taryn smiles and scratches the goat between the horns. "Hey, buddy. It's all okay now. Wait until you meet your brothers and sister." He turns to me. "You've got a lot of explaining to do, but first, we need to get you some health potions."

Laojin wraps my arm over his shoulders and helps me to my feet. Another troll takes position on the other side. I've pushed my exhaustion to the limit, nearly to the same point as I did after Ismora was stabbed so long ago. Back then, I'd passed out when we made it back to the forest and had to recover for almost two days. Luckily, this won't be as bad.

They lead me into a cave and sit me down on a bed covered in fur blankets. A table against the wall is filled with vials and clay pots. The next thing I know, a health potion is being pressed against my lips. An elderly female troll shakes her head as she looks down at me. She knows I pushed myself too hard, but I'm a hero, it comes with the territory. Immediately, a warm tingle spreads through my body and my energy returns fraction by fraction.

Laojin watches me intently, and Limery sits on my stomach. I smile at the imp, and his small shoulders relax.

A moment later, Taryn enters the cave. "I just put Michael Jordan with the other pets. I was worried he might attack them, but he seems much calmer than the ones we saw in Whitgard. Stompy actually acknowledged him."

I lift my head off the bed, certain that I must have misheard him. "Did you just call him Michael Jordan?"

Taryn gives me a devilish grin. "I was thinking Mikey or Jordy for short. I haven't decided."

The exhaustion must be playing tricks on my brain. "Why Michael Jordan?"

Taryn's grin grows wider. "Because he's the G.O.A.T."

I roll my eyes, not even willing to dignify his statement with a response.

Laojin looks at him with a confused expression. "Is Michael Jordan a dwarven name?"

Taryn's smile fades. "No, it's, uh, you know what? It's not important." He turns his attention to me. "Want to explain to me why I now have another pet and a twenty percent chance that they won't obey me? Stompy is stubborn enough. It's bound to rub off on little MJ."

"Oh, come on. He'll make a great pet. And you said yourself it's not like they'll refuse to listen, they just might be a little more creative in how they do it. Don't sweat it." With more of my energy replenished, I sit up on the bed. "I'm famished. What's for dinner?"

After three bowls of stew and an entire boar leg, I finally feel like myself again. Taryn and Limery both slurp at their bowls beside me. When we're finished, we'll meet Chief Laojin and the others in the council room.

I catch lots of glances and outright stares from the villagers. A young troll stalks around like a monster, his two hands mimicking horns on his head. None of the looks are hostile, but I'm sure I'm quite the sight to them, especially when I didn't have these monstrous horns a few days ago.

I toss the bone from my boar leg to Berry. He snatches it up and lumbers away.

"What have you two been up to while I was gone?"

Taryn wags his finger at me. "No, you're the one who stumbled in here with a damn ghost leading the way. I don't care how awesome my news is, and it is awesome, you owe us an explanation.”

“Yeah,” Limery echoes, his mouth full of food. “Yous owes us an explanations.”

I give them my best pleading look. “Come on, you know I’m going to have to tell this story to the council. Can’t you wait five minutes?”

Taryn narrows his eyes. “Fine. Go ahead and analyze me.”

I do what he says, focusing on him until his gamertag appears.

Taryn Jones
Level 25
Shadow Druid
Ebony Dwarf

“Holy shit! You hit level twenty-five already. And what’s a shadow druid?”

Taryn smirks. “Yeah, and Limery is level twenty-four. We’ve been busy while you were frolicking through the snow. Even Berry and Stompy leveled up nicely.” He tilts his bowl, finishing the last of the stew. “Shadow druid is my subclass. I’ll tell you more about it later when we can really talk it over, but I think it will be good for us. I still have one ability point to use and can’t decide what to spend it on.” He stands up. “Alright, let’s get the interrogation over with.”

After taking Taryn’s pets back to the cave, we go to the council room. The council is already at the table when we arrive, in the middle of a heated discussion.

Laojin slams his fist against the table, rattling the empty bowls. “It is no coincidence that—” He cuts his words short when he sees us, and his glare softens. "Chod, Taryn, Limery. We were just discussing you."

Sounds like that was going well. My shoulders stiffen. If they are talking this heatedly about us behind our backs, it can't be good.

"The horns suit you." Senzala winks at me.

I drop my gaze to the floor, and heat rushes to my cheeks. I've never done well with compliments on my appearance, and I'm suddenly aware that in spite of being a troll, the shaman has incredibly feminine features. Her eyelashes are long and wispy against her piercing eyes, and the way her short tusks peek above her lips gives her a mischievous look.

When I sneak a peek at her, she's still staring at me with a wry smile.

"Thank you," I mumble.

Taryn nudges me in the side, and I shake my head to clear my thoughts. Now is not the time to get flustered by a pretty girl.

The chief clears his throat. "Congratulations on finding your spirit beast. The frost goat is a respectable creature. One full of strength and determination. They are not easily intimidated and attack their opponents without hesitation of defeat. I trust that you have found the knowledge to continue down your path?"

I nod. "It was a process, but I'm happy with the results. Thank you for all of your guidance."

Oyanna straightens out a piece of parchment and holds a feather quill in her other hand. "I would like to record your adventure for our library. There is nothing better for scholars than a firsthand account of advancement."

I tell them my story, which consists mostly of me waiting around and staring at animals until I found the frost goats. Her pen moves rapidly, and though she doesn't have an inkwell, it never runs out of ink.

When I get to the part where I find the dying frost goat, Senzala raises a hand for me to stop.

"It is strange to help an animal that has already resigned itself to its fate. Why did you do it?"

I shrug. "I've been asking myself that a lot. It would have been easier to leave it there. But I don't really know. I guess maybe because I thought I could, that if I could bring him here then his story didn't have to be over."

She smiles, and my cheeks grow red again. "I think his story is just beginning."

"Speaking of stories..." Laojin sets my satchel on the table and pulls out the green egg I took from the vault at Seascape. "I'd like to know how a troll came into possession of a dragon egg?"

CHAPTER 35
MYSTERY LOVES COMPANY

"Dragon egg?" I exchange looks with Taryn, who seems just as surprised as I am, before returning my attention to the chief. "How do you know?"

Chief Laojin frowns. "Do I look like the type not to recognize a dragon egg when I see one?"

I picked the egg up in King Orso's vault because I thought it looked cool and its stats were nothing more than question marks. I thought it was a trinket, some item that would prove useful in the future. Not once did I consider there might be an actual living creature inside. Every time I analyze it, it just says Mysterious Green Egg. I focus on it again, but this time, there is a description.

Item. Green Dragon Egg. *Green dragons rule with impunity over the forests they inhabit. They are the most territorial of all dragon species and capable of spewing toxic gas in lieu of flames. Wherever a green dragon calls home, a dense fog is said to follow. Green dragon eggs may only be hatched in the heart of an ancient forest.*

Wow. I've been carrying around a dragon egg all this time and had no idea.

"How do we hatch it?" Taryn blurts out, his eyes filled with greed.

Laojin laughs. "You have eyes for it already."

He lifts the egg, admiring its beauty. The egg is slightly larger than Limery's head, bright green like freshly-mowed grass. Thick, diamond-shaped scales lap over one another like a pine cone.

Laojin places it carefully on the table. "Green dragons can only be hatched in the heart of an ancient forest, where the life aura can infuse it."

I pick up the egg. It's so lightweight that it's hard to imagine it ever being something as big as Nesira. "Where can we find an ancient forest?"

Limery reaches over my shoulder for the egg, tracing his claws along the scales.

Chief Laojin's expression is unreadable. "There are only two that I know of. One is in Wandermere, home of the centaurs."

"And the other?" asks Taryn.

The chief's face goes serious. "Mosstar."

Taryn's eyes go wide. "Wait, isn't that—"

"Home of the dark elves..." He pauses for a long moment. "And birthplace of Valmar Worren, the one you call the dark wizard."

Everywhere we go, it's a constant reminder of what's coming. I don't know much about ancient forests, but if they have the power to hatch a dragon egg, there's no telling what Valmar has waiting on the other side of those portals.

I take my satchel from the table and place the egg back inside. "Considering the portals are still closed to Mosstar, I don't think we'll be going there anytime soon. But there's no way we can turn down the possibility of having a dragon on our side." I lock eyes with Senzala. "Which I'm sure you understand. So, after Boneholde, we will set our sights on Wandermere."

Laojin strokes his beard. "Very well. I hoped we would have

more time with you, but you have an opportunity few in Mythos ever experience—to witness the birth of a dragon." He turns to Taryn. "Another day in the dungeon is little compared to a dragon on the battlefield. I advise you to leave for Boneholde at dawn. Tonight, we will celebrate your good fortune."

Tzane rubs his belly, a massive grin on his face. "I'll have them prepare the sweetwater."

***

Taryn lifts his cup of sweetwater in the air. "To dungeons."

"And dragons!" I shout, tapping my cup against his and we both take a large gulp of the famous troll brew.

"And Limmy!" The imp hovers before our faces, holding his mug with both hands.

"And to Limmy," Taryn and I both echo, toasting him in turn.

The sweet, frothy liquid burns as it trails down my throat. It tastes just like I remember at the troll village. Even though the tribes are different in many regards, it's nice to know some things remain the same.

I can't help but think how far I've come since then, back when my top priority was not getting killed by other heroes.

Trolls spill out from the caves, and the village looks like the site of a yeti festival. Drinks flow freely, and drums echo off the mountain. Pets roam the village, and I'm surprised by how social MJ has become. He's like a completely different animal compared to the frost goats in Whitgard. Stompy lays next to the mammoth at the entryway to the caves sharing his carrot. Every time they finish one, he returns to hover over Taryn until he gets another.

"This is the last one you get tonight." Taryn pulls a carrot from his satchel. "Tell your girlfriend to mooch off someone else."

Stompy snorts as he heads away, and Taryn grins like a proud father.

Laojin has made an ice slide for the children to play on that descends from the caves down into the village. It even has a loop in the middle and a ramp at the end that launches the children into a snowbank that Senzala created. Young trolls run from the snowbank at the bottom back to the caves to slide again and again.

"Limmy wants to slides." The imp finishes his sweetwater and zooms toward the top of the slide.

I'm glad he's having fun.

Across from us, Senzala and Laojin stand side by side. The chief whispers something in her ear, pointing to one of the children as the young troll comes to a stop against the snowbank at the end of the slide. Senzala laughs, spilling some of her drink in the snow.

Taryn elbows me in the side. "You gave me so much shit about Lady Brollen when we were in Sandholde and look at you, swooning over some hairy titties."

I shove him away. "Dude, it's not like that. She's just, I don't know, I think she's kind of cool."

"So that's your type?" Taryn smirks. "I thought you didn't have time for women."

"I don't." I focus on the children playing to keep from looking at Senzala. "We'll be gone in the morning, off to our next adventure."

Taryn scoffs. "All adventuring and no play makes Chod a dull boy."

A loud roar draws our attention as Rhaz beats his chest in the center of the village. "Who will challenge the mighty Rhaz?"

There's chatter before a deep roar answers, and Tzane emerges from the crowd with a mug of sweetwater in each hand.

He chugs them both back-to-back before tossing the mugs aside and slamming a fist against his own chest. "A few days in the dungeon and you think you are king of the mountain." He cracks his knuckles. "Let's see what you've got."

Cheers and roars echo as a circle forms around the two challengers.

Rhaz and Tzane lock hands, to the delight of the crowd, each one pushing with all their might as they try to overpower the other. The two trolls grunt, their muscles bulging as they hold each other at a stalemate.

After several minutes of neither one giving an inch, steam starts to rise from Tzane's body. A few of the onlookers catcall as the challenge shifts in Tzane's favor. He grunts louder, and Rhaz starts moving in the other direction. His feet dig into the earth, but the pot-bellied troll keeps pushing. Tzane unleashes a mighty roar and shoves Rhaz onto his back.

Tzane flexes for the crowd and asks for another mug of sweetwater, and then he extends a hand to Rhaz.

Rhaz slaps it away. "No fair, you raged."

Tzane shrugs. "The mountain favored me today. A worthy fight."

"Hey, look. Now's your chance." Taryn points across the way to where Senzala is standing alone drinking her sweetwater. "Bro, live a little. It's just a conversation. It's not like you have to worry about her dragon biting your arm off or anything." Taryn steps behind me and pushes me forward.

Well, I hadn't been worried about that.

I know Taryn won't shut up until I talk to her, so I concede. As I walk over, I feel the same nervous energy I used to get when I was called to the front of the class, keenly aware of every step and afraid I might fall on my face. I don't know why I'm so nervous. We've talked before, but we've never just chatted, and

I'm no good at small talk. All I can think about is how stupid this is.

"Want some company?" I ask, thankful for the cold air against my warm cheeks.

She smiles. "Sure. Are you enjoying yourself? The little one certainly is."

I take a large swig of sweetwater and let the burn wash over me. "You mean Limery or Taryn?" I laugh. "I'm having a good time. I love a good troll party."

She runs her hand along one of my horns, letting the tip poke against her finger. "Too bad you're leaving soon. We'll be having our spring festival before long. Now, that is a party you don't want to miss."

My pulse races at how close she is to me. "Sounds like fun, but we have a dragon to hatch." I pull the egg from my satchel, admiring its beauty. "Want to hold it?"

"It's beautiful." She lets go of my horn and takes the egg, admiring it like some precious jewel. "You have no idea how lucky you are to have this. Dragons are a true wonder. Nesira is my totem, but she will never be mine. She lends me her power and allows me in her presence, but she has a mind and will of her own. I never got to see her as a hatchling, back before she realized the world bowed before her."

"You could come. See the dragon hatch and join us on our travels. We could use someone with your power for what's coming."

She shakes her head. "A shaman belongs with her people, no matter how tempting the offer. Plus, the ring wouldn't hold with me being so far away."

Everywhere I go, there's always a reason for inaction, a reason for people to stay stuck in their ways. "Don't you think your tribe deserves more than hiding away in the mountain?"

She frowns, handing the egg back. "What I think doesn't matter. It is not my decision to make."

I put the egg away before I crack it in frustration. "But you're on the council."

She sighs. "I offer guidance and wisdom when I can, but our place in this world is a matter that was settled long ago."

"Wheeeee!" Limery shouts as he speeds down the slide, interrupting our conversation and eliciting laughter from the crowd.

He launches off the end, but instead of plowing into the snowbank, he flies into the air, his molten form a beacon in the sky.

"Showoff!" Taryn shouts. "If you think that is cool, watch this."

He lifts his staff and a beam of silver energy shoots down from the sky, exploding against the snow. The way he wobbles back and forth, I can tell he's feeling the sweetwater. For several seconds, the moonbeam radiates sizzling energy, melting a crater in the snow before eventually dissipating.

The crowd cheers in response to his theatrics.

I decide to let our conversation fade, summoning my spirit guide and letting it run through the crowd. Michael Jordan runs over to the spirit goat, lowering his head in respect. A drunken Taryn gives me a thumbs-up.

The trolls playing the drums increase the rhythm, beating in rapid succession until everyone quiets. Chief Laojin starts a slow clap as he walks up the pathway to the ledge overlooking the village. Several male trolls follow him, joining in with clapping.

Once at the top, the others continue to clap as they fall in behind him until there are at least thirty trolls standing behind the chief. The drums beat louder and faster. The claps fall in sync until it all sounds like a rapid rumble.

Chief Laojin raises his staff in the air and the village goes silent. "Tonight, we celebrate the accomplishments of our guests, and knowing that whatever role they play in the future of Mythos, we had a small part in that. Tonight, we will send them off in style."

The chief slams the butt of the staff to the ground, and the ice slide crumbles into a million tiny shards. It sounds like rain as they pitter-patter down the mountain.

There's an audible inhalation just before the trolls unleash a thunderous roar that has my hair standing on end. In perfect unison, they all stomp with their left foot, clap, then stomp with their right. They lower into a squat and roar again, making faces that would keep children up at night.

Then they perform their tribal dance, a beautiful display of grace and power. Stomps, roars, and thunderous claps echo across the night. Senzala grabs my arm as she watches, and I'm thankful she can't see my blushing face. I lose sight of the performance as I focus on the warmth of her touch.

Their final chant brings me back to the world as they all tilt their heads back and a brutal scream escapes into the night. The scream ends, its echo calling back to them again and again.

And then the dragon answers.

A powerful gust of wind blows across the village as snow pours from the heavens. In a matter of seconds, the clear sky is a whirlwind of white. Nesira's shrieking roar cuts above it all, and though I can't see her, I can feel her presence.

Senzala squeezes my arm. "I think the celebration is over."

CHAPTER 36
ON THE ROAD AGAIN

THE NEXT MORNING, we say our good-byes to the tribe before Senzala and Laojin escort us down to the ring. I'm surprised that Taryn seems more well-liked by the arctic trolls than me. He and Limery both have a crowd of trolls wishing them well on their journey.

It feels like the chief and Senzala are the only ones I've really connected with since being here. Even though I got my class advancement, I can't help but feel like I missed out on an amazing experience inside the dungeon.

Taryn balls his fist, teaching Rhaz how to fist-bump. The muscled troll then tests out his new greeting on Limery. He bumps a little too hard, sending the imp somersaulting through the air, before tilting his head back in raucous laughter. I guess the best bonds really are forged on the battlefield.

Stompy nudges Taryn in the side, almost knocking him over.

"Fine." He pets the moulhaug on the snout before pulling a carrot from his bag. "They won't last forever, you know."

Stompy takes the carrot and drops it at the feet of the mammoth. She grabs it with her trunk and tosses it in her mouth.

Taryn puts his hands on his hips. "They grow up so fast."

Oyanna loads us up with health and mana potions, and after Taryn struggles to get Stompy to leave his new mammoth girlfriend behind, we set off down the mountain.

I take one last look at the village in all of its icy glory. The fresh layer of snow from Nesira makes it more picturesque than ever. I take a mental picture, because in all likelihood, I'll never set foot here again.

"Alright, Jordy, lead the way!" Taryn slaps the frost goat on the hindquarters, and he trots to the front of the party, snorting at Berry and Stompy as he passes.

Limery swoops down, landing on the goat's back. Taryn climbs on Berry, and I elect to stay on foot with Senzala and the chief.

"Is that what you settled on? Jordy?" I ask.

"Yeah, Mikey just didn't have the same ring to it." He grins. "I can't wait to see him in action."

Laojin grunts. "You will have many opportunities on the journey to Boneholde. But beware the hobgoblins of Greypeak. What they lack in intelligence, they more than make up for in numbers and tenacity. They have a certain fondness for ambushing unsuspecting travelers."

"I thought the hobgoblins stayed hidden in the mountain?" I ask.

He nods. "They do, but there are always hobgoblin scouts roaming Frostmoor, so be wary."

"Let them try and ambush us." Taryn puffs out his chest. "They aren't the only ones who can scout ahead."

Taryn and Laojin get lost in talk of pets, scouting, and all things druid, so I walk beside Senzala. We haven't spoken since our time together was cut short by Nesira. I open my mouth half a dozen times to say something, but I can't seem to find the right words.

I know I have bigger priorities, but I did enjoy her company. It's a shame it has to end so soon.

"You know, I never got to see you in action," I finally manage to say.

She smirks. "Consider yourself lucky."

"Oh yeah?" I can't help but grin. "Why's that?"

"You'll understand when you hatch your own dragon."

If it weren't for our promise to King Orso, I'd be tempted to head straight to Wandermere without even visiting Boneholde, but maybe we can end our stay in Frostmoor on a strong note. We've made friends in Whitguard and Hornryx, but what we really need are allies.

The conversation flows smoother the rest of the journey, and before I know it, we're only a few hundred yards above the ring. The massive snowstorm rages around the mountain, obscuring our vision of what lies below.

"I'm glad I met you, Senzala." I extend a hand.

She grasps me around the forearm. "As am I. Perhaps one day, we will meet again." She winks, and I feel like there is more to those words than she is letting on.

"Travel safely." Laojin places a hand on my shoulder. "I sense great things from you all. Let the other tribes know that we have not perished. If they wish to find us, then you know the way."

I shake my head. "If you want the other tribes to know you remain, then it is you who must find them. I respect you, but I will not be your messenger."

The chief narrows his eyes. I can't tell if he's surprised or angry, but he nods. "Very well."

I summon my spirit guide, and it takes position next to Jordy, ready to lead us into the depths of the ring.

"Good-byes!" Limery shouts as the snow swallows us whole.

"Hell yeah!" Taryn shouts as Moonbeam finishes off a wild boar. "That's what I'm talking about."

"Congrats, you're finally useful," I tease as I start skinning the boar for our dinner.

He flashes me a rude gesture. "No need to be salty because you have to wait for your new active ability. Speaking of which, I still need to allocate my last ability point."

"Hey, I'm not salty." I use my claws to separate the skin from the meat. "My spirit guide has already proven useful. And now that my attacks deal splash damage, I can probably sell or trade Sea Scorpion at the next town we get to. It should get a nice price." Taryn squirms as I pull the skin from the boar's body. "So, what ability were you thinking?"

He scrunches his brow. "I don't know. I've narrowed it down to four, but they all seem so useful. Scry could be good for tracking our enemies. Mind Warp can help turn a fight in our favor. Shadow Cloak gives me more utility, especially for sneaking around. And then Endless Night can really turn things on their head."

"If it were me, I'd think about which one is going to be the most useful right now. Tracking our enemies is cool, but do we have need of it at this moment? Do we even have anything to use to track them with? I'd save that one for the future, but keep it in mind going forward." I point to Limery, who is clearing an area for a fire. "We can finally put his greedy little hands to use for good."

Limery looks up from his work with a devilish grin.

Taryn scratches his forehead. "If we want to look at it like that, then Endless Night is the easy choice. I can use it offensively to blind the enemy while we bombard the area with spells, or we can use it as a quick getaway if things get hairy."

"Sounds like a good plan." I finish gutting the boar and empty the innards into a large pot from my inventory. "Summon us a shelter for the night and I'll get our meat cooking."

Our little shelter is more crowded than ever now that Jordy has joined the mix, but it still beats sleeping in the open air. The goat tucks his legs beneath him, sandwiched between Berry and Stompy. Ruby sits in front of the fire next to Limery, eyeing the meat as it sizzles.

At the base of the mountain, the ring that hides the arctic trolls once again towers above us. Tomorrow, we will abandon the enchanted trail and cut through the snow toward Boneholde. It will probably take us at least two days to reach the Snowwalker Tribe, and that's with Taryn casting Strong Wind.

Taryn reaches for a piece of meat and jerks his hand back. "Ouch! Hot!" He kisses his fingers gingerly. "First mana flames, and now food. Why does everything have to be so damn hot?" He grimaces at the puffy red skin. "You really think we're going to be able to hatch a dragon?"

I shrug. "Who knows, but I figure it's worth a shot. Not like we have anywhere important to be once we leave here."

Limery sticks his hand into the open flame, grabbing a piece of meat and tossing it straight into his mouth. "Limmy wants to sees the baby dragons."

Taryn places his hands on his hips, and Limery mirrors his

expression next to him. "Look, it's thirty seconds. If we want to use my abilities to their limits, then we need to test them."

I summon more horrors so that we can properly test the effects of Endless Night. "Fine, let's get it over with."

The next thing I know, everything is pitch-black. I can't see. I can't hear. Not even my night vision can penetrate the darkness. I can sense my horrors' presences, but I can't even begin to guess their location. It's unnerving to feel so helpless. So lost. I summon my spirit guide, but even it can't cast light through Taryn's spell.

When the darkness fades, Taryn looks at me expectantly. "Well?"

I use my hand to shield my eyes from the sudden brightness. "It's OP. No sight, no sound. Nothing. I can think of a handful of ways to use this to our advantage."

After an hour, the ability is off cooldown, so Taryn casts Endless Night on himself and his pets. The darkness fades again, and Taryn grins from ear-to-ear. "This is good."

We discuss strategy as we walk, testing out new theories every hour as the ability becomes available. As we get closer to Greypeak, Taryn and Limery take turns scouting ahead for any signs of hobgoblins.

As the sun begins to set, we pass the enchanted path that leads up to Greypeak.

"Want to go beat up on some hobgoblins?" Taryn gestures up the mountain.

I shake my head. "I want to hit up Boneholde and get out of here. It might be a good idea to scout the area before we camp."

"Aye-aye, Captain." He mock-salutes me. "You and Limery get dinner ready, and I'll scope out the area."

An hour later, Taryn returns. "I flew up to some of the ruins. There's no signs of hobgoblins anywhere."

I hand him a piece of roasted boar. "Maybe they're all inside the mountain."

The next morning, Taryn scouts the area again, but there's still no sign of the hobgoblins. As cold as everything is in this climate, I'd probably be content to hide away in the mountain as well. At least it's one less thing we have to worry about.

By midday, the features of Boneholde begin to come into view. It's the shortest of the five peaks, and the skeleton of some ancient beast can be seen half-buried around the base of the mountain. Long ago, the hobgoblins made their homes in the shadow of the skeleton. Now, it belongs to the Snowwalkers.

Eventually, we come across the fifth enchanted path, and we're on a straight shot to the village. As we get closer, I can make out smoke rising from the massive bones. Judging by the positioning of the sun, it'll likely be dark when we arrive, but I think I have a plan that will get us a warm welcome.

"Think anything will come of this?" asks Taryn.

"I don't know. Gherhardt says they're more tribal. I don't want to judge them before we meet them, but I doubt that will work in our favor."

The sun finally sets, and small orange dots appear along the mountain. The Snowwalker Tribe has made their home much lower than Whitgard, so the fires can be seen burning from where we are. These guys must have a flare for the dramatic, because the eye-holes in the massive skull glow ominously from above the village.

"That's not foreboding at all," mumbles Taryn.

"Ready to let them know we're here?" I ask.

"Go for it."

I summon my spirit guide, and the ethereal frost goat lights the way as we approach Boneholde. I'm hoping the spectacle gains us at least a little favor with the natives.

We must be a sight to behold as we make our way up the mountain—with the glowing frost goat leading the way, followed by Jordy, with Limery holding onto his horns, then Taryn and Ruby riding Berry, and finally me lording above them all on Stompy's back. All we need is some whacky music and a little dancing to set the scene.

A slight incline leads up to the village, where a wooden palisade forms the boundary. Inside the walls, the ancient skeleton towers above all. Wooden huts are built along the bones, using them for structural support, and some of the buildings are several stories tall along the rib cage.

At the gate, two massive pyres burn, casting the figures watching us from the lookout in a shadowy silhouette.

I halt my spirit guide about fifty yards from the gate. Something definitely feels off about this.

Mana pulses at my fingertips, but I fight the urge to summon my horrors. The villagers might not be welcoming, and I don't want to give them a reason to attack.

"What business do you have in Boneholde?" one of the shadowy figures asks.

"We come seeking allies on behalf of King Orso of Seascape," I shout.

The two figures laugh, and it chills me to the bone.

"You just won't stop, will you?" There's something familiar about the way the man spits the words out. "You should have stayed in the forest where you belong."

My hair stands on edge as the pieces fall into place.

"We need to go," Taryn whispers.

"I'm surprised you found us, but you made a big mistake coming here. There's no one to save you this time. You're finally going to pay for all the damage you've done."

The man takes a step back, and the light of the fire reveals his face. Jude Duggan, the hero who has had it out for me since Vanaria. Shaggy black hair falls just above his dark eyes, and his lip curls up in a snarl.

If that's Jude, then the other figure must be—

"Good to see you again, troll." Glenn smiles as he steps into the light, but the smile doesn't reach his eyes. His cheery disposition is nothing like the monster underneath.

He's as plain-looking as ever, and his mismatched armor has been replaced by leather and fur. If I didn't know any better, he'd look exactly how I'd imagine a tribesman to appear.

He pulls out a dagger with a bone hilt, and the blade catches the light of the flames. "I think we have some unfinished business."

Taryn inches Berry backward, but I hold my ground. I refuse to be intimidated by these assholes.

"What are you doing here? I demand to speak to the Head of the Snowwalker Tribe."

Jude cackles madly. "You hear that? He demands to speak to the head of the Snowwalker Tribe." He lets out a sigh of pleasure. "Oh, that's good. Well, go ahead. I'm listening."

"I'm not here for your games, Jude," I snap, urging Stompy forward. "We're taking you back to Seascape to face your crimes."

Glenn shakes his head. "Stupid troll. You don't understand. You have no power here."

I take a moment to analyze both, just so I know what we're getting into.

Glenn Orickson

   Level 21
   Warrior
   Human

Jude Duggan

Level 24

Fighter

Human

Whatever they've been up to, they've been busy. At those levels, they are definitely dangerous. There's no telling what abilities they've unlocked. And if Glenn has somehow convinced the Snowwalker Tribe to follow him... I clench my fist, trying not to think about how they earned those levels.

Regardless of how strong they are, we're still stronger. I'll carry them back to Seascape on my shoulders if I have to.

"We can't leave," I whisper to Taryn. "I've seen what Glenn is capable of. First with the townspeople of Lynchton, and then the dwarves at the portal. Jude might just be an asshole, but Glenn is dangerous. We can't let him do anything to these people."

Taryn frowns. "What can we do? They're already inside the wall."

"Then we lure them out." I jump down from Stompy and equip Destroyer, waving it in the air at the two heroes. "Why don't you come and fight me like a man?"

Jude leaps down from the lookout. He lands with one knee to the ground like a superhero. "Don't mind if I do. Then I can mount your head on the gate like all the rest."

All the rest?

"Dear god," Taryn whispers.

That's when I notice the heads mounted along the palisade.

Dozens of heads top the spikes that make up the wall of the village. Men, women, and children stretch for as far as I can see. So many lives gone forever. How did I not notice until now?

Fresh rage consumes me. "Why?" My voice cracks when I ask,

though I'm not expecting any reasonable explanation from these two.

Glenn jumps down, landing next to his demented partner and flashing me an unsettling smile. "Don't worry, Boneholde is in good hands now."

"Enough talking." Jude touches his palms together and four shadow doppelgängers spread out from him, two flanking each side. "Let's fight."

He pulls two daggers from his waistband, and the clones wield shadowy weapons of their own.

Glenn grins with delight. "You heard the man."

His body erupts with a golden glow, and he charges at us.

CHAPTER 37

BONEHOLDE

A WAVE of shadow and light washes over us as Glenn charges alongside Jude and his four doppelgängers. The two heroes are dressed similarly in fur clothing and wield blades with hilts made from bone. Jude has several daggers and knives strapped along his body. Glenn grips a shortsword.

I turn to Taryn. "You and Limery take Jude. Glenn is mine!"

Taryn's face is set in determination. "I don't like this. It feels like a trap."

"Look what they've done!" I snap. "How many more have to die before they're dealt with? We can end this now."

He bites his lip, then nods. That's all the confirmation I need to summon horrors as I rush into battle.

Sparks run along Glenn's arm as he slashes his sword at me. I raise the frosted buckler that Taryn looted from the dungeon to block the blow.

His dagger connects and lightning explodes. Electricity courses through my body and jumps from me to my horrors, stunning us in place. For a moment, I can't move. Glenn stabs for my throat, but I quickly activate my Tiger's Eye Pendant, cleansing the stun from myself but not my horrors.

I block Glenn's attack with the buckler, and he raises his sword for another swing. With his Dexterity cut in half thanks to my buckler, he thinks twice. Instead, he takes a few steps back and smirks.

My horrors press onward, but he makes short work of them with his sword.

"Big, bad troll, always pretending to be the hero." He keeps smiling. "Pretty soon you'll all be food for the worms."

I ignore his comment. I'm not here for a conversation. The only thing that matters is making him pay for all the people he has hurt.

Lightning crashes nearby, where Taryn and Limery have the upper hand against Jude. The fighter is on the defensive, along with his doppelgängers, as they dodge fireballs and the whipping vines of Sapling Staff.

Jude somersaults backward with his clones mimicking his every movement. When he lands, he swipes his arm in front of him, and three shadow blades shoot toward Taryn. The doppelgängers each shoot three of their own, sending a barrage of dark blades.

Stompy steps in front of Taryn and Berry, taking the brunt of damage as fifteen shadow attacks bury themselves in his flesh. He bellows in pain, and anger flares in Taryn's eyes.

Limery yells, hitting one of the clones with a fireball and setting it aflame. A simultaneous Lightning Bolt and Moonbeam disintegrate another doppelgänger.

Blood pours from Stompy's wounds as he favors his left front leg, but the stubborn moulhaug refuses to quit, charging toward Jude.

Glenn attacks while I'm distracted, but I see him out of the corner of my eye. I swing Destroyer up in time to meet his blade. The force from the warhammer is enough to knock the weapon from his grip. It flips end over end, landing point down in the snow.

I press the attack while he's weaponless, and he equips a small shield made from the skull of some monster. He parries my first attack, backpedaling as he reaches for his weapon. I bring my weapon down on his head with all my momentum, but a silver dome forms around him at the last second, absorbing the blow and reflecting it back to me. The reverberation launches me like a cannon blast.

I crash to the ground twenty feet away, crawling to my feet as Glenn kneels to retrieve his weapon. Jordy rams into him at full speed, drilling Glenn in the chest and tossing him like a ragdoll.

Nearby, Taryn and Limery still have the upper hand. Jude uses some sort of shadow-step, leaving a trail of blurry figures as he barely dodges consecutive fireballs. He pauses for half a second too long as he casts more doppelgängers, and a fireball hits him in the chest. He loses a chunk of health but manages to get the spell off, and more doppelgängers appear.

"Time to finish this!" I shout.

Taryn nods, but a loud bellowing note blares over everything. I turn to see Glenn with a horn pressed to his lips.

He removes it, and his smirk is more punchable than ever. "You're right. It is time to finish this."

Jude falls back, laughing hysterically as he does.

A dull rumble forms from inside the village, and snow cascades from the roofs of buildings.

At first, I think he's learned how to summon an avalanche—until I hear the growls that accompany the unmistakable trampling of feet.

There's scratching on the other side of the wall, and then

dozens of round heads with pointy ears climb over the heads mounted along the palisade.

Hobgoblin. *Level 20. Full of more anger and rage than traditional goblins, hobgoblins do not bow to those with greater power. They trample them.*

They leap from the palisade without fear, landing in the snow and setting off at a sprint. Each hobgoblin is about three feet tall, with dull gray skin, putrid yellow eyes, hooked noses, and long pointy ears.

It all makes sense now. The reason there were no hobgoblins in Greypeak is because they were all here.

"Run!" I shout.

Taryn is already leading Berry in the other direction as I summon more horrors and send them at the hobgoblins to buy us some time. Ruby and Jordy sprint ahead of the group, but Stompy is slow to follow with his wounded leg.

More hobgoblins spill over the wall by the second, and the gate shakes as countless more beat against it from inside the village.

Taryn's eyes are full of panic as he casts Strong Wind. I immediately move faster, but Stompy continues to limp noticeably.

He glances over his shoulder at the influx of hobgoblins. "Hold them off while I heal him."

He casts Stonewall, forcing some of the hobgoblins to leave the path and go through the snow. This slows them some, but they continue to climb the palisade. Meanwhile, Glenn and Jude retreat toward the village.

I meet the hobgoblins in the snow, smashing them with Destroyer until it is molten hot. Limery peppers them with fireballs and summons flame walls. I try to keep them as close together as possible. With my new passive, every hit deals damage to those around my intended target.

Jordy joins the fray, headbutting, stomping, and kicking hobgoblins to death. Berry rips one's head clear off.

Taryn leans over Stompy, casting the moulhaug in a golden glow, when a black dagger stabs him in the shoulder. The aura of Restoration fades.

"Not so fast," laughs Jude.

Taryn grimaces as he tries again, but another dagger hits him in the back.

The gate to Boneholde bursts open, and countless hobgoblins spill through. These carry stone clubs, bones, and other blunt force weapons.

"We have to go now!" I smash Destroyer into another hobgoblin, caving its head in. "I'll clear what I can but get moving now."

I activate Berserker Rage, using the increase to my stats to fight off goblins as we retreat. Stompy moves a little faster with some of his wounds healed, but he's a long way from healthy.

Taryn summons another Stonewall, separating me from the horde. "Let's get out of here."

He lifts his staff, and a cloud of darkness forms over our pursuers. Strong Wind hits me again, and my feet move faster.

By sheer numbers, the hobgoblins push through Endless Night, looking dazed and confused as they emerge from the dark cloud. More and more continue to pour out of the village like ants.

Glenn blows the horn again and the hobgoblins refocus on us once again. My heart pounds in my ears as I sprint after Taryn and the others. Even with Strong Wind, the hobgoblins are gaining on us. There's no way we'll escape if they continue to pursue.

"The Frost Bombs! Toss them!" I shout.

I pull both frost bombs from my inventory and toss them at the horde. They explode upon impact, freezing a dozen or so in place, but more hobgoblins trample over their frozen brethren.

Taryn hits more with his own frost bombs, but it's not enough. There are just too many.

I summon horrors and watch them get swallowed by the horde. There are so many hobgoblins that Horror of Vitality's slow can only affect a few at a time.

Stompy comes to an abrupt halt, and I crash into his backside.

I pat him on the leg. "Come on, boy. Let's go."

He snorts, turning to face the horde.

"Uh, Taryn!" I yell over the approaching chaos.

He brings Berry to a halt. "Stompy, let's go."

The moulhaug huffs, taking a step toward the approaching hobgoblins.

"Stompy! Now!" Taryn yells. His face is contorted in confusion and anger.

I grab Stompy by the reins and pull hard, but he refuses to budge. He paws at the ground, pulling against my grip with all his power. I pull back just as hard.

The reins snap, and he charges back toward the horde, leaving me holding the torn leather. I'm at a loss for what to do.

"Stompy!" Taryn pleads.

In all my years, I've never seen Taryn with such a pained expression.

He jumps down from Berry, running after the moulhaug.

I step in his way, wrapping him in a bearhug. "We have to go."

He struggles against my grip. "I can't... Stompy... I can't!"

Stompy swings his horn from side to side like a battering ram as he collides with the horde. Hobgoblins fly in every direction like bowling pins. For a moment, he wreaks devastation on the smaller creatures like a bull in a china shop, but they continue to swarm him as a steady stream continues to pour through the gate. They pile on him until there's nothing but a mound of hobgoblins.

Taryn's struggling fades, replaced by heaving sobs. I lift him onto Berry's back.

Limery hovers in the air with a look of grim confusion.

I squeeze Taryn's leg. "We have to go now."

Tears stream down his face. He looks at me, but it's like he can't see me.

I grab him by the cloak. "Now, or we all die!"

His eyes focus, and he glares at me as he whips the reins.

CHAPTER 38
THE ULTIMATE SACRIFICE

WE WALK FOR HOURS, and no one says a word. Empty silence, aside from Taryn's occasional sniffle or Berry's groans, and the crunch of gravel beneath our feet. Limery clings silently to my shoulder. Even he is at a loss.

I look over my shoulder constantly, but nothing follows us, at least as far as I can tell. Either way, we won't be resting any time soon. I've already reached the point where my stamina is waning, but how can we rest knowing that there are hundreds of hobgoblins out there?

I still can't wrap my head around what happened. Not just losing Stompy, but all of it. The last time I logged out, I remember watching Jude and Glenn lying in a cave through the monitor, but I never would have suspected this. Glenn must have used the hobgoblins to overtake Boneholde.

An entire village wiped off the map. And Whitgard could be next.

I need to warn them. Maybe it will be the push they need to

talk to King Orso. Maybe not, but they need to know what they are up against.

The arctic trolls can hold their own. They have the ring. They have a dragon. No one even knows they still exist.

"Limery," I whisper. "I need your help."

He looks up at me with bulbous yellow eyes. "What is its?"

"I need you to fly to Whitgard. Tell Gherhardt what happened and then meet us back at the portal. We can't stay here, but they need to be warned."

He nods, and tears well up around his eyes. "Chods."

"What's up, buddy?"

"Is Stompys coming backs?"

The words hit me like a punch in the gut. The moulhaug's last moments replay over and over in my mind. That look of stubborn defiance as he snapped the reins from my grip. He was loyal until the very end, sacrificing himself for the person he loved more than anything in this world.

I blink back tears. "No, he's not."

He wraps his warm arms around my neck. "Limmy will miss hims."

Yeah, we all will.

Limery says good-bye to Taryn before taking off into the night, but there's no response.

Taryn continues to cast Strong Wind whenever it's available, but he hasn't said a word or even acknowledged my presence. I give him his space. I can imagine what he's going through, what it would be like if I lost Limery, but I'll never really know how it feels unless it happens.

I pray that day never comes.

Jordy, who normally leads the way, clings next to Berry. The two walk so close together that there's barely any space between them.

After a few more hours, I finally break the silence. "Taryn."

No response.

"We should probably rest soon."

Silence.

"Hey, man, I know you're hurting right now, but if we pass out from exhaustion, then we're screwed."

There's an angry sigh as he guides Berry off the path. He leads the bear toward a group of trees, where he casts Stonewall. During the time it takes him to summon three more walls, he never looks in my direction. His posture is stiff as a board.

Without Limery, there's no fire. Taryn sits against Berry with Ruby in his lap. Jordy attempts to nuzzle Taryn, but he ignores the goat.

I sit against the opposite wall aimlessly cleaning my claws. "You know you can talk to me, right?"

He glances at me, and I don't know if I have ever seen so much hatred in his eyes. I know he's upset, but I don't understand why he's taking it out on me.

"What?" I snap. "You're not the only one upset. I cared for Stompy too, you know! I tried to get him to run. I fucking tried!"

Taryn is on his feet in an instant, pointing in my face. "I told you I had a bad feeling about that place but you didn't listen. And if you hadn't brought that stupid goat down the mountain, this never would have happened. I didn't want to make him my pet. If I hadn't added another pet, then maybe Stompy would have listened to me. Maybe he would still be alive right now. You—" He presses his finger against my chest. "—You caused this."

I smack his hand away and jump to my feet, towering over him. "Don't you put this on me." My vision blurs, and hot tears run down my cheeks. "No one forced you to do anything. I'm not the reason Stompy is dead. Neither is Jordy. Stompy had a mind of his own, regardless of what your stupid stats say. He never listened to anyone unless he wanted to. You want to know why he ran back in? Why he didn't listen?"

Taryn continues glaring.

I clench my fist, but the tears keep flowing. "He did it because he loved you. He sacrificed himself so that you could live. So that we could all live. If you want to hate me, go ahead, but you know I'm right."

He looks up at me, brow furrowed, and for a moment, I'm sure he's going to hit me. Then his lip quivers and his shoulders collapse. He grabs my cloak and buries his head into my chest. "I just miss him so much. I didn't even get to say good-bye," he wails. "This isn't fun anymore, Chad. Games aren't supposed to make you feel like this."

His body shakes violently between sobs, and for a moment, I just wrap my arm around him and hold him tight.

When his sobs fade to sniffles, he lets go. "They are going to pay for what they've done?"

I wipe away the ice crystals that have formed around my eyes. "One day, but right now, we need to worry about getting to safety."

He nods, wiping his nose on his sleeve, then he reaches into his pocket and pulls out a black leather glove. "We'll get them when they least expect it."

I analyze the glove, but it's nothing more than a simple garment. "What's that?"

His eyes narrow as he stares at the glove. "I took it off Jude during the fight. Once I unlock Scry, they're both dead."

After a short rest, we're back on the road. We're a far cry from normal, but some of the tension is gone.

Taryn reaches into his satchel and pulls out a carrot. He leans down from Berry's back and offers it to Jordy. "I'm sorry I called you a stupid goat. None of this is your fault."

Jordy takes the carrot from his hand.

"How many of those do you have?" I ask.

"Gherhardt gave me an entire box before we left. I used to give them to Stompy—" He chokes up, and there's a long pause before he clears his throat. "I used to give them to Stompy as treats."

Jordy crunches the carrot in his powerful jaws. When he's finished, he bleats, and the wavering cry carries across the night.

We elect to rest in short doses, never camping for more than a few hours before moving on. One of us is always on alert, watching and waiting for any sign of trouble. During my watch, I keep a full army of horrors ready at all times, just in case something shows up. Eventually, the sun spills over the horizon, setting the snow ablaze with light and allowing us to see for miles in every direction. The coast looks clear, but it does little to ease my worry.

Taryn slows his pace until we are side by side. "What are we going to do about Whitgard?"

"What can we do?" I shrug. "We don't have the forces to fight that many hobgoblins. I sent Limery to warn them. We can make sure they are prepared, but that's about it."

"Maybe we should stop in Seascape before going to Wandermere. We can tell the king what happened. Maybe he'll send his forces to capture Jude and Glenn, or at least offer protection."

I scrunch my brow. "You wouldn't want to join?" After everything that's happened, that doesn't make sense to me.

He shakes his head. "It's too raw. I know for certain that if I saw them now, I would do something stupid." He pulls Jude's glove from his pocket. "When the time comes, they'll get theirs."

I pat him on the back. "I'll be right there with you."

He suddenly lifts his hand to his forehead and squints in the direction of Hornryx. "What the hell?"

A dark splotch moves along the enchanted path toward the portal. I curse. They're going to try and stop us from leaving Frostmoor. The hobgoblins must have had time to flank us while we were resting.

I search the sky for Limery, hoping he might arrive before they do, but I see nothing. Not that I'd be able to pinpoint his small frame against the sea of white.

I turn to Taryn. "You should fly through the portal in your bird form. The king will send help if he knows we're trapped. I'll go stay with the trolls until you return."

"Don't be crazy." His eyes are focused on the approaching hobgoblins. He says it so nonchalantly that I'm worried where his head is at right now.

"Don't be crazy?" I throw my hands in the air. "We can't win this fight. You just said you aren't ready."

He stares into the distance. "It doesn't matter."

I grab him by the cloak, causing Ruby to jump and nearly pulling Taryn from atop Berry. "What do you mean, 'It doesn't matter'? I know you're grieving, but there's no need to be stupid."

He pushes my hands away. "It doesn't matter because those aren't hobgoblins. They're trolls."

I do a double-take, but I can't make out anything for certain without enhanced eyesight. "What are they doing this far down the mountain?"

He shrugs. "Your guess is as good as mine. Want to go find out?"

Taryn flies ahead in his bird form to check on the situation, leaving me with his pets. Berry whines the entire time, but by the time we arrive at the portal, Taryn and Limery are waiting along with the entire population of arctic trolls, including all of Chief Laojin's pets.

Berry, Jordy, and Ruby pile on top of Taryn, tackling him into the snow. For the first time since the battle with Jude and Glenn, he laughs.

Rhaz frowns when he sees us. "Where is the big one?"

"He— Stompy didn't make it. We were attacked in Boneholde." I go on to tell them about Glenn and Jude and their army of hobgoblins.

Chief Laojin kneels next to Taryn, placing a hand on his shoulder. "He was a fine pet, and a strong warrior. I am grateful for the time I shared with him."

Taryn blinks back tears. "Thank you. That means a lot."

I don't want to cut into their moment, but I still don't understand why the entire tribe is at the portal. "What are you all doing down here?"

Laojin sweeps his arms in an arc, gesturing to the tribe. "Fighting alongside Taryn in the dungeon awakened something in the trolls. We have decided it is past time we reunite with our brethren."

"Really? That's great." I look over my shoulder at the distant mountain. "But what about Boneholde?"

He scowls at the mountain. "If your words are true, then this dwarven king will send his army to Frostmoor. And if not, that will be a matter for the council to decide."

I turn to Limery. "Did you warn Whitgard?"

He nods. "Limmy did. Theys was not happy."

"Yeah, I don't imagine they would be." I take one last look up the mountain. "Alright, let's get going. I can introduce you to both King Orso and Chief Rizza when we get to Seascape."

Senzala steps forward, shaking her head. "Nonsense. We can make our own introductions." She grins. "You have a dragon to hatch."

"But we need to tell them what happened in Boneholde." I extend my arm in the direction of the village.

"Do you think us incapable of delivering a message?" She touches my arm. "Go where you are needed. Let the forest heal your broken spirits."

I place my hand on top of hers. "I like the sound of that."

She winks. "I'm sure our paths will cross again."

Chief Laojin is the first one through the portal, riding atop his giant mammoth. The council follows next, and then one by one, the rest of the tribe steps through to Seascape.

"You think they'll be okay?" asks Taryn.

I wrap my arm around Taryn and stare into the maelstrom of energy. "I do. Now, let's get out of here."

I focus on the runes for Wandermere, a triangle with a V that cuts through it. The runes ignite, and we step through to our next adventure.

EPILOGUE

Valery sat in the corner of the break room staring into her cup of steaming coffee. Her head pounded, but that was nothing new these days. Time was running out, and she needed to decide what to do about Chad Johnson.

Footsteps echoed down the hall just before Thompson entered. The technician sighed, tossing his tablet onto the table, oblivious of Valery.

He sat down, placing his head in his hands. "Fucking Glenn."

He kicked one of the chairs so hard that it rocketed across the room. It crashed into the wall, startling Valery. She yelped.

Thompson looked over with wide eyes, immediately standing up. "I am so sorry. I didn't see you over there." He picked up his tablet. "Sorry. I'll get back to work."

She waved a hand for him to stay. "Don't worry about it. I know it's a little tense out there right now. What's bothering you?"

He looked at the floor. "Oh, it's nothing. Really."

She softened her expression. "Thompson, talk to me. You're

normally so calm and collected, that's why I hired you. So how about you tell me what has you so upset?"

He stood there for a moment like a deer in headlights. Valery wondered if he might run out the door and never come back.

Thompson sighed, then he took a seat at Valery's table. "It's Glenn. I don't— I just don't get it. We're letting him run around and hurt people, and we aren't doing anything about it. I thought this program was supposed to help him?"

Valery smiled. There were a lot of things she didn't have answers for at the moment, but this wasn't one of them. When it came to Glenn, she knew exactly what she was dealing with.

"He's something else, isn't he?"

Thompson's eyes narrowed. "He's a monster."

She nodded. "He has compulsions to do things most of us never experience. Do you mind if I ask you a few questions?"

He nervously tapped his tablet. "Uh, sure."

"You've been watching Glenn's progress since he was immersed, correct?"

"I have."

"Do you think he's changed at all?"

"No. He slaughtered an entire village earlier today. If anything, he's getting worse."

"I can see why you might think that. But you have to remember, those villagers are NPCs."

"Does he know that?" asked Thompson.

"I think he knows it far better than you do." She sat up, taking a sip of her coffee. "Let's take a look at him for a moment. In the months since he's been in Mythos, he has made it his mission to destroy a monstrous race. While his methods might not be ideal, he has not directly killed any of the human NPCs without provocation. This village he killed, they attacked his army first. The only living player he has attacked has been Chad, hero of a monstrous race. He's made an ally in Jude. He is doing exactly as the AI has intended. What we're working with here, it's not a quick fix. It's not a fix at all. It's a reframing of how these individuals interact with the world. Glenn is the hero of his own story. And so far, his violent tendencies have been directed at NPCs. I'd say that is a step in the right direction."

Thompson sighed. "It'd be a lot easier if they didn't feel so realistic."

"If they weren't realistic, this wouldn't work."

He scooted back in his chair. "I suppose you're right. Sorry again for my outburst."

"Don't worry about it."

He'd done what she'd felt like doing on many occasions.

He stood and started to leave, but then turned around. "Can I ask you a question?"

She smiled. "Go for it."

"What are you going to do about Chad Johnson?"

She froze. That was the million-dollar question, and everybody knew it. "I don't know."

Continue the adventure in Sentenced to Troll 5!

Acknowledgments

Congratulations! *You have finished* Sentenced to Troll 4.
    4 of 6 completed.
    +1 stat point to distribute.
    +1 Review to leave.

Thanks for reading! I hope you had as much fun reading about Chod and his adventures as I did writing them. This adventure is just getting started. If you enjoyed the book, please consider leaving a review. Reviews and word-of-mouth are the lifeblood of indie authors. The more positive reviews I have, the more likely it is that others will take a chance on this series.

There are many wonderful people that played an integral part in making this book a reality. You all have my sincerest thanks.

First, I would like to thank Cindy for reading through my earliest drafts. There are pieces of your wisdom scattered throughout this series.

I'd like to give a shoutout to my brother Davey for being the first in the family to read all of my books. Keep your head up, bro.

And to Caroline for the constant belief and support.

Thanks to all of my amazing Patrons, you'll never know how much your support has helped the past two years.

Gold Patrons: Michael Percell, Randy Duckworth, Robert Schaefer, and Eric Sprague.

Silver Patrons: Jim Devito, Justin Thomas James, and Nick Kelly.

Bronze Patrons: Cindy Koepp, Frank Pisauro, Rachael Osterhout, Rickie Brookes, Roxanne Baechler-Gill, and Wayne Lyons.

As well as all of the Wood Patrons.

A final thanks goes to my team of amazing beta readers for keeping everything in check: Paul Tuson, Loren Foster, Ted Roberson, and Robert Schaefer.

If you're looking for more books similar to my own, check out LitRPG Books.

ABOUT THE AUTHOR

S.L. Rowland is a cozy fantasy and LitRPG author known for crafting immersive worlds filled with adventure, heart, and a touch of humor. A lifelong gamer and fantasy enthusiast, he draws inspiration from tabletop RPGs, video games, and the fantastical. When he's not writing, he enjoys weightlifting, hiking with his Shiba Inu, and enduring the heartbreak of being an Atlanta sports fan.

SLRowland.com

Patreon-For signed paperbacks, advanced chapters, exclusive short stories, art, merch, and more.

Newsletter: For updates on new releases, sales, and behind the scenes content!

Email: slrowlandauthor@gmail.com

Find out more at https://linktr.ee/SLRowland

ALSO BY S.L. ROWLAND

Tales of Aedrea

Cursed Cocktails

Sword & Thistle

The Halfling's Harvest

There Be Dragons Here

Pangea Online

Pangea Online: Death and Axes

Pangea Online 2: Magic and Mayhem

Pangea Online 3: Vials and Tribulations

Sentenced to Troll 1-6

Path to Villainy: An NPC Kobold's Tale

Collected Editions

Pangea Online: The Complete Trilogy

Sentenced to Troll Compendium: Books 1-3

Sentenced to Troll Compendium 2: Books 4-6